GU01048751

THE
BLACKEST DEATH
Volume II

Edited by
The Staff of
Black Death Books

Black Death Books
an imprint of
KHP Industries
www.khpindustries.com

THE BLACKEST DEATH VOLUME II
edited by
The Staff of Black Death Books

Black Death Books
is an imprint of
KHP Industries
http://www.khpindustries.com

This is a work of fiction. Names, characters, places and incidents are either products of the author's imagination or are used fictitiously. Any resemblance to actual events or locales or persons, living or dead, save those clearly in the public domain, is purely coincidental.

Keeper of the Streets Copyright © 2005 Mike Adamson
The Little Plastic Devil in a Bottle Copyright © 2005 Douglas T. Araujo
The Debt Copyright © 2005 Diana Bennett
Jesse Wept Copyright © 2005 Eric S. Brown and D. Richard Pearce
The Little Boy Who Came Back From the Grave Copyright © 2005 Tim Curran
Séance.net Copyright © 2005 Peter Ebsworth
A Twist of Hate Copyright © 2005 Christopher Fulbright
Where The Dead Men Lose Their Bones Copyright © 2005 Kenneth C. Goldman
Where Secrets Fester Copyright © 2005 T. M. Gray
Payback Copyright © 2005 Derek Gunn
The Return of the Ba Copyright © 2005 Angeline Hawkes-Craig
The Empire of Sleep Copyright © 2005 Davin Ireland
Enter Sleep Copyright © 2005 Nancy Jackson
Longing Copyright © 2005 Brian W. Keen
Bad Hand Man Copyright © 2005 Karen Koehler
Keeper Copyright © 2005 Aurelio Lopez III
Minion Copyright © 2005 A. L. MacKinnon
In Shadows Copyright © 2005 Paul Melniczek
Revenge of the Roach King Copyright © 2005 C. Dennis Moore
Veils Copyright © 2005 Marc Paoletti
Perhaps I'm Not Dark Enough Copyright © 2005 Stephanie Simpson-Woods
Demon Dreams Copyright © 2005 Lavie Tidhar
The Space Between Copyright © 2005 Erik Tomblin
Keepsake Copyright © 2005 Ray Wallace

All rights reserved. No part of this work may be reproduced or transmitted in any form or by any electronic or mechanical means, including photocopying, recording or by any information storage and retrieval system, without the prior written permission of the Publisher, except for short quotes used for review or promotion. For information address the Publisher.

ISBN: 0-9767914-0-4

Cover art by KHP Studios

Printed in the United States of America

10 9 8 7 6 5 4 3 2 1

CONTENTS

KEEPER OF THE STREETS

Mike Adamson

W ell-informed didn't even come close to describing it. The man just *knew* things.

Pure and simple. He knew things about people he'd never met, about situations he had no involvement in. He knew his neighbourhood. He knew the streets. Yet the strangest thing of all was that no one knew *him*.

The man was a shadow. A virtual ghost of knowledge floating around the streets. Picking up a bit of gossip here and there. Things went on and he knew about them.

The man kept track of things. If something caught his attention, or if something just *came* to him, as was frequently the case, he would keep a close watch on it. He'd find out everything he could. Then he would wait.

People were dying all the time, and for someone in his line of work, that was a good thing. There's an endless supply of business. Evil is his client list. And anyone who hasn't been living in a cave for the last forty years will know that's a damn big list.

The man knows what he is. He is a beacon. He is a receiver for someone. Or something. He knows his purpose. He considers himself fortunate to have been selected. He feels chosen. He belongs.

Right now he sits alone in his tiny flat. Staring at a computer screen. There are literally hundreds of files and folders scattered about. There are old newspapers everywhere.

One file is open and on his lap. This one is complete. All the info has been gathered and documented. This one is ready to go. He is ready to go to work.

All he has to do is wait. Soon he will fall asleep, and by morning, he will know what to do.

Howard Kellner woke at 7:30 am. A policeman was banging on the door of his cell.

The small slit in the heavy steel door dropped open. A pair of eyes glared through at him.

"Get up Kellner, you're solicitor's here," a voice growled.

"Solicitor?" Kellner mumbled, sitting up. His back was aching and his arse was numb from trying to sleep on a concrete bed. He rubbed a hand through his hair. His neck creaked. God, he fucking hated police stations.

"Move it, sweetheart." The policeman said and pulled the door open.

Kellner moved out of the dimly lit cell. His shoes, minus the laces, were outside the door. He slipped into them.

The policeman walked ahead and Kellner followed. He walked with a slight limp in his left leg. Kellner's narrow eyes darted about nervously as they walked down the corridor.

"Who did you say was here?" Kellner asked, still a little confused.

"Your fucking lawyer, how the hell am I supposed to know who he is." The policeman spat back without looking over his shoulder.

He stopped and opened a door on the right.

"In there. One hour," he said, standing near the door with his arms crossed.

Kellner shuffled into the room almost expecting the policeman to punch him.

The small room was painted blue. There was a desk in the middle and two chairs.

On the back wall there was a long thin window. Sunlight was streaming through it. The table shone. The sun was in Kellner's eyes and he could only make out the back of another person standing behind the desk.

"Hello." Kellner said.

"Have a seat, Howard, may I call you Howard?" a man's voice spoke. It was a very soft voice. Almost soothing.

"Er, sure." Kellner said. He moved over to the desk and sat down. The sun was still in his eyes and he could only just see the outline of the man.

"So, who are you?" Kellner asked.

"I'm the cavalry, Howard. I'm not technically your solicitor, but that doesn't matter. I am so much more to you than that. I help people solve problems."

"Look, I'm sorry, but the sun's in my eyes, I can't see you," Howard said, moving his chair.

"Doesn't matter, Howard, but why not." The man turned and sat down.

Howard almost recoiled. The light looked as though it had somehow moved. Suddenly the guy was shrouded in darkness. Howard could tell he was wearing a suit. There was nothing prominent about the man, he could only make out very soft features. A heavy shadow lay over him. The man's eyes were shrouded in darkness as the sun beamed down behind him.

"What's going on?" Howard said, startled.

"Relax, Howard. I'm going to help you." The man laced his hands together and rested his right ankle on his left knee.

"You're a murderer, Howard. You know it and I know it. The police know it too. They just can't prove it yet. But someone else knows, Howard. You have been chosen or I would not be here. Why you, I don't know. Doesn't matter to me."

Howard started to protest, "Hey, I already told the cops I was nowhere near that place…"

The lawyer raised his hand, cutting him short. The man's hand sparkled in the sun. His nails were manicured and Howard could see a golf cufflink near his wrist.

"Yes, Howard, I know what you told the police. But you lied. So listen close, Howard, I won't repeat myself. If you want to get away with this, if you want to get out of here, then you'd better tell me that you killed those girls. You'd better tell me exactly how you killed them. Because if you don't, I walk. You'll get life in prison. The choice is yours, Howard."

Howard opened his mouth, but before he could say anything the lawyer cut in.

"Just bear one more thing in mind. Think about my suit, do I look like some legal aid reject? Did you call me? And think about just what *is* going on with the light in here. Strange things happen, Howard. Sometimes it's best to just get on board and roll with it."

Howard wasn't dumb. He knew what he'd done and what he was facing. So why the hell not. Roll with it. You're fucking-A right, my strange new friend, he thought.

Forty-five minutes later, Howard had laid it all out on the line. Yes, he'd murdered six teenage girls in the past year. Yes, he was the psycho that everyone was talking about. And, oh yes, he'd done all manner of ghastly things to them. Howard was amazed at how relaxed he felt as he was talking. He wasn't remorseful, not at all. He enjoyed killing them, why should he feel sorry about it?

The lawyer was very interested in the specifics of how Howard had chosen the girls. How he chose where to take them. And, of course, what he'd done to them, that hadn't been released to the press.

The lawyer didn't write anything down. He just sat with his arms folded and listened.

"So how is that going to help, then?" Howard said.

"Well, Howard, the real problem the police have is that they just don't have any *physical* evidence that you did it. You're problem is that your alibis are hardly watertight. You knew two of the victims, and there is, I believe, a witness who saw you with Julie Crag on the night she died."

The lawyer leaned across the desk toward Howard. A shadow spilled over it in front of him. Then he went on.

"So let's say that what if another girl died tonight? What if she was linked to all the others and died in the exact same way? Well, then, you couldn't have killed her, could you? And what if this time, the killer slips up? He *does* leave behind some evidence, a hair, semen. And, lo and behold, the police find out he's done it before, they know who he is. They rush out to catch him, but, oh dear, he seems to have killed himself. And everyone forgets about Howard Kellner. Case closed. That's how I do business, Howard. So you just sit tight and sleep well. I promise you tomorrow this will all be over."

The lawyer stood up. The sunlight blazed around his shoulders.

"Don't ask me why, Howard. I'm afraid that's one thing I don't know. But there is a reason, and when the time is right, he'll let you know." he said.

"Who will?" Howard said, suddenly a little scared.

"Think about it," the lawyer said, then he was crossing the room and pulling the door open. He was perfectly illuminated by the sun, but his back was turned.

Howard tried to get up.

"Goodbye, Howard," he said over his shoulder. The he was gone. Howard almost caught a slight glimpse of the side of his face. He *thought* he saw the lawyer smile, and beneath that smile Howard *thought* he saw one long sharp blood-dripping fang.

Detective Bruce Haver, who was in charge of the murder case, walked into the station that morning ready for a fight. He was meeting with Kellner's solicitor. Some dopey legal aid junior who was going to waste her time trying to convince him that Kellner was innocent. No chance. He would have the bitch shitting bricks.

The meeting was set for 11:30. It was 11.35.

Haver stopped and spoke to the desk sergeant.

"Is Kellner's Solicitor here yet?"

"Been and gone, sir." The sergeant replied.

"What?" Haver said.

The desk sergeant looked down at the log sheet in front of him.

"Yeah, he, erm, came in this morning, early. Erm, it was PC Davies, I think..." The Sergeant was stuttering as he scanned the sheet.

"What is the matter with you?" Haver said, frowning.

"Well, I can't find the entry here, sir. I wasn't on this morning. PC Davies was, and I don't think he's written it down."

Haver let out a heavy sigh.

"But he's been and gone?"

"Well, I presume so, sir, I saw him leave and Davies told me who he was."

"Right, get PC Davies down to my office now." Haver was flushing red under his collar. This he did not need.

PC Davies stepped into Haver's office looking like a rabbit caught in headlights.

"Oh, for god's sake, Bill, you only forgot to enter it on the log sheet, it's not court martial time. Just tell me what went on," Haver said when he saw the worry on PC Davies's face.

Davies was in his mid-thirties and he'd been on the force a long time. He was paunchy around the middle. He sat down, scratching his head.

"Yes, sir, I know, it's just, well, I don't know what happened. I didn't speak to him. I only let Kellner in there, and then picked him up when the solicitor left."

"Mayston, right. Kerri Mayston?" Haver said.

"Sir?" Davies replied with a dazed look on his face.

"Good god, Bill, Kellner's lawyer, Kerri Mayston, right?"

"Oh no, sir, it was a man. Real flash suit, you know the type," Davies said.

"Ah, finally, so what's his name? I want to know what he's playing at." Haver reached for the phone.

Davies didn't answer him.

"Hello, Bill, what's his name?"

Davies was visually squirming in his seat. "I don't know, sir," he said.

"Are you taking the piss? What do you mean you don't know?" Haver was ready to blow a gasket, his chest was puffed out and he was tapping his left leg. He still held the phone in one hand.

"No, sir, I mean I forgot to write it on the log sheet and, well, I can't remember."

"Unbelievable." Haver dropped the phone.

"So you didn't log him through, you can't remember his name and all you know is he was wearing a flash suit. Are you sure this actually happened?" Haver said, rising out of his chair.

"Yes, sir, it's just weird, I just can't remember the bastard," Davies said. He appeared sincere. He had the look of a man who didn't have a clue what was happening.

"Fuck it, get me a copy of the tape from the interview room. I'm going to see Kellner."

With that, Haver stormed out of his office and headed for the cells. PC Davies hurried away to get the cassette.

Haver pulled the door open and marched into Kellner's cell.

"Morning, detective." Kellner said.

"Enough of that shit. What are you playing at, why did your lawyer turn up early this morning, and who the fuck is he?"

"How should I know, guy shows up, say's he's my lawyer. We talked, he said he'd be in touch. What do you want, I didn't know he was coming."

"Who is he? And don't you dare tell me you don't know." Haver towered over Kellner with his hands on his hips.

Howard had been thinking.

"Mr Avery Waters. That's what he said his name was."

"Whose office is he from?"

"I don't know, I thought I was getting some legal aid monkey. At first I thought one of us was in the wrong room."

Haver turned and stormed out of the cell.

When he got back to his office Bill Davies had the tape player set up.

"Go on then, Bill, let's have a look," Haver urged.

Davies pressed play on the video and a security camera view of Interview Room 9 came onto the screen. There was a lot of white fuzz at the top of the screen.

"Sort that out, I can't see him," Haver said.

Davies played with the tracking but the interference refused to go away. All they could see was Kellner sitting down and talking to someone. Davies span the tape forward. Eventually they saw Kellner move to get up. Davies pressed play. Very slowly, the interfering snow began to slide down the screen. It moved all the way to the bottom and then vanished. When it disappeared Howard Kellner was on his own.

"Now just what the fuck was that?" Haver said.

They rewound the tape several times, but it was always the same.

"That is bloody stupid," Haver said after a few moments. He looked worried. His anger had been replaced with a light layer of nervousness.

Davies almost jumped as the telephone on the desk rang.

"Detective Haver," he said, snatching up the phone. He listened for a moment, thanked whoever it was, and then hung up.

"Well, apparently Mr Kellner's solicitor is here. Miss Mayston." Two days later and Howard Kellner was sitting at home. All charges dropped.

It happened just way the lawyer had said. His real lawyer, a tasty young thing, played things beautifully. As he reclined on his couch, sipping a cold beer, he wondered about what the other lawyer had said. There was a reason why he, Howard Kellner, was on this earth. The lawyer said he didn't know, but Howard had an idea. Someone was obviously looking out for him in his war against the sluts. He must have impressed a lunatic or something, and so he'd been sent a guardian angel to get him off the hook. Now Howard wasn't dumb, and he knew that things like this didn't happen twice. He resolved to be much more careful in the future.

Starting with that nice young solicitor of his.

The man sat alone again in his room. Howard Kellner's case file lay closed and forgotten. He was watching a new one now. Someone in the south was getting a little bit careless and the chants of "serial killer" looked just about ready to start up.

He was almost there, soon he would know.

Until then, he simply had to wait. It was easy.

Business was good, and with him in charge, it would stay that way.

The man waited.

Smiling.

MIKE ADAMSON is a UK author living in Warrington. He divides his time between the office and the world of horror writing, unsure of which scares him more. He has had six short stories published and one poem. Mike is hoping for a busy year ahead. After recently turning 28, he hopes to prepare a collection of his short works, make a move into the world of proofreading/editing and complete his first novel. The highlight of the year came when Mike met with Jeffery Deaver in Manchester. "It is always a tremendous rush to meet a person that you admire. I met a legend. Try to imagine that."

THE LITTLE PLASTIC DEVIL IN A BOTTLE

Douglas T. Araujo

1

Norman stepped back, the chisel in one hand and the mallet in the other, and stared at the half-carved piece of wood that lay on the bench in front of him. It was not even close to the result he was imagining—his model was a picture of Jennifer taped to the wall, smiling, her hair waving in the wind—but it was already taking a form that slightly recalled a human being.

Maybe I will finish it on time, after all, he thought, and his eyes unconsciously moved to the wall at his right. A calendar was posted there, and a date twelve days in the future was highlighted with a red circle.

Norman sighed. He had only twelve days to finish the bust before their wedding anniversary.

"I should have begun earlier," he said to himself in a low voice.

But despite his concerns about the time, Norman knew he shouldn't work anymore this Saturday. The sun was already hiding behind the roof of Mr. Thompson's house at the other side of the street, and the garage was getting darker and darker every minute. The dim light, added to the fact that he had been carving since early morning and was already very tired, could lead to disastrous happenings. Just one too-strong blow of the hammer was needed to ruin all the work he had already done. Besides that, he could smell food coming from the kitchen, and he knew that Jennifer would call him to dinner any moment.

Considering all this, Norman decided it was time to stop working for the day. He covered the piece of wood with canvas and took the picture of Jennifer from the wall. While he looked at it, his thoughts went back to the day when he had taken that picture. It had been two years ago, when he and Jennifer had spent a weekend at the beach. He remembered the way her blue eyes matched the color of the sea that day, and a smile appeared on his lips.

"God, I love that woman!" he whispered to himself, and it was really true. They had been married ten years, and he still loved her as much as on the first day. Maybe even more now. That's why he wanted to give her a special gift on their anniversary. Something that was *his*. Something that he had done *himself*.

With this thought, his mind focused on the bust he was carving for her. While he stored his tools back in his toolbox, Norman kept wondering how his wife would react. With his mind's eye he could see her expression when he give her the bust, the way she would raise her eyebrows and part her mouth in surprise. He could see the shining in her eyes when she realized that he had done it all by himself...

Then an unexpected event broke Norman's chain of thought.

He had been so distracted thinking of Jennifer that his fingers stroked a chisel he was trying to get and flicked it down the far end of the bench. It was a small chisel, and Norman watched it fly across the edge of the bench, hit the floor with a metallic sound and slip under the old blue freezer that stood abandoned at one corner of the garage.

As soon as the chisel disappeared from sight, Norman walked toward the freezer, kneeled and peered under it.

That old blue freezer had already been in the garage when Norman had bought the house ten years ago. Jennifer had already asked him two or three times to take that "dinosaur"—as she used to call it—to the junkyard, but Norman had always escaped with an excuse. Although the "dinosaur" had already been broken when he bought the house, Norman liked the way it looked among the tools, old magazines and other stuff stored in the garage. Its old-fashioned shape and color kind of reminded him of his childhood, and, in his opinion, lent a pinch of old elegance to the environment.

However, he couldn't remember having ever cleaned under it. Let alone moving it from that place. So when Norman peered under the freezer what he saw was a world of dust and cobwebs, so dense that he could barely see anything else.

At the left, however, the wooden handle of the chisel contrasted with the grayish tone of the cobwebs. It had cleared a path through them, and several of them were wrapped around the tool, as well as flocks of dust.

With a grimace of disgust, Norman prepared to put his hand under the freezer and get the chisel. But before he did so, he scanned the space again, just to make sure there were no spiders ready to bite him once he put his hand in there.

It was during this last scan that Norman saw the box.

The size of a shoebox, it was resting against the wall at the far end of the space under the freezer, and seemed to be wrapped in newspaper. Norman didn't feel surprised at not having seen it in the beginning. It was so covered by dust and cobwebs that it was barely visible.

"What the hell is this?" Norman said to himself, looking at the box.

By the way it looks, a voice inside his mind answered, *it must have been there for years. Probably it belonged to the Rubensteins or, who knows, maybe even to whoever lived in this house before them.*

Norman kept looking at the mysterious box for some moments, wondering what could be inside it, and what would lead somebody to hide it in that place.

Maybe it's just full of old documents, or love letters from a cheating wife. The same voice inside his mind spoke again, and this time it seemed more guttural, very different from his normal inner voice. *But what if it's full of money and jewels? It would be nice to find a lot of money hidden under the old freezer, wouldn't it?*

"Well, there is only one way to find out," Norman said aloud, and put his hand under the freezer.

The cobwebs enveloped his hand and arm like a shroud, and his whole body shivered at their touch. But it lasted only a second; the next instant Norman pulled out the box, got to his feet and took it to his bench. He blew on it and cleaned its surface with his hand to knock away the dust and cobwebs still attached to it.

The newspaper it was wrapped in was old and yellow. Norman saw, amazed, the date printed on it: October 31, 1946. Apparently the box had been hidden there for much longer than he had initially thought.

Carefully, Norman unwrapped it. The box itself was made of cardboard, and really did seem to be a former shoebox. He scanned its surface, looking for any mark, but there were none. He could feel, while he turned the box in his hands to look at the sides, that something solid moved inside.

Putting it again on the bench, Norman opened the box's cover.

There was no money or jewelry inside the box. Instead, what he saw made the hair stand up on his arms and a shiver run down his back.

From the box, a little devil inside a bottle looked at him.

Of course, it was not real, as Norman noticed immediately after the initial shock. It was just a plastic doll put inside a bottle by some clever artisan.

Whoever did this, Norman thought, raising the bottle to the level of his eyes, so he could inspect it better, *did a great job. It really seems real at first glance.*

The little devil was about three inches tall, and its trunk, arms and head were painted in a light red, almost pink, color. Its trunk was that of a very thin man, and its arms were long and thin and ended in big hands with long fingers. Each finger had a claw that was as sharply pointed as a needle. From the waist down its body was not human. It had the legs of a goat, covered with dark brown fur, and hooves instead of feet. It also had a long thin tail, without any fur, whose end was coiled around the left leg. Its hooves were glued to the bottle in such a way that it wouldn't fall even if somebody turned it upside down.

But what really grabbed Norman's attention was the devil's head. It was big, much bigger than what would be expected with such a thin body. From the sides of it protruded big curved horns, like those of a ram, so big that their tips almost touched the devil's chin. At the top of its head, in the space between the horns, there was a line of black hair that resembled a mane. Its ears were slanted, and inside its mouth, which was opened in a grin, it was possible to see its teeth. It had a long nose, and its eyes were big and blood-red and seemed to shine when you looked straight at them.

Norman turned the bottle in his hands, wondering how somebody could have put that doll inside it. He thought that the glass must have been cut and glued again at some point, which should have left a mark, but he couldn't find any sign of it. The only opening he could find was the bottleneck, which was firmly corked and was too thin for the doll to have been pushed through it.

Norman put the bottle back in the box, carefully, then kept looking at it for some moments.

"Well, well," he said to himself, "what am I supposed to do

with you? I don't think Jennifer would like to have you in the house…"

But he didn't finish the sentence. A sudden dizziness overpowered him, and the whole world spun around him while the little devil's eyes seemed to glow. Norman had to hold the bench to keep from falling to the floor.

This is a wonderful piece of art, the guttural voice spoke inside his head again. *How could you even think of throwing it away?*

The little devil's eyes looked like red-hot coals. They were the only things steady in the spinning world.

It will go perfectly with your home office, the voice continued, and Norman suddenly realized that was absolutely right. *It's just what you need to create the exotic atmosphere you were looking for. I'm sure Jennifer will understand that.*

Then, as suddenly as it had come, the dizziness disappeared. The little devil's eyes stopped glowing. The world came back into focus.

Norman got the bottle from the box again.

"I'm sure Jennifer will understand," he said to himself. "She's such a wonderful woman. She'll understand this is just what I need in my office."

Norman left the garage and walked toward the kitchen, taking the bottle with him. He couldn't wait to show it to Jennifer, and while he walked he was already seeing the bottle on the upper shelf of his home office.

Under the old blue freezer the fallen chisel remained, totally forgotten among the cobwebs.

2

Jennifer was finishing dinner when Norman entered through the door that linked the garage to the kitchen. The front of his shirt and shorts were covered with dust. Something that looked like a long cobweb was hanging from his hair and seemed to fly behind him at each step.

"Oh my God, what happened to you?" she asked, a smile on her face. "You are *filthy*!"

Norman didn't answer. He didn't seem to have even *heard* the question.

"You won't believe what I found under that old blue freezer in the garage," he said, and extended something he had been carrying in his arms like a baby. "It's amazing!"

Jennifer turned her eyes from the cobweb on her husband's hair and looked at the thing in his arms.

It was a bottle. And from inside it a little devil stared at her with bloody red eyes.

Jennifer jumped back as if she had just suffered an electrical shock. Her eyes widened and her heart raced. She put a hand on her chest and said with a trembling voice: "What is that *thing*, Norman?"

"It's a devil in a bottle. I found it under the freezer, wrapped in a newspaper from more than five decades ago," he explained with a smile on his face. "It's amazing, isn't it?"

"It's *disgusting*! What are you going to do with it?"

"I was thinking that it would fit perfectly in that blank spot at the upper shelf in my office…"

"What? Are you thinking of keeping this thing *in our house*?"

The smile disappeared from Norman's face.

"It's only a plastic doll, Jennifer. It's a piece of art. It must have some value."

"I don't want it in our house," she said in a matter-of-fact tone.

"Come on," Norman said and, passing an arm around her waist, pulled her body against him. "It's only a plastic doll. What harm can it do?" He kissed her on the cheek.

"I don't like it," she said, but her voice was not so inflexible anymore.

"You know I was looking for something special to fill that blank spot on the upper shelf," he said, and kissed her again. "And I think this is special. I've never seen anything like this."

Jennifer looked at her husband, uncertain about what to say, and then peered at the bottle in his hand, at the little devil that seemed to be staring at her again.

A shiver ran down her spine.

But now that she knew it was just a plastic doll, it didn't seem so threatening as before. Norman was right: what harm could it do?

"All right," she said, still not totally sure about it. "It can stay. But I don't want to touch it. Do you understand?"

Norman gave her another kiss on the cheek, this time a stronger one.

"Don't worry, honey," he said, "I'll take care of it."

And he went toward his office, carrying the bottle in his arms like a baby.

3

The next morning, Norman went to the garage as soon as he finished his breakfast. Now, he had only eleven days left to finish Jennifer's anniversary gift.

He uncovered the piece of wood that was just beginning to resemble a human being. Then he took the picture of Jennifer he was using as a model and fixed it to the wall with duct tape. After that, he took a step back and looked at the wood he had been working on over these last few days.

Suddenly, he wasn't so sure what he should do next.

I don't feel in the right mood to work on this today, he pondered to himself. *And it's not a good idea to work on it without being motivated. If I got distracted, I might easily waste all the work I've already done.*

He looked again at the piece of wood on the workbench and at the picture on the wall. From the picture, Jennifer smiled back at him.

There is still plenty of time. The same guttural voice he had heard the day before spoke inside his head again. *You still have eleven days to finish her gift. Why don't you give yourself a rest today? You surely deserve it.*

Norman hesitated for a moment, unsure if he could finish the work on time for their anniversary.

Of course you can do it, the voice continued. *You're a very skilled handworker. You can finish it easily next weekend, or during the next week, after work. Eleven days is a lot of time.* The voice paused for a moment, and Norman felt a slight dizziness overpowering him. *Why don't you rest today? Go to the office, choose a book and make yourself comfortable on the couch. Just enjoy yourself for the day.*

The dizziness disappeared as suddenly as it had come.

Norman wiped the sweat from his forehead and approached the workbench. With a hand that was visibly shaking he removed the picture from the wall and put it on his shirt pocket. Then he covered the wood.

"I still have plenty of time," he said to himself aloud. "Eleven days is a lot of time."

Norman turned his back on Jennifer's wedding gift and entered the house. He went straight to the office, picked a book from the bookcase without even looking at which one it was, lay comfortably on the couch and opened the book on his chest.

Before he started reading, however, his eyes moved toward the upper shelf where he had put the little plastic devil the night before.

And from inside the bottle, the little devil stared back at him with its red-painted eyes.

4

"Norman?" Jennifer asked, standing at the office door. The dim light coming from their bedroom upstairs was barely sufficient to let her see her husband lying on the couch in the dark office, a book resting on his chest. "Are you awake?"

"Yes, I am," he answered in a voice that seemed somewhat different, distant.

"Aren't you coming to bed? You've been in this office all day. It's late."

A little pause. As if he were hesitating before answering. "I just want to stay here one more minute," he said. "Go to bed. I'll follow you in a moment."

But Jennifer didn't move.

"Are you all right, Norman?" she asked hesitantly. "You've been lying on this couch the whole day. You barely ate. Are you feeling sick or something?"

"I'm fine. I just wanted…to be here for awhile. To read a book. To rest. I think I worked too hard on your gift yesterday."

She stood silent for a moment.

"Are you sure?" she finally asked.

"Of course I'm sure. Go to bed and don't worry. I'll be there in a moment."

Jennifer hesitated for some seconds, feeling slightly uneasy about something, but unable to clearly point out what it was.

Finally, without a word, she went to their bedroom, never realizing that what had made her feel that way was the fact that during the whole conversation, Norman's eyes had never left the bookcase's upper shelf where the little devil was.

5

Norman was dreaming.

In his dream, he was a little boy again, and he was very happy. And the reason why he was so happy was that he had found a brand new toy, one that none of the other boys in the street had.

A toy that was very special.

Then he went out of his house to play with his new toy. He wanted to show it to the other children; he wanted them to know how special his toy was.

But, as soon as he stepped out of his house, the other children surrounded him. He didn't see where they had come from, but he could feel the hate that emanated from them. He could see on their faces how envious they were of his new toy. How much they *wanted* it.

Norman embraced his new toy harder, trying to protect it from them.

"You need to get rid of it, Norman," a girl spoke from the middle of the crowd, and he looked at her.

It was Jennifer.

Yes, it was Jennifer, but at the same time it wasn't. He could recognize his wife's adult features in that tiny child face, but her eyes...he had never seen so much hatred in Jennifer's eyes.

"Get rid of it, Norman," she said, and her childish voice was full of threat, "or we will do it for you."

Norman looked around at the faces of the children around him, and through his wet eyes he recognized them. They were his neighbors, his parents, his relatives. His co-workers, his boss, even the clerk he used to talk to once in a while at the newsstand. Everybody he knew was there, their features changed into those of children, but still recognizable.

And he recognized them all. Every single one of them.

They all looked at him, hated him, wanted his new toy.

"Give me the toy, Norman," the childish Jennifer spoke again, and this time she seemed much taller, much more *adult*.

All the other children-adults stepped forward all of a sudden, tightening the ring around him. They raised their arms toward him, trying to take his new toy from him, scratching him, *hurting* him.

"NO!" Norman screamed, but his scream seemed to die as soon as it left his lips. "It's MINE!"

Then he looked down at what he had been holding tightly against his chest, and for the first time he saw his beloved new toy. It was a bottle.

And inside it, a little devil grinned at him, licking its lips with a snake-like tongue.

Norman awakened.

He didn't scream, although his mouth was dry and his jaw wide open. He didn't sit up suddenly in bed, although his whole body was covered with sweat and his heart was racing so hard he thought he would have a stroke.

Instead, he just opened his eyes and looked at the ceiling. One moment he was asleep, and the next, fully awake.

His body shivered.

He remained that way for several minutes, unable to move, paralyzed by his own fear. He felt lonely, angry, fragile, all at once.

They wanted to take it from him. His little devil. They wanted it.

Norman slowly moved his head and looked at Jennifer, totally asleep beside him.

At that moment, he hated her. How could she be sleeping, so peaceful, so calm, when they wanted to take his devil from him?

You can't count on her, the guttural voice said inside his head again. *She doesn't like the devil. She told you so. She wants them to take it from you too.*

Norman felt the anger grow inside his chest. Making a decision, he jumped from the bed. His bare feet slapped the cold floor and Jennifer turned on the bed, but didn't wake up.

Norman left the bedroom as fast as he could, as if he was afraid that someone would prevent him doing so. He almost ran down the stairs, and when he entered the office his heart was racing again and he could hear his pulse in his temples.

He stopped in front of the bookcase and looked at its upper shelf.

There it was.

His little devil.

Norman immediately started relaxing. With his little devil staring back at him, its eyes gleaming slightly in the dim light, he felt all the anger and fear disappear. Soon, a soft sleep subdued his senses and, without even thinking about it, he lay on the couch and slept.

That night, Norman didn't have any more nightmares.

6

Jennifer woke up with the sound of a door closing downstairs.

"Norman?" she asked, still half asleep, while the noise of a key being turned in a keyhole came to her from downstairs.

Jennifer turned and looked at Norman's side of the bed, but it was empty. Then she sat and looked around.

Her husband wasn't anywhere.

"Norman?" she asked again, this time louder.

From outside, the sound of a car engine being started broke the silence.

Jennifer jumped to her feet, ran toward the window and peered outside just in time to see Norman driving away in their car, clearly dressed for work. A somewhat suffocating feeling grew inside her chest while the car slowly moved through the street and turned at the next corner.

But it was only when it disappeared from sight that she suddenly understood what was bothering her.

Within ten days she and Norman would complete their tenth year of marriage, and this was the first time during all those years that he had gone to work without giving her a good-bye kiss.

7

"Norman, what is happening to you?" Mr. Johnson asked. "You've made a mistake in the accounts again. It's the third time today!"

Norman looked into the pig eyes of the little fat man standing in front of his desk, and asked himself for the thousandth time how such a man could be his boss.

So he'd made a few mistakes on the accounts this morning. So what? Wasn't he allowed to make mistakes? Wasn't he good enough for Mr. You-Made-Three-Mistakes-In-A-Day up there?

He wished he could be at home with his little devil.

But what really upset him was the shine in those little pig eyes. Norman knew Mr. Johnson was pleased to call attention to him in public. He was taking pleasure in humiliating him that way.

A sudden anger burned inside Norman's chest.

He looked around him. In every direction his co-workers were looking at him, pointing at him, talking about him. Although they were pretending not to, Norman knew they were. Certainly they would burst into laughter as soon as he turned his back.

They all hated him. He *knew* it.

They wanted to humiliate him.

The anger grew inside his chest. Norman hated them all.

But he knew they couldn't humiliate him. Not anymore.

After all, he was the only one in that office—maybe in the whole world—who had a little devil in a bottle.

Now, he had something special. Now, *he was special.*

"Are you OK, Norman? You look a little bit pale." Mr. Johnson handed back the report Norman had just finished.

Norman opened his mouth, ready to tell Mr. Johnson to shove that report right up his fat ass, but he thought twice. Maybe this was just the opportunity he had been looking for. Maybe he could take advantage of this situation.

"To tell you the truth," Norman said, and took the report from Mr. Johnson's fat hand, "I'm not feeling very well this morning. I think I'm a little bit feverish…"

"Maybe you should take the day off," said Mr. Johnson. "Go home and rest, so you can come back tomorrow in good shape."

"Thank you, Mr. Johnson." Norman smiled at him, and Mr. Johnson took a step back, as if he had seen something scary in that smile. "You're a very good man."

Mr. Johnson turned and went back to his office, glancing at Norman over his right shoulder with an intrigued expression. Norman followed him with his eyes, and when his boss locked himself in his office, he looked around again. Again, he didn't see anybody looking at him, but he was sure they were only waiting for him to leave so they could start the gossip.

But it didn't matter anymore. Soon he would be with his little devil again, and everything would be all right.

8

Jennifer entered the office, leaving the vacuum cleaner she was pulling behind her at the door. She walked toward the window and opened it.

"Now it's better!" she said to herself when the sun illuminated the room.

She got the vacuum cleaner and pulled it inside the office, looking around the walls for the nearest socket. Then she plugged it in, turned it on and started cleaning the carpet while the roaring sound of the machine filled the room.

At first, Jennifer's thoughts wandered through the tasks she still had to do that day: she needed to wash the bathroom, prepare lunch, and then she needed to go to the market to buy some lettuce…for some minutes, these thoughts occupied her mind completely.

After awhile, however, her thoughts started drifting away from these mundane tasks and she found herself thinking about Norman again.

Something was not right, she knew that. Although she couldn't clearly define what it was, she felt inside her heart that something was wrong. Norman had spent the whole previous day on that couch, reading, and she had never seen him do that. She knew he liked to read, but he was a very active man, the kind of man who is unable to stay quiet for long. Norman liked to be doing things. He was a handyman. He just wasn't the kind of man who would spend the whole day lying on a couch, reading.

But that's what he had done.

Maybe he's sick, she thought. *Maybe he has the flu, or something.*

Because yesterday he certainly hadn't seemed like the Norman she knew. He had looked as if he was somebody else inside Norman's body.

A chill ran down Jennifer's back at this thought.

"He must just be tired, as he said," she said to herself aloud.

But these words didn't diminish the anxiety she was feeling. And it seemed to increase somehow when she saw the book Norman had been reading the day before had fallen on the floor beside the couch, as if it had been thrown there. She knew how much Norman cared for his books.

Another chill ran down her back.

Something was wrong. And whatever it was, it had started since Norman had found that bottle under the old blue freezer.

Instinctively, Jennifer glanced at the bookcase's upper shelf where the bottle was.

Her heart jumped in her chest. For a crazy moment, she thought the little devil's eyes were glaring.

But then the moment passed and she noticed what was really happening, and she smiled to herself. The devil's eyes were just reflecting the sunlight that was falling directly upon it through the open window.

"You're making a fool of yourself," she said, and resumed cleaning the carpet.

However, the image of those blood-red eyes staring at her remained on Jennifer's mind, and another feeling soon started dominating her thoughts.

The feeling of being watched.

Jennifer pulled the vacuum cleaner faster and faster behind her, suddenly wanting to get out of that room as soon as possible.

It was observing her. Watching her. She could feel it, although she was making a conscious effort to not look toward the bookcase.

It's just a doll, an inner voice said inside her head. *It's just a plastic doll, for God's sake.*

But it didn't matter. She could feel its gaze on her back, she could feel its red eyes following her through the room, she could feel the evil that emanated from those eyes burning her skin.

An irrational fear started overpowering her. She pulled the vacuum cleaner faster and faster, her eyes fixed on the carpet, sweat pouring from her forehead.

Then, through the corner of her eye, she saw a movement.

Jennifer stopped, paralyzed by fear, her heart skipping a beat while an icy rock seemed to form inside her stomach. The vacuum cleaner's hose was in her hand like a sword, its noise still filling the whole room, but she wasn't cleaning anymore.

Like a person in a dream, Jennifer raised her eyes from the floor and looked at the little devil inside the bottle on the bookcase's upper shelf.

9

Norman had just parked the car inside the garage when he heard a terrified scream coming from inside the house.

Oh, my God, the thought crossed his mind as soon as he heard the scream, *the little devil.*

He jumped from the car and entered the house as fast as he could. When he crossed the kitchen toward the living room, he almost ran into Jennifer, who was coming the opposite way.

"Thank God you're here," Jennifer said between the sobs, and embraced him fiercely, "it was horrible."

"What happened?" Norman pulled her away from him so that he could see her face. "What happened, Jennifer?"

"It was that disgusting devil." Her whole body shivered at the thought. "I was cleaning the office…"

"Did you break it?" Norman interrupted her.

Jennifer started sobbing again.

"Did you BREAK it?" Norman shouted, shaking her by the shoulders.

"NO!"

Norman released her and ran toward the office, his heart racing. *If she broke it,* he thought, *I'll kill her.*

But then he entered the office, and his eyes rested on the bottle. It was still on the bookcase's upper shelf, the same way he had put it two days before.

Norman approached the bookcase and looked closer at it.

From inside the bottle, the little plastic devil was grinning at him, its red eyes shining.

Norman smiled and returned to the living room. Jennifer was sitting on the couch, still sobbing.

"What happened?" he asked, his voice as cold as ice.

"That bottle," she said. "I was cleaning the office, and I started getting the feeling that someone was watching me. Then I looked at the bottle, and the devil...the devil..."

"What?"

"It *moved*!" She looked at him with eyes full of terror. "It turned its head and looked straight at me, and its eyes were shining and its tongue came out of its mouth as if it was a snake!"

Norman smiled at her. "It's only a plastic doll," he said, and the disbelief was clear in his voice. "You must have imagined it."

"I *saw* it!" she said, and her eyes pleaded with him to believe her. "It *moved*!"

"It's only a plastic doll," Norman repeated. "It can't move."

"We need to get rid of that thing, Norman. To take it away from our house."

Norman face contorted in a furious expression. "I won't get rid of my little devil just because you've been imagining things, Jennifer."

Jennifer remained silent for a moment, stunned.

"Don't you see what's happening here, Norman?" she finally said. "You've been a different man since that thing entered our house!"

"That's not true!"

"Yes, it is! Even now, you were more worried about your little devil than about me!"

"Stop ranting! You are making a fool of yourself."

"You need to get rid of it, Norman."

"I WON'T!" he shouted, and his face turned red with anger. "All you've talked about since I found that bottle is throwing it away. Know what? I think you're *envious*! You're envious because for the first time I have one thing for myself, a thing that I found! A thing that is MINE!"

"Norman, I..."

"SHUT UP! LET ME ALONE!"

Norman went to the office, closing the door behind him with such force that it trembled on its hinges. Seconds later, he turned the key in the keyhole, locking himself in with his little plastic devil.

Norman was dreaming again.

It was the same dream. Again, it started with him happier than ever for having found a new toy, a special toy. Again, he went out of his parent's house to show it to the other children. Again, the children surrounded him, threatening to take his toy from him. Again, he recognized every one of those children; he saw the adult features on every one of their childish faces.

"Give me the toy, Norman," child-Jennifer said again, and this time she seemed much taller, much more *adult.*

Once more, all the children-adults stepped forward, tightening the ring around him. Again, they raised their arms toward him, scratching him, *hurting* him.

"NO!" Norman screamed as he had before, and again his scream seemed to die when it left his lips. "It's MINE!"

He looked down at what he had been holding tightly against his chest, and again he saw his beloved new toy.

Inside the bottle, his little devil grinned at him, licking its lips.

But this time, Norman didn't awake. Instead, he screamed again, "It's MINE!"

But the children-adults didn't listen. They continued to scratch him, to shred his clothes, to hurt him.

"Free me!" the little devil said to him from inside the bottle with a hissing voice, its eyes shining. "Free me and I will protect you! I will make them pay for what they have done to you!"

Norman got hold of the cork with his childish fingers and pulled it from the bottle.

A deafening shriek made the children step away from him, covering their ears with their hands. Most of them started crying, pleading for mercy. Other just ran away. Jennifer remained where she was, paralyzed by fear.

Then, as if coming from nowhere, the devil was beside him. But it wasn't little anymore. Instead, it seemed taller than a house.

"Let's start the fun," it said, and grinned at Norman. Its tongue moved from side to side amongst its needlepointed teeth.

Norman smiled back at it. He felt safe now. Powerful.

Without a word, the devil ran toward Jennifer, its red-hot eyes shining.

Norman smiled.

11

Jennifer approached the office's closed door. She stood beside it, trying to hear something from inside, but unable to. Finally, after some seconds of hesitation, she knocked at the door.

"Norman?" she asked, trying not to show the concern in her voice. "You spent all night locked in this office. Are you all right?"

No answer.

"Norman?" She called again, this time louder, and knocked at the door once more. "Aren't you going to work? Are you feeling well, Norman?"

"GO AWAY!" he shouted, and his voice was so full of such anger that Jennifer unconsciously took a step back, frightened.

"Open the door, Norman," she said. "I was thinking about yesterday, and…well, it's just a plastic doll, right? I must have *imagined* it was moving. You know, I was a little bit nervous, and I think I overreacted…"

Silence again.

"You need help, honey," Jennifer continued. "Let me help you. Open the door."

No answer.

"Don't you see what's happening?" Her voice was louder now. "You've been acting weird since you brought this bottle to the house, Norman. Maybe I have just imagined that I saw that plastic devil moving, maybe I have really overreacted, but despite all that there is something wrong about it, Norman." She paused. "You're…obsessed about it, I don't know."

She heard a sound from inside the office, what seemed like murmured words. She decided to continue.

"You need to get rid of it, sweetheart. Let me in and we can throw it in the garbage can…"

"NO!!!" he shouted with such violence that it caught Jennifer completely off-guard. "That's all you want, isn't it? You want to take the little devil away from me, because you're ENVIOUS! But it's mine! It's MINE, do you understand that? MINE!"

"I don't…" she started, but he wasn't listening.

"*I* found it!" he continued. "And you won't separate it from me! It is MINE!"

Then he stopped shouting, but she could hear him breathing hard on the other side of the closed door.

"Norman, you need help," she said hesitantly. "Look at what you're saying! You never talked to me like that. Please, open the door. Let's talk to a doctor."

Silence.

Jennifer's eyes filled with tears "Norman, please…" she said in a trembling voice, while a tear ran down her cheek.

Norman didn't answer.

"If you don't open this door now," she said, making a decision, "I'm going away from this house. Right now."

Silence.

Deep, deathly silence.

Jennifer waited for three full minutes. Then, when she had convinced herself that Norman wasn't going to open the door, she turned and ran to their bedroom, crying.

12

Through the locked office door, Norman heard Jennifer crying, and the steps on the linoleum when she ran to their bedroom.

After that, silence.

And then, after awhile, he heard the sound of something heavy being pulled along the stairs and through the living room. With his mind's eye he pictured Jennifer dragging a bag full of clothes toward the door. He imagined her breathing hard, sweating, her eyes red with crying.

He smiled.

After some minutes, the dragging sound stopped, and he supposed Jennifer had reached the front door. He could imagine her standing there, looking at the office door, unsure about leaving, unsure if she should talk with him once more.

As if to confirm what he was thinking, he heard the sound of steps on the linoleum again. Slow, hesitant steps approaching the office.

Suddenly, they stopped.

All became quiet again. Seconds passed by.

Steps again, this time going away. Almost running now.

Then the front door closing with a loud thunderous sound, and a key turning in the keyhole.

Silence again.

Jennifer had gone away. She had really left him.

Norman looked at the little devil inside the bottle he had in his hand and smiled.

"She was envious," he said as if he was talking to an old friend, "because *I* found you, and she didn't. Because you're *mine*." He caressed the bottle as if it was a treasure. "But now we don't need to worry about the old bitch anymore."

His laugh echoed off the walls of the closed office.

"Now," he added, "it's just you and me."

From inside the bottle, the little devil stared back at him with red glowing eyes, its mouth open in a demonic grin.

13

Five days had passed since Jennifer had left, but Norman didn't know that. Closed up in the office with the lights off and the windows closed, he wasn't aware of the passage of time. He didn't even know if it was night or day, nor which day of the week it was. A strong stench of urine and feces emanated from his clothes. His beard was grown, his hair was untidy, and he had started losing weight since he hadn't eaten anything during those three days. If somebody looked at him, they would have certainly thought he was a beggar.

During those three days, Norman had spent most of the time on the couch. Sometimes he had stood and walked around like an animal locked in a cage, and sometimes he had thrown books and other objects against the walls, but most of the time he had just lain on the couch, looking at the bottle on his desk.

Staring at the little devil inside it.

Talking to it.

He had talked about himself, about his childhood, about the boys who used to humiliate him. He had talked about his father, his mother, his sister. He had talked about Jennifer, how he had met her, how they had kissed for the first time, how he had proposed to her. He had talked about his work, his boss, his co-workers.

During those three days, Norman had told the little devil inside the bottle everything about his whole life, including the smallest details he could remember. He had told it about all his fears, all his hopes, all his deepest secrets.

And after that, Norman cried.

He cried as he had never cried, not even when he was a small child and the other boys humiliated him. He cried as if a dam he had built inside himself had suddenly ruptured, letting all the pain and grief escape.

"You're my only friend," Norman said to the little devil when he finally stopped sobbing. "The children, the men at my work, Jennifer, *everybody* is always wanting to hurt me. Jennifer even wanted to take you away from me." He paused, and his face contorted in an expression of disgust. "I *loved* her, and she wanted me to throw you in the *garbage*."

He paused and wiped away the spit that was dripping from the corner of his mouth.

"They're envious. Now that I finally found you, they're envious, because we're friends. Because you're *mine*. And they know that they can't hurt me anymore while I'm with you. You're *mine*."

Norman took the bottle from the desk and stared at it, and the devil's red eyes stared back at him. They seemed to glow in the office's dim light.

"We will be together forever," Norman said. "Now that we have found each other, nobody can separate us anymore. We now are one, you and me. You're *mine*." He paused, and then added, "and I'm *yours*."

Silence followed.

In the dim light, Norman suddenly thought he had seen the devil's eyes turn brighter and the grin on its face enlarge, revealing a snake-like tongue that moved from side to side, licking a multitude of needle-pointed teeth.

"Yes." Norman heard a hissing voice emerging from the bottle in his hand. Its tone was bass and muffled as if it was coming from a deep hole in the earth. "You're mine. Forever."

14

Jennifer looked at the calendar on the kitchen wall and her eyes filled with tears.

"What is it?" Marcia asked when she saw the expression on her face. Marcia was her best friend, and Jennifer had been staying at her house since she had left home. "Are you thinking about Norman again?"

Jennifer nodded.

"You need to forget him."

"Today is our anniversary," Jennifer said simply, and started sobbing.

"Oh, dear, dear." Marcia embraced Jennifer, trying to comfort her.

"I keep remembering," Jennifer said while tears ran down her cheeks, "how he was a good husband. He was funny, loving, tender. How could he change so much, so fast?"

"I don't know, dear."

"He's sick. He must be. It's the only explanation."

"You need to forget him, Jennifer."

"But I *love* him," she said, and wiped the tears away with the back of her hand. "And now, when he needed me the most, I left him. What kind of wife am I?"

"You did all that was possible…"

"Yesterday," Jennifer interrupted, "I called him at work."

"You what?"

"I called him at work. I just wanted to hear his voice." Jennifer blushed slightly. "But do you know what I discovered? Norman hasn't gone to work for the last ten days."

Marcia remained silent.

"He is sick, and he needs me, Marcia," Jennifer said. "I'm his wife, and he needs me."

"All right. But I don't think you should go there alone."

"But I need to. Maybe I can convince him to seek medical assistance. Maybe…" She paused, then added, "I don't know. But I feel I need to go there."

"When are you thinking to go?"

"Right now," she said, and stood up.

15

"Everybody hates me," Norman whispered in the dark office to the bottle in his hand. "Everybody hates me but you. They want to get you away from me. They hate me."

"Yes," the hissing voice answered from inside the bottle. "They all hate you. I'm your only friend. I'm the only one you can trust."

Norman eyes filled with tears.

"Why?" he asked, and tears ran down his cheeks. "Why do they hate me? I'm a good boy. Why didn't the other children like me? Why do they always laugh at me?"

"Because they're envious," the hissing voice said. "Because you're smarter than them. Because you have *me*."

"Yes," Norman wiped away the tears and smiled, "yes, I have you. We're friends."

"And friends take care of each other, right?"

"Friends take care of each other." Norman nodded.

"I can make them pay," the hissing voice continued. "Now that we're together, now that we're friends, I can make them pay for every time they mocked you. I can make them pay for every time they made you suffer. Every one of them."

"Can you?" Norman didn't seem so sure.

"Yes, I can. Wouldn't you like to see all them suffering as you did? Those children, the people at your work, your wife…wouldn't you like to hurt them as they have hurt you?"

Norman nodded again.

"Friends take care of each other," the hissing voice said again. "And I can take care of you. But first, I need you to do me a favor."

Norman looked at the little devil and raised his eyebrows, curious.

"I need you to take that cork out," the hissing voice said, and Norman saw the little devil's eyes glow in anticipation. "Then I will be able to make them pay for what they did to you."

Norman looked at the cork, not so sure of it.

"If you do this," the hissing voice continued, "I will make you strong, powerful. More powerful than any man on earth. Then you will be able to take revenge on all those who have hurt you."

Norman touched the cork, and for the first time he noticed there was a small cross carved on its upper side.

"I don't know," he said. "What if I take the cork out and you go away from me?"

"We're friends," the voice said; Norman felt that strange dizziness overpowering him again. "And friends help each other."

Norman held the tip of the cork with his fingers, and the dizziness suddenly disappeared.

"You need to hurry, my friend," the hissing voice said, and its tone was soft and commanding at the same time. "She is coming. She wants to separate us, to take you from me. She is coming already. Can't you feel it in your bones?"

"Yes, I can," Norman said, and he started pulling the cork from the bottleneck. "She's coming."

"Free me, my friend, and she will not be able to separate us. Release me, and she will not be able to take you away from me. Because I'm yours, and you're mine. We are one, and we need to be prepared for her. Free me, and we will be prepared. I won't let her hurt you again. I won't let anybody hurt you again. Free me. Free ME! FREE ME!"

Norman pulled the cork with more strength, and it moved slightly.

"YES!" The hissing voice screamed, exultant. "FREE ME! NOW!"

With a loud popping sound, the cork was yanked from the

bottleneck.

An exultant scream filled the dark office.

16

Jennifer opened the front door and entered the living room. It was much darker than outside, and she stood some seconds beside the open door until her eyes got used to the dim light.

"Norman?" she called, closing the door behind her. Her voice seemed to spread over the silent house like a shroud. "Norman, are you there?"

She waited for a moment.

No answer at all.

She moved slowly toward the office, wondering if he was still locked in there, wondering if he was all right, suddenly afraid he had fainted or suffered a stroke or something.

What if he had fallen dead on the office carpet? What would she do?

Jennifer walked faster.

Then she noticed the office door was open, and felt a little bit relieved. At least he wasn't locked inside the room anymore.

"Norman?" she called again as she reached the open door. The stench of feces and urine made her cover her nose with a hand.

Nothing. The only sound she could hear was her own breathing.

Jennifer peered inside the office, which seemed somehow darker than the living room, as if a shadow was covering everything like a fog.

Norman wasn't there.

Her eyes moved immediately to the bookcase's upper shelf as if they had a life of their own.

Jennifer's heart jumped in her chest.

The bottle with the little devil wasn't there either.

She remained there for an instant, framed in the office doorway, her eyes fixed on the spot where the bottle should have been, and wondering where Norman could have gone.

It was only when she turned to leave the office that she saw it on the floor, among a pile of fallen books.

A cork.

She stepped inside the office to get it, and a sudden shiver ran down her back as if she had stepped into chilled water.

She didn't like to be there. She didn't *want* to be there. She could feel evil pouring from everywhere around her—from the furniture, from the objects, even from the walls. This room was impregnated by it, and it seemed to emanate toward her in waves that made her nauseous.

A sudden dizziness threatened to overwhelm her.

But she forced herself to kneel beside the cork and touch it with the tip of her finger. Her whole body trembled when she did so, and she withdrew her hand as if she had suffered an electrical shock. Then she quickly stood and stepped out of that room.

As soon as she stepped outside the office, the nausea and the dizziness disappeared.

"Norman, what have you done?" she asked in a low voice. Suddenly, she wasn't so sure anymore that she had only imagined the little devil moving. "What is happening here?"

The sound of a door closing came from somewhere inside the house. In the silence, it seemed like thunder, and made Jennifer jump.

"Norman?" she asked, putting a hand over her racing heart. "Is that you?"

No answer.

Maybe I should go ask for help, Jennifer thought. *Maybe I shouldn't be here alone.*

But instead of doing so, she started walking toward the kitchen, the place where the sound seemed to have come from.

17

"She is coming," a hissing voice whispered inside Norman's ear. "Be quiet. Be prepared. She is coming, and now we are going to make her pay."

From his hiding place, Norman smiled in anticipation, his green eyes seeming to glow in the dim light.

18

Jennifer entered the kitchen.

It was a little more illuminated than the other rooms, which was a relief, but Norman wasn't there either.

She walked toward the door which led to the garage, and opened it.

"Norman, are you there?" she asked the dark garage, and stepped inside it.

No answer.

She took another step and looked around. Even in the dim light she could see the shapes of the tools on the walls, the piles of magazines in a corner, the old blue freezer in another corner. Jennifer kept looking at the freezer for a second, wondering who could have hidden the bottle under it, and wishing Norman had never found it.

Then she looked at the other side, toward Norman's workbench. It still had the gift Norman was preparing for her on it, covered with a canvas.

Jennifer's eyes filled with tears. Suddenly, she felt an urge to remove that canvas, to see what Norman would give to her, even knowing it was not ready.

She stepped toward the workbench.

But she didn't reach it.

Jennifer had only walked half the way when somebody—a shadow—jumped her from a dark corner. She was thrown down and fell to the ground near the freezer, hitting her head with such force on the floor that her sight blurred and she saw light points floating in front of her eyes. For a terrified moment she thought she would faint, but somehow she didn't.

Before she could react, however, the person—the shadow—was over her, sitting on her chest and squeezing her neck with his hands.

With her heart beating hard, Jennifer looked at his face.

It was Norman. But, at the same time, it wasn't.

His hair was disheveled, his clothes and face were dirty, and he stank of urine and sweat. His mouth was contorted in a crazy smile that showed his teeth, and his tongue kept moving from side to side, like a snake's. His whole face was a grimace of hate and pain, and a shadow seemed to surround his features, turning them darker.

But what really attracted Jennifer's attention were his eyes. They were wide-open and unfocused, and their green irises seemed to glow in the dim light. When she looked into them, she felt as if she was being dragged into an abyss. There was no trace of a human soul behind those eyes.

They were the eyes of a madman.

"I'm going to make you pay," Norman said, and his voice had a hissing tone that Jennifer had never heard before. "You are going to suffer for everything you did to me."

He tightened his hands around her neck.

Jennifer tried to pull his hands away, but they wouldn't move. She could feel the coldness of his fingers penetrating her flesh.

"You tried to take it away from me," he continued, "but it's mine. Are you hearing this, you bitch? IT'S MINE!"

She couldn't breathe anymore. She tried to talk, to beg him to release her, but from her mouth the only sound that came was a groan.

Norman smiled.

Jennifer started kicking and pounding as hard as she could, trying desperately to make him release her, but her blows seemed to have no effect on him. He seemed to feel no pain.

He seemed possessed.

"I'm going to kill you, bitch," he said with his hissing voice, and spit flew from his mouth.

Her lungs seemed to be on fire. Her heart raced as if it would explode at any second. Black dots floated in front of her eyes. Her limbs started to go numb, and her kicks lost their strength.

Norman's green eyes seemed to glow brighter.

He laughed.

Desperate, fighting for air, Jennifer moved her head from side to side, trying to free herself from her husband's grip.

At that moment, she saw it.

Under the old blue freezer, within arm's reach, there was a small chisel. It was pointing away, but its wooden handle was clearly visible.

Jennifer stretched her arm toward it and felt the cobwebs brush her skin. Every movement was difficult now, as if she was moving under water.

Suddenly, everything blackened for a second.

Norman's laugh filled her mind.

I can't faint, she thought desperately. *God, help me.*

Suddenly, she touched the chisel. She grabbed at it as if it were a lifeboat, and looked at Norman's face.

He was still laughing.

"I'm going to kill you," he whispered when he saw she was looking at him.

Mustering her last strength, Jennifer pulled the chisel from under the old freezer. Norman was still laughing when she buried it deep into his neck.

Norman's eyes widened and his mouth dropped open in an expression of incredulity. His hands released Jennifer's neck and touched his own. He looked at his fingers, soaked with blood.

Jennifer gasped violently for air, rubbing her own neck. Although she couldn't see it, dark bruises were already visible all around it.

Norman was trying to talk now. He looked at her, incredulous, his shirt already soaked with blood. Then he moved his eyes and stared at the place where he had been hiding before.

"You said..." he whispered, and his voice didn't have that disgusting hissing tone anymore. "You said that you would help me to make them pay..."

Norman fell forward, his body covering Jennifer and his blood bathing her. With some effort, she pushed him off and freed herself. Then she touched his neck, looking for the pulse.

There was none. Her husband was dead.

Jennifer started crying, and her tears cut a path through the blood on her face. She remained there, crying beside her dead husband on the garage floor, for a long time.

Then, when finally her sobs subsided and her tears started drying, she stood. Supporting herself on the workbench, she walked toward the place where Norman had been hiding.

And there it was, as she had suspected.

From the floor, near the wall, the little plastic devil stared at her from its place inside the bottle. It was grinning as always, but this time Jennifer thought its grin seemed larger, as if it was mocking her.

With a trembling hand, Jennifer took the bottle from the ground.

"Now," she said, looking at the little plastic devil inside the bottle, "I will do what I should have done since the first time I saw you."

But as soon as she said these words, a dizziness overpowered her. It was so strong that she needed to hold herself to keep from falling to the floor again.

Why are you blaming this plastic doll?" Jennifer thought, but somehow the voice in her mind seemed strange, as if it wasn't her own inner voice. *It's just a doll. It's inoffensive. If you need to blame somebody for what happened, blame Norman. He was crazy.*

The dizziness became stronger yet. The whole world was spinning around her.

Besides, her inner voice continued, and now its tone was slightly hissing, *now that everything is over, you could turn the old office into that studio that you always wanted.* It paused. *Now that you don't need to worry about Norman anymore, you could just throw all his things away and redecorate it. It would be great, wouldn't it?*

"Yes," Jennifer said in a low voice, "it would be great to have my own studio."

And this little plastic devil would fit nicely in that studio, wouldn't it? the hissing voice continued. *It would give a special touch to the decoration, don't you think?*

Jennifer nodded, and looked at the bottle in her hands. Inside it, the little devil's red-hot eyes seemed to glow.

But before you start redecorating, the hissing voice said again, *you know you need to do one more thing...*

"Yes, I know," Jennifer whispered, and put the bottle carefully on the workbench as if it was a treasure. She smiled at it, the same way a mother would smile at her newborn baby.

Then she stepped to the left and got an ax from its hook on the wall. As soon as she took it in her hands, the dizziness disappeared.

"Just one more thing before I start redecorating," she whispered, and approached Norman's dead body. "It will be nice to have my own studio. I always wanted it, and now it's MINE."

She raised the ax over her head and brought it down with all her strength.

Blood sprayed on the walls and on her face when the blade chopped into flesh and bones.

Jennifer smiled and raised the ax over her head again, her blue eyes seeming to glow in the garage's dim light.

THE DEBT

Diana Bennett

"Y ou owe me."
The voice rang incessantly in her ears. For weeks now it never gave her a moment of rest. Overriding every thought, canceling out all other emotions, it never ceased. Even though the sound was beautiful, more that any angelic choir could ever be, it still filled her ears night and day. If only it would stop. Even just for a second.

At first, it was a surprise. She wondered if others heard it, but soon found out it was for her ears alone. She tried to find comfort in the beauty of the sound itself, ignoring the meaning of the words. It worked for a while, but soon even the heaven of the tones became a hell. She tried to ignore it, but it would get louder and more demanding. Even sleep offered her no solitude. There was one dream that would appear night after night, after night. A dream of the terrible night not so long ago.

It was a party for a co-worker, who was retiring after far too many years. To celebrate, she had some champagne, maybe a glass or two, no more. She was just starting to feel the slight buzz that comes with alcohol and wanted to enjoy the feeling. Then, out of the corner of her eye, she saw him, the guy in shipping, who tried to hit on her every chance he got. Tonight was sure to be the latest attempt, considering he was trying to walk over to her. Trying was the proper term. He should have stopped drinking the fifth before the one in his hand. She looked for a conversation to try to join, but found none within easy walk. She was stuck.

The smell of booze preceded him. He might have been considered by some to be attractive, there might have been those who think he is handsome, but she was not among those followers. He was short and unkempt, with a mustache she always thought looked drawn on with eyeliner. His belly showed one too many Big Macs had visited in the past and to say he did a comb over was not to do justice to his hairstyle. He stood trying to look as suave as the alcohol led him to believe he was. In her eyes, he was barely standing; his words garbled and slurred, at times no more than mumbles. That was bad enough, but when he started to reach for her breasts, grabbing them like some prize awarded at a two-bit carnival, that was the last straw. She slapped him with such force the entire room was silenced by the sound of the blow. She glanced around and saw she had now become the focus of attention. No doubt she was also the topic of the ensuing whispers.

She stormed out of the room and fumbled for her keys, as she ran toward her car. How would she ever be able to show her face again to those people? Maybe the others were too drunk themselves to notice what had happened, but she knew better. She found the key and as the engine roared to life, she slammed it into drive and took off from the parking lot and onto the highway.

She hadn't driven very far when she glanced into the rear view mirror and saw two lights in the distance growing larger with each passing second. She knew who it had to be and what he wanted to do if he caught her.

With the lights so close it was starting to light up her car, fear began to grip her. She could still feel the residue of the slap upon her hand; no doubt, it was even stronger on his cheek. She had to do something, but what?

Her eyes scanned the surrounding countryside, praying for the first time in her life that the police would catch her speeding. There were none around, were there ever when you wanted one. She noticed somehow she managed to turn off onto a side street and was entering a neighborhood. Perhaps, she reasoned, she could lose him in there, with all the twisting streets. However, she dare not slow down or he would be upon her in an instant. She had seen enough people do high-speed turns in movies and on TV. She felt it couldn't be that hard. She might just pull it off, as long as she kept control of her vehicle. She wrenched the wheel to the right and her car did as commanded, taking the turn without effort. The lights were still behind her, shining on houses and cars she had past far too recent.

She stepped on the gas and began to turn haphazardly left and left and right and left, until the lights were no longer behind her. At last, she had lost him and she smiled a smile of relief and joy, grinning like a child with a new toy. She didn't notice the parked car in front of her before she hit.

In the hospital, she learned from the detective, the car held a young boy and girl, just getting back from their first date. She didn't know it was the girl's first car date. Nor did she know it was with a boy she had loved since sixth grade. It was her sixteenth birthday and she had been saving herself for just that boy and just that moment. Before that moment happened, they were struck by a car doing seventy-five in a twenty-five zone. Sixteen. Just a few years younger than she was herself. For the young lovers to be, death was instantaneous. Their supple bodies pried away from where the metal had melded into their flesh.

The true irony was the 911 call came from the man who had been following her. Not to have his way with her, as she feared, but to apologize for what he had done. He had gone from oafish buffoon to concerned friend, even going as far as sending flowers to her room, during her recuperation. At the subsequent trial, he confessed under oath that he was the reason for the accident and he, not this scared frail woman, should be charged. She was found to be not guilty of vehicular homicide because of his testimony. She was released and he was charged and convicted. Soon after, the voice began.

She decided that maybe therapy would help. Maybe someone with a friendly smile and a warm demeanor would believe her and not think she was insane. Maybe even if she were deemed to be suffering from a mental illness, she would be given the help she needed to make it stop. She would even settle for drugs, legal or otherwise. Any price would be worth it, no matter the cost. Just make it stop. Please, for the love of God, make it stop.

For the next year, she went twice a week, an hour each time. The doctor was a nice old gent, with a gruff sounding voice and a scraggy looking beard that seemed to fit him. He looked to be old enough to have known Sigmund Freud as a child. For nearly a year, twice a week, an hour at a time, he would sit, listen and nod while scribbling in his ever-present steno pad. She found out why her and her parents did not get along, why she hated green beans and there were not really monsters under her bed, waiting to eat her when the light was turned out. Nevertheless, the voice continued.

Watching TV one night, she saw an interview with a man who claimed to be able to speak to the departed. She sat glued to the set, hanging onto every word he spoke as if it were gospel. The next morning, she went to a nearby bookstore and picked up his latest best seller. She took it home and devoured each line, like a man who was being fed for the first time since a yearlong fast. Still she was hungry for more, not finding what she was craving. In the back of the book was a list of titles by other authors. She bought each of those and read them with the same fervor, excited by each new glimmer of knowledge she gained. Before long, she had amassed quite the library of dark works and the knowledge of the arcane to accompany them. At last, after a long dark path down many dead end leads, she found the tome she needed at an ancient used bookstore, on the Internet. It was rare and cost more than she had, but it had to be hers. She put a second mortgage on her house and soon the book was in her hands.

She took the dusty book and cracked open the cover, turning to the table of contents. There, in old script that appeared to be written by hand, was the spell she was looking for, 'How to banish bothersome spirits'. She turned to the page, sat down on the floor and began to read.

Later that night, she locked herself in the closet she had converted into a chamber of ungodliness, as the book said. She drew the diagram on the floor and lit the surrounding candles, saying the proper prayer, as each new flame burst into life. Then, wearing her robe and standing in the center of her sigil on the floor, she started to speak. At first, her voice was weak and faltering as she tried to speak the words of a tongue that had been dead for many millennia. However, they started to come easier to her the more she spoke them, her voice growing stronger and more commanding. Soon she was no longer just saying the invocation, but demanding an audience with the spirit causing her such never-ceasing aggravation.

The air inside the room seemed to swirl about her as she continued to call back into reality one so soon departed. She could feel the temperature dropping, the room getting colder. She saw the flames on the candles beginning to dance around on their wicks, changing colors, getting dimmer with each change of hue, until they were but miniscule points of light, not far from burning out. Yet, she continued in her recitation, never relinquishing her drive to put an end to the voice. The candles at last extinguished themselves and the room was enveloped in blackness.

Without any warning, an explosion of light engulfed her, forcing her to close her eyes. All trace of darkness in the room vanished, replaced by a pure white light emanating from the center of the pentagram on the floor. At last, she was face to face with what was causing her such torment.

"Who are you and why have you been doing this to me?" she demanded from the light.

There was no response.

Again, she issued her demand, more forceful this time.

"I command you, in the name of Xcajatm, Foemithr and Zoftctileum, they whose names are spoken as a whisper even by Mighty Lord Satan Himself, to answer me now. Who are you and why have you been doing this to me?"

She waited what seemed an eternity and was about to begin anew when she heard the sound that had been plaguing her all these years.

"I am she who you caused to be here. I am she who lost her heart's desire. I am she who is cursed because of your actions. I am she whose debt you are in. I am she who will never leave your side until the debt is paid in full."

She tried to see into the light, to make out the features of the one who spoke but it was no use. The light was too bright. It must be, it has to be, the spirit of the young girl that died in the car she hit.

Just then, she remembered the book in her hand. Glancing at it, she turned the page and began to speak.

"No, unclean spirit, there is no debt. It was an accident, nothing more."

"You owe me."

"No, again I say to you, there is no debt," she said and began to read from the ancient tome, "By all that is evil, by all that is unclean. By all that is dark and unholy. By all that creep along the dank bowels of the bottomless pit of Hell, I command you to be gone from my sight and from my side. I banish you away from me, never to find the peace you desire. In the name of Yartehict. In the name of Halitide. In the name of Bratetome. The power is mine and I command you to abide by my decree. Be gone!"

"NO! You cannot do this! Where is my justice?" the voice screamed.

"There is no justice, save for what I exact upon you. Be gone from me!"

With those words, the light that overpowered the room faded to nothingness. The blackness returning for moments, until without warning or explanation, the candles re-lit themselves. However, what amazed her was not the candles or what she had just experienced. No, it was that she was alone inside her head. For the first time since she woke from the hospital, all those years ago, there was no voice droning on, overpowering her other thoughts. She fell to her knees and wept with joy at what she had accomplished.

Time passed and she soon put all of the black arts behind her, she no longer had need or desire for them. She had done what she wished to do with the knowledge. She moved to another town, got a new job and even changed her name. She even forgot about the voice that once haunted her every moment. She was never happier than the day she met her true love. Swept up in a whirlwind courtship, she found herself giddy like a schoolgirl when he proposed.

At the wedding, she wore white, as entitled by tradition. It was a beautiful ceremony; she was radiant in her gown, as well as relishing being the center of attention. Moreover, she couldn't wait until that evening when she would at last give herself to the man who won her heart.

The evening came and they retired to their honeymoon suite. The lights were off and she slipped between the sheets, to join their bodies, as well as their hearts. They were quick to lock in passion's embrace and she reached down to feel his manhood that yearned for her touch. He stopped her, gazing down into her eyes. The demeanor on his face was changing from one of lust, to one of snarling animalism. He rammed himself into her, causing her to scream in pain, as her inner flesh was inhumanly torn asunder. She tried to fight him off, but he overpowered her with each attempt. Then the backhand slapping started. Each thrust was accompanied with a quick slap to her face and breast. Each stinging smack he caused spurring him on to more violent acts. His fists soon replaced the backhand. As blood began to flow and bone and cartridge splintered under the pounding, his thrusts increased in speed and intensity.

After exploding inside her, he looked at his handiwork. Her beautiful face now splattered with blood. Her lips split and teeth fragments imbedded within them. Her nose flattened beyond recognition, eyes swelling shut. Through the slits that remained, she looked up at the man who she loved. She saw him pick up a heavy vase that sat beside the bed and raise it in the air. She knew it was about to land on her head, taking her life. She managed to get out one quiet whisper.

"Why?"

He stopped and looked at her, the vase still held above his head. In a voice she had not heard in a long time, a voice more beautiful than any angelic choir could be, he answered as he brought down the vase upon her skull.

"You owed me."

DIANA BENNETT currently resides in Orlando Florida, with her daughter Jaquelyn, an ever-growing number of cats, one ladybug, which followed them home from camping, and a fish that just died. Her first novel, His Father's Son: Dante's Rage, and her collection of short stories Consternation, are now available. The second novel will more than likely see print in 2005. She is the editor of the anthologies, Monsters Ink, Raging Horrormoans, and UK, and writes a column for both Camp Horror and The Corpse. For more information about these or upcoming endeavors please visit her website at www.dianabennett.com.

JESSE WEPT

Eric S. Brown & D. Richard Pearce

Jesse took a long drag from the cigarette dangling loosely between his lips as he checked the chamber of his Colt. He slammed the full chamber into the gun and spun it, watching the dark streets below his window.

The dirty sheets on the bed were still turned up and unruffled. He would find no rest in this cheap excuse for a hotel tonight. Through the dusty windowpane, orange flames flickered in the night on the edge of town, casting eerie shadows across the room. If Jesse squinted hard enough, he could see the shadow things out there, dancing around the burning church.

X'ah had followed him here, and soon this quiet little town would be fighting for its life. Even now, Jesse imagined Reon's residents being dragged from their beds by X'ah's creatures, their flesh rent from their bones by the demons' razor-sharp claws—their despair as their physical bodies were eaten alive while their very souls were consumed by mouths that could not be seen.

A shotgun thundered somewhere down the street from the hotel. Horses reared and kicked out against the walls of their pens. They felt the evil as deeply as he did.

He should not have come here. The blood being shed in the darkness was upon his hands.

He wondered why he'd come, perhaps in search of protection? Some vain hope that mankind could or would rise up to save him as he had for them time and again? But he realized with certainty that in coming to Reon, he'd only brought death to their door. They could do nothing to help him—the limbless preacher dangling from the steeple of the church across the street was proof of that. Reon's destruction would do nothing but buy him a few precious moments to prepare for what lay ahead.

Jesse tossed the butt of the cigarette aside and pulled another from the tin in his shirt pocket, striking a match against the room's rough wooden wall to ignite it. There would be no more running. It would end here, tonight.

The door to his room burst open, nearly ripped from its hinges, as Matthew entered. The fat hotelkeeper was sweating like a pig and his skin burned a deep red from fright and exertion. "Mister, you better clear out! There are things out there in the street! They ain't human, killing everything in their path. They're working their way through the whole town!"

"I reckon if I was you, I'd be runnin' then." Jesse smiled.

Matthew stared at him for a second, befuddled by his calmness, and then shook his head, vanishing back out into the hall. Jesse listened to his shouts as he roused his other guests, warning them to the danger.

The streets below Jesse's window were alive now. Six-guns and rifles barked in the darkness, their short bursts a sharp contrast to the longer cries of the wounded and dying. Dark shapes flowed from the shadows and back into them, unhindered by the gunfire. Several other buildings were aflame now and the town outside the window reminded Jesse of Richmond of a few years before. He felt helpless, now as then. But maybe this time he could save the men from the Dark, even if he couldn't save them from each other.

Jesse shattered the window with a quick blow from the butt of one his twin revolvers and took aim at one of the moving shadows below. The gun's muzzle flashed and the shot was followed by a howl-like shrieking, high pitched and monstrous. A white body materialized and fell with a thud onto the walkway of the general store across the street. The thing was barely four feet tall and hairless from head to toe. It wore no clothes and a yellow puss leaked from the wound on its scalp as its body twitched and thrashed about in the throes of death.

"X'ah!" Jesse shouted, "I'm here! Come out and face me like a man!"

Shadows moved and leapt. Dark forms hurried through the chaos below toward the window and the hotel. Jesse opened up, blazing away with his Colts as white demons suddenly appeared as they died, littering the streets.

His Colts clicked empty. He flung the chambers open, spilling spent cartridges onto the floor with a clatter, and began to reload. Quickly, he packed six silver rounds into each of the twin chambers. He kissed each of the chambers, a gentle, patient blessing completely at odds with the chaos around him.

"J-E-S-S-E," a voice colder than the deadest winter echoed in the hotel below. The sound of an army of tiny feet climbing the stairs told Jesse all he needed to know. The Devil didn't believe in a fair fight. Neither did he, not this time. He climbed out the window, tossing his cigarette underneath his bed. As he half jumped, half fell to the street below, his room exploded in a shower of broken wood and flames. He heard the squeals of the demon-things behind him as they died in the blast. "It's amazing what a few well-placed pounds of TNT can do," he laughed to himself.

He rolled with his fall, barely managing to avoid breaking his legs as he hit the ground. He was on his feet and running even as the hotel buckled inward on itself in a fiery collapse. He didn't delude himself with the notion that he'd been lucky enough to get X'ah too. At best, he'd merely evened the odds a bit.

Reon's survivors still ran about in the streets, panicked and terrified. A few had managed to find horses or wagons and were hotfooting it out of town. The Shadow things were there also, though their numbers were smaller, patches of blackness descending upon the innocents as they tried to flee.

Jesse stumbled in his haste for the stables and went tumbling into the dirt. Cursing loudly, he got to his feet as he saw the glowing figure of X'ah standing outside the remains of the hotel. A halo of light surrounded him, and though the angel should have been beautiful in his white robes, the effect was marred by the glistening blood of the damned dripping off of him. His eyes held an infinite blackness, and long blonde hair spilled down over his shoulders. He stood with his arms spread wide as if to embrace the carnage before him.

"Jesse, it is time," his voice called out inside Jesse's head, though his lips never moved.

Jesse stood his ground, his hands resting on the butts of the Colts tucked in the holsters on his belt.

"Go back to hell and leave me alone!" Jesse screamed at the figure in white.

"Not without you," X'ah floated an inch off the ground as he swept towards Jesse. "Not without my son."

"I am not your son!" Jesse wailed as tears welled up in his eyes. With blinding speed, Jesse's Colts cleared their holsters, but X'ah merely waved his hand and they flew from Jesse's grasp.

Jesse turned to run but X'ah was upon him, his arms snaking around him with blinding speed. "Are you not?" the demon asked as he drew the man close to him. Jesse struggled, but was helpless in the tentacled embrace. X'ah turned the man around, deposited him on the ground before him. "Are you not?" he repeated. "And who else would have you? The Creator?"

Jesse looked up, tears creating little channels on his soot-darkened face. He said nothing.

"Oh, yes, and will the Creator come and claim you as his offspring, haul you down from the tree where you hang amongst thieves and criminals? You made that mistake before, did you not? How many fathers will you call upon before you recognize me?"

"You cannot be my father." Jess stubbornly shook his head. The demons surrounded him, visible now, leaving off their sport with the humans and leering at him maliciously.

"Cannot? How can I *not* be your sire? Again I ask you, how many times will you be reborn, how many times will you give yourself to these sheep, calling on whatever god they hold dear at the moment to recognize you? Did Zeus save you when you were chained to the rock, as I came every day to feed upon your liver? Will you give away more palaces, more riches, more kingdoms? Who else came for you—Brahma? How many incarnations will you have, Lughnasadh? Or shall I call you Adonis, or Tammuz, or Enkidu or Quetzalcoatl?"

Jesse said nothing, defiance on his face, but despair in his heart.

"Who is there with you, son of man, at every death? Who is the father of the Hanged Man, if not the Devil?"

Jesse wept. "Enough," he said, "It is as you say. What do you want of me?"

The demon leaned forward, eagerly. The stench of ten million corpses was in his breath as he stretched forward to embrace his 'son.' "Finally, you will acknowledge me?"

"No."

The voice came from behind X'ah, and the demon whirled around, dragging the unfortunate gunslinger with him. "Who dares?" he started.

A small girl-child stood there, tattered and dirty in her nightdress, ash on her face. "No!" She shouted up at X'ah. "You let him go!"

Jesse clamped his eyes shut, desperately praying to whatever god might be watching this generation, praying to the child. *Run, child, run.* "Leave her, X'ah, you have me."

X'ah released Jesse, who slumped to the ground. He snaked his tentacles toward the child. "I have you both, Jesse. And this one I will enjoy."

"No! Mama says you can't hurt me, not when my angel is watching. I know who you are, old Scratch. You have to go, 'cuz my friend's tougher than you."

X'ah caressed the girl's face, dragging his tentacle along her cheek. "Really, child? And who is your friend that is so tough?"

"He is." She was pointing to Jesse, who was standing again. He had quickly looked for his guns, but realized now that he didn't need them. He stood behind X'ah, wrapped his arms around the demon, breathing into his ear like a lover. "She is right, you know, X'ah. I am stronger than you. You will always be here for them, but so will I. Despair is strong, but Hope is stronger."

X'ah screamed, lashing out at the girl, but his tentacles bounced off of her like she was under glass. Then he lashed back at Jesse, who calmly ignored the tentacles tearing at him. X'ah kept striking, and pieces of flesh and clothing were flayed from Jesse's back. But Jesse didn't seem to notice. He leaned in, and seemed at first to be kissing X'ah on the neck, but his mouth kept opening wider, and he drew X'ah in, slurping the demon's grotesque form into his mouth, slurping the tentacles in last.

He turned to the screaming demons. "Be gone," he said, and they were.

The girl wrinkled her nose at him, "You *ate* him. Yuck."

"It *was* yuck. He tasted awful."

The girl laughed. "I have to go find Mama."

Jesse nodded.

He turned and found his guns, slung them in their holsters. He patted his stomach, and opened a door to nowhere, "Come, father, we should get you home."

ERIC S. BROWN is the author of the paperback collections: *Dying Days, Space Stations and Graveyards,* and *Portals of Terror.* His fourth collection, *Madmen's Dreams,* will be released from Permuted Press in April, 2005. Eric's first novel, *Cobble,* is also due out in 2005 from Mundania Books. Other works by Eric S. Brown include the chapbooks *Zombies the War Stories*, *Still Dead*, *Flashes of Death*, *Blood Rain*, *Bad Mojo*, and *Dark Karma* as well as the e-book *Poisoned Graves*. His short fiction has been published over 250 times in a wide array of markets ranging from places like *The Book of Dark Wisdom*, *Post Mortem*, and *The Blackest Death* anthology series to *The Eternal Night*, *The Milestone Literary Journal*, and *Cyberpulp* magazine. He lives in North Carolina with his wife, Shanna, and his cat, Howard.

D. RICHARD PEARCE has been seen lurking here and there around the web. He is a slush reader for Creative Guy Publishing and a slush writer for whoever will pay. He is pleased to have written a few stories with Eric S Brown, and is looking forward to *Madmen's Dreams*, which include a couple of his own. He lives on the West Coast of Canada.

THE LITTLE BOY WHO CAME BACK FROM THE GRAVE

Tim Curran

One moment Reed was alone, the next there was something with him.

He was drained from another day hawking insurance to bored, plastic faces, and then the air shifted, moved, turned in on itself. It went cold and dank like a dungeon and there was the rank stench of rotting leaves and stagnant water.

That's when Reed saw his visitor.

And seeing this, his breath came rushing out and his heart hitched painfully. There was an explosion of noise in his skull and his flesh went tight and rigid. His vision blurred, then sharpened and made him look, made him take in what was sitting on the sofa, dripping black water into the carpeting.

It was a boy.

And he was dead.

Reed was certain of that. Maybe ten or eleven years old, the boy was dressed in a muddy, mildewed suit gone to rags. His face was bleached white, hung from the bones in flaccid flaps and folds, was set with numerous holes or punctures like something had been burrowing into it. There were leaves in his hair, dirt streaked over his ashen complexion, and his eyes were compressed hollow moons.

And he was grinning...fetid water running from the holes in his face.

Reed thought he would fall from his chair, hit the floor, and knock himself out cold. But that didn't happen. He remained upright, staring, watching, sucking it in like a sponge, filling himself with a blackness that was absolute. He could not move. Could not think. Could not do anything but listen to that tearing sound in the back of his head which he was certain was the sound of madness, the sound of reality finally ripping open and him with it.

Wetting his lips, blinking his eyes, Reed said, "Who...who are you?"

The boy kept smiling that black, evil grin, the frayed corners of his lips pulling up farther and farther until his face was slit open and all those gray, crooked teeth were jutting from the gums like splintered pegs. Reed saw something squirming behind those teeth...maybe a tongue, maybe something worse.

The boy stank and dripped and leered.

There was a silence in the room that was thick and green and pregnant. Reed could hear the blood rushing in his head, the sound of water dripping from the boy, and a ragged, rasping sound that might have been breathing.

The boy moved, stood up with the sloshing, pulpy sound of wet linen. His puckered face kept grinning, those eyes oozing with water and silt. He held out one hand, the fingers white and bloated and wrinkled. There was something in his palm, something shiny trapped in clots of dirt.

The boy spoke and his voice was one of river mud and poisoned tidal pools, lake weeds and pale things washed up on beaches: *"I brought you something...Tommy..."*

And that voice, the thing knowing his name, this is what made Reed slide out of his chair, made him begin to shake and whimper. A scream was born in deep in his belly, rising up in a shrieking, demented wail that exploded in his throat but could not get past his sealed lips.

"I brought you this."

And the dead boy tossed what was in his hand.

Gray water splashed over Reed, made him shudder. Something struck his chest and fell into his lap. And when he looked up, the boy was gone. There was just Reed, ass on the carpet, that noisome stink in the air, the sofa soaked with dirty water. There was a puddle of it on the cushion, a water bug squirming in it.

It had not been a hallucination.

Reed reached down and picked up what the boy had tossed him. With trembling fingers, he brushed the dirt away. It was a bracelet, tarnished but still shiny, an earthworm tangled in it. Reed shook it away with a weak cry.

Saw what he was holding.

He knew that bracelet.

His mother had been wearing it when she was buried.

The next evening, Reed met Nicole at the Firehouse Grill, sat there numbly while she talked about the wedding. Nicole always talked about the wedding. Like some little girl trapped in a princess fantasy, oblivious to the world around her. Reed always listened, always loved to hear her plan their life...but now, now it all sounded empty, impossible. Like some story he had heard too many times and simply couldn't believe any more.

So their food came—broiled whitefish for her, barbecued chicken for him—and Nicole talked and talked, did not see or listen, her voice a loom that knitted fabrics and worlds around her. The caterers and wedding dress. The champagne glasses and the timeshare in Tahiti. She talked, pausing only to swallow a bite of dinner, then charged right back in.

Wonderful, pretty Nicole. Her with the big emerald green eyes and choppy short red hair. She taught kindergarten and had no use for spooks unless it was Halloween. Bless her heart.

Reed tried to eat. After the dead boy had visited him, he tried to do a lot of things and each one was a failure. His chicken was rubbery, corrugated-looking like the boy's face, and once that occurred to Reed, he set his fork down and could not pick it up again.

Finally Nicole said, "I want you to come to school on career day."

Reed shook his head. "No...no, I can't."

"And why not? The kids would love you."

"No, they wouldn't. I sell insurance for chrissake, Nicole, I don't chase down bad guys or put out fires. I'd bore them to tears talking claims and pending litigation. Jesus, baby, that stuff bores adults, let alone five-year-olds."

"Oh, come on," she teased. "You're not that boring."

But Reed would not rise to the bait. What was inside him now, what he had seen and felt and experienced...it was eating a hole straight through him. All he could smell were waterlogged corpses, and all he could see were dead little boys, water dripping from them.

"You seem kind of distant, Tommy," Nicole said. "Is

something bothering you?"

Boy, that was a good one. Here it was, Reed's opportunity to lay the whole stinking, insane mess at the feet of his beloved. But he couldn't do that to her. He couldn't bear the look in her eyes when she saw that he was crazy.

"No, I'm okay. Just tired, I guess."

But it was a bad lie and he couldn't even dig up the ambition to yawn to reinforce it. He felt...flat, used-up, gray inside and out. Maybe that didn't make sense, but that was how he felt. Last night, he'd been terrified. This morning, disturbed. And now? Just gray. Gray as rainwater being sucked down a street drain.

Nicole wasn't eating now, either. "You wanna try telling me the truth here, Tommy Reed?"

"The truth?"

"Yes, you know. As opposed to bullshit."

He managed a weak smile at that. "I think I saw a ghost."

She started to smile herself, a mischievous look in her eye. It was the way she looked at her kids. The way she gazed on one of them when they said, *Miss Braden, I saw a ghost. I really, really did see a ghost.* So Nicole smiled. And then she saw that her fiancé was dead serious and the smile just fell from her lips. Something else replaced it, something unpleasant. "Tommy...what do you mean you saw a ghost?"

So he told her. It didn't take very long. He found that he could not look her in the eyes as he reeled it out, had to stare at his plate, his hands, the tablecloth. Because, honestly, it all sounded a little ridiculous when put into words. That was, unless you'd experienced it.

Nicole just sat there and the look was in her eyes, that look that said, well, let's put on the brakes here, because I'm not marrying a crazy man. Maybe it wasn't that extreme. But there was concern there, maybe worry and pity, too. A sense that Reed had just crossed some barrier of trust, of believability, or reliability, and there could be no going back.

"Well?" he said to her, seeing that look and not hating her, but surely hating himself. "You think I'm crazy. Great. So do I."

Nicole sighed, wetted her lips so maybe they wouldn't crack open or her voice wouldn't squeak. "Maybe you've been working too hard or you hallucinated or...Jesus Christ, Tommy, I don't know. But dead people are dead and...I can't believe I'm having this conversation."

Reed couldn't believe it either. He pulled out his mother's bracelet, showed it to her. She would not touch it, like maybe there was a germ of madness on it and she might catch it. He set it on the table. "She was buried with this twenty-five years ago. Maybe I lost my mind, maybe I fucking hallucinated that little zombie, but I sure as hell didn't imagine this."

Nicole swallowed. Swallowed a couple more times. "There's someone I want you to talk to."

"Oh, for chrissake."

"Please, Tommy, please do this…"

A psychiatrist, of course.

That's whom Nicole wanted him to speak with. She was a real big believer in therapy, encounter groups, 12-step programs. Whereas some people were afraid to bare their soul, Nicole was the original soul-nudist. No shame, she bared it all, flaunting every saucy disfunctional curve of her life. She was from a broken home and her sister had committed suicide when she was thirteen and her first husband had beaten her. So, being more than a little spunky, Nicole had brought it all out, talked and dissected her demons until they slinked away, heads hung. You had to hand it to that girl, nothing kept her down.

But Reed wasn't that way.

Never had been.

His thoughts, his memories, his demons were kept under lock and key like priceless collectibles, and only taken out rarely, viewed, but never touched, never handled. Slipped back in their protective wrappers and tucked away in a strongbox.

But now Nicole wanted to change that.

Jesus.

Reed sat there thinking about this, staring at the TV, a warm Molson in his fist. Talking to the psychiatrist, the therapist, that's all Nicole wanted. It would make her happy. But what would it do to him? What would it do when he started unwrapping all the private goodies and this therapist started sorting through them like a marble collection? Deciding, after he or she heard Reed's tale of the dead boy, that this collection was a few marbles short.

Reed thought: *Why don't you be honest with yourself? Why don't you admit to a few things here? Why don't you just admit that you know who the boy is?*

No, no, that wouldn't work at all. There were certain things in a man's life, in his past, that had to stay buried. Maybe they felt like they had to crawl out of said graves now and again, but what you had to do was kick them back in and bury them even deeper.

The phone rang.

It was midnight.

Nicole would not call so late. All of Reed's wild friends had moved on after they learned that he was having a relationship; nothing frightened them more.

The phone kept ringing and Reed kept telling himself that this was not good, not good at all.

Setting his beer down—eyes watching that sofa as they had been all evening, waiting perhaps for something decayed and obscene to sprout like funeral lilies from the cushions—he picked up the phone. Picked it up and held it in his hand at arm's length like maybe it was something that might bite him.

He put it to his ear. "Hello?"

There was a breathing on the other end, ragged, phlegmy, hollow…like air sucked through a swamp reed. And a voice, that same evil voice of wet things and dead things and things drowned in leaf-caked pools: *"Tommy, Tommy, Tommy…guess what I did to your mommy…"*

And Reed standing there, cold steel links tightening in his belly, remembering things he'd tried so hard to forget. "Fuck you," he said, his voice weak and airless, but controlled despite it all and filled with threat just as sharp as razors.

On the other end, a high deranged laughter that was shattering glass and forks scraped on tin plates, screams echoing through clogged pipes and fingernails on blackboards. It was a lot of things and none of them good, but mostly it sounded like a boy vomiting out his intestines down a mineshaft. Reed threw the phone against the wall.

When it didn't break and the laughter still squealed from it tinny and distant, he stomped it to pieces with his foot. Then he got a carving knife from the kitchen and waited.

He didn't wait very long.

The therapist's name was Kathleen Brogan, who sounded less like a shrink and more like an Irish barmaid. Reed went in to see her, took in the books on the shelves, the antique desk, and the obligatory leather couch.

"Ah," he said. "The couch. The fruit of all evil."

Brogan laughed. "It's really not that bad, Mr. Reed."

"You telling me you never had any psychopaths on it with a Norman Bates complex? Oh, doc, you're destroying my illusions and preconceptions. All those old movies I watched, too. So much for drama."

Kathleen Brogan was thin, thinner, dressed in a skirted business suit. There was a sternness around her mouth that was in great contrast to her huge brown puppy-dog eyes. Had she gained maybe thirty pounds, rounded out what nature gave her, she might have been attractive. But as it was, you could have picked your teeth with her.

"Go ahead, Mr. Reed. Sit on the dreaded couch," she said, enjoying the banter apparently. "It doesn't bite...at least not at first."

Reed was looking at the art on the walls, mostly impressionist stuff like fruit in bowls and peasants carrying sheaves of wheat on their backs. Nice, inoffensive stuff. There were a couple expressionistic works, too. Reed found them creepy. But that was the wide, wonderful world of psychotherapy, he supposed, a little impressionism and a lot more expressionism.

Reed sat on the couch and despite his lagging spirits and world-view, which had been thrown into the cellar, he had to suppress an urge to giggle madly. "Before we get into my Napoleon complex and the little men who keep stealing my Jujyfruits, I think we should get a couple things straight, doc. I'm a husky guy and I want my straight jacket in extra large, also make sure there's lots of straw on the floor of my cage at the laughing academy because I gotta weak bladder. And, would it be too much to ask, do you think, to tell Dr. Happy not to shave my head when they do the lobotomy? I'm already losing my hair and I don't think it'll grow back if you take too much off."

Brogan just smiled thinly, sitting behind her desk. "Well, Mr. Reed, I'll see what we can do. Generally, for the lobotomies, we just use a drill with a half-inch bit and as far as your cage goes, you'll be in the community room with the other nuts living in your own filth. Now and then, an orderly will spray you down with a firehose to keep the nits off you."

"Fair enough. One more thing, get that letter-opener off your desk before I lose control here. You gotta keep sharp objects away from my kind. Don't they teach you people anything?"

Brogan just watched him and Reed had to look away. Those eyes of her were very intense when she turned on the steam. He could already feel them looting around in his head, picking at the rusty locks up there.

He stretched out on the couch. "Well, where should we start? I had a typically morose childhood. There were seventeen of us living in a squalid, rat-infested steamer trunk. My father was a rag-picker and my mother—"

"All right, Mr. Reed. That'll do."

Reed sighed, turned off the faucet of his amusement and, without looking at her, knew what she was thinking. "The people who are laughing the most on the outside are crying the hardest on the inside, eh, doc?"

"Do you mind if I call you Tommy?"

"Please yourself."

"Why don't you tell me about yourself, what you do, where you came from."

"Not much point in that, is there? What did Nicole tell you about me? Other than that bit about me being loony, that is."

Brogan said Nicole had told her nothing. "There's something on your mind and we both know it…why don't you just tell me about it. I won't judge you."

Reed felt the gloom taking him back over, the sense that Mr. Reality had bent over too far and ripped the ass out of his pants. He licked his lips and tried to think of all the "safe" bullshit he had planned on telling Brogan, but like a soft penis, it just wouldn't come. "Okay, you want some dirt, lady. I've got some for you. But before I begin, maybe you ought to get that room ready at the state hospital."

Brogan sighed. "Already phoned it in."

Reed nodded. "Do you believe in spooks? Ghoulies? Vampires? Boogeymen? You know, any of that comic book shit that don't have the sense to stay in their graves?"

"I've never seen any," she said diplomatically. "But that doesn't mean they don't exist."

"How about ghosts?"

She shrugged. "Have you seen a ghost?"

"You could say that."

"I'd like to hear about it."

Reed cleared his throat. "I was sitting at my apartment. I had a long day, I was tired. Not tired enough to hallucinate. I wasn't drunk. I'm not on any medication. I don't do drugs. I don't even smoke anymore...at least that I'm willing to admit. Anyway, the air felt funny all of a sudden..."

When he was finished, Brogan scribbled a few things on a pad. "Okay. That's sounds very traumatic...but why would this ghost target you? I mean, I would think ghosts of little boys don't harass people at random. There must be a reason behind it."

"Hmm. You're right. You're very good," Reed told her. "There *is* a reason and I know what it is...I just can't believe it, is all."

"Why don't you tell me about it?"

Reed tensed. There, she was picking those locks. For 25 years he'd kept these things secret and now it had all come back to him. Since he figured he was insane anyway, he began to talk, letting it flow. "We lived in a tenement, Northside Milwaukee. And it *was* a tenement. Cold water walkup with rats and bedbugs. My mom and I lived there. I never met my father. My mom was a great lady. She held down two jobs, was always scrimping and saving, trying to get us out of that shithole. I don't mind saying that we had it tough. The neighborhood was dirty, full of winos and bums and, later on, drug dealers. But for all that, the people who lived there were a pretty tight bunch. They watched out for each other."

"Sometimes that's the way it is," Brogan said.

"And sometimes it's not," he reminded her. "Anyway, when I was ten this Hispanic family moved into our building. No big deal. There were other Hispanics in the neighborhood and they were okay. My best friend was a kid name Louis Armados. His old man was Puerto Rican and his mom was black. They were good people." Reed paused, remembering it all. "Anyway, this Hispanic family moves in. Their name was Lupero. Mom and dad, this weird old guy who might have been a grandfather, and, Chimmy. Chimmy was my age. Chimmy is what this is all about, you see.

"Chimmy was a weird kid. He had just a hint of an accent, but it almost sounded more European than Hispanic. He was small for his age, pale as cream, with black hair and blacker eyes. One of those kids with the central eyebrow, you know? I tell you honestly, doc, the first time I saw him something crawled up my spine. I didn't know what it was then and maybe I wasn't entirely sure later, but it was there, all right. Like driving by a cemetery at night...it gets to you, but you're not sure why. Maybe it was my imagination. Who knows? My memory has gone to hell with my sanity.

"Anyway, this Chimmy was weird. He liked to fool around like the other kids, but he just didn't know when to stop. He was a little monster, I'd guess you'd say. He did a lot of fighting out in the playground and mouthed off to the teachers, spent a lot of time in the principal's office. He was a little thief, always stealing things and threatening the other kids. I remember he punched this little black girl in the stomach hard enough to drop her and was kicked out of school for like a month. But I suppose you can't blame everything on that little deviant. His family was weird. His mother was crazy and would scream a lot in the middle of the night. His grandpa—or whoever the old guy was—was no better. He was always peeking around the shade, tapping the glass with his fingers, watching us with those dead eyes of his. Chimmy said he was a witch and we believed him. But the worst one there was Chimmy's father. He was a brute. Always nice to us kids outside, but behind closed doors he would beat the living hell out of Chimmy. Maybe the kid deserved it."

Reed paused and Brogan watched him. "Do you really believe Chimmy deserved it, Tommy?"

"You didn't know that kid, doc," he told her. "Maybe none of us really did or wanted to. But his father did, I'll bet, and maybe that's why he did those things. Chimmy told us once that his dad beat him to drive the devil out of him. Crazy shit, I guess. Bottom line, Chimmy was frightened of only one person and that was his father."

"His father was probably the reason he was so vicious," Brogan said.

"Maybe. Maybe not."

"Tell me some more, if you want," Brogan said.

Reed did. He had to pause a moment, pull something from deep inside himself and, whatever it was, he didn't like handling it. "My friend Louis did not like Chimmy. Louis was a tough kid, but a good kid. He decided Chimmy was trouble and decided to ride that little freak for all it was worth. He used to pick on him, push him around. Once, after school, he beat him pretty good. About a month after that, Louis disappeared. Just vanished. Nobody ever saw him again. It was all over the news, in the papers." Reed was having trouble with this part, the memory of it was like knives in his belly. "Um…a couple months later, some utility workers found some bones down in the sewer, human bones. They figured it was Louis. They tried to keep it from us kids, but we heard, all right. Louis had been stabbed and cut, dumped down in the sewer...probably still alive...and left for the rats. Jesus, Jesus Christ. And you know what made it worse?"

Brogan shook her head. "Tell me."

Reed chewed his lips, ran stiff fingers through his hair. "What made it worse is that I knew who killed Louis."

"Who?"

"Chimmy. Chimmy killed him. He told me so. Said something like, 'Hey, that prick Louis, I kill him pretty good, eh? The rats strip him to bones.' No, don't ask me if I told anyone because I didn't. I wasn't about to rat out Chimmy. I didn't have the guts."

"Were you afraid of him?"

Reed managed a thin, brittle laugh. "Yes, I was. Lots of kids were. There were some big mean kids in that neighborhood, but sometimes the small ones were the worst. Chimmy definitely was."

"So what happened?"

"Lots of things happened, lots of nasty things, but there's no point in going into it all. Suffice to say that somebody was robbing the apartments during the day while people were at work and my mother saw who it was: Chimmy. She saw him coming out of a flat down the hall with a TV. She told me he was smiling at her. That's how my mom got killed, see. I came home from school one day, an awful feeling in my guts. The cops were there and they wouldn't let me go into our place. My mom had been cut up, her throat slit."

Brogan wasn't writing now. "Dear God...that's terrible."

"Yes, it was and it is," Reed said coldly. "And I knew who killed her. I knew it was Chimmy. I just knew it. Anyway, I was dumped in a foster home and stayed there until I was seventeen and joined the Navy."

"And what happened to Chimmy?"

Reed looked at her. "I killed him."

"You killed him?" Not a question and not an accusation, maybe something in-between.

"It was two years later. The Menominee River in Milwaukee. Lots of us kids would swim there. We weren't supposed to. A bunch of us were there, fooling around. I saw Chimmy and he saw me. I was getting pretty big, pretty tough. He saw that and he knew it was trouble. He was right." Reed had his teeth clenched now and his voice was coming out with sharp gasps of air: "That little sonofabitch…he laughed at me. Kept swimming by me and *laughing* at me. There were a lot of kids there, dozens of us splashing, and when he passed by me again…Christ…I took hold of his head and put him under, held him there until he quit moving. Nobody noticed. And you know what? They're wrong about dead bodies floating…Chimmy sank like a brick."

Maybe Reed was expecting Brogan to comment on this, but she did not. She just watched him, let him go about it at his own rate. Reed used to wonder if maybe he would have felt better confessing all this, purging the sin and guilt from his soul…but he did not feel better. He was shaking and sweating and his hands were sore from being balled into fists.

"Do you want some water?" Brogan asked him. "Maybe… maybe something stronger?"

He shook his head. "I'm not done. I've already dug myself a deep hole here, admitting this crap. No going back now. Just hand me a bigger shovel. Might as well finish the job."

"Just take your time."

Reed sighed. "You're probably wondering if killing that evil little shit made me feel better…well, it did not. I left the river, told the other kids I wasn't feeling so hot. I made it maybe a block until I ducked into an alley and threw up. I laid on the pavement awhile, scared white, sick to my stomach until some guy put out the garbage for a restaurant. He took me inside, called a doctor…or some guy in that neighborhood who claimed to be one."

"Did you ever tell anyone?" Brogan asked.

"Hell, no! You're the only person besides Jesus and my mother that knows about this mess. I know what you're thinking, that this makes me a killer. No better than Chimmy—"

"I'm thinking no such thing, Tommy," she admitted to him, and he believed it. "Trust me on that. Yes, there's possibly a crime involved here, but nothing I hear in this room goes beyond this room. Besides, Tommy, you might not have killed him at all. You were young, you were overwrought, and, take my word for it, memory can be a deceptive thing. And particularly those memories we hold the strongest."

Reed nodded, said, "I want you to understand what Chimmy was even if I'm not sure myself. Calling him a 'boy' is like calling a man-eating tiger a kitty cat. Believe me. Maybe it was environment and maybe it was heredity and maybe the devil was in that kid, but I'll tell you something, and this from an adult's viewpoint: Chimmy

Lupero was black and rotten right down to the core. There was nothing remotely good or decent about him. If you think a kid like that who went around setting fire to houses, throwing dogs poisoned meat, and trying to push other kids in front of buses is just a normal, healthy child, then you're crazier than I am. Way I saw it at the time, I was crushing something dangerous, something that had already caused a lot of suffering and would cause a lot more if left to his ways. Chimmy was a leech, doc, and he fed off of pain.

"But don't think, even so, that it was easy on me. I had some rough spots as a kid and I could be pretty mean if you cornered me. Shit, I was a street kid, you had to be tough. But I never hurt anyone purposely...not until I stomped that little insect. Like I said, tough as I was, it was hard on me. I was sick for weeks, could barely eat. I lost a lot of weight and ended up with some kind of fever that I barely pulled through. By the time I came out of it, well, I thought maybe I'd dreamed it all. Nobody ever found a body in the river. None ever washed up. Chimmy's family probably never mentioned the fact that he was missing, were just happy with the fact. I don't know. A current probably sucked him out in the deeps.

"For years afterwards, I would have nightmares. Awful, scary nightmares about him coming for me. I'd wake up at three in the morning, sweating and trembling, certain that he was standing over me, breathing maggoty breath in my face..." Reed was breathing hard, trying to hold it together and not doing a real good job of it. "But time passed and, eventually, I left it in the past. Sometimes, though, I'd remember and feel sick inside."

"Do you think your own guilt might have something to do with this apparition?"

He shook his head. "No more than I think my thoughts color the sky, lady. Sure, I'd love to believe this was some headcase gobbledegook about repressed guilt manifesting itself in the image of my crime. And maybe I could even believe that. Maybe I could swallow that nonsense if I only saw the dead boy once..."

"You saw him again?" It was obvious Brogan did not care for this. Maybe it was tossing some pat theory she had into the wastebasket or maybe she was thinking that Reed *was* crazy.

"Last night. Last night he called on the phone. I knew it was him before I even picked it up...isn't that something?" Reed's voice dropped now a few octaves into a dead, uneasy monotone. "Yes, he called, said something about my mother."

"What did you do?"

Reed laughed, rubbed his hands together like there was something on them. "I got a knife from the kitchen and I waited for him. See, I knew he was coming. And he did. One minute I was alone and the next...that little horror was standing behind me, giggling. I turned and I wanted to scream. He was all white and bloated, pulled and stretched and swollen-up, his face full of holes, things squirming inside him. Not like a boy, but like some grotesque Halloween scarecrow just standing there, stinking and dripping and making gurgling sounds in his throat. That smell, doc, like sticking your head in a garbage can full of rotting fish." Reed paused, kept swallowing like he couldn't get his throat wet enough. "Sure, I was scared, I was terrified. That thing...it disgusted me on levels I can't even explain to you, made something inside me curdle like cream. But I hated, yeah, I still hated that wicked little monster. So I grabbed him by the hair...except that hair was greasy and crawling like newborn snakes, and I gave him the knife. I sank it right in his belly, right into that *filth*." Reed let go with a high, hysterical laugh. "You ever stab a ghost, doc? You can't stab 'em. Chimmy wasn't solid like you and me or transparent like on those dumb ghost movies, he was...Christ, I don't know. The knife went in him right up to my wrist and he was cold and wet inside, crawling and dirty, like wet rags and dank mists...moving and slithering. I...I dropped the knife, I guess. It fell right from my fingers because inside Chimmy was cold like nothing you ever felt. My arm went numb right up to the fucking elbow and he started laughing, all that black polluted river water running from his mouth..."

Brogan let him compose himself. He was wringing wet, shaking, his teeth chattering. Finally, she said, "What happened? Did he go away?"

"I guess...I woke up on the floor like an hour later. I was drenched and cold. He must have been standing over me, dripping on me..."

Brogan let the silence hang, let Reed sob under his breath. It was pathetic watching him try to rein his rioting emotions in. The smug, sarcastic man who'd come into her office had been replaced by this: a wreck. A man drained physically and emotionally, his soul ripped wide open and bleeding poison.

"You realize," she said after a time, "that this is a serious... condition you have, Tommy. That we'll need to talk again. The sooner, the better. Because you can't go on like this. Something has to happen."

He stood up, fixed her with a steely, caustic glare. "Oh, something is going to happen, doc. I'm going to send that little monster straight back to Hell..."

"Well?"

"Well, what?"

Nicole gave him the look and Reed knew exactly what she wanted, was just wondering how in Christ's name he was going to tell her any of this, or maybe not tell her at all.

"What happened with Kathleen Brogan?"

Reed said, "She thinks I need to be locked up. I'm a danger to myself and society. She recommended a full frontal lobotomy... they want to pull my brain out my ass with a dessert spoon."

Humor. It was funny and he knew it was funny, yet there was nothing funny about this business and surely nothing funny about what his life had become. Yes, stark and haunted and insane. That was Tommy Reed's life in a nutshell.

He was sitting with Nicole at a restaurant again. This time not the Firehouse Grill, but a swank seafood joint called Clementi's. They had a clam linguine there to die for. Fresh bread. Bottled their own wine. Cooked shrimp and steaks over open flame, Sicilian-style. Right then, Reed was staring at a hot loaf of bread in the wicker basket before him.

The smell of it made him nauseous.

He cleared his throat. "She wants to see me again and probably again after that. I'm really fucked up and she knows it."

Nicole took hold of his hand and squeezed it. "We'll work through it. Did she...I mean, does she believe—"

"In my ghost?"

"Yes."

"She didn't say. She seems pretty open-minded about spooks, though. Maybe she believes and maybe she doesn't. She said it doesn't matter if it's real or not, all she cares about is what it's doing to me."

"She's good. Didn't I tell you she was good?"

Reed just nodded, wanting to say so much more to Nicole, but afraid to on some basal level. Afraid if she knew what he had done as a kid, she'd run away and never come back.

Nicole kept squeezing his hand. "I'm worried about you, Tommy. You were always so strong. This is scaring me."

He pulled his hand away. "Scaring *you?* You got any idea what this is like for me? It's hell. I know what's happening, but nobody will believe me. Even you won't believe me...I can see it in your eyes, you think I'm fucking nuts. Do you have any idea how that feels for me? What that does to me?"

"Tommy..."

"No, piss on it. Let's talk about something else. I need to hear you talk about something else."

Nicole chewed her lip, looked at just about anything but him. She started going on in a hollow voice about what was going on with her kids at school, which was a lot with the spring program coming up. Costumes to make, songs and dance moves to rehearse.

When she paused, Reed said, "Keep going, honey. It's nice to hear something...*normal,* something that doesn't involve my screwed-up head or ghosts and ghoulies."

She started to talk again, tears in her eyes now. And the food was coming, the waiter setting it all up on a little stand. Steaks smothered in mushrooms, still sizzling from the grill. Side orders of bacon-wrapped shrimp and fettuccine. The smells were heaven, but Reed was not moved. His voracious appetite which had survived numerous diet attempts and given him a good paunch, had finally been stilled. He was losing weight rapidly and there was no end in sight.

The waiter said he'd forgotten his pepper mill and danced away to get it.

Nicole wrapped her arms around herself. "Does...does it feel really cold all of a sudden?" she said.

And it did.

You could feel it plummet ten degrees in a matter of seconds. And there was a good reason for that: Chimmy was there. Standing there, watching Reed. His eyeballs were blanched white with pinprick pupils that stared from muddy sockets, one huge and glaring, the other only partially open. He was dripping and stinking, draped in seaweed and drawing in waterlogged, bubbling breaths. Each time he exhaled, foul water ran from the holes in his distorted, blubbery face.

"What?" Nicole said, alarmed now. "What is it?"

The waiter returned with the pepper mill and she waved him angrily away and it looked like he was glad to go, like maybe he'd stepped into something or it had stepped into him.

Nicole, watching Reed staring into space, feeling that dank cold on her like fog off a pier, said: "He's here...he's here, *isn't he?*"

Reed tried to nod, tried to answer, tried to do a lot of things. But he was powerless to do more than stare and shiver and feel his soul going to a stew of rot.

Chimmy saw the horror crawling on Reed and grinned a black, crooked smile, his white face hitching up and quivering. Black, oily tears ran from his eyes. He made a sound like a backed-up drainpipe, opened his mouth and pulled something out of there with tumescent fingers. Pulled something from deep in his throat like a strand of red licorice.

Something wet and looping.

A worm. A ten-inch segmented mud worm, slimy and wriggling. He dropped it onto Reed's plate where it coiled fatly in the juice of his steak, writhing and corkscrewing.

Then Chimmy began to dissipate like smoke.

And Reed began to scream.

Reed was an underwriter at Southern Wisconsin Insurance. Although it was hardly a glamorous job, he was good at it and he made a good living. Around the office, he was known to be the guy with all the answers. Only today he had a lot of questions. When he went in to see Marsha Bricole, a claims-file adjuster, two days after the nightmare at Clementi's, he had lost ten pounds since the last time she'd seen him. His eyes were staring, glassy balls sucked into hollows and he smelled like whiskey and cigarettes.

"Jesus, Tommy," Marsha said. "I heard you took a leave of absence...what'd you do, go on a toot?"

He just stared and stared. "I need your help."

"Close the door," she said, feeling what was coming off him and knowing it was nothing to joke about.

Reed came to see her because she was the only one who might be able to help. Marsha was into new-age spiritualism. Believed in the tarot, numerology, and the power of crystals. She planned out her life according to the phases of the moon and would happily admit as such.

"Marsha…you're into all that…that spooky shit," he said in a rasping voice. "That new-age shit, right?"

She raised an eyebrow. "I guess."

"I need help. Supernatural-type help."

Marsha suppressed a wicked urge to laugh. "You? Mr. Skeptic? Oh boy, this is gonna be good."

"You're the only one who can maybe save my life." Reed dropped that and it sobered her very quickly. "You know people, right? People who channel and have powers or think they do. You know people like that, right?"

Marsha leaned forward. "You're serious, aren't you, Tommy?" Seeing that he was, she said, "What do you need?"

"I think," he said, "I need a witch."

Reed wasn't sure what Dara Troon was, but she wasn't a witch as such. Marsha warned him against calling her such. When Reed got to Troon's place—an apartment in an upscale high-rise, of all things—she answered the door in an old gray sweatshirt and jeans, both spattered with white paint. He could smell the latex in there.

"Don't mind me, Mr. Reed," she said, "just doing a little redecorating."

Nope, no pointy hat or witch's dress. No candles burning atop skulls or simmering cauldrons. Just an ordinary woman in an ordinary, though expensive, apartment with a stunning view of Midtown. Here he'd been expecting Marsha to send him to some old shack at the edge of the marshes. No such luck.

Dara Troon was barely five feet tall, was chubby and had beautiful blue eyes like azure reflecting ponds. She poured them both a glass of Chianti and asked him what he wanted.

"I'm being haunted," he said, feeling foolish saying such a thing on a bright, sunny day in this woman's airy, modern flat. "A little boy is haunting me, tormenting me. I want you to…what do you call it…get him off me."

"Exorcise him, you mean?"

"Yes."

Troon sipped her wine. "Give me some details. Everything you have."

Reed did, giving her everything but the childhood bit. "That's all there is."

"Sorry, but I don't believe that. These things are not just coincidental, Mr. Reed. They happen for reasons. If this little boy is haunting you, then there is a tie between the two of you. You might not recognize it as such, but it's there."

This then is why Marsha had called Troon, not a witch, but a wiccan, which meant either "wise woman" or "cunning woman". And obviously Dara Troon was these things.

"Try again," she said.

So Reed did, wrenching it all out of himself with a certain bitterness. "I guess I've just admitted a crime to you. As a good citizen, you should call the police."

But Troon just shook her head. "And what could they do but make a bigger mess of this than it already is?"

"Can you help me?"

She set her wine down on a glass table. "I can try. Just understand that what you will have to do is dangerous and I can't do it for you. In fact, you couldn't pay me enough to do it for you. You have either one of two things here, Mr. Reed. Either a malignant ghost or a vengeful elemental pretending to be that boy. Take your pick."

"What do I have to do?"

So, taking her time, she spelled it out for him…so to speak.

Friday. Midnight.

The witching hour.

Reed stood there in his living room, feeling mad and disoriented and having trouble remembering when he hadn't felt that way. He thought of Nicole and himself, the way things had been and the way he wanted things to be again…but he didn't believe it anymore. He just didn't believe in fairy tale endings. What was happening to him now…this sort of stain, you could spend a lifetime scrubbing and it still wouldn't come off.

He had torn up the living room carpet now, drawn a big circle in chalk, a pentagram inside of it. He placed the black ceremonial candles at each point of the star and lit them. He was standing in the center of the pentagram now. Carefully, he set down the things he would need at his feet.

Dara Troon had given him specific instructions, and he followed them to a tee. He had not eaten in 48 hours now. Had bathed only in the salts she had given him, had drank nothing but spring water. Purity was important, she said. It all seemed silly to him, but he did it, believing it would work.

And belief, the yuppie witch said, was all-important.

After meditating for a time, Reed took out his mother's bracelet, said a few words over it. The bracelet was the avatar and Chimmy would not be able to ignore its pull on him. Reed slit his left thumb open, let a few drops of blood touch the bracelet. He took out the slip of paper Troon had given him. Then he read the words. Read them three times as instructed.

He waited.

Nothing.

If the entity does not show itself, you may have to make things more personal.

Yes, Reed thought. Yes.

He read the words three more times. Then he looked around the room, said aloud: "Okay, you stinking little fuck, show yourself. Show yourself or I'll summon up your old man to beat your ass…"

There was a crackling in the air as of static electricity. It went thin and cold, became hard to breathe, then went thick and sodden and oppressive. Reed felt something tangle in his stomach. Felt a chill at his spine. The room was alive with shadows, with a distant dripping, the sound of wind howling through empty churchyards and vacant houses.

Chimmy appeared.

He did not grin. He just wavered there, corporeal yet misty, a flux of tissue and gas and malefic hunger. His shirt was open and his belly was white and pustulant, set with crawling green worms like the teats on a goat. Reed did not look him in the eyes. He read the words three more times and Chimmy became more ethereal, more insubstantial, filmy and rippling like liquid. As Reed read more of the words there rose in the room a noxious stench first of sulfur and steel, then wormy decay, and finally sewage.

Chimmy began to hiss.

Began to scream inside Reed's head about how he had killed his mother and fucked her in Hell, how he still fucked her. How they all fucked his mother in Hell.

Reed pulled out the little doll Troon had made. Looked like a burlap gingerbread man, but weighty, stinking of spices and rotting things and graveyard dirt, all the dark wonders sewn up inside. While Chimmy raged and taunted and filled the room with the screams of the damned, Reed dropped the image of Chimmy into a brass bowl. Then, carefully, he uncorked the bottle of undiluted hydrochloric acid.

"Chimmy Lupero," he called out. "You will dissolve as these fibers dissolve..."

The acid hit the doll and it began to twist and undulate like it was alive. Maybe it was Reed's frantic, overheated imagination, but it seemed to make a tiny, agonized mewling sound like a sick kitten. And then the acid found it and devoured it, dissolved it, turned it into a black and muddy soup that bubbled and spattered.

Chimmy was like a slug hit by salt. His flesh sputtered and smoked like hot grease, became a lurid red wax that ran and puddled. He became a running, fluxing clot of color that paled and grayed, turned in upon itself and pissed out a vile yellow steam. Then he was just a tower of screeching rags, billowing and blowing like a sheet in a tempest. Then even that curled-up, blackened, became ash and dust that died in its own whirlwind.

And that was it.

Reed stayed in the circle another hour, holding his mother's bracelet and chain-smoking.

When he finally stepped out of it, the air smelled fresh and clean.

"It's been some time since we talked," Kathleen Brogan said to him two weeks later. "I know you've been through an awful lot, but sometimes it does help to talk."

Reed, looking much thinner and somehow older than the last time she'd seen him, just nodded. His eyes were distant, depthless like smoky glass. "I suppose it does. But sometimes there are things all the talking in the world can't cure."

"If you mean Nicole..."

"I'd rather not talk about Nicole," he said. "That's all over and I have to let it be over."

"It won't do you any good to bottle it up inside, Tommy. Trust me on this. I'm saying this not only as your therapist but as Nicole's friend." Brogan didn't get any response on that, just those eyes that were more haunted than old houses. "We were all shocked by her death—"

"Oh, were you? Were you really shocked? Well, I was a little more than shocked, doc, I was fucking traumatized. What happened to Nicole...Jesus...that's a table I sit down at every day, every night. I sit down and I eat and fill myself with guilt and horror and I can't tell you all what."

"Precisely why you can't live with it day in and day out, all alone..."

Reed uttered a high, splintered laugh. "I don't have a choice, I don't really have a choice." He studied the prints on the walls. "When they found her...when they found Nicole strangled, I was the first one they questioned. Did you know that? For three fucking days those dumb shit-eating cops kept stopping by at all hours. You know what those dumbasses did? They showed me morgue photos of Nicole, told me how she'd been strangled with a rusty chain..."

Brogan was not untouched. "That's unacceptable, Tommy, in fact that's out and out bullshit. The DA is a friend of mine. Tell me the names of those cops and I promise they'll regret what they did."

But Reed just shook his head. His eyes were like open, bleeding wounds. "It doesn't matter. None of it does. Let's...let's change the subject, if we can."

Brogan took her time. "Well," she said, "I suppose you know what I'm going to ask you about?"

"Chimmy." That got another shallow, humorless chuckle from Reed. He began to smile and he couldn't seem to stop. "I hired a witch. She told me what to do."

"Which was?" Brogan asked, not surprised at the depths of despair in this man. Not surprised at all, really. He was draped in agony, inhaling suffering and exhaling torment.

Reed told her about it very calmly. What was there to get excited about?

"And...and did that work?"

Reed really started laughing then and couldn't seem to stop. It was a bitter, twisted shrieking that echoed through Brogan's office, finally broke down to a breathless, broken sobbing. "Oh, lady, it worked. It worked real, real well." Reed wiped his eyes with shaking fingers, studied the tears on his fingertips. "Until last week, that was. You see, Chimmy came back again. Except this time he's not alone. He's got a little girl with him. Her name is Marnie. Somebody dumped her in the river, chained her to a cement block...she carries that chain with her and it's all rusty...she calls it her necklace..."

TIM CURRAN lives in Michigan, works in a factory by day, and writes horror, crime, and westerns by night. A member of the HWA, he has appeared in nearly a hundred different magazines and anthologies, including *Flesh and Blood*, *City Slab*, and *Black October*, as well as in anthologies such as *Vicious Shivers*, *Sick*, and *Darkness Rising*. His supernatural horror/western novel, *Skin Medicine*, is available from Hellbound Books. You can find Tim Curran on the web at: http://www.darkanimus.com/curran.html

SÉANCE.NET

Peter Ebsworth

E verything was done. Fresh flowers on the grave, sealed letters on the hallway table, he had even cleaned the house. Somehow it seemed appropriate, he knew they would assume that his mind had been warped by his grief, but maybe the cool logic contained in his letters combined with his meticulous preparation would make them reconsider. The front door was unlocked, so that they wouldn't even have to break in to find him. There was a reference to that in his letter to the police, in case they thought that he'd just forgotten.

For the final time, he logged-on to his computer, no longer feeling any impatience with the time delay as Windows booted up. No experience might ever again hold quite the fascination that it did the first time, but sometimes the thought that it might be the last came close. Once the hour glass told him the process was complete, he clicked on Outlook Express, which automatically checked for new messages, although he no longer had any interest in whether he did or not. There weren't any. Going to 'read mail', he called up the e-mail from Séance.net to confirm that his appointment time in the Server was 6:00 pm; then closed the screen to enter the Net on Explorer.

After subscribing the previous day, he had dropped the web address into Favourites, so now he highlighted and single clicked to take him to the site. When the welcome page loaded, he typed in his name, then 'memory', which was his password for everything. Clients were taken to wait in the chat room—'reception' was the name they called it in the e-mail that had given him his joining instructions. Immediately, a message appeared in the room box saying, 'Password: memory, please enter consultation link five on the options above.' Lining the top of the page were six link buttons. His hand was trembling on the mouse, making the cursor arrow move in small random jerks. Only after pausing to take a deep breath did he succeed in pressing number five. Before him the page opened up into one full screen blank page with a grey outlined text input box at the base. Then words began to appear. His mouth felt dry and his heart quickened as he realised that he would never log off from this page. Once this last task was completed, it would be his time to die.

Amethyst: Thank you for subscribing to Séance.net. I am Amethyst, your personal medium and guide. Together we will connect with the spirit world and communicate with the one you seek. May I have your name please?

Paul: Paul Underwood.

Amethyst: Welcome, Paul. Have you ever used a Medium before?

Paul: No. I've always thought that you were a bunch of charlatans and frauds. But then I've never been this desperate to contact anyone before.

Amethyst: That's not unusual, Paul. When the *Titanic* finally went under, I would guess that she didn't take any atheists down with her. Cynicism is always emotional thin ice; it can't bear much weight. Who do you wish to contact?

Paul: My daughter, Becky.

Amethyst: When did she pass through?

Paul: Die, you mean? When did she die?

Amethyst: Yes, if you prefer. But die is such a final word for what is, after all, only an evolution from physical to spiritual consciousness. The universe is alive with the life force; our living bodies channel and focus our awareness like a signal through a radio. Death is only the transition back to the original spiritual world from which we came. Becky has not stopped 'being', she never will. None of us ever will. So when did Becky make the transition?

Paul: Three weeks ago. She died three weeks ago in a car accident.

Amethyst: That is a very recent transition, Paul; she may not have had time yet to find her place on the spiritual plain. I may have to use a spiritual intermediary already known to me to establish contact. What were Becky's interests? It will assist our spirit guide to calm her if he can remind her of familiar and well-liked things.

Paul: Horse riding, discos, boy-bands, she liked all the usual teenage girl stuff, but most of all the Internet. She absolutely adored the chat lines and e-mails. She even built her own web site so 'cyber friends' could find out all about her.

Amethyst: Thank you. That will help. If we are able to find her, what are you wishing to ask?

Paul: I don't need to ask anything. You only have to get a message through to her. I thought that maybe, just maybe, this site could be real, that you might be a genuine medium, that in spite of all the smoke and mirrors there could be a little real magic. So I'm giving it a try, giving you a try.

Amethyst: I am genuine, Paul, but I warn you now, not infallible. Spirits are still people, often lost and bewildered people, especially after only a few weeks on the other side. I may not even be able to find her. Is the message to say you're sorry? It so often is. Sorry things weren't different; sorry you didn't try harder. If so, she will already understand and, indeed, she will be feeling the same. Believe me.

Paul: No. I want her to know that I'm coming to get her. I'm going to make the 'transition.'

Amethyst: I'm sorry, Paul, *Dad*, but I don't understand.

Paul: Well, you should understand; it's very simple. She's only fourteen, and I'm not leaving her there on her own.

Amethyst: But, Paul, she's not *Daddy, is that really you* on her own, she's with all the family that have gone before. It's natural to be upset, but the pain will ease over time. Please don't do anything foolish.

Paul: Why is it foolish? You tell me the spirit world is real; well I have a Smith & Wesson Home-Defender next to my keyboard that's my ticket over. But I want her to know I'm coming, to not be afraid anymore because she will know that I'm on my way. How can I know how long it will take me to find her? Maybe it'll be hours after I'm dead, maybe days. However strange and frightening the place, at least she will have the comfort of knowing that her dad's coming through for her, she'll know that I'm going find her whatever it takes. I've thought it through and realise that she needs me now more than ever.

Amethyst: Look, Paul, tell me where you are, you need help. *Daddy, I'm not dead. I'm at home, but where are you?*

Paul: Becky?

Amethyst: No, we will be unable to make any contact today. My temporal connection has faded; the spirit guide has left.

Paul: Honey?

Amethyst: Paul, you must understand that I am not saying that *Dad, was it a mistake? I knew that you couldn't be dead, I just knew it all along, but no one would listen to me* the spirit world is an actual place, think of it more as a state of mind.

Paul: What's happening, have you made contact with my daughter? Is that her speaking to me?

Amethyst: There's only me, Paul, this is a one-to-one chat room with no observers and no other participants, I'M BECKY UNDERWOOD FROM CEDARS AVENUE, WINSTON AND I WANT TO KNOW ARE YOU MY DAD OR NOT but I need your address to get you some assistance. Is there anyone else in the house?

Paul: Yes, it's me, Becky. It's Dad. But you're not at home Hon, not anymore.

Amethyst: There's no point in trying to talk to her, I can't make contact with your daughter, believe me, Paul, I honestly can't.

Paul: I've been trying to reach you through a medium and it seems like it's worked. Don't worry, sweetheart; I'll soon be with you.

Amethyst: Stop it, Paul, you're frightening me. Look, I'll be honest; I'm just someone trying to earn a living on the Net. I thought that this website could be a money-maker. I have no more link with the spirit world than anyone else, which is none. You were right, it is only smoke and mirrors; it's all illusion. *No Dad, I'm at home on the computer. I logged onto Séance.net to see if I could make contact with you. We were in a car accident on the way back from Michele Richards' party, and when I came round in the hospital they told me that you had died. I knew it was a lie, I knew that you couldn't really be dead, but it's been so long since you've been home that I started to think maybe you could be. Did you loose your memory or something, like in a movie?*

Paul: I did crash the car bringing you back from the party. It was my fault; I was tired and didn't react quick enough to avoid the truck. I'm so sorry, so desperately sorry. But it was you who died, honey; I just wish that it had been me instead.

Amethyst: PAUL, READ WHAT I SAY! THERE IS NO SPIRIT WORLD. IT'S MADE UP TO COMFORT PEOPLE. IF YOU KILL YOURSELF YOU WILL GO NOWHERE. YOU WILL JUST BE DEAD. DO NOT COMMITT SUICIDE. *Dad, maybe we are both OK. Do you remember that dead boring show that you made us watch on the Discovery channel that said every possible outcome might really happen, but then split into different worlds?*

Paul: Yeah, I do, based on Quantum Theory. Every possible timeline actually exists. The Multiverse Theory, you're a clever girl to remember that. But, sweetheart, they were different dimensions or something. There's no way to communicate between them.

Amethyst: PLEASE LET ME GET HELP! *Maybe we've found one. I'm fine, Dad, I really am. Missing you will never end, but as long as I know you're alive somewhere, then I'll be content. Stay where you are, Dad, messages within cyberspace may cross over dimensions but people can't.*

Paul: Are you really alive somewhere, Becky?

Amethyst: *Of course I am, silly, the dead can't type. Now promise me you won't hurt yourself.* I'm sorry, I've done what I can, you are obviously in great distress and very confused but I must insist that this finishes now. *Promise me, Dad.*

Paul: I promise. But you must swear in return that you are truly alive and safe, not only Becky's spirit returned to stop me killing myself.

Amethyst: That's enough, if you do not disconnect immediately, Mr Underwood, I am going to close down this site at the server feed.

Paul: NO STOP. SHE'S HERE WITH US NOW, CAN'T YOU SEE? CAN'T YOU READ HER? FOR GOD'S SAKE DON'T CUT US OFF.

Amethyst: I'm sorry, but you've left me no choice, I can't be responsible for this. Goodbye, and please, don't end your life; there is, honestly, nothing else. I LOVE YOU DAD!

Paul: Becky, swear to me…

Sorry. This Web Page is now unavailable.

A TWIST OF HATE

Christopher Fulbright

The depth in his eyes is what hit me first. When he answered the door, it looked as though someone had used his face for a punching bag until I realized the sockets were just greasy with sleeplessness and chemical inhalation. His eyes were more than alert; his pupils were so dilated you couldn't tell the color of the irises.

Garrett Frier looked a hell of a lot different than he did on the picture in my pocket. In the picture he stood outside on a warm day in checked golf shorts, pink tank top, one arm propped on his metallic green convertible Miata. In the picture, Garrett Frier had the face of a successful man.

The Mr. Frier who now stood before me had the face of a man who was low on sleep, high on meth, and had frowned most of his life. But more than that showed in his eyes; this man's soul was very old, and much of its inherent knowledge was wisdom of the mind's darker sways. The majority of my victims have this same aura. I can only remember one out of hundreds who didn't—the first one.

But that was a long time ago. And right now, I had some pending business with Garrett Frier.

He stood framed in the doorway of his home wearing a large plaid robe. Wisps of silvery hair were pushed back behind both ears, wet from a recent shower. He smelled like Irish Spring and Old Spice. His eyes squinted at me and joined the curl of his freshly shaven upper lip in a sneer. The look seemed to fit him just fine.

"Can't you read?" He snapped and stabbed a thumb at the sign plate above the doorbell.

NO SOLICITING.

I gave him a distant smile.

Garrett Frier waved his hand in front of my face. He snapped his fingers.

"You stupid, buddy?"

I squinted my eyes at him. The summer sun was hot on my shoulders and the back of my neck. Sweat dripped into my eye and stung. I blinked it slowly away.

As the heat of the sun soaked through my skin, the emanations of his presence twisted in my guts and I felt a surge of rage. This guy was spit. Worthless junkie sicko. I ground my teeth, set my palm stiffly against his broad chest, and shoved him back into the foyer.

"What the—?" Frier stumbled backward as I followed him in. I slammed the door behind us without turning my back on him.

It took a moment for my eyes to adjust to the darkness of the foyer. None of the curtains were open in the house, and beyond the foyer the veil of shadow slowly dissipated to reveal a sitting room full of vacant furniture. The walls, the staircase, and the hall tables were dark knotted wood to match the cheap paneling.

The knots of wood began to swirl and darken, peepholes from the beyond. An audience of demons to witness the kill.

Garrett Frier moved to get up and fell short of the task. He panted from the feeble effort. Fifty-two years can take a heavy toll on a junkie.

"Who the fuck do think you are, you son of a bitch?" He growled.

I balled my right hand into a fist. I explored the backs of my teeth with my tongue. My teeth were still grinding, but now I'd stolen his sneer. I leaned down and jabbed his cheek with a quick left, then floored him with my right. My blow crushed the cartilage of his nose. Crimson drops spattered the white marble of the entryway.

He rolled over, a fat sow of a man, his white flesh peeking obscenely from beneath the plaid robe. One thatch of gray hair had come dislodged from behind his ear. His frown-creased face was bewildered. His bloody hands wandered between his nose and his unbelieving eyes.

"You..." he whispered, "I'm...bleeding."

"Yes, you are."

He narrowed his eyes and tried to probe me, to get some intuitive insight on the situation. I let down my psychic shield and gave him a glimpse.

When the fear dawned in his expression, his face resembled that of a day-old corpse.

"I know you," he whispered.

As he lay transfixed by my image, I pulled the 9mm Beretta from my sling and felt the weight of its devastating power in my hand. The dark energy of the gun surged into my veins and fueled the building rage within. It came from the core of my being in waves, taking over the automation of my body.

A sound like that of strong winds and rushing waves filled my ears and the power of death flew from my molten core. I pulled the trigger. The Beretta kicked.

The bullet pierced his skull clean between the eyes.

Shredded lumps of brain sprayed through the back of his head, which fell with a wet splat to the marble floor. The grout seams of the entryway slowly filled with blood.

My rage subsided. The psychic rush dropped off, and I felt suddenly beaten and out of control, as though the entire meaning for my existence had emptied of purpose and I knew I wasn't lucky enough to die.

The stabs of pain struck me as I stood there in the dead man's entryway. Garrett Frier's energy filtered through me as it snapped free of its mortal coil. His sins and hate felt like hot iron rods piercing my body. His energy flowed through the web of my soul as I absorbed what part of that energy was mine. A rush to the head knocked me to my knees, blacking my vision. Still I clutched the Beretta in my right hand. It was my handle on the world. It was a talisman to boost my power, my tool I used to feed, and even though I fell to the cool, blood-painted tile in a fetal position from the ferocious intensity of the pain, I would not let it go.

Sight returned to my eyes slowly. The pain ended abruptly. It left behind a tingling of warmth, contentment. New strength filled my veins, but it wasn't the same surge of power that had overtaken me before the kill. This was fresher, cleaner. It was an awakening. The Enlightenment. That's all I've ever called it. It's the only word that ever seemed to fit.

Natisha sat on the green floral print couch in her small studio apartment, somehow managing to look relaxed. The sofa—divan, actually—was the product of a Goodwill drop-off theft, but was still in good condition. The back and arms were curved with decorative wood trim, but the cushions themselves were too hard for me. Most of the time I just leaned in front of the TV whenever I stopped by. It ensured her attention when I spoke to her. I'd never seen anyone get so lost in television as Natisha. That was the main reason I stood in front of it. The other reason was that she usually wore short skirts, and didn't seem to mind giving me an innocent flash of those delicious slices of flesh between her thighs.

I wondered if she could feel my desire for her. But then, it was foolish to assume that she couldn't. We were connected.

I wondered if there were times when she physically wanted me. I wondered if she would sometimes dream of me when sleep was creeping near, and her bedroom filled with those whispering shadows which told her of things to come.

Natisha looked up at me with half-closed eyes. A used syringe lay next to a spoon and open bindle in front of her. She slouched on the couch with her arms wide open, as if expecting someone to lie down on top of her so she could embrace them. I knew better. Tracks scarred the pits of both arms; one irritated red mark stood out at the inside of her wrist. She probably didn't have much luck finding veins there either. But while the scars of Natisha's addiction marred her arms, those were the only things it seemed to have touched. Her skin was flush with new sun on top of an already bronze tan. Her complexion was healthy. Her breasts and waist and hips scored a perfect 36-26-36, and the shape of perfection was only heightened by the best pair of legs this side of Traci Lords. The way she was sprawled on the couch, arms open, legs open and spread wide on the coffee table before her, she looked like dessert.

"Well, Cade," she said conversationally, propping her head on one hand. Her hair flowed in shining waves of black velvet around her. "Did you do the job for Kalley? The old man?"

I nodded and folded my arms in front of me. The TV emitted the melodramatic classical theme music to some old 40's black and white. I still leaned with my back against the screen. Natisha's pupils were swimming with heroin and she tried to focus her thoughts on my recent whereabouts. I knew she couldn't have known—the heroin seemed to stifle her intellectual probes. Normally, her perceptions would have been acute enough to simply know without having to ask, and I'd subsequently volunteer the details. That was on a normal visit though. She wasn't normally high, despite her appearances. The tracks had never gone away from when she'd been living on the streets of Phoenix years ago. She'd quit the heroin completely when she moved here. Or so I'd thought. Looked like she'd taken it up again.

"Yes," was all I said. I contemplated asking her about the drugs but decided against it. Her business. I got a little happy with meth from time to time myself. We both had our vices. "I did the Kalley job."

"How was he?" Natisha sighed. She looked as though the greatest feeling in the world just coursed through her body, her eyes still peering deep into mine. I looked away from her hypnotizing gaze to where she slipped the narrow fingers of her right hand into the low neck of her dress. Her fingertips traced circles around her nipple for a few moments, arousing the other breast at the same time. When she stopped to reach for a Marlboro Light, both nipples showed like sharp nubs beneath the thin fabric of her dress. She went to cross her ankles on the table, but spread her legs farther apart at the knees. I caught a glimpse of golden chain wrapped around the highest part of her thigh. Her snatch was still partially hidden in shadow. I knew she would be hot to the touch. I knew it.

"It did the trick, but I have to say the quality of substance has taken a significant decline on these past two kills for Kalley." I met Natisha's eyes. Psychic and sexual excitement danced like playful flickers in her eye as she watched me, looking to see how long I could withstand the urge to take another peek. Despite what I'd just told her though, I still felt the strength and cleansing revitalization filtering through my soul into my consciousness and getting me high. The reality of Natisha's cozy one-room apartment grew sharper edges as I stood there, feeling better than any man-made drug alone had ever made me feel. My mental acuity sharpened along with the detailed visual effects. I smiled at Natisha, moving up to the edge of the coffee table, still blocking her view of the TV, towering above her in a show of my hunger to dominate her.

She sensed it. She felt my spider-like probes soothing the pleasure centers in her mind. She leaned her head back on the sofa, closed her eyes, and breathed deep. Her shining red lips curled into a smile. Her hips twisted, as though she were writhing to the rhythm of deep penetrating sex.

"Oh, my God, Cade," she breathed, reaching up to unbutton and peel away the satin material of her low-cut black blouse. Her breasts were firm, rounded mounds that barely sagged when she pulled down the material, exposing them. The blouse was bunched around her slender waist, just below her belly button. Her left nipple was pierced with a small golden ring, its chain attached to a similar hoop on her belly button. The chain glittered with facets on the slope of her breast, falling into the valleys of her abdomen. "Cade," she whispered desperately, "Please share it with me…" she gasped and opened her golden eyes again, pinning my center, trying to manipulate my will. "I haven't fed in so long, Cade…I need some of your light, so I can see again. Uh! OOOoooh!!! Cade, please…so bad…*let me in…*"

Surrender your energy to me, Cade…surrender…let me in…submit…

I reached down and took her right foot into my hands, massaging the tender flesh of her arch, working my way up to the balls of her feet. A violent shudder ran through her body. Goosebumps rose over the sweat sheened surface of her skin. Natisha's hand finally went to her clitoris, blending sweat and excretions of pre-orgasmic cum like oil in a nest of trimmed black hair.

I felt some of the strength began to trickle in moderation from the light within me, down the conductors of my arms, through the bones of my hands and into my fingertips. I continued to massage the balls and heel of her foot, paying close attention to the heel. It was one of the most receptive points of the body for transferring energy.

I gave Natisha a taste of the old man's strength.

I charged her with a portion of what good energy I had absorbed from the man. I forced my thumbs deep into the softest part of her foot until I felt the connection between our hungry souls and let it flow.

I closed my eyes to envision the transfer.

My soul is stretched taught, a tattered spiderdemon's web constructed between two gnarled, bare trees in a silent, windless forest in Purgatory. The uppermost membranous section of my soul is colored red, which fades into violet on a clockwise spiral, which bleeds into blue, and a smaller band of green, followed by a circular yellow-golden bullseye at the center of the tapestry. As my body connects with Natisha's body, so too does a ray of light beam forth from the brightest center of my soul, cutting through the ashen timelessness of Purgatory to find its mark at my Earthbound shell, which serves as a conductor into Natisha's own life force. Her mind in turn projects a diffused shower of yellow energy, misting her own soul with its light.

I see her soul.

I follow her through the familiar Silent Forests of Purgatory, where my own soul has been stretched between those ancient gnarled trees for two centuries now. I wholly expect her astral form to pause at her own web, claiming one of the uncounted millions which hang in the forest as one of her own.

Natisha's astral form continues through the forest, however, and my spirit experiences a new region of Purgatory, where none was thought to exist. Natisha's form clears the forest and emerges into a valley. The valley sweeps upward into a horizon of gray and featureless mountains, against a twilit azure sky. I have never seen the skies above Purgatory. They are much as I had speculated they might be; no sign of Earthlike wispy clouds, only clear views to the cosmic activity that takes place above the world of the damned. Nebulas span the skies, red and silver and orange with blue mists groping like phantom tendrils. Layers of the fantastically lighted gases and glittering dust and debris form the ever-changing shapes of the Watchers Above. The demigods began simply in the shape of glittering nebulas or clusters of stars which could have been distant galaxies. Then the shards of light began to shift, as though an ethereal wind had blown through space, stirring them from their natural course through eternity, forcing them to take the shape of nine-headed hydras, of flying dragons with smoky fangs and ancient beards, of dark angels with clawed wings spanning the Universe…

"…Cade…"

Natisha's call to attention drifts through time and space to the consciousness of my traveling spirit. I have been wandering the heavens while allowing Natisha to feed off the lightness of my soul.

Give it to her. Give it all to her…

Something tells me that. Someone. Another me.

Give her all the light…

But I cannot. Though she needs even more, I save the last for my own. A soul needs light to stay alive. Even mine. Though my power is drawn from the greater darkness of my soul, inherent wisdom tells me there must be light in the center of my web for the soul to conduct Earthbound life. Survival instincts make me sever the beam.

Energy collapses along our trails. The landscape of Purgatory zooms by in reverse. I am alone. Clutching her foot. Alone again in the forest. My soul, tattered, not much light left at the center.

No more.

No more.

"No more," I said aloud, and released her foot, setting her trembling leg gently to the table.

Natisha's beautiful body convulsed before she opened her eyes and gasped, golden irises alive with the afterglow of the transfer. She breathed heavily, undoubtedly losing the effects of the heroin in combination with the ecstasy of Enlightenment. She licked her lips, looking around the shadow-darkened interior of her apartment as she tried to refocus on reality.

Twilight had given way to nightfall, and the only light in the room was that of the flickering television casting upon her a ghostly pallor. She reached absently between her legs. Her fingertips came back wet. Then she sighed and leaned back on the couch, once again relaxed. Her dark eyes came to rest on my face, then skipped down to the bulge in my jeans.

"Thank you," she whispered. Slowly she sat up on the couch, and swung her cascade of hair behind her. It fell onto the back of the couch like unfolding satin as she straightened her skirt to conceal the glistening dampness between her legs. She closed her knees and sat topless, turning to stare at the movie.

I walked around the coffee table to sit beside her, and she barely acknowledged me.

She wanted more.

I relaxed and placed my hand on her thigh.

She kept her knees closed, and was unresponsive. Her eyes reflected the movie. It was an old movie that I remembered having seen over here a couple of weeks before, Hitchcock's *Strangers on a Train*.

The character of Arthur Ash, a famed tennis player, had just finished elaborating on the troubles between he and his wife to his psychotic train-car companion, when he suddenly stops talking to the stranger and proclaims:

"Oh, forget it. It's not easy realizing you've been a schmuck."

I glanced over at Natisha, testing my hand higher up on her thigh, creeping up beneath the hem of her dress. Her eyes were glassy and staring into the television. The golden chain hanging from her nipple ring looked like tinsel in the pale blue light. I touched it gently. Its facets sparkled. I touched the tip of her left breast, then grabbed it in my palm, enjoying the firmness.

She still did not respond.

I knew she wanted more.

The thought occurred to me that she might not have cared had I completely extinguished the light of my soul to satisfy her needs. I removed my hand from her breast, curled it into a fist. She didn't move, didn't even seem to be breathing. I checked her pulse. Her heart was still beating. I sank back into the couch and watched the rest of the movie with her. When it was over, she closed her eyes and fell away from me, dead asleep.

I pulled on my coat and shut off the lights. I left the television going, because it was her companion and helped her fight off the darkness. On my way out, I turned the lock and closed the door tight, making sure it was secure before walking away.

I was thinking I might not come back. Walking along that hallway to the stairs and out into the night as I had done a hundred times or more, the thought was all too familiar. But we were linked, and I could not deny her the feast. It was as if we existed to serve each other's purpose—I gathered the energy to feed her voracious soul. It was something deeper than love that bound us together...mere love was not this eternal. We were psychic symbiotes. The collection of energy within would destroy me without a way to channel it elsewhere. And the void in Natisha's own tainted soul made the perfect receptor for all of that.

I awoke to a roar of thunder. My window was open, and the curtains were soaked. They billowed inward, slinging drops of water across the carpet. It was dusk. The red numbers of the digital clock beside me read 6:45. I closed my eyes and rolled over, listening to the rain, drifting back into dreamland.

The phone began to ring. I let the answering machine do its job; it was in the other room, and all I could hear was a woman's voice muffled through the darkness of the hallway. Then there was silence again. And the rain. And I suddenly wasn't tired anymore.

I got up and went over to close the window. The carpet gushed water beneath my feet. I locked it and pulled the curtains closed, fetching a towel from the bathroom to sop up the mess. I didn't turn on any lights. I didn't feel the need. This house was my sanctuary from the world. As such, I was familiar with its every twist and turn, and I hadn't rearranged the furniture in two years. I figured that would work to my advantage if I ever woke up blind.

The phone rang again.

This time I picked it up.

"Cade," a man's gravelly voice. Kalley.

I grunted a reply, feeling spent. Empty. A dull throb in the core of my being. She'd nearly taken it all, and still hadn't given it up. The bitch. The stupid soul-sucking, beautiful bitch whom I couldn't live without. Sucked me dry and sent me home with a dull ache in my loins.

"Got another one for you," he said.

"Uh-huh."

Of course he did. There were always more. And after Kalley died years from now, there would be someone else who needed death done. Some other sorry piece of shit who couldn't do it himself.

He gave me the information and I dropped the phone into its cradle. I stood there for a moment, watching the storm, awash in the strobe flashes of lightning.

My mind strayed back to thoughts of Natisha. Wondered if she were all right, knowing that she was. We were connected, forever. Fate, with a twist of hate. A poison love.

I stepped into the shower and tried to wash it all away. Would have cried if I'd had the energy. I got out, dried off, and cleaned my gun instead.

Another day, another one dead. One more stop on the road to eternity.

Time to recharge.

WHERE THE DEAD MEN LOSE THEIR BONES

Ken Goldman

"I think we are in rats' alley
Where the dead men lost their bones..."
—T.S. Eliot, The Wasteland (1922)

G *etting a little piece of ass on the subway during the middle of the* *night...Hell, what kid wouldn't nurse a woody just thinking about* *doing it right there on the MTA?*
["Oh my God, Billy...hold me...Oh my God....!"]
It seemed like a good idea at the time...

Midway through the Labor Day weekend Billy again felt like a horn dog, and he knew that tonight Miss September and a Kleenex would not suffice. Hungry for someone who did not have a staple in her navel he found himself cruising the East Village nightspots.

Frankie Blue's was awash with human bodies, but this holiday weekend the shark frenzy on the dance floor seemed especially fierce. Spotting a likely candidate, Billy mashed out his cigarette at the bar and ran his fingers through a buzz cut which, like so many in the crowd, contained streaks of hair gone prematurely green. He moved in for the kill among the throng packed ass-to-ass.

Although the girl in the denim skirt would not have been his first choice a few weeks earlier, she outclassed the Goth types and tongue-pierced Vampirella wannabes who frequented Frankie's. Her face might have been plain and maybe her tits belonged more properly on a pygmy, but in Billy's eyes the girl with the mousy hair and the prominent overbite would do nicely. He tapped the beanpole who was her dancing partner and waited for him to perform a disappearing act.

"I'm Billy."

"Cecilia. Call me Cee. You into scavenging other guys' girls, are you, Billy?" she shouted to him over the din of a throbbing bass without losing the tempo of her gyrations.

"Carpe diem, Cee," he answered with a Billy Idol sneer, although he hoped to seize a lot more than the day. That thought kept his hard-on twitching through several spasmodic numbers by The Roots and Beenie Man while the couple joined the group gasm that passed for dancing at Frankie's. After fifteen frenetic minutes of dance floor convulsions and a couple of cold draughts from Suzette, who tended bar, Billy managed a semblance of focus, enough to catch the fragments of Cee's conversation he could hear from his stool.

"*...sales rep at Mandee's near Hutchinson Parkway...saving for my own apartment...*"

Working girl in the city, direct from central casting.

Yadda, yadda, and yadda...

When time arrived to determine just how congenial this salesgirl really was, Billy slugged down the last of his Coors. His kiss came from out of nowhere like some kind of sucker punch, but Cecilia-call-me-Cee didn't push him away. His teeth scraped her overbite and the girl didn't really respond much to him, although her tongue tentatively brushed against his. The brief taste of her proved encouragement enough to advance to Phase Two.

"It's warm as a bitch in here. Let's get some air."

The girl could not mistake the irony of Billy's suggestion of getting fresh air in the midst of a sanitation workers strike. With an ephemeral blush, she smiled and mumbled, "Why not?" Her consent was as good as a checkered flag waving Billy in. Within two minutes both were through the door.

Because the garbage strike was into its third week Avenue A was hardly conducive to a midnight stroll. Crud overflowed the dozens of receptacles that lined the alleyways, creating a stink that made it all the way to the curb, and Billy wondered if New York flies ever slept. On 2nd Avenue a bloated brown rat scampered across their path, the remnants of some thick scrap of mystery meat hanging from pointed teeth. It stopped for a moment to stare belligerently at them, then continued towards the teeming bins.

"Filthy little fuckers get pretty ballsy with all this shit lying around, don't they?" Billy muttered. He slipped his arm around Cee and she clung closer to him. In the Village this passed as a romantic moment. Somewhere between a walk-down Caribbean candle shop and another that specialized in gimmicky bar mitzvah items, the girl stopped cold.

"So where are we going, William? You planning to have your way with me here in some alley? Just you, me, and the rats? I can't tell you how wet the thought is making me."

Billy had no idea where they were going. He wanted to take her anywhere reasonably private that provided opportunity to slide his hands south of her bikini line. But discounting the demands of his hot wired hormones, he was beginning to like Cee and the paradox of her being so wise-assed while looking like the girl who always raised her hand in Algebra class.

"I was thinking maybe the park. Stop at Starbuck's, find a bench and just sit for a while, discuss your Beanie Baby collection, strangle a rat or two."

"Tempting," Cee acknowledged, turning towards the derelict sleeping on the subway grate she had practically tripped over moments earlier. A tone of genuine foreboding kicked in. "Look, Billy, for real. I'm not sure we should..."

Passing the darkened crevice of an art gallery, a semblance of clear thinking returned, and Billy weighed the logistics of Cee's point. Could he get something going surrounded by winos, scavenging fur balls, and three weeks of garbage? On these streets it was difficult to feel much of anything except the urge to puke. Worse, his appearing like some drooling school kid out to cop a feel might bogus the entire situation. A passing subway rumbled beneath them, its thunder reverberating from the grate near his feet. In that moment Cee spoke his very thoughts.

"You said you lived in Queens...?"

He wasn't sure where this was going, uncertain if the girl's mind operated on the same frequency as his.

"Uh huh..."

"I live on the way. We take the same subway home, the A-train from Washington Square. Late nights the Spring Street Station is open. It isn't far."

The girl's smile oozed peaches and cream, suggesting possibilities entirely incongruous. If the effect were intentional, Billy had struck the mother lode.

Maybe she wanted a little taste of him right there on the subway? Possibly wanted to do it balls out the second time on her couch alongside her high school graduation photo with Mom and Dad asleep upstairs and the dog resting on the carpet? Hell, past midnight an empty subway car seemed a creative alternative to a quick dry hump in the back of a taxi.

It took all of his effort not to drag her along the sidewalk like some life-sized love doll so they would not miss the next train. If luck and the MTA were with him, they might catch an express, and there was a long interval between the JFK and Broad Channel stations during the hour's ride to Queens. Maybe, if the last car were empty and the girl wasn't just yanking his chain...

"Come on!" she said. "We have a train to catch!"

Cee raced ahead of him.

It seemed like a good idea at the time.

They stood at the tracks beneath Spring Street, Billy surveying the entire length of the station. He saw no one on the dim platform, and satisfied that luck remained with him, he kissed Cee again. Her response proved considerably more enthusiastic now. Wrapping her fingers around his neck, she drew him closer while her tongue explored his mouth. He continued kissing her as the subway rumbled into the station, illuminating it with strobing light and making the impassioned couple appear part of some flickering old-time movie.

This train was one of those dinosaurs belonging to the older fleet from maybe the early '50's that the Transit Authority sometimes used late at night when riders were sparse. The cars were noisier and rumbled a lot more than the modern models, but there was something genuinely picturesque and I Love New York about them. As Billy had hoped, the last car was completely empty, but both waited for the doors to slide shut before taking a seat. The two were yanked backwards as the subway howled into the vacant darkness.

Billy craned his neck to view the forward car, which also seemed empty, and turning to Cee he noticed she was checking too. They shared smiles during a moment that seemed so free of bullshit that kissing her again convinced him this weekend belonged in the win column. Billy slid his hand to Cee's breast. "Maybe I should make a few local stops along the way." That earned him a giggle.

"No need to stop," she said, smiling, and leaned into him. They kissed for several minutes, and Billy kept right on going even when the train took a sharp and unexpected turn. With his tongue still deep inside her mouth a realization slowly sank in. He managed to pull himself from the girl.

[No need to stop...No need to...stop...]

"We haven't stopped," he said.

"What?"

"There are supposed to be stations along here. Canal Street. Chambers. This train hasn't—"

"I wasn't paying attention," Cee giggled. "I was a little distracted, you know. Anyway, maybe this is an express. Like your hands on my ass."

He looked through the dusty window into the darkness and his jaw dropped. Something clearly had gone gonzo. A couple of beers and a stiff one might have dulled his perspective. Maybe they had stepped inside a train that was supposed to be out of service.

"There's no Southbound track going the other way," Cee pointed out. "I think we're in some kind of utility tunnel. Has this ever happened to you before?"

"Shit, no."

A rancid stench filled the rail car. Billy turned to Cee.

"You smell something funny?"

She sniffed.

"There's nothing funny about *that* smell..."

Garbage. There was no doubt about it. Billy tried to smile but he felt his lip twitch. "We may be under one of those refuse sites the city is using during the strike. Christ, if New York has a butt crack, I think we found it."

The lights flickered once. A moment passed and they flickered again. The train slowed.

"Billy? What's—?"

He stared through the window as the wheels came to a squealing stop. The doors remained closed while yowling subway echoes resonated through the tunnel, fading like distant ghosts. A lengthy silence followed, a stillness as empty as the tunnel was huge.

They had arrived at some kind of platform that could not properly be called a station. There were no street indicators and few lights—dim bulbs, really—not enough to provide any decent illumination of the murky shadows impossible to determine as either posts or people.

Billy could not see anything in motion outside, but he had the uneasy feeling there was something in the darkness moving with a determined slowness, something watching and perhaps waiting. He sat frozen, unwilling to run the risk of revealing himself and sweating even in the cold damp of the tunnel. Cee must have been feeling the same. She did not move.

The lamps inside the train again strobed wildly as if they were shorting out, replacing the couple's confused expressions with colorless stop-action masks. In the next instant the lights blinked out altogether and the subterranean world went black.

"Billy!"

"It's okay. They'll probably be back on in a minute."

But light did not come, and inside the darkened rail car Billy instinctively reached for Cee's hand. Hers felt clammy with cold sweat, and she squeezed his hand hard.

"Jesus Christ, Billy! What's happening?"

"Maybe I should go to the first car, see what's going on," he offered, not certain he favored his own suggestion. "There's got to be someone running the train, right? Maybe if I can just find—"

"No, Billy! Don't leave me here! Please don't—!"

A *whoosh!* interrupted her. The subway tube's dank coldness filled the car with the chill of a meat locker. Billy could not clearly see it happen, but he knew doors had slid open.

"Power failure, maybe?" Cee offered.

"I don't think so. Something opened the doors. And that means there's someone running this train. There's lights on inside the tunnel too, not that they're lighting much. See for yourself."

She looked through windows caked with black dust.

"See what? I don't see anything! Aren't there other passengers bitching anywhere on this whole goddamned train? Who's driving this thing? What's going on?"

"I don't know."

"Shit, Billy. Shitshitshit..."

He heard thumping on the floor pads like something scurrying through the open door. Coming through and coming through and coming through, there was a scampering at their feet so close that if he probed the floor with his Nike Billy knew he would touch...

...touch what?

Cee heard it too, a scampering accompanied by shrill squeaking sounds like violin strings plucked by a madman.

"Something's in here with us! Oh Christ, Billy, they're all around—!"

Instinctively they pulled their legs from the floor, crouching together on the seat like huddled children.

"Shhh!"

Billy pulled his Bic from his pocket. Snapping it on, he already knew what he would see. Still he gawked when he spotted them.

At first there were only the eyes and teeth in the undulating darkness, but then lumpy shapes formed and Billy recognized for certain what had been keeping them company inside the stalled subway train.

Huge bloated brown rats squirmed along the floor in squeaking furry heaps, their tails thick tangled strands of flesh. There were dozens of them, and they crawled over one another, skulking in stop/starts toward the couple cringing on the seat. More of them were wiggling from the platform and into the train, their movements on the floor pads a cacophony of light thumps, their legion swelling in dark waves.

"Garbage must've brought them out of their holes," Billy whispered. "For weeks they've had themselves one hell of a banquet, got themselves good and fat. Goddamned disease carriers eat anything, even each other. Now they want more than garbage."

The lighter, low on fuel, flickered. A heavy rat that felt like a small dog catapulted itself into Billy's lap. The boy remained perfectly still while his heart did the funky chicken. The chunky rodent paused upright on his thigh. Billy could hear it sniffing the air. Then it sprinted off.

Cee's screams suddenly filled the old railway car. Billy fumbled, trying to reactivate his lighter. Getting it going he saw the husky rat had flung itself on her. The fat little fur ball was agile and had attached itself to her face, the scaly tail extending past the girl's eye, while its mouth snapped wildly at her lips. Cee tried tearing into it, her nails digging deep into rat-flesh. The creature squealed in pain and fury, but it did not release its grip. Thick veins of blood dripped down Cee's cheek, purple rivulets that smeared her complexion gone pale in the firelight.

"Billy! Oh my God, Billy! Get it off! Please, get it off!"

The rat continued gnawing as Billy squashed the flame into sticky matted fur, the rodent's barbecued pelt giving off a rotted stink. Shrieking, the rat still would not budge. Tearing blindly at it with both hands, Billy felt a damp trickle along his wrist that he realized was Cee's blood. Tugging harder, he feared he might shred the flesh right from the girl's face. He pinched the rat's jaws, and it struggled, trying to shake itself free. Finally the rat loosened its grip. Billy tossed it like a ticking grenade clear across the aisle, then heard it thud against a window, its protesting squeak cut short.

Cee could not stop flailing at the air as if she expected the next one to drop from the ceiling.

"Get them away! Oh God, get them away!"

Another rat climbed up Billy's chest, tearing through his shirt and embedding taloned claws into his skin like thick needles. He felt the cold snout poke his throat. This one wanted *his* face, wanted to sink its teeth deep into the soft flesh of *his* neck.

"Get off me, motherfucker! Get—!"

He managed to twist the claws from him, ripping shreds from his own skin as he did. The rat hit the floor like a kid's deflated toy.

But now other rats snapped near his ankles. One, more ambitious than the others, climbed into his lap. It tore and chewed its way towards his face even as he shook another from his foot. There were many more on the way. Billy could hear a platoon of them thumping along the floor.

[...thub thub thub...]

[...thubthubthubthud...]

The rats would not stop coming until they had wrenched the skin from their bones like sticky cheese, tearing at them as if he and the girl were serving up a buffet. Struggling to keep the lighter's flame alive to fend the new intruders off, he felt a sudden stabbing pain as a corpulent rat sank a string of sharpened pencil points into his wrist.

The Bic fell to the floor. Darkness and Cee's screams filled the rail car.

Panic overtook him. Billy slammed the rat against the window and kept slamming. It clung stubbornly with the persistence of an adhesive, shaking its head and clenching more firmly. Smashing the tenacious bastard into the Plexiglas Billy felt something inside the rat crunch. Seizing his chance, he squeezed the head hard, twisting the rodent's thick neck like a bottle cap until the bone inside snapped. When the animal's vicious squirming stopped cold, Billy tossed the bloodied creature into the writhing pile swarming the floor.

He turned to Cee in a blackness so pitch he could see only a charcoal sketch of her.

"You okay?"

"I'm bleeding so bad, Billy."

"We'll get out of here," he told her, aware of the idiocy of his remark, aware too that he hadn't the slightest idea how to do it.

"There's someone out there…" Cee said.

"What?"

"Someone's outside the train, there in the tunnel. People…a lot of them are walking on the tracks straight ahead! Look!"

Cee was right. Billy couldn't tell how many were approaching further up the tracks. He saw only the long trails of light beams bobbing in the darkness. There might have been a dozen flashlights, maybe more. They were some kind of rescue party come to find them, maybe tunnel workers or passengers from one of the other cars. Billy didn't care. The two pounded on the windows.

"In here! The last car! We're in here!"

A wash of light at the sliding door caused the rodents to scatter towards the other exits. A tall stick-figured man silhouetted in shadows entered first, and stomping his heavy boot he nailed one of the rats on the run. The creature made a dull farting sound like a crushed water balloon, writhing on the floor and kicking ridiculously at nothing. The man kept stomping until its writhing slowed, then stopped.

"Thank God…oh, *thank God!*" Cee muttered. Billy held her close, uncertain if her shudders were hers or his.

Other shadowy figures entered the car behind the leader, stomping at anything that moved near their feet as if the entire group were doing some grotesque square dance. The activity must have scared the rat shit out of the mangy swarm. In thick rows they scurried from the train.

The tall man removed his cap and wiped his forehead. "Grubby little subway cooties. Must be a million nestin' inside these tunnels, but I ain't never seen 'em do this before. Refuse site upstairs prob'ly made 'em bolder and more 'thusiastic for some midnight treats. These track rats can't never seem to get enough, and runnin' in packs they'll do some serious damage. You the only ones in here?"

His lantern's high intensity light revealed only tattered seats and a few dead rodents on the floor. The man's companions silently entered the train, their faces hidden in the wash of illumination as their lamps pierced the darkness like searching beacons. Satisfied the rail car had emptied, the cluster of rescuers ventured forward into the aisle.

"You two okay?" the stick-figured man asked.

"This girl was bitten pretty badly. I think she needs a doctor," Billy said.

The man's filthy clothes suggested he had seen a lot more of the underground transit system than most would care to. When he leaned forward to examine the girl Billy noticed he wore the tattered hat of an MTA train conductor.

"Are we in some kind of utility tunnel?"

"That's just where you are," the man answered. He aimed a high-powered wash of light into her face to inspect the girl's cheek closely. "Naw...she ain't hurt."

"Of course she is!" Billy shouted. "Christ, look at her! She's bleeding!"

"Ain't hurt, I'm tellin' you," the stick-man insisted. He aimed the light again at Cee, smearing his thumb on the girl's bloodied cheek. "You see? It's just a scratch. You're not hurt, are you, little girl?"

Cee stared uneasily at Billy as if she expected him to speak for her, but the boy had no ready response. He managed a semblance of composure that seemed all the more uncertain for his attempt.

"Mister, she's hurt pretty bad," he tried again. "A few minutes ago a rat the size of a bread loaf was chewing on her face. I wrestled one of those bastards off me too. These rats are rabid and I'm pretty sure we both need some medical attention."

The tall man scratched the oily hair beneath his cap as if this information took a powerful effort to assimilate. Finally, he turned to those who stood behind him, addressing a tub of lard with a wispy beard, whose belly spilled from his soot-streaked T-shirt like a fleshy beach ball. "We'll ask my boy, here. These kids look hurt to you, Jeremiah?"

The husky kid stepped forward, bringing his face level with Cee's. He spread another wash of light on her. Leaning in, he licked a thick stream of blood from her chin.

"This one seems fine to me, Pa. 'Least she's a whole lot better than this rat here."

He scooped the rodent from the floor. It was still alive, although barely, but it shimmied wildly in his pudgy hand as he held it close to his face. "Then again, I guess most anything looks fine compared to what you find livin' down here in these tunnels."

He bit off the rat's head. Billy said nothing, just sat by Cee, nodding in agreement like an idiot.

"You get to understand them garbage-eatin' fur sacks, though," Stick-man continued. "Sometimes you learn from 'em how to play real dirty just to get some food to feed your family. This city don't act too kindly towards its vagrants, you know? You sometimes got to set your own rat traps, so to speak. Like I been teachin' my Jeremiah when these old trains go clunkin' through these tunnels so late at night..."

He handed the conductor's cap to the fat kid.

"All aboard!" the boy said, smiling through teeth that resembled smashed crockery.

The bearded kid urged those behind him forward, and in the shadows Billy couldn't determine how many were inside the rail car. He could barely make out faces belonging to those who stood muttering in the brightness of the hand-held lamps. They hardly seemed like faces at all. It was impossible to tell their features as male or female. Their shapes were all wrong.

The man knelt to pick up the rodent he had stomped into pulp, sinking his teeth deep into what meat remained of its stomach. Sticky ropes of entrails dripped down his chin.

"'Course these little graybacks sometimes will do as appetizers. Ain't that much substance to 'em, though, nothin' no sane man would ever call tasty. On the other hand..."

The tall man snapped off his lantern. Taking his cue, his family did the same, each high beam in turn yielding gradually to the shadows. In moments the rail car went as black and silent as a tomb.

Billy trembled cold and shivering in the darkness. He could hear Cee whimpering to herself.

"Billy...oh God, Billy..."

[It seemed like such a good idea...such a good idea...]

The couple crouched together, holding each other. For one wildly irrational moment Billy wondered if he should kiss Cee a last time, try to salvage something, anything.

You set your own rat traps, so to spea...

Together the tall man and the tub of guts named Jeremiah moved toward the pair.

"You go first, son. We'll leave the girl for the others. Ain't good to be greedy."

"Thanks, Pa."

"Oh God, Billy....please hold me...oh my God....!"
Cee's shrieks turned to hysteria. Billy could not stop himself from screaming too.
Then they were on him.

KEN GOLDMAN resides in Pennsylvania and the Jersey Shore. His stories appear in over 350 publications in the U.S., Canada, the UK, Ireland, and Australia, with over twenty due for publication in 2005. He won 2nd place in the Rod Serling Memorial Foundation Writing Contest (1993), 1st place in the Preditors & Editors Best Poem In The Universe On The Internet (1997) Readers Poll Contest, and 2nd place in the Preditors & Editors Horror Short Story Contest (2003) ; 2nd place "silver" in the Salivan Short Story Contest, Horror Division (2000), 2nd place in the Horizon Literature Awards Contest (2000), 3rd Place in The Rose & Thorn Writers Contest (2000), 1st Place in the Red Writer Hood Contest (2001), and Second Place in the Harrow Murder Contest (2001). He received honorable mentions in Datlow and Windling's Year's Best Fantasy and Horror 7th and 9th Annual Editions, and Datlow and Kelly Link & Gavin J. Grant's Year's Best Fantasy and Horror 17th Edition.

WHERE SECRETS FESTER

T. M. Gray

Towering like a great mountain, the pile of organic matter triumphed over the lesser heaps of debris at the town dump in Howell, Maine. Despite truckloads of its composting sections being hauled off by farmers and groundskeepers, it grew larger with each passing year, and because of the paper and plastic it contained, it took a long time to break down and rot.

Dump man Virgil Felton managed to pick out the larger pieces of non-degradable material, but truth be told, he wasn't terribly selective unless it was something he could use.

So the mountain grew, and along with it, so too did Virgil's status as a social outcast. He knew this in the way the townspeople looked at him, wrinkling their noses, and in the way their conversations stopped whenever he came around. Sometimes he considered telling them he was onto their darkest secrets, but always he'd clam up, unable to share such information lest it come to a stop altogether. So to relieve his tension, Virgil shot rats as he was doing tonight.

His eyes narrowed as he peered down the shotgun's barrel at the rat dead center in the crosshairs of the scope, chowing down on rotten food scraps. Virgil couldn't help but think what a repulsive animal it was, large as a puppy with mangy fur, beady eyes and a long hairless tail. Such vermin were the bane of his existence; no matter how many he killed, more took their place.

Bastards breed like rabbits, he thought, pulling the trigger.

The rat exploded in a spray of flesh and fur. "Another one down," Virgil called out. "Anybody else want a turn?"

The remaining rats, of course, did not answer...but *something* did. The noise was wet and slick, almost a burp, lasting a few seconds before falling silent.

What the...? Virgil whirled around at the sudden sound, reaching into his pocket for the buckshot. He reloaded the gun, his eyes scanning the slowly composting mountain under the yellow glow of floodlights. The other piled sections of the dump, the rusting appliances, construction scraps and hazardous materials, were unlit and relatively free of vermin because rats only liked the rotten stuff. But that noise couldn't have possibly come from a rat. Whatever it was, it was big. A bear maybe? Black bears sometimes scaled the chain link fence to steal a bite to eat, and Virgil had no reservations about shooting them, even off-season. In a good year, the meat of three or more bears filled his freezer.

It wasn't a bear, though, of that Virgil was certain as he slowly walked around the great mound. He eventually concluded the sound must have been caused by the release of compost gases rising from within. With a shrug, he headed back to his shack at the edge of the dump.

It was humble, but it was home. Built solely of scrap materials and furnished with pickings other people had thrown away, Virgil had made it quite comfortable and was proud that he hadn't bought a stick of furniture in over three decades. He seldom had to buy anything, for that matter. Linda Royal's cast-off curtains hung in his windows; she'd thrown them away because the sun had bleached them. He ate his meals with Vivian Rolland's old silverware. Some of the forks were bent and the silver plating had worn off the spoons, but Virgil didn't mind using them because he wasn't out to impress anyone. Debra Carson's dinner plates and mugs lined his cupboard; every one of them was chipped or cracked, but it mattered little as long as they were useful.

People throw away good stuff all the time, he mused, seating himself in Jed Milford's discarded easy chair. Sure, there was a cigarette burn on the right arm and stuffing kept tumbling out of the bottom, but it was comfortable and he'd managed to save it just before the spring rains.

And people wonder why they go into debt, he added in thought. Always having to buy new, usually on credit. He reached down beside the chair and picked up last month's issue of *Gent* magazine. The pages were wrinkled and the cover boasted a large oily stain, but the parts that mattered were still readable. Virgil could almost set his clock by Chet Lyman's trash; the first week of the month came *Playboy*, the second week, *Hustler*, the third, *Gent*, then *Penthouse*. Ever since his divorce in '93, Chet had taken up with the paper harem, much to Virgil's advantage.

Oh, Virgil Felton knew all kinds of secrets about the folks in Howell, Maine…like Bud Quincy's short but torrid affair with Debra Carson. He'd found their love letters in the trash, among the coffee grinds and kitchen scraps. He knew about Debra's husband, Emery Carson, how he kept two sets of books from the mill…one for himself and another for the IRS. He also knew about Jed Milford's obsession with photos of young boys and Arlie Wilbur's health problems…a multitude of syringes could always be found among the newspapers he threw away. In the Rolland's garbage, Virgil usually found empty liquor bottles. Rum, mostly, but lately there'd been several dead bottles of aftershave and mouthwash as well. That scared him a bit because Dwain Rolland was the town cop and Vivian taught Kindergarten at Howell Grammar School.

Still, Virgil kept these things, these secrets, to himself. Although he'd lived his entire life in Howell, he had no friends, like the kind who'd drop by for cards and coffee. The only person who'd ever been inside his home was Jed Milford, the mailman, and he'd only stayed long enough to deliver a package.

Virgil thumbed through the girlie mag, then retired to the couch to sleep, giving no more thought to the strange noise he'd heard earlier.

Something was burrowing in the pile of organic matter. Virgil stared at the movement, unable to comprehend what it might be. A nest of rats, perhaps? Or gophers? He supposed it could even be snakes, maybe big garters drawn to the warmth of the rot.

Disgusted, he went to his shed and brought out a trap with steel jaws. Whatever it was, without a doubt, this would ensnare it. He set the trap carefully by the spot where he'd seen the movement and stood there, watching, waiting for something to happen.

He turned when he heard a car drive up, its horn blaring, and he groaned. The Cadillac Seville belonged to Emery Carson, Howell's richest man and founder of Carson Millworks. Reluctantly, Virgil walked over to the gate and opened it.

Emery rolled down his window and stuck his bald head out. "Mr. Felton," he said in his typically haughty tone, "it seems we have a bit of trouble."

Virgil knit his brows. "What's going on?"

"The stink, Mr. Felton, from *your* dump. My workers are complaining because the stench of it is all through my mill. You'd better do something about it or I'll go to Thurman Royal and *he'll* do something about it."

Virgil frowned. Town manager Thurman Royal was a worse pain in the ass than Emery Carson, always reminding him that the town owned the dump and Virgil was only an employee hired to tend it. *You can be replaced,* Thurman often told him, but Virgil couldn't imagine anyone vying for his job.

"It's just because of the hot weather," he told Emery. "That's why it smells kind of ripe right now, but I'll do what I can."

Emery rubbed his nose in disdain. "You'd better, Mr. Felton." With that, he rolled his window up and backed out of the driveway. Virgil stood there watching him with his hands in his pockets.

If he complains to Royal, that will be the last straw. I'll report him to the IRS, he decided. That would serve the bastard right.

So Virgil returned to his tool shed to get a bag of lime. It wouldn't solve the odor problem, but it might help.

By the time he went back to the organic pile, his trap was gone. There were no more movements within the debris, so he had to assume the animal had been caught, likely burying itself in its death throes. Virgil considered digging it up to retrieve his trap, but thought better of it. *Best wait to make sure it's really dead.* He remembered the deep bite he'd gotten, years ago, when he'd tried to remove a mink from the trap. The mink had seemed dead, but was merely stunned and rewarded Virgil's efforts by sinking its teeth into his wrist.

He pulled back his sleeve and looked at the scars, tiny white spots among the freckles and hairs. No, he wasn't going to risk it again, so he spent the better part of the afternoon sprinkling lime to cut down the smell.

That evening he returned, armed with his shotgun and a shovel, but something wasn't right about the shape of the mound; he could see it under the floodlights and as he got closer—a huge hole had materialized in the side of it.

The smell was even worse now, a fouler stench than he'd ever thought possible.

Gagging, he raised his gun, ready to fire. The hole was big enough that a good-sized bear could fit inside and still have ample room to move. But could a bear have made it? Oh, sometimes they dug through the pile, looking for food, but they never tunneled into it. Not like this. Virgil scratched his head, dumbfounded, and decided to go back for his flashlight, thinking maybe then he could see what was there.

He left the shovel by the pile and was on his way back to the shack when he saw blue lights flashing, making their way towards the dump. *Oh, what now?* he wondered. No doubt, Emery Carson complained to Howell's finest about the stink.

The black and white cruiser pulled up to the front gate, and officer Dwain Rolland stepped out. "Virgil," he asked, "where have you been all day?"

Virgil cradled his gun in his arms. "I've been right here. Why?"

"Did you see Emery Carson today?"

He nodded. "Yep, he came by only for a minute, then he left. What's going on?"

Officer Rolland paused and shook his head. "I was hoping you could tell me. He's dead, Virgil. Someone murdered him, from the looks of it."

Stepping back, Virgil's eyes narrowed. "Murder? I hope you don't think I had anything to do with it. Carson came here, complaining about the smell, and I told him I'd take care of it, but I didn't kill him, that's for sure."

"What time was he here?"

"Oh, about nine or a little thereafter."

"And you've been here all day?"

Swallowing, Virgil nodded. "That's what I said. Trash pickup is tomorrow morning, so I'd have no reason to go anywhere today. What's with all the questions, Dwain?"

Officer Rolland shot him a distressed look. "He was smothered, completely covered in filth. Rotten garbage."

Virgil reached up and rubbed his chin. "Wonder who'd do that to Emery Carson?"

"That's what I'm trying to find out."

Thinking about the hole in the organic pile, Virgil considered sharing this find with Officer Rolland, but decided he'd best not. What if word about the stink got back to Thurman Royal?

Turning back to his cruiser, Officer Rolland glanced over his shoulder. "Well, keep your eyes open, Virgil. You see or hear anything, you come to me, okay?" He wrinkled his nose and added, "And for God's sake, use some lime."

"I will," Virgil said, nodding. He watched the cruiser retreat, then hurried to his shack. No, he wouldn't be going back out there with the flashlight tonight. What if Thurman's killer was hiding inside that hole in the pile?

And who, in their right mind, would hide there? Virgil knew his own sense of smell had been somewhat numbed to the odor of garbage over the years...but this kind of stench was downright gut-wrenchingly rank. Vile, going way beyond rotten.

All that night, Virgil thought about the odor and worried about the hole. What if the killer was there, plotting his next kill? What if he was creeping around the dump, waiting for just the right moment to pounce? Virgil knew he wasn't the sharpest tool in the box, but he had a keen sense of intuition.

Someone's there, he thought, and it's up to me to stop them.

The next morning, before dawn, he awoke and slipped into his overalls. He considered checking the pile, but admitted to himself that he was just too damned scared. Besides, today was Wednesday, trash pickup day in Howell, and he had to get going in order to be done before the town started waking up. No one wanted to see his smelly old truck, or him tossing bags into it; they all wanted it picked up, gone, as if done by magic.

The townspeople didn't like Virgil, and he had little use for them either. The few times a month he'd go to the local store, folks would look the other way and step aside, giving him a wide berth. Was it because he wore clothes he'd picked from the trash? *Maybe it's just because I'm the dump man,* Virgil decided on his way out to his truck. *I'm a reminder that they aren't as neat and tidy as they think they are, and I know this because I take care of their garbage.*

His first stop was at Bud Quincy's farm. Three dark green plastic bags with yellow ties lined up on the curb. Before tossing them into the truck, Virgil carefully opened them to examine their contents. There was nothing good in any of them, just typical garbage. Since Bud had ended his affair with Debra Carson, his trash had been rather boring, but maybe now things would change since Emery was out of the way? Virgil retied the bags, heaved them into his truck and kept going.

The next stop was Arlie Wilbur's place. Arlie lived in a camper trailer when he wasn't on the road. He was a trucker and his big rig was parked in the drive. Virgil was careful with his trash. He didn't know what kind of disease Arlie had, but he didn't want to get stabbed with one of those syringe needles.

When he pulled up in front of the Rollands' home, he noticed Dwain's cruiser parked right next to the curb instead of in the drive. Its radio was on, playing a country western song. But why was it turned up so loud? And where was Dwain?

Virgil climbed out of his truck and went up to the driver's side of the cruiser to see what was going on, but under the streetlight, he could see Dwain slumped against the door, covered in slimy filth.

"Oh my God!" Virgil said, gasping as he tore open the door. Dwain tumbled out onto the curb, filth all around him. The smell was horrendous, like the stench of the pile, and Virgil wanted to vomit, but instead gathered his courage and ran across the street to bang on Thurman Royal's door.

"Who's there?" he heard Thurman call out. "Hold your horses, I'm coming." The door opened and Thurman Royal stood there in a blue bathrobe, with wet hair, his lower face covered in shaving cream. "Virgil Felton," he said, "what the hell are you doing here?"

Virgil gulped to find his voice. "It's Dwain Rolland. I think he's dead!"

Thurman gave him a fearful look. "Okay, I'll be right there. I have to find my shoes." He disappeared for a moment and Virgil heard him call out, "How do you know he's dead?"

"I opened the cruiser door and he just kind of fell out. But I didn't touch him."

"Well, then, you don't *know* he's dead. Go back and check for a pulse," Thurman ordered. "I'm calling an ambulance."

Virgil did as he was told, but he didn't like touching Dwain, who looked like he'd been dipped in muck. Muck that contained bits of shiny paper, parts of labels, maybe, and something that sparkled in the dark greasy filth…broken glass. Shuddering, Virgil pulled off one glove and pressed his fingers to Dwain's neck. His skin felt cold and slimy; a pulse was not to be found.

Thurman Royal ran up and shouted "What the hell is this?" as soon as he saw what had become of Dwain Rolland. "He's—he's all covered in garbage." He gave Virgil a hard look. "Did you have anything to do with this?"

Virgil stood up, wiping his fingers on the rag he pulled from his back pocket. "No, of course not."

Thurman raised a brow. "Well, I wouldn't be leaving town if I were you."

Meeting his stare, Virgil replied, "I won't. But I didn't do it."

Even though he said nothing else, Thurman looked like he didn't believe him. The ambulance arrived and left, taking Officer

Rolland's body in it, along with his wife, Vivian, who was quite hysterical. Thurman followed the ambulance in his car, leaving Virgil standing there in shock. After a few moments, he realized he was supposed to be working and went back to his truck, but he couldn't shake his fears, afraid of what he'd find next and thinking about the hole in the pile at the dump.

Later that day, someone knocked on the door of his shack. Surprised to have a visitor who'd come in past the front gate, Virgil scrambled to open it.

"Hi there, Virg. I got something for you here," said Jed Milford, handing him a brown package.

"Thank you." Virgil reached out and took it, turning it in his hands. There was no return address and the handwriting was strange, all curly-cue, written in heavy black marker. The package itself was wrapped in wrinkled brown paper, marred with oily stains.

"What do you suppose it is?" Jed asked, stretching his thin neck to peer over Virgil's shoulder.

"Don't know. Guess I'd better find out." He ripped away the paper and lifted the top from the box. It contained his trap, the one he'd set on the pile yesterday, and it was covered in filth.

"Geez," remarked Jed, backing out the door, "why'd anyone send you something like that?"

Virgil shook his head. "I haven't a clue."

Before he left, Jed added, "Oh, did you hear about Mr. Royal?"

"What about him?"

"He's dead. They found him in his car and he was covered in money. Bills all torn up, looked like they'd been put through a grinder. They say he smelled real bad, too."

Virgil took a step backward. "I didn't do it!"

Jed gave him a strange look. "I didn't say you did, I only thought I should mention it since you were the one who found Dwain Rolland this morning. Don't look so surprised; everyone's talking about it. Oh, and I should also tell you, there's an emergency town meeting today at three. Everyone's expected to be there. You'll come, won't you?"

"I suppose."

Jed gave him another weird glance. "Well, okay then. See you at three."

Virgil nodded, watching him return to his car, acting rabbit-nervous. *He knows something's here*, he thought. *He can sense it, too. I should go out and take another look at the pile...but I just can't. What if it gets me, too?* He grimaced, knowing today's garbage was still sitting in the back of his truck and that he'd have to deal with it soon.

But not today.

For the town meeting, Virgil wore his best suit, one of Chet Lyman's cast-offs. It was brown tweed and went nicely with Emery Carson's old set of dress shoes. He went to the meeting hall and took a seat in the back. That's when the Bitch Committee found him.

Debra Carson attacked first, pointing a manicured finger. "You!" she yelled. "It's your fault my husband's dead!"

Virgil sat back in the metal chair, not quite knowing how to react or what to say, and before he could think of something, Vivian Rolland drew second blood.

"Explain the garbage," she demanded in a shrill voice. "Why were our men covered in filth? Filth that could have only come from one place: *your* dump."

Linda Royal joined them. "I don't know how or why you did it," she said, her eyes dripping with hate, "but you're responsible for their deaths. And we'll make you pay, Virgil Felton, just see if we don't."

At this, he jumped to his feet and fled. Why were they blaming him? True, he hadn't been friends with those men, even strongly disliked two of them, but he had nothing to do with their murders.

Now he was certain the killer was living in the dump pile. *I'll have to end this*, he promised himself, and returning home, he decided he'd best gather his courage first.

The rum was old, the bottle untouched for over a decade. Virgil had found it in the Rollands' trash during one of the few times Dwain had tried going on the wagon. Although he wasn't much of a drinker, Virgil twisted off the cap and took a swallow.

It burned going down his throat, and when it hit his stomach it brought a sudden warmth to his chest. *It's got to help quell the fear*, he thought, taking another swig. *And with any luck, it'll give me back my guts.*

An hour later, Virgil lifted the bottle to the light. It was half-empty and he was feeling quite giddy. He sat on the floor of his shack, blinking, trying to think.

There was one way to stop the murderer for sure. Dynamite. He had several sticks out in the tool shed, ancient leftovers from

1938 when Jed Milford's father shut down the old silver mine.

They must be pure nitroglycerin by now, he thought, wiping his chin with the back of his hand. His lips felt numb and he set the rum bottle down. *I bet just one of those sticks going off would be like an atomic bomb. That should blow the murderer to kingdom come.*

Virgil struggled to his feet and staggered toward the door. His vision had become quite blurry but he vowed not to let it prevent him from accomplishing his mission. It took him a while to locate the dynamite, and he tried to handle it carefully, knowing that just one drop and the stick would go off, blowing *him* to kingdom come.

He carried it out to the pile and knelt to fiddle with the fuse.

The smell was even worse now, making his belly flip-flop, and he tried to concentrate on what he was about to do. That's when he heard it again…the strange burping sound coming from within the mountain of garbage.

Virgil set the dynamite down and stood up, his legs unsteady. "Who's there?" he called out, fishing for the lighter in his pocket.

"Come," said a deep voice. "I'm in this hole and I need your help."

Virgil stiffened at the murderer's voice. "Who are you?"

Another wet burp followed. "Please, come and talk with me. I'm not who you think I am. You're the only one who can help."

Virgil took a halting step forward, toward the hole in the pile. "Are you gonna hurt me?"

"It's not my intent to cause you harm. Please, come inside. We must speak."

Covering his nose and mouth with his hand, Virgil stepped closer.

"Do not be afraid," the voice said.

But Virgil was very much afraid. He didn't want to go into the hole and meet whoever was inside. Still, he was drunk and drunken men don't always reason very well.

The hole was dark but surprisingly solid. Whimpering, Virgil went into it, slowly, feeling his way with his hands.

"Stop where you are," said the voice. "This is hallowed ground."

"It's so dark in here." Virgil gave an involuntary shudder.

"Then let there be light." Instantly, the hole became bathed in red. Virgil stared at its source: stringy veins of crimson running off in all directions. Then he saw, oh God, he *saw* the speaker.

At first, he thought it was a baby. It sort of looked like one with chubby little cheeks, big blue eyes and a head of fine golden curls. It sat atop a throne-like chair fashioned of garbage.

"Who are you?" Virgil asked as soon as he could find his voice. "*What* are you?"

The baby clasped its pudgy hands. "I am Belphegor," he said in that deep voice which didn't match his appearance. "You ask what I am and I shall tell you. My kind is older than this planet. Throughout human history, we've been defined as gods, angels, darklings, aliens and demons. Such labels have little meaning. We are what we are."

Again, Virgil sought his own voice and found it. "So what are you, really?"

Belphegor smiled like a cherub. "Guardians, the keepers of secrets. As you are, so once were we. As we are, so shall your kind become. But first there must be a universal transformation. That's the heart of the matter, and why I have brought you here."

Virgil coughed into his fist. "Why me?"

The baby blue eyes opened wider. "Why *not* you? You know many secrets, yet your heart is pure and true. Others can learn from you, and where prophets have failed in the past, you shall succeed. You'll bring in the birth of a new religion."

Frowning, Virgil said, "But I'm not the one. I don't have a religion."

"Perfect!" Belphegor said, again clasping his hands in delight. "You've come to me free of preconceived notions. An honest man, I like that."

Virgil opened his palms. "But why here? Inside this dump pile?"

Belphegor sighed, a perfect baby sigh. "Each guardian was given something to rule. Not a tangible object, such as an army or a country, but rather an *idea*. And we were designated as Lords. I am, for all practical purposes, the Lord of Sloth. I surround myself with filth and rot as a constant reminder of the work I must do. And you, Virgil Felton, will become my greatest accomplishment!"

"I'm not sure I want to be," Virgil mumbled.

At this, Belphegor leaned forward. "You assume you have a choice in the matter? The plans for the present, past and future were written long ago, in stone, I might add. So it shall be, now and forever. You must not deny your true destiny!"

With watering eyes, Virgil looked at the creature. "But I'm just the dump man…"

Sitting back, Belphegor nodded. "And that's precisely why you're so important to me. You know the decay inside others. Yes, you take care of their external garbage—and yet, you do nothing about their internal filth, their darkest secrets. It's up to you to help humankind sanitize to prepare them for the great transformation. I have faith that you can accomplish this."

"But I only know a few secrets," Virgil maintained. "Stuff about some people they'd rather not have anyone else know about."

Belphegor nodded with a frown. "I'm well aware of the secrets that you keep. Those secrets are killing your people. The decay growing inside their hearts will pour forth, as it has for some already."

"But what can I do about it?" Virgil asked.

"Kneel, human, and I'll tell you everything. We'll talk about secret things. Dark things. And then you'll know what you have to do."

"I'm afraid," Virgil admitted, holding onto his knees to keep them from shaking as he knelt.

Belphegor smiled like an innocent babe. "Of course you are. But you're under my protection now and nothing shall ever harm you. Now come forward and let me touch you."

Slowly, his heart quaking in fear and awe, Virgil inched toward the great throne of trash.

He awoke the next morning on the floor of his shack. The rum bottle beside him was empty, lying on its side. His stomach heaved, as if remembering having drunk from it, and Virgil rolled over, crawling on his belly toward the door.

His skin felt hot and sticky, and his head hurt worse than it had ever hurt before. *It's just a hangover,* he assured himself, rubbing his temples. When he opened his eyes, he saw clumps of hair sticking to his fingers. He ran his hands over his head, then stared at them. *I'm losing my hair,* he thought. *That isn't supposed to happen like this. Oh dear, my head is killing me.* He reached up and rubbed at his eyes. His eyebrows met the same fate as his hair, sticking like whisker shavings to his knuckles.

Could I be losing my hair because of what happened last night? he wondered. *It seemed so real...what was his name? Bel-something. God, I need an aspirin.*

Virgil stood up, his vision wavering, and stumbled back inside. He managed to locate the aspirin on a shelf over the sink and popped a couple tablets into his mouth. Something didn't feel quite right and he looked at his reflection in the mirror.

He stared in horror at his teeth. The ones in front were loose, several just hanging by thready veins. *What's happening to me?* he wondered, holding onto the sink to keep from screaming, but he was shaking so badly two of his teeth fell out.

That's when he heard them coming. He looked out the window at the pickup trucks and cars winding their way down the dump road toward his shack. Men were standing in the back of the pickups, holding rifles and shotguns. He could hear their angry shouts over the blaring of the horns.

When Bud Quincy rammed through the front gate with his farm truck, Virgil staggered out the back door of his shack. *They've come for me,* he thought, his mind racing. *And they plan to kill me. Bel-something said he'd protect me, didn't he? Hope to hell it wasn't a dream.*

As the trucks began pouring into the town dump, Virgil ran stumbling toward the mountain of organic matter, thinking, praying: *If I can only get back in the hole, I'll be able to hide from them—and Bel—if he really exists, will save me.*

"There he is, boys!" someone yelled. Virgil tried to sprint but a shot rang out, then another, and then there was fire on his back and he became airborne, flying, landing facedown at the foot of the pile. The flames were deeper now, spreading inside him, growing hot and wet.

"I think we got him good," he heard Chet Lyman say.

"Yeah, serves him right, killing those three women," Arlie Wilbur added.

What women? Virgil wanted to ask, but he couldn't seem to breathe. *I didn't kill nobody!* He could smell the scent of blood over the stench of garbage. His blood.

"What should we do with him?" Bud Quincy asked.

Jed Milford spoke up. "Just leave him alone. Let the dump take care of him."

Darkness followed, drowning out their voices. Virgil felt something big and warm embracing him and was barely aware of a sinking sensation.

He had no idea how long it lasted, for time ceased to have any meaning, but when he opened his eyes again, he saw red lights and felt life being breathed back into him. The fire in his back was gone, replaced by a fire within.

Sometime in the night, the pile of filth gave birth to a new creature, white as a maggot and shaped like a man, its sole purpose:

to root out the rot within each human heart.

Virgil stretched his new body in the moonlight, a modern-day messiah bent on saving the entire world. Transformation would take place soon; he could feel its coming zinging in his limbs, and it would be a beautiful thing indeed. But for now, he must take up where Belphegor had left off, beginning in Howell, Maine.

Knowing everyone's darkest secrets would make it easy.

PAYBACK

Derek Gunn

T he man passed through the rusted turnstiles, and the shriek
of neglected metal reverberated off the narrow corridor
walls. A small, bare light bulb held the darkness at bay valiantly
around the entrance gate and was reduced to a dull glow further
out on the platform. The reek of unattended toilets hung heavily in
the air and the retreating lights of the 10:45 illuminated the
platform briefly before they disappeared round a corner and
plunged the area into twilight.

The man sighed. He really shouldn't have allowed himself to
fall behind schedule, but his last victim had been unsettling. He had
never been happy about the hit, not that the killing itself bothered
him. In the years he had been plying his trade he had killed many
people and his conscience had long since fallen silent, but there
was something about the victim himself. It wasn't anything he
could put his finger on; maybe it was the victim's reputation for
dabbling in strange arts or maybe it was the strange atmosphere in
his home that reminded the assassin more of a mausoleum than a
house, but something had made him uneasy from the start.

Normally his victims were so terrified that he enjoyed baiting
them, watching the fear in their eyes and relishing the way their
whole bodies shook uncontrollably before he finally slit their
throats. Even those he had killed at a distance felt that instant of
realisation as death enveloped them. But tonight his victim hadn't
run or pleaded.

There was no one else on the platform and that suited him
fine. He hated being around people, seeing them pace nervously or
impatiently up and down the platform as they waited for the next

train. He hated their tuneless whistling and their incoherent mumblings as they talked incessantly among themselves or read inane advertising billboards out loud because their tiny minds couldn't filter the message without hearing the words.

He hated them all.

He reached into his pocket for a cigarette and the darkness retreated violently around him as he struck a match and lit the end before creeping back and settling around him like a familiar blanket. He inhaled deeply and held the smoke briefly before letting it—and his inner tension—seep away. He saw a faded *No Smoking* sign on the wall beside him and flicked the burnt match at it contemptuously before returning to his musings of the night's hit.

He remembered the eyes of his victim as he drew his knife slowly along the man's throat. For a second nothing had happened, then a thin red line appeared and then suddenly a torrent of blood flowed as the man fought for breath and began to choke. His victim had shuddered violently as his body fought for air, but the assassin had held him firmly and watched the man's eyes as death took hold. He loved that part the best. There seemed to be transfer of a spark between his victims and himself, and he always felt stronger after a kill. Tonight, though, there had been no transfer, only a bone-aching tiredness and a recurring image of his victim's eyes that continued to send a shiver down his spine. There had been no fear in those eyes, no fatal resignation, just a defiant, even mocking, glare that still unsettled him.

At some level he was aware of his growing addiction. He had completed four kills this month alone, where one had always been enough before, but he ignored this inner voice and was confident that it would grow silent soon enough.

Suddenly the light in the corridor flickered and died. The darkness was total except for the lit end of his cigarette, and he felt his earlier unease begin to gnaw in the pit of his stomach. Darkness had always been his friend. It allowed him to stalk his victims with impunity, adding to their fear as he teased them before the kill, but this felt different. Normally he had control, he was the one using the darkness, but the total blackness that had suddenly enveloped him was beyond his dominion. He suddenly realised that he couldn't see the edge of the platform. How far had he stopped from the edge? What if he fell onto the tracks?

His heart began to hammer in his chest, and he drew on the cigarette repeatedly until he burnt his lips as the burning tobacco reached the filter. He jumped and dropped the butt, and then even that small comforting glow was gone. He plunged his hand deep into his pockets, searching for another, and his hands actually shook as he retrieved the pack and struggled to light it. He tore a match from the book but his fingers fumbled it and the book dropped to the ground.

"Shit!" he muttered and bent down to feel along the ground for the book. Nothing! He reached a little further and then moved his groping fingers in an arc around him. His fingers brushed against a still moist and sticky mound of gum and he cursed the person that had so carelessly discarded it. He reached further out, nearly overbalanced, and had to move his left foot forward to prevent himself from falling.

How far was he from the edge now?

He strained his eyes, trying to make out the edge, but gave up as his head began to pound. He abandoned his search and rose slowly to his full height and gingerly balanced on one leg while he used the other to try to find the edge of the platform. He really hated not being in control. He hadn't felt this helpless since his father used to lock him in the basement, but of course he couldn't do that anymore...

A slight breeze touched his cheek and he pulled his overcoat up around his collar to keep out the chill, but he shivered regardless. Suddenly a train thundered into the station as a flood of blazing light and screaming brakes assaulted his senses viciously. The interior lights of the carriages exploded outwards, bathing the entire platform in painfully bright light. He paused for a second as he tried to regain control of his senses and blinked furiously to clear the spots that swam in front of his vision. The sudden darkness from before must have confused him more that he had thought as the train had come into the station behind him. He shrugged, reasoning that he must have turned around while searing for the matches. His eyes cleared and he noticed the matchbook on the ground, picked it up, and walked onto the next-to-last carriage. The odour hit him as soon as he walked through the doors and he quickly retrieved his cigarette, lit it to drown out the smell, and then sat on the nearest seat. He brought his legs up onto the seat opposite and sat back and looked out the window. The doors closed silently and his heart had already slowed to normal by the time the train smoothly accelerated from the station. He dismissed his earlier unease as tiredness, maybe four killings in one month were too much, he thought absently.

The tunnel was dark and the light of the carriage threw his reflection up onto the glass. The face that stared back at him was gaunt. His thinning hair was slicked back with oil and accentuated the sharp cheekbones and hawk-like nose. A weak chin and a thin mouth, permanently straight like a tight strand of rope, gave him a perpetual snarl, and the dark clothes he wore only emphasized the paleness of his face. He liked to think that his appearance added to the aura of danger that emanated from him, and so he purposely dyed his hair dark and avoided sunlight as much as possible.

He finished his cigarette and flicked the butt to the ground where he let it smoulder and turned his attention to the interior of the carriage. It was surprisingly clean; he marveled at the fact that there was no graffiti at all, either on the walls or on the back of the seat. In fact, if it weren't for the aged stench that clung to everything, he would have thought that the carriage was new. He tried to breath through his mouth only but the reek of urine, vomit and something that he couldn't quite place still caused bile to shift uncomfortably in his stomach.

He yawned again and felt his eyes grow heavy. The slight seesaw motion of the train relaxed him and, despite the cloying smell, he drifted off to sleep.

He woke with a start. He had never slept in public before and his heart hammered as he thought about the implications of such a lapse of control. He ran his hands expertly over his body, checking his weapons and the tools he used for his trade, and relaxed a little when he found everything still in place. He paled as he realised that he had been totally helpless while he lay there and he decided then that he was definitely going to take a long break once he got home and reported the conclusion of the hit.

He looked around and saw that the carriage was still empty and peeled back his sleeve to check the time. The hands had stopped at 11:11 and he shook the watch and brought it to his ear but heard nothing.

What time was it? Had he missed his stop?

The questions swirled around his head and his usual cool indifference began to fray. It really had been a strange night. He pressed his face against the glass and peered out into the darkness, hoping to see a landmark or a station that would give him his bearings. The darkness outside was impenetrable and all he could see was a shocked and pale reflection staring back at him. He recoiled at the image, backed out of his seat and looked around for some clue before striding purposely to the front of the carriage.

His earlier unease had returned and he felt a stab of pain in his chest as tension gripped him. The carriage seemed inordinately long, as if he was walking the wrong way on an escalator, and it was with some relief that he finally gripped the door handle and peered through the dividing glass.

The carriage appeared to be the same as the one he was in, but he could see the heads of other passengers bobbing above the seats to the rhythm of the train and a small gasp of relief escaped his lips. He pulled at the door handle and it slid open easily. He stepped through between the cars and a painful roaring noise filled the cramped area. He muttered a curse, gripped the second handle, and wrenched the handle with a little more force than he had intended. The door swung easily and he stumbled through into the carriage where he let the door slide closed behind him and sighed as the roaring noise disappeared.

He looked quickly around to see if anyone had witnessed his undignified entrance and straightened his jacket as he rose to his full height and made his way forward. There were a number of passengers throughout the car, but he saw a ticket collector about half way up the aisle with his back to him and made his way towards him with renewed assurance.

The ticket collector was busy stamping a passenger's ticket as he came up behind him so he turned to a female passenger instead. "Excuse me," he asked as he tapped her on the shoulder, "could you tell me if we have passed Coulter Avenue Station, please?" He forced his mouth into a smile as he spoke. Although he would not normally be so polite, he had no wish to make a scene after the day he had had so far.

The woman turned towards him and smiled. She was pretty, blond hair cut straight and framing an oval face and piercing blue eyes that seemed to pull at him. There was something familiar about her, but before he had time to think further about it she opened her mouth and hundreds of yellow-green maggots spewed from her mouth. The creatures poured over her clothes and onto the ground. Some wriggled over his hand. He recoiled backwards and clamped his mouth shut as the bile rose in his throat. He shook the maggots from his hand and continued to rub it against his jacket long after the last of the creatures were gone.

He looked back at the woman. Her pretty smile had become grotesque, and he stumbled back and tripped over the legs of the man sitting opposite. On impact, the other passenger's head fell forward and then tumbled down his chest and thumped to the ground where its glazed eyes stared up at the assassin. He had no time to react or even to wonder about what was happening as a hand touched him on the shoulder. He spun around. The ticket collector stood before him in a neat, red uniform but his face was a mess of bone and tattered flesh. One eyeball hung stubbornly by a thin tendon and bounced against his cheek with the motion of the train. The other socket was empty except for a small white worm that squirmed deep in the socket.

The assassin stumbled back and watched in horror as the conductor reached up with a gnarled hand, plucked the remaining eye from its tendon and offered it to the assassin. He screamed and turned his back on the creature and fled back down the carriage. He slammed into the door and pulled hard at the handle. It slid open easily and he rushed through back into his own carriage and continued on down to the last door.

It wouldn't budge! The first door had slipped easily open and he had passed into the noisy space between the cars, but the second door was completely stuck. He wrenched at it repeatedly as he looked back down the carriage in time to see that the conductor had followed him. He was about fifteen feet from him, and he turned again to the door and pulled at it with all his strength. The noise was painful in the small alcove and his scream of frustration was lost to the thunder of the wheels. He frantically looked for a catch but the door was bare except for the handle.

Ten feet.

He jammed his back against the door jam and pulled with all his strength. It moved! Only about two inches, but it moved. He looked back and the conductor was only eight feet away so he redoubled his efforts and pulled again. The door moved another inch and the conductor closed to six feet. Sweat broke out on his brow and his heavy clothes were drenched with the exertion.

The conductor was so close now that he thought he could feel his hot breath on his neck as he tried one last time. Suddenly the door flew open, and he was so surprised that he flew through the opening and landed in a heap on the floor of the last carriage. He lay on the ground, breathing deeply, and tried to ignore the pounding in his head. He looked up at the door and the conductor beyond and tensed his muscles to flee further down the carriage when the conductor stopped at the second door, pulled it closed and retreated back into the other carriage.

The assassin slumped against the first seat with relief and closed his eyes briefly as he concentrated on slowing his pulse. He breathed deeply and ignored the fantastic rationalisations that his mind began to conjure. That could wait, for now he concentrated purely on his pounding heart and shaking hands.

He felt his body begin to recover and immediately his mind flooded with questions as he tried to make sense of the last few minutes. He checked the door again and then rose slowly to his feet and peered back into the other carriage. It appeared empty. He fully expected to wake up any minute. It had to be a dream, he reasoned. A very realistic one, but a dream nonetheless.

He laughed with relief and turned to find a seat. He had never felt such fear before and the surge of adrenaline had been intoxicating. Was this how his victims felt just before they died? He had never imagined that the moment of death could be made so exhilarating.

The carriage had been deathly quiet since he had stumbled in, so he was startled when he turned and noticed that most of the seats were actually occupied.

He scanned the faces before him and felt his heart tighten again in his chest. There was something not quite right...then he noticed it. Each of the figures had terrible deformities. A woman beside him wore a bright pink dress more suited to summer evenings than midnight train journeys. Then he noticed that the dress wasn't pink at all; it had been another colour at one time but had been drenched in blood that had now dried and faded. She turned towards him and smiled. He took a step back. His mind might be convinced that he was dreaming, but he wasn't taking any chances. He saw a man opposite her, and as the man turned he could see that most of the left side of his face was missing and blood and brain matter had congealed down his shoulder and into his lap.

The assassin looked frantically around and began to notice each of the passengers' wounds. Just then he saw a familiar face and he blanched. Three seats down from him sat the man he had killed tonight. The man sat and smiled, his wide grin grotesquely matching the open wound along his throat. The assassin's eyes darted from face to face, and he began to recognise faces from dossiers. Names popped into his mind of all his victims over the years, and he began to match each one with a face.

He stumbled back towards the door and reached for the handle. It was gone! He palmed the door, feeling along its length, but it was completely smooth. That's impossible, he thought, and then he heard the sound of the passengers rising. He whirled around and saw the mass move towards him. He flattened himself against the door and began to scream, hoping that he'd wake up. He hugged himself as he started to giggle uncontrollably. He felt the gun strapped under his shoulder. How could he have forgotten?

A cold fury seethed through him. No one made a fool of him. He ripped the gun from the holster and placed his first two shots expertly through the foreheads of the nearest two passengers. The bullets both entered just above their eyes, drilling neat holes in the flesh and then exited in fist sized chunks at the base of their skulls. The assassin laughed as he continued to place shot after shot into the approaching hoard. His mind was numb and he acted purely on instinct. But he failed to notice that those he hit didn't actually stop advancing. He also didn't notice the dull click of his automatic as the hammer continued to fall on an empty magazine as he kept pulling the trigger and laughing maniacally long after the bullets ran out.

The laughter turned into a scream as the first of the passengers reached him and bit into the soft flesh above his wrist. He dropped the gun and swung towards his still-smiling attacker. Fresh blood poured down its chin and the creature chewed the flesh slowly. He stumbled backwards and shot out his arms to regain his balance, but suddenly another passenger gripped his arm and tore the flesh on the back of his hand.

Pain shot through him and he screamed as he felt other hands groping at him, pulling his jacket off and tearing at his flesh with wickedly sharp teeth. He pressed himself against the door, willing it to disappear, and screamed until he was hoarse. His mind snapped but the pain continued. There was no plateau of pain where it blended into a constant numbness; each tear and rip was fresh and excruciating. He prayed for it to stop, for unconsciousness or even for death, but all were denied him. The victims continued to move forward and each one extracted their pound of flesh.

The assassin watched the last one approach. The man he had killed tonight still smiling as he came abreast and ripped the flesh from his throat and then retreated back into the pack. The assassin slumped to the ground, every fibre of his body was in agony, but death remained elusive. Suddenly he felt his ruined body begin to knit itself together, blood began to congeal and then stopped pouring from his wounds. The process was agonising and it brought him to a new level of pain. Then his eyes widened as he saw his body begin to heal. Blood rushed through ruined arteries and intense pain came with it.

He felt his strength return and then watched in terror as his victims lined up and began to approach once more.

"Oh God," he screamed, "Not again."

DEREK GUNN was born in 1964. He lives in Dublin, Ireland where he works as a Global Communication Network Specialist for an international communications company. His first novel, *Vampire Apocalypse*, is forthcoming by Black Death Books. You can also find short stories appearing in the November 2004 issue of *Corpse Magazine*, the upcoming anthology *Chimera World 2* due out in January 2005 and the anthology *The Undead* in August. His next two novels, *Holmes's Destiny* and *The Estuary* are finished and currently being considered. You will find sample chapters and news of upcoming books and stories on his website at www.derekgunn.com.

RETURN OF THE BA

Angeline Hawkes-Craig

"That the new one?" the intern asked.

"Uh, yeah—real beaut, huh?" Dr. Cranston said, looking up from the clipboard he was writing on.

The awed intern walked around the well-preserved mummy laying on the gurney. "Wow, the linen on this guy looks fresh enough to unwind, no problem," Nick, the curious intern, said with a hint of excitement in his voice.

"That's the plan," Dr. Cranston mumbled.

"No joke? Are we really unwrapping this one?" Nick had seen so many mummies go in and out of the lab, but each one could only be x-rayed, catscanned or have very small samples taken from it for analysis. Just once he wished they could actually unwrap one and see the mummy inside with their own eyes.

"No joke. We start now." Cranston smiled and set the clipboard down on the chrome metal desk next to him.

Nick and Cranston put on masks and gloves. Dr. Cranston spent a moment looking this way and that at the wrapped mummy and sighed. "I think we might have to cut some of the strips over here—see where the resin has made the linen hard? I don't think it will separate."

Nick shrugged. "Still, the majority of it should come off intact."

"We'll see about that the further in we go. The inside layers might be hardened up with resin like that section." He pointed to the hardened strips.

Slowly they unwound the bindings, beginning at the feet, around and around. Several metal bins were waiting to hold the some 400 yards of linen they would need to remove. The more that came off in intact strips, the better.

Somewhere up around the knees the resin that the ancients had used had hardened the linen into one solid sheet. Dr. Cranston reluctantly pulled out the scissors and cut from underneath, trying to keep the top intact in case of later restoration. It took six hours to gingerly unwrap the first layers. They took a break and grabbed some sandwiches and sodas from the machine in the lobby.

Chewing his tuna fish on wheat, Nick asked, "So, what do you expect to find in the wrappings?"

"Same ole stuff. Scarabs. Ankhs, amulets, wouldn't expect anything out of the ordinary in that department."

Nick nodded. "What do you know about the mummy aside from what we've recorded so far?"

Dr. Cranston took a swig from his soda can. "Well, if the sarcophagus is accurate, and assuming the mummy wasn't placed in someone else's sarcophagus or tomb, then the markings that I've deciphered so far indicate that this was one of Ramses the Second's lesser wives. According to the hieroglyphics, she committed some sort of a betrayal against Ramses and the goddess Maat came around and demanded our mummy be partially prepared and buried alive for her crimes."

"Damn! Why didn't you tell me all of this to begin with? I thought we were dealing with your average Joe—buried alive! How grotesque. The mummy doesn't look disturbed in anyway, though, maybe it's all a bunch of hype." Nick swallowed the last bite of bread crust.

"Not disturbed because, apparently, the priests drugged her first. Then they wrapped her and dumped all the nitrate and fun stuff in there and sealed her up before she woke up—probably never woke up. Not much air in a sealed sarcophagus or in a sealed tomb." Cranston wiped his mouth and tossed his crumpled-up paper napkin into the trashcan along with the rest of his trash. He got up and deposited his empty can in the recycling bin.

Nick drank the remainder of his soda. "So, let's go see what our cursed mummy has to yield!"

Cranston smiled, rolled his eyes, and followed his exuberant intern back to the lab.

They had barely cut into the second group of layers when they began to hit amulets, scarabs, and ankhs. All sorts of little spells written on small papyrus tags were embedded in the wraps as well.

Then above the mummy's breast they found something quite remarkable.

"Looky here." Nick handed the copper vile to Dr. Cranston. "Looks like it opens."

Cranston studied it for a moment and then sat on a stool and carefully opened the jeweled top. Inside was a roll of papyrus. "It's a scroll," Dr. Cranston said, his eyes lighting up.

"What's it say?" Nick asked enthusiastically.

"You keep unwrapping. I'll need a few minutes to write it all out." Cranston pulled out a chart and started to decipher the scroll.

Nick ran into amulets with the eye of Horus, which was used for protection, and scarabs that ensured that the dead would be resurrected in the afterlife. This mummy seemed to have an exorbitant amount of amulets and doo-dads wrapped up with it.

"I'm at 201 scarabs and such—someone was really worried about this chick."

"Maybe it was someone who believed she had been unjustly punished," Cranston muttered.

"Why? Does it say that? Does the scroll say something like that?" Nick continued to cut the strips, removing them carefully.

"Hot damn, almost got it!" Dr. Cranston laughed.

Nick stared with saucer eyes and then stopped. "Okay, down to the last layers, want me to keep going?"

Cranston looked up momentarily. "Yeah, go on."

Nick raised his eyebrows. "Must be some scroll." He laughed.

Cranston whistled. "Remarkable!"

"Something looks different with the abdomen on this mummy," Nick said while working.

Cranston looked up from the scroll and from his notebook. "She was pregnant."

"Hmm. Buried alive and pregnant. Wonder if the two had something to do with each other. Can't see a Pharaoh burying alive his own offspring…unless, it wasn't his," Nick added the last part with a sudden understanding.

Cranston nodded. "That's it. But, there's more. Here's what I got. It seems our mummy here, Imiu, is a lesser wife of Ramses the Second."

"So, the sarcophagus is correct," Nick said.

"Yeah. And she had an affair with a high priest. Now, remember that the high priests would wear terra cotta masks of Anubis while watching over embalmings? Well, it seems that she went to meet up with this unidentified high priest and instead, according to the scroll, the actual Anubis shows up and knocks her up. Well, Pharaoh gets wind of it from the goddess Maat, who is the goddess that regulates the natural order of things—like how the gods and mortals interact and things like that…" Cranston took a deep breath and continued excitedly. "Well, Maat gets mad because Anubis laid with Imiu and got her pregnant, and Maat thinks that Imiu is responsible because she should have been able to tell a god from a mortal man. So, she orders that both Imiu and her unborn child should be partially prepared for burial and placed alive in the sarcophagus and tomb. The unidentified high priest is the one who has recorded all of this and adds that the enclosed spell will resurrect his unjustly punished lover. He himself inserted the amulets and this vile with the scroll to ensure Osiris, the god of fertility and the afterlife, would resurrect Imiu and her child."

"Osiris? He called in the big guns." Nick laughed. "Is that all it says?"

"Apparently, he hid all the stuff on her before she was sealed up, and from the looks of things, he never got caught." Cranston sighed. "Remarkable."

Nick unwrapped the fingers, which were wrapped individually, and unwrapped the arms. "Whoa. Got another vile here." Nick shook his head in disbelief and passed it to Dr. Cranston.

It had the same jeweled lid and same proportions. Dr. Cranston opened it and found another scroll. He whistled. "This must be the spell. Keep unwrapping and get the camera ready while I work on this scroll."

Nick gingerly unwrapped each toe, and leg. The mummy was so preserved that her hair was still attached to her leathery skull. It hung in long, skinny braids pulled back at the nape of her neck. Not the usual shorn head of a noble who was used to wearing wigs all of the time. Nick took some measurements of limbs, fingers, shoulder width, cranial measurements—all of the standard measurements recorded to determine age, height, general health and all of the everyday information scientists liked to record. Cranston was frowning noticeably.

"What's wrong?" Nick asked.

"Says we can't read the scroll out loud. So, I'll just have to give you the general idea of what it says."

Nick laughed. "What do you mean it says we can't read it out loud? And you believe whatever hocus-pocus has been threatened, should you read it?"

Cranston frowned again. "I take the religion of the ancient Egyptians very seriously. There are reasons for not reading it out loud."

Nick laughed and waved his hand, saying, "Go on, then."

Cranston looked at his notes and pushed his glasses up further on his nose. "Basically, it's a spell to resurrect Imiu. It seems her lover, the high priest, wasn't entirely sure Osiris would do it on his own, so he added the powerful resurrection spell to her corpse. He believed that Imiu had been tricked by Anubis and should not have been punished for his trickery." Cranston cleared his throat. "I think we should have another look at her sarcophagus. There were several lines of hieroglyphics that I could not read due to dirt and grime, but it is supposed to have been cleaned up. I think I'm going to go take a look at the sarcophagus down the hall while you take all the photos and load them into the computer." Cranston picked up his clipboard. "I'm wondering if there is more to the story than just the perspective of the lover of the supposedly unjustly punished woman."

"Like the court version or non-biased version is written on the sarcophagus?" Nick asked.

"That's what I'm hoping." Cranston smiled and headed down the hall.

Nick finished the photographs and loaded them into the lab computer. From the data he had collected so far, he was guessing she was around twenty-five years old. She was beautiful, even now all shriveled up and mummified. She still retained that realness and natural beauty to her person. She was big pregnant even shrunken up. Her abdomen still retained a rounded shape, probably was very near her due date at the time of death. Pity they couldn't allow the child to have lived. The child was the innocent victim in all of this; but according to the nameless priest, Imiu was innocent too—not of adultery, but of whom it was committed with. Then Nick theorized that looking at it from a rational point of view, the baby was probably the unnamed high priest's child, not the spawn of Anubis, and Ramses knew that and was pissed that not only did she sleep with someone else, thus betraying him, but she went and got pregnant with the other guy's kid. Ramses was probably just really pissed off. Nick had to feel for the woman, though. Ramses had like, what, one hundred or more wives and concubines? She was probably lucky if she got to see him once a year. What was a gorgeous woman like her supposed to do—sit around and grow old? With Ramses' fifty or so sons, even if Imiu managed to have a son the odds were incredibly slim that her child would ever assume the throne. A lonely woman's desperate act ended up costing her life.

Nick finished with the computer data and wandered over to Cranston's desk. He had left his translation of the spell behind. He had also left the original scroll. No stranger to reading hieroglyphics, Nick picked up the scroll and began to stumble through the phrases, reading them aloud. He reread the bottom line a few times, struggling with a symbol or two. In Egyptian he spoke the words for each symbol: "Oh, Osiris, you are a busy god. I have left this spell to aid you. Oh god of the fertile, god of that which comes after life—take Imiu to your bosom, she is a lost daughter wrongly accused and unjustly sent from this life. Send her Ba back to her; breathe your gust of living breath into her so she might live again. Maat and Anubis have conspired against her. Let her live for she has been sorely used by all she has loved."

Having read it through, Nick read it through smoothly the second time in an even tone, clear and concise. The actual spell made little sense to him but he read it over in chanting Egyptian. Cranston walked in as Nick was concluding the passage.

"Was that the spell? Did you read it out loud?" Cranston demanded, grabbing Nick by the coat sleeve.

"Yes, calm down. I read it while you were gone so you wouldn't listen and get all concerned."

"That's not the point, Nick. You read it aloud. The scroll specifically warns on its seal not to read it aloud! Did you bother reading this part, the introduction?" Cranston pointed to the paragraphs before the spell that Nick had not been interested in reading. "Reading this scroll out loud sets it in motion with dire results!"

"Such as?"

"It didn't say. But do you want to take such a chance?" Cranston frowned. "I told you that I didn't want it read aloud and you violated my wishes."

Nick sighed. "Did you find anything on the sarcophagus?"

"No. They're still cleaning it. I recorded the legible parts, and I'll go back tomorrow and read the rest. You're changing the subject. You violated my wishes. How can I work with you if you don't take what I say seriously?" Cranston was beyond pissed; little veins were popping out and throbbing on his neck.

"It's just a piece of paper!" Nick exclaimed.

"To you. To me—and to her," Cranston waved towards the mummy, "it is very real. I have seen things that you haven't concerning these ancient beliefs. After the things I have seen you learn to take things seriously. I'm going to have to ask you to remove yourself from this project. You purposely violated my wishes. I cannot trust an intern that chooses to become some rogue scientist in my lab."

"It was one paragraph!" Nick couldn't believe Cranston was being so irrational.

Cranston took off his lab coat, and pulled on his sports jacket, and, loosening his tie, he pointed at Nick. "You're very talented, and you have a lot going for you—but I cannot work with someone who chooses to disregard my wishes and beliefs. I'm going home. Close up the lab and don't come in to the lab until the committee calls you back." With that, Cranston picked up his clipboard, slammed it into his briefcase, and clomped out. Nick listened to Cranston's heavy footsteps clack down the tiled hall until they were muffled, then gone. Nick sighed. Great. This wouldn't look good on his record. He booted down the computer and got a plastic sheet to cover the mummy. He rolled the gurney into the climate-controlled storage room and closed the door. He started to put up the equipment when he heard a noise. He looked around briefly and reasoned that it must be the janitorial staff out in the hall.

He continued placing items in their appropriate places when he heard another noise. Nick froze where he stood, sucked in a deep breath and listened, hoping to locate the origin of the sound. It was a thumping sound. He listened closely. It was coming from the storage room. Did someone put something alive in there? Mix-ups happened occasionally but he was surprised whatever it was in there hadn't made any sounds earlier. Probably a lab animal in a cage being used to test something. Nick frowned, flipped the switch to the room and opened the door.

He didn't see anything out of the ordinary. He glanced around, shrugged and reached out to turn off the light and leave.

Then he heard it. Raspy breathing like someone was struggling to breathe. Then he heard the thumping and saw that over on

Imiu's gurney the plastic sheet was rising up and down and moving this way and that as if the mummy under it was trapped and needed air.

Nick stared at it in shock.

The mummy flailed frantically.

"Oh my god!" Nick uttered as he slowly crept up to Imiu's side. He reached out a hand—slow, slow, ever so slowly, and grabbed the plastic. In one swift yank he ripped off the sheet and threw it aside, jumping backwards defensively at the same time.

Imiu's eyes opened in a flash.

Nick jumped again and bumped into another gurney behind him. He grasped it with both hands.

Imiu seemed to study him. Nick studied Imiu from her head to her toes. He saw the flesh regenerating before his eyes. Her feet were still withered, the skin seemed to be moving downwards in a cascade of flesh, unfurling down her body. Where the mummified leather of former skin had been, new flawless flesh had grown. Her body was a golden parchment color. Her eyes a chocolate brown and the braids on her head became silky and glistening, black and perfectly plaited. Nick stared, too shocked to speak.

Imiu felt her face all over and moved her hands down her body and over her very pregnant belly. She smiled. Slowly, she pushed herself up to a sitting position, swinging her legs over the side of the gurney as she looked around the room, eyes finally returning to Nick.

"I am not dead?" Her voice was musical.

Nick smiled at her amazement. He spoke back in Egyptian as she had done, "No, you're not dead. Well, not anymore, apparently," he stuttered.

"What do you mean, not anymore?" Imiu looked at her outstretched arms. "I am alive, am I not?"

"Uh, yes. You do appear to be alive."

Imiu sighed heavily. "I feared Ramses would have me buried, he said that it was to be so." She touched her belly again.

Nick stared at her partially in awe and partly in horror. "Ramses, uh, did have you buried. Uh, I don't know how to say this, so I'm just going to say it. Ramses had you buried, partly mummified, you've been in a tomb for like three thousand years," Nick blurted, the Egyptian words rolling off of his tongue.

Imiu blinked as if she did not understand. Then she frowned. "This cannot be as you say," she said and held out her arms again,

"Look! I am alive, and see, see how my babe kicks within me!" She touched the bulge at her side happily.

Nick watched the babe within her kick and move under her flesh. "Your lover—the priest—put a spell in your linen wrappings that were meant to assist Osiris in resurrecting you." Nick passed his white lab coat to Imiu and she wrapped it around herself like a cloak.

"How do you know about my lover?" Imiu whispered. "You must be silent. Ramses will kill him if he ever finds out who he is."

Nick laughed. "Ramses is dead."

Imiu frowned again. "Panaet is safe, then?"

Nick shook his head. This chick just wasn't getting it. "Panaet is dead too. You were dead. You were dead for three thousand years. I read the scroll meant for Osiris, your Ba was returned, and here you are, alive," Nick said, held out his arms towards Imiu and then shrugged. "I don't understand it myself."

Imiu looked around the room again, startled. She got up and walked to the other mummy lying on the gurney behind Nick. She touched it.

"I, I looked like this?" she asked absently.

"Yes. Just like that. Then I read the scroll and now you are alive."

"Can I see this scroll?" she said quietly, looked up at Nick and then back at the mummy on the gurney.

"Yes, yeah, hold on, I'll go get it," he said, running out and picking up the glass case that Cranston had put the papyrus in before leaving, brought it back to the storage room and passed it carefully to Imiu.

"This is Panaet's pen," she said slowly.

"Yes. He wrote it. He must have loved you greatly to risk putting it with you before you were sealed up," Nick said and smiled.

Imiu nodded. "And I him."

Nick took the papyrus and put it back in the box. He returned it to Cranston's desk, but kept glancing back through the door of the storage room half expecting Imiu to disappear in a hallucinatory pouf. But so far, she hadn't.

He walked back to her side, terror mixed with sympathy for this beautiful, sad woman staring at a dried-out mummy lying on a cold, steel gurney.

"If it is any consolation, Panaet's name is never mentioned. I don't believe Ramses ever discovered who your lover was."

Imiu smiled across her whole face and placed a hand over her heart. "Such joy I feel. I refused to tell, this angered Ramses so. He only knew that it was one of the high priests. I believed he would discover who he was after my death."

Nick shook his head, "Well, according to everything we've got, he is only identified as a high priest. Ramses must never have determined which priest it was."

Imiu smiled. "Then he lived. Through him, I lived."

"He lived. He mourned for you." Nick put his hand on her arm. She was real. He needed to confirm this fact for his brain. She was truly real.

Imiu politely withdrew her arm. "Touch not the wife of Pharaoh," she said quietly.

"Dead, remember?"

Imiu made a confused expression. "To you. To me—it is like yesterday. I laid down to rest my swollen ankles, and woke up—now."

Nick raised his eyebrows. "Do you feel different?"

Imiu shook her head no. "Everything is as it was, even this one kicks as hard!" she said and rubbed her belly.

"When does he come?" Nick pointed to her swollen abdomen.

"Any day! Ramses was fast to put me in the tomb, he did not want another man's bastard to remind him of my betrayal!"

Nick frowned this time. "The scroll that your lover, sorry, that Panaet, enclosed with you said that you had been tricked by the god Anubis and that he had gotten a babe on you. And that it was Maat that told Ramses to entomb you and your child while you were alive to atone for your crimes."

Imiu looked at him with a mixed look of horror and amusement. Then she burst out laughing. She covered her full lips with tiny hands as she continued to laugh. "That is what he said?" she asked.

"That's how he explained it. You were wrongly punished for the misdeeds and trickery of Anubis."

Imiu laughed again. "Besides Ramses, Panaet was the only man I had lain with. Ramses had me entombed because of my adultery. Poor Panaet!"

Nick scratched his neck. So, they had a lover who tried to persuade Osiris into resurrecting his lover out of pity for her unjust treatment, and it was all a lie! Maybe Osiris knew that from the beginning and that was why Imiu had never been resurrected. Until now, because of his "rogue" ways, as Cranston believed.

"Damn," Nick hissed under his breath. So, he had evoked a powerful spell for a completely typical chick that was grieved for by a heartbroken and magically inclined lover. Cranston wouldn't like that, not that he was going to believe any of this. He would probably accuse Nick of stealing the mummy or something out of revenge.

"What would happen if Anubis had a son by a mortal?" Nick asked curiously.

Imiu laughed. "Legend says that the human son of Anubis comes to destroy the world. That he would eat man like a jackal does a ripe pomegranate and spew out man's bones like seeds."

Nick laughed. "Nice image. Glad Panaet was just being dramatic!"

Imiu laughed musically again. "He had a flair for the dramatic. He was a high priest, after all."

Nick smiled. "Well, strange as all this is, you can't stay here overnight. Let's find you some clothes, and you can sleep on my couch for the night until we see what Dr. Cranston thinks we should do."

"What is couch and Cranston?" Imiu followed Nick into the lab and Nick closed the door to the climate-controlled storage room.

He found a pair of sweat pants in a locker and a man's t-shirt. "Here, these might be a little tight—but they'll do until we can get back to my place and see what I can find for you."

Imiu stared at the articles, not knowing how to use them. Nick figured this out. "Here, put your arms up above your head."

He tugged the shirt over her arms and head, trying not to ogle her round full breasts with chocolate-hued nipples. He showed her how to put a leg in each of the pants legs and pull them up over herself. She looked down at herself and laughed. "These are peculiar clothes three thousand years now," she struggled to say what she meant.

"I bet you'd feel better in a dress. I'll get you one on the way home." Nick remembered his sister saying that in the last month of her pregnancies all she could wear were dresses because she was so big. He'd stop by a discount store on the way home and pick up a couple of maternity dresses for her. She'd been pregnant for 3000 years, and that was the least he could do for her. "Okay, now.

We're going to go. You might see very strange things. Try not to scream or act too surprised. I'll explain everything to you and I will keep you safe," Nick reassured her and started to take her arm but withdrew his hand and instead pointed through the door. "This way, follow me." He flipped off the light.

Imiu jumped. "What magic is this?" she whispered.

"No magic. We don't use fire or oil to make light now. We have something called electricity. It goes into those white things you see," he pointed to the florescent lamp above them, "and illuminates them like a candle."

This seemed good enough for Imiu at this point. She stopped in front of the soda machine and stared at it. "What is this? It has two mouths!" she said and bent down and looked into the place where the cans came out.

"Oh, watch this!" Nick took a dollar and fed it into the machine. It sucked the money up and clunk! The soda dropped into one of the "mouths". Imiu jumped again and covered her own mouth so she would not scream.

"Is it angry?" she whispered.

Nick laughed. "No. No. Here…" He popped the can. "We drink this." He took a drink and then passed it to Imiu. She felt the can.

"It is cold," she stated. Then doing as she saw Nick do, she hesitantly raised the can to her lips and tasted of the brown bubbly liquid inside.

She laughed. "It tickles my tongue! It is sweet," she said and took another drink. "It is cold." She seemed most impressed with its temperature.

Nick indicated for her to follow him. She stared at everything on the way out. The Egyptian statues in the hall she seemed to notice most of all. "This is from the temple!" she whispered. "They should put this back. It is a crime to steal from the temple, from the gods!" she hissed.

Nick nodded. "I'll tell Cranston," he whispered back and hoped this would make her feel better.

"Who is this Dr. Cranston? He is a healer?" she asked.

"No. He's…he's like a teacher." Nick hoped that helped.

Imiu nodded.

The night air was warm as they walked to his car under the starry ebony sky. Imiu stopped and stared up at the stars. "They are different," she said slowly.

Nick sensed the sadness in her voice. "A lot happens in three thousand years."

She sighed and started walking again. "No sand?"

"No. Not here. There are places. And Egypt. It looks much like you remember. Little has changed in some parts."

"We are not in Egypt?" Imiu obviously hadn't thought about that before now.

"Uh, no. Sorry. We're in a place called America," he said slowly so she could learn the name.

"I know not of this place," she said, a bit frightened.

"It is far from Egypt, but maybe we can take you back to Egypt. You have much knowledge that you can share with the Egyptian people."

Imiu shook her head in the negative. "I am shamed. I am not a good wife. They would only entomb me again."

Nick saw his car. "We can talk about all of that later. Here we go. This is my car," he said, realizing that she would know nothing of cars.

"Car?"

"Like a chariot that doesn't need horses to make it go." Nick unlocked the door for her and helped her in.

She sat down apprehensively. "It is much softer than a chariot," she stated and smiled.

Nick got in and warned her before he turned on the engine. She was amazed by the speed of the vehicle, even though he barely went over forty miles per hour. She held onto the seat for dear life. He swung into the parking lot of a discount store.

"Now, I'm going in there to get you some things to wear. You stay right here. I promise I will return. Do not get out of the car," Nick said and locked the doors. He practically ran inside. He had a 3,000-year-old living mummy in his car that had a prior history of disobedience. He had better shop quickly. He found the maternity department, grabbed two dresses and some panties that he judged to be about her size, snatched a pair of fluffy pink house slippers on the way to the checkout, saw a small teddy bear which he tossed into the basket, paid and nearly ran back to the car.

She was still sitting, face almost smashed against the glass, just where he had left her. He handed the bag to her and got in.

She started feeling the plastic, crunching it in her hand repeatedly. "What is this?" she asked.

Nick laughed. "Oh, that's called plastic. You want what's inside of the plastic. Go on and look in," he said while driving.

She pulled out the dresses and seemed to understand a bit more. The pack of panties she put back into the bag, not understanding what they were for. Then she caught sight of the bear.

"What is this?" She held up the bear.

"For baby," Nick said and smiled.

"A toy?" She suddenly understood.

"It's called a teddy bear, it's a stuffed bear." Nick smiled. "Kids, babies love them."

"When I was a girl I had a crocodile that my mother made for me out of linen. She stuffed it with grass. I also had a wood doll named Merit." Imiu smiled. "I loved Crocodile best, though."

"I had a stuffed doll named Ernie." Nick laughed.

"Is that an animal, an Er-nie?" she asked, still looking at the bear.

"No. Just an orange doll." Nick laughed again and pulled into the parking lot of his condo. "Here we are," he said and turned off the car.

"Is this your palace?" She looked over the condominium complex.

Nick looked around and laughed. "No. I just live in one of them. There are many rooms. Many people live here."

"Your servants?" she asked, following him up the brick steps.

"No. Just people like, uh, like me." He had started to say like you and me, but caught himself. No one here was like her. No one here was a 3,000-year-old ex-mummified wife of a pharaoh! He flipped on the light, again to Imiu's amazement, and ushered her inside. They spent the next couple of hours playing "What is it?" with Nick explaining and demonstrating every appliance in the house.

She washed and dried her t-shirt three times. He found her a frozen fish fillet in the freezer and cooked it for her. He didn't have anything else she would be familiar with. She ate everything he offered without complaint and drank a few more sodas. He got her a glass of milk. She seemed especially happy about the milk, so he showed her how to get her own and she did, frequently.

Two days passed, and to his surprise he hadn't heard from Cranston, nor had the police come busting through his door to arrest him for mummy theft. Maybe Cranston was so wrapped up in reading the hieroglyphics on her sarcophagus that he had not looked in on the mummy. How unbelievable would that be? Nick didn't know, but he was enjoying his time with Imiu and had kept a journal of every bit of information he had learned from her. He could see why she had been one of Pharaoh's wives. She was beautiful, but her personality was magnetic. It would be hard to turn down the advances of such a persuasively clever woman like her. No wonder Panaet was so passionately in love with her that he had embellished the truth to bring honor back to Imiu's name throughout eternity. Nick wondered if Panaet's spirit was still looking for his long lost love—now walking the earth again because of his undying love for Pharaoh's wife.

Nick grew concerned when Imiu began to complain of pains. She refused to leave the condo to see a doctor. He didn't know what to do. He was one year away from a doctorate in Egyptology, not in obstetrics.

He pulled up all the info he could on the Internet and frantically combed the yellow pages for a midwife. He called six before he found one who would come with such short notice, no interview, no nothing. Nick secretly wondered if the broad was on the up and up, but having no other options but to deliver the baby himself, he gave the midwife the instructions for his condo and begged she be quick about arriving. She asked a few questions that Nick translated for Imiu and answered the midwife, and then they hung up.

Imiu smiled. "He comes!"

Nick put up his hands. "Whoa, girl. No 'he comes' until the midwife gets here!"

"Midwife?" Imiu said between a grunt and a stifled cry.

"Is that good?"

"Yes! That is good," she said while she moaned. She rocked back and forth on all fours on the floor as Nick nervously paced the floor. Nick nervously looked out the window, anxiously watching for the midwife—there she was. A short, stocky woman knocked on the door.

"Oh my god, I am so glad you're here," Nick said nervously.

"First the money. Then the baby," the woman spoke in a thick accent and held out her hand.

Nick gulped and went to retrieve the money. This well-preserved mummy was costing him a lot of money. He paid the impatient woman, who crammed the wad of bills into her bra and then went to Imiu.

Nick continued to pace. He began to wonder if he should call Dr. Cranston.

The midwife had Imiu in the center of the living room, an old sheet spread beneath her. Nick doubted the sheet would be very effective in protecting his carpet, but what could he do? Twice he found himself with the receiver in his hand. Finally, he called Dr. Cranston.

"Hello, Dr. Cranston?" Nick asked nervously.

"I was wondering when you'd call, Nicolas. Do you have the mummy?" Cranston said in an exasperated voice.

"Uh, yes and no. She's not exactly a mummy anymore. That's why I'm calling you. She's, Imiu, is having her baby in my living room," Nick said, throwing a glance over his shoulder.

Silence.

"Uh, Dr. Cranston?"

"Nick. Stay there. Do not let Imiu leave. Keep her right there!" Cranston commanded.

"Uh, like I said, she's in the middle of having her baby, I don't think she's going anywhere." Nick sort of laughed.

The line went dead.

"Dr. Cranston? Hello?" Nick frowned and hung up the phone.

He leaned against the bar and watched the midwife instructing Imiu. She panted and pushed, groaned and cursed in Egyptian.

A pounding on the door turned everyone's head. Nick ran to the door, relieved that Cranston had arrived.

He flung open the door. Dr. Cranston shoved Nick aside, sending him crashing into the hall table and onto the floor. He leaped over the back of the couch, and before anyone could protest, whacked off Imiu's beautiful head with a curved sword.

"What in the hell?" Nick said, scrambling to his feet.

Cranston bent over, out of breath, and panted, "The baby is cursed. He is destined to destroy mankind—the son of Anubis—it was on the sarcophagus—warning on the side, not to resurrect—son of Anubis will destroy man."

"No, you don't understand! It's all a lie! It's a..." Nick stopped as he heard the cries of a newborn, then a yelping sound and the scream of the midwife filling his ears.

Cranston and Nick snapped their heads in the direction of the midwife who sat between the legs of the decapitated body of Imiu—the body began to darken, wither, bones caving in, breaking down from flesh to mummified leather to dust—bits blowing about in the breeze from the ceiling fan.

The midwife screamed again as the newborn kicked and cried in her outstretched arms.

Nick and Dr. Cranston looked at the squalling infant—fully formed and healthy, kicking and yelping, the body of a baby boy and the head of a jackal.

"The son of Anubis!" Cranston shouted in horror.

Nick fell to his knees. He had been tricked, beguiled just like Panaet had been deceived into believing Imiu's innocence. The midwife swayed to one side, then fainted. The baby landed on top of her ample bosom and pushed itself up to her face, licking her cheek and yelping its dog-like cry.

Nick and Cranston stared in terror, speechless, with mouths agape. Horrified, Nick watched as Cranston turned his head slowly towards the curved sword he still held in his sweaty hand—and then looked at the barking baby—the son of Anubis.

ANGELINE HAWKES-CRAIG received her B.A. in Composite English Language Arts in 1991 from East Texas State University where she was a member of Sigma Tau Delta (English Honor Society). She is a former secondary education teacher. Angeline is a member of the Horror Writer's Association. Her fiction crosses many genres but primarily Angeline writes Horror, Fantasy and Speculative fiction. With publication credits since 1981, her work can be found in many anthologies and collections. Her novel *The Swan Road* was published in 2002. Cyber-Pulp Press will release her novel *Far From The Tree* in 2005. For more information visit: http://www.angelinehawkes-craig.com.

THE EMPIRE OF SLEEP

Davin Ireland

S erendipity. *The faculty of making happy chance finds. I wonder if Arnold Bright would have named the cottage so had he forseen what violent caprices retirement had in store for him. Certainly, the old man did little to deserve the untimely lot that befell him. Just worked hard his whole life, scrimped and saved what change he could spare, whilst carefully nurturing the ideal of a place in the countryside and a fitting epitaph to his dream.*

I can see the name clearly now, branded into the little cherry-wood plaque above the letter-box as I wade through the gathering dusk. It is framed by an untended stand of rose trees that bracket the path to the unlit porch like stooped ushers in florid evening wear.

Knowing that the door is always locked, I step forward and grip the handle anyway. I jiggle it with my hand, the urgency of my efforts rattling hollowly among the eaves. A fluid stream of squeaking, membranous shapes swirls forth from the shadows, copperplating the air with a series of loops and meaningless curlicues.

Something tells me that time is running out. As if to confirm this, the last of the daylight haemorrhages from the sky. Then the furtive scrape of wood on wood issues from deep within the house. Yeghnazar is coming awake. Courage deserts me at this point. Retreating, stumbling, I discover that the sharpened stake in my belt has vanished along with the sinking sun.

This is only one of several recurring themes.

I emerge from sleep heavy-limbed and weary, like a drowning man crawling onto a riverbank. I stagger into the hall, the narrow kitchen beyond. My eyes hurt. My throat is constricted. I down glass after glass of water, then vomit a mixture of blood and bile into the sink. If I don't bring this malignant fiasco to an end soon, exhaustion will kill me as surely as any gun.

This is only to be expected, of course. I am a reflection of that which surrounds me, and this town is dying on its feet. May have expired already, for all I know. In the hours of daylight, the shrinking numbers of the living trickle dazed between the shops and houses like spring run-off after a light rain. At night, jeering rivers of the undead flow through the streets, seeking nourishment and amusement in equal measure, never giving up, never tiring of their jaded gallows humour.

Haywood told me that I was crazy to stay, that I should have left when the going was good. Only those already touched by the promise of death, he added—the aged, the infirm and the sick—will remain until the winter, for they are as shadows to the blind. The others, those who retain the irrecusable tang of life, will be hounded into the shadows and converted as mercilessly as a ladybug gobbles aphids. Who will say he is wrong?

All I can be sure of is that the battle is not yet lost, despite so many signs to the contrary. Granted, there are too many of them for any one man to stop. But I have drawn up a contingency plan of sorts. If I can destroy Yeghnazar, if I can eliminate the host, then perhaps his brethren will expire of their own accord. I have no evidence that this be the case. In fact, my theory has no more grounding in science than it does in folklore. But still I must try. And I have a weapon, too. My dreams.

Thanks to these nightly visions, I felt Yeghnazar's presence the moment his entourage set foot in the village all those months ago. Pawing aside the drapes, I peered into the raw light of morning, blood zinging, a taste like shorn metal at the back of my throat. A fat August sun peered back at me over the sagging roof of the old Calverton homestead, casting a shadow the shape of a rotten molar across the lane that separates our two properties. Propped up in a wheelchair, my new neighbour's exhausted form was bandaged from head to foot like an outpatient from a burns unit, dark glasses sewn into the fabric of the gauze above his ears. Yet still he mewled and whimpered like a tormented kitten when the rays of the newly risen sun pierced his wrappings.

A week later the live-in housemaid fled, but not before chalking a single word on the pavement outside her employer's new abode. *Stregoa.* This curious item of graffiti piqued my interest, and with the endeavour of a trained scholar, I set out to verify its meaning. Variations on the word crop up in several European languages, but they all seem to hold a common source. The nearest

The New Oxford Dictionary of English comes is Strigose, which means 'covered with short, stiff ad-pressed hairs'. I puzzled over this at first. Italian, French, Romanian, Hungarian—all reveal a similar association: hairs, bristles, brushes, yet little else. Only the original Spanish provides the first hint of a deeper meaning. A supplementary interpretation of the word, plucked from an online archive, reads 'stiff-bristled brush; *blood-sucker*'. Unsurprisingly, it is the latter part of the definition which harks directly back to the Latin cognate.

Needless to say, Yeghnazar vacated his new home not long after this and went to ground—quite literally, I was later to discover. Nine members of a local neighbourhood watch found him curled up in a natural hollow at the base of a dead whistle-wood tree near the village outskirts. Badgers and foxes had further excavated the hollow for him before being desanguinated and disposed of themselves, their matted husks strewn about the twilit wood like spent waterskins. And now the emaciated form of the Dark Master, draped in roots and dry clods of soil, had taken their place. Naturally, he bested the villagers and fled again, but by that time a pattern had been established. Yeghnazar was vulnerable, he could be hurt. His perpetual flight since proves it beyond any doubt.

And so to the present day.

The dream of Arnold Bright's retirement cottage—poor, dead Arnold Bright, who only ever wanted to end his days in the countryside, a wish now long-granted, of course—has revealed the current lair to me. A happy chance find, indeed. And so enough is enough. I have a personal score to settle with Yeghnazar, and I have bluffed and fretted and procrastinated on this issue for far too long. The time for words is over. I must achieve that which I have failed to achieve in every dream sequence thus far. To confront and best he who would consume us all in eternal darkness.

I gather my wits.

Murky grey light streams through the fanlight at the far end of the narrow hall, puddling weakly on the carpet. I know not if it is dawn, dusk or noon of an overcast day. It matters little now. The strength is returning to my limbs, but nowhere near fast enough. As I collect my canvas toolbag, with its cargo of pointed sticks and aerosol mace canisters (the latter having proven far more effective than garlic, it has been discovered), I am forced to appreciate the ultimate irony of my situation.

I am last of those willing to fight the scourge that has invaded our ranks, yet in appearance I lack even the vitality of the freshly interred. My sore eyes itch from lack of sleep, my jaw is fuzzed with week-old stubble, the ashen face I last witnessed this Friday morning can have grown no more healthy in the interim. But I need not fear. The good Lord has spared me the horror of my own countenance. As I move the through the hallway, the gilded mirror opposite reflects only stained wood panelling and the sunburst clock I inherited from my grandmother at age eleven. Any sign of my physical aspect has vanished entirely.

Once again I am reminded of what Yeghnazar has taken from me and why he must be destroyed.

Since his debut in 2003, DAVIN IRELAND has sold over two-dozen short stories to print magazines and anthologies around the world. Recent credits include fiction published in *Albedo One, Revelation, Black Petals, Zahir, Neo-Opsis, Dark Animus, JupiterSF,* and *Futures Mysterious Anthology Magazine,* with more tales following soon in *Horror Express, Underworlds, The Journal of Pulse-Pounding Narratives, Here & Now, Agony in Black,* and the upcoming *Dark Elation* anthology.

ENTER SLEEP

Nancy Jackson

"Just sleep," she said out loud. "Let me get some sleep tonight."

Sighing, she focused on lead, bricks, and pounds of sand, anything to will her eyelids to grow heavy. Shutting off her mind was not an easy task and she fought for total silence. After several restless turns beneath the sheets, she felt the first signs of her body relax. A faint noise brought her back to semi-consciousness. Looking into the mirror beside her bed she watched the reflected hallway nightlight filter in, her door opening on its own. She shrugged and closed her eyes, trying to get back to the sleep zone she had entered.

"Why did you leave!" cried a voice.

Heidi jolted straight up in bed, her pulse raced. She turned on the bedside light, and almost knocked it over. "What?" she said. "Who's there?"

Scanning the room she didn't see anyone, and got up to close the door. She figured it had only been a dream.

"How could you do that to me!" screamed the voice.

Heidi looked down and froze. The dinner of meatloaf and potatoes churned in her stomach, a taste of bile formed in her throat.

"Mom?" she whispered.

On the floor lay the head of her mother; eyes wide open in anger.

"I waited, young lady, and you never came back!" she cried.

This was the same conversation she'd had with her mom three years earlier when she moved out.

"I am asleep, I just have to be," she told herself. "None of this is real."

"Oh, I'm real all right, I just haven't been the same since you left," said her mother. "I've fallen to pieces and you don't even care!"

Heidi looked back at her bed and crawled in, throwing the covers over her head. Nightmares were nothing new for her, but this one was far too disturbing.

"Wake up, I just need to wake up," she repeated.

"Get the hell out of that bed!" shouted a man's voice.

Heidi sat up and stared. Her father stood at the doorway, an axe in his hand.

"Daddy? What are you doing here?" she cried.

His eyes were bloodshot and looked like he hadn't slept in weeks.

"It's time for you to be a good girl," he said.

"How do you mean?"

"I need you to help me with your mother," he said. "Some things have happened."

Heidi shook her head. Was she awake or asleep? She couldn't tell. Sitting up, she looked into the mirror and still could see her father standing in the doorway, blood dripping from his axe to the floor, staining her carpet. From underneath the bed, her mother's head peeked out.

"Don't tell him I'm here," she whispered.

Heidi turned back to her father.

"I couldn't stand the guilt anymore," he confessed. "The look in her eyes was enough to drive any man crazy."

"What are you talking about?" she asked.

"That woman scrutinized every move I made!"

"You were the one who cheated on her," she said. "It's a natural response to betrayal."

"What would you know about betrayal?" he asked.

"I am an adult, I've been through it with boyfriends, and whether you like it or not, you betrayed me as well," she said. "Because of what you did I left."

"What's done is done," he said, and shook the axe.

"And what did you do?" she asked.

He took a step in and the bedroom changed. A thickness coated the air, making it stale and difficult to breathe. Thin lines of blood streamed down the blue wallpaper and pooled at the bottom onto the floor.

"I lost patience with her," he said.

The muscles of his arms flexed while he wrung the axe between his hands.

"I told her I was going out and she said she didn't care. I knew what that meant; she figured I was going out to be with another woman. Something inside snapped."

Heidi rose from her bed. The smell of death enveloped the room.

"I was ready to get into the car and leave, but instead I decided it was time for a change. No more guilt, no more distrust, neither of us living in such pain and torment," he explained. "It seemed like the logical thing to do."

"Tell me this isn't real," she said. "Just tell me I am in the middle of some morbid nightmare!"

"It's my nightmare," he said. "Trust me, it's real."

The walls of her room moved in and out, in rhythm with the raspy breath of her father. Closet doors slid open and revealed an empty space where the floor should have been.

"I grabbed the nearest thing I could find and went back in the house," he continued, waving the axe in the air. "She was typing on the computer to someone and my first instinct was another man she'd met online. I realized the guilt would always hang over my head and I'd had enough. If I couldn't make it work with her, no one else would have a chance."

His words filtered in and out, her mind unable to fully grasp what he was saying. Wisps of smoke drifted out from the hole in the floor of the closet, arousing her curiosity.

"There were other ways to change it but I was in too deep, you understand?" he asked.

A long silence followed before she could even blink. She couldn't believe her own father was a killer.

"It was so easy," he said. "Just like slicing through melted butter."

"I don't want to hear anymore!" screamed Heidi.

"You have to, I can't keep it inside any longer," he said. "Before I knew it, I'd knocked her head clean off! It went flying, hit the wall and rolled. At first I was in shock, her fingers remained poised to type on the keyboard, her body sitting tall and proud. Then it leaned over and crumpled to the floor, and I realized what I'd done."

"Stop it!" she cried. "I know this is just a stupid, crazy, fucked-up dream that I'm going to wake up from any minute!"

She stood above the hole and looked in. A river of lava moved in fury, emitting smoldering heat upwards into her face.

"It's a mess in the study," he said. "Blood is everywhere and her body has been rotting in there for a week now and I don't know what to do."

"Call the police, you idiot!" she cried.

"I need your help, Heidi. I cannot find her head. I need you to come home to help look for it," he said.

"Like hell," she whispered.

The room blazed intense heat, and melted everything in sight. Her CD collection bent and warped, the mirror reflected her distorted image. He took a step closer and gripped the axe tighter. She watched his jaw clench tight and his lips moved in a mumble, some sort of private conversation with himself. As hard as it was, she had to remind herself this was her father.

"You need to go home and turn yourself in," she said.

"I can't do anything until I find her head," he said. "How would I explain that?"

"You figure it out," she said. "I have nothing to do with this."

"Yes, you do. If you had stayed, I wouldn't have given up so quickly," he said. "You were an incentive to keep trying. With you away I had no one left to prove anything to." Heidi shook her head; this man was a complete stranger to her and she wanted to wake up and make him go away.

"Get out of here or I'll call the police myself!" she retorted.

"No daughter of mine talks to me like that!" he bellowed, storming towards her. Heidi dodged a swipe with the axe and speed-crawled along the carpet until she hit the doorway. Scrambling to her feet she raced downstairs, his footsteps thundering behind her. Grabbing her keys she ran into the garage and got in the car. Her father came in and tore open the door.

"Get out now!" he roared.

She turned the key in the ignition and sharp stabs of pain broke out all over her body. Heidi looked down and saw hundreds of tiny needles poking out through her skin. She tried to move but the needles pinned her to the seat. Her father waved the axe around, blood flinging and coating the windshield of the car.

"I won't hurt you if you come home with me," he said.

Heidi shook her head; she didn't trust him anymore than her mother had.

She tried to pry herself away from the seat, but the needles stretched her muscles, and ripped them further apart. Her screams of pain reverberated off the windshield and it shattered. She closed her eyes as glass shards covered her body and face. When she looked again, her father was gone. Heidi buried her face in her hands, trying to hold back the tears. She couldn't understand why there was no blood coming from the holes in her body.

"If you don't come home with me, I will slice off your head and put it on your mother's body," he said from the backseat.

Startled she jerked, more needles tearing her apart. He grabbed her hair and pulled her head back hard, the blade of the axe resting against her throat.

"If I can't find that head, I'll need to replace it," he said. "You two look so much alike. Now, you don't want your father to go to jail, do you?"

"No," she whispered.

The needles released from her body.

"Good girl," he said. "I knew you would do the right thing."

"I don't want you to go to jail," she said. "I want you to go to Hell!"

Reaching back, she raked her nails against the back of his hands and dug them in as deep as she could. He hollered and let go. Heidi ran out of the car and back into the house. She couldn't leave her mother again.

Re-entering her bedroom she was shocked at how much the blood had risen. She knelt on the floor, the crimson pool reaching just above her waist. She looked under the bed; worried her mother was drowning. She could just barely make out the thin strands of blonde hair that poked out. Reaching in she pulled out her mother's head, and cradled it in her arms.

"Are you okay?" she asked.

"I need you to do something and then you must leave me," she said.

"I can't," cried Heidi. "Look what happened because I left the first time! I never should have left you."

"I don't blame you," she said. "None of this is your fault."

"How can you say that?" asked Heidi.

"Look, honey, your father was just too scared to leave and start all over," she explained. "He hoped to kill his conscience, but it backfired. He won't have his wish while my soul is still intact."

"What do you mean?" Heidi asked.

"As long as he is alive I will remain in this form. I made a solemn vow when I married your father, until death do us part," her mother said.

"I'm confused," she said.

"Until we both die, we are in this marriage, one way or another," she explained. "My death will not undo the promise I made, but once he is dead, our union will end completely. I need you to kill your father for me."

She placed her mother's head on the comforter and stepped back.

"I am not capable of killing anyone!" she cried.

"Sweetheart, I cannot live like this," said her mother.

Heidi blinked back tears. This had to be real; she hurt too much. Her mother had been in enough pain, how could she be expected to endure more?

"I have to think about this," Heidi said. "I'm not sure I could live with myself."

"You will find a way, you are strong like me," she said. "Life is full of tragedy and traumas that we must face and survive. If you don't kill your father then I'm afraid he will kill you."

She heard her father walk up the stairs, dragging the axe against each step. Her heart pounded, blocking out all other sound. She looked from her mother to the closet; its doors opening again, revealing the river of lava, the doorway to Hell.

"One last chance," he boomed from the doorway.

Heidi threw a blanket over her mother and ran to the closet. "Come and get me," she challenged.

He lunged at her, axe raised high above his head. For a moment time moved in slow motion. She watched his veins throb from his forehead, his neck strained tight as his lips sneered. His body moved close; the axe bobbed as he ran towards her. Blood filled the room up to her knees and made it difficult to move. Her eyes reverted to the bed, picturing her mother's head lying there, willing her to save them all from one another. The axe was upon her and he was so close she could smell the foul odor of his breath.

Time resumed its normalcy and Heidi moved just as her father leaned forward to deliver the blow. "No!" he cried as he lost his balance and went down through the floor of the closet. His hand grabbed her foot and pulled her along with him. Heidi screamed as the inferno of flames devoured both their bodies.

The melodic sounds of birds interrupted her horrific visions and she opened her eyes. A faint image of her beautiful mother floated on the ceiling. "You have been saved," she said. "I made a deal with the devil and you are alive and well."

Sunshine poured in through the blinds, bringing in warmth and security. Her room was back to normal and her shoes lay along the closet floor.

"Thank you, baby," she said and vanished.

Heidi wiped the sweat from her forehead, the room still quite humid. Nothing made much sense, but she was glad to still be alive. Somehow she knew everyone would be okay now. She felt drained, and for the first time knew she could fall right to sleep. Ignoring the daylight, she pulled the covers up over her head and closed her eyes, willing herself to enter sleep.

"Heidi," cried a voice. She bolted upright. On the floor was the head of her father, his eyes flashing fear and confusion.

"Why did you do this to me?" he cried.

Looking towards the doorway, the headless figure of her father stood swaying, a burnt and bloodied axe in hand. Was this a dream? Or was she in Hell?

NANCY JACKSON'S work can be read in *Corpse Magazine*, *Macabre*, *Cthulhu Sex*, *The Hacker's Source*, and various anthologies including *Embark to Madness*, *Maelstrom I*, *Small Bites* and *Trip the Light Horrific*. She is also a book reviewer, editor, moderator, interviewer and avid reader. Lurk at her website http://www.nancyajackson.com if you dare.

LONGING

Brian W. Keen

T he sound of a fist hitting wood awakened me in the middle of the night. I sat up in my bed and stared at the beaming red numbers on my cheap clock radio. 11:47 they screamed out. I wasn't accustomed to having guests, and certainly wasn't expecting any at this hour. I sat up in my bed, pondering if I was truly awake or merely dreaming. A second set of knocks broke the silence and discarded any hope that I was still asleep.

The knocks echoed through the apartment. A thud, a pause, then two more knocks. The unmistakable familiarity grasped my heart, and before I opened the door, I knew it was Karen. She looked so cold standing there with her arms crossed, and only a light jacket and a pair of sweat pants protecting her from the blustery New York winter night. I squinted under the glare of the lights from the hall shining off her pale skin. She had never been dark, but now her face wore a dull, deathly white. She stared at me silently through swollen eyes. As she stood there, my lost angel, my love, my mind journeyed in all directions. I remembered the day I met her. We were standing in line for movie tickets. Both alone. I was going to see *Pulp Fiction*. A racey film for my tastes, but highly recommended by a friend of mine. Karen smiled at me. We chatted and decided we could both use some company on such a dreary, rainy night. The movie entertained, for the most part, though we talked during the majority of it. She was free-spirited, rock-and-roll, black-and-white, and marijuana. I was cautious, Mozart, khaki, and a six-pack of Heineken. She showed me her world. I showed her mine.

I began to enjoy an occasional toke off of a joint on a Friday night. She went with me to the opera. And somehow it all meshed. The lovemaking was like none I had ever known. And I think it was special for her too. We vowed that no matter what, we would make love when it rained. Many a fight was interrupted by the soft pitter-patter of the rain against the window. I would take her in my arms, press her lips hard against mine, and our difference of opinion would dissipate, only to resurface later. This worked for a while. But as is always the case, the differences soon took center stage and the relationship was laid bare. She was always smoking, insisting we go out, partying, and searching for that next thrill. I, on the other hand, enjoyed quiet evenings, a good meal, a glass of wine, a fine book, and some good conversation for Christ's sake!

Then one moonless October night, I came home from work and she was gone. Clothes, make-up, perfume, all gone. I stood silent in my lonesome one-bedroom apartment, holding the necklace I had bought her for her birthday. I had "Love Conquers All" inscribed in a gold heart. This was the first day since I gave it to her that she didn't have it on. I cried for days, but somehow made it through. I hated the rain. Damn the rain! And now here she was, damaged and frail. It looked like she had lost at least twenty pounds. Twenty pounds she couldn't afford to lose. And so damn pale.

"Can I come in?" she whispered.

I felt embarrassed. My mind often wandered. How long had we been standing there?

Once inside the apartment, Karen reached in her purse, produced a pack of Marlboro's
and took one out with a shaky hand.

"Got a light?" she asked.

"In the third drawer, same as always," I answered.

"Oh, I forgot. I'm sorry."

I mixed myself a white Russian while she lit up. I had graduated to liquor during her absence. She exhaled through her nose, something I always despised but never told her.

"You sure you don't want a drink."

"No, a drink is the last thing I need," she answered.

"What's got you so shook?" I inquired.

"It's my boyfriend, or ex-boyfriend," she said, apparently not too sure.

"What's his name?"

"Jacob. He's just so…so…so different. I know you hate hearing this, but I just don't know if I could ever make you realize how different."

"Different good or different bad? How different?

She paused. "Neither good nor bad." She frowned. She seemed as confused as I was. "Just different. It is something you have to see for yourself to understand. Words could not do it justice."

"I thought we were talking about a guy, Jacob, remember? What do you mean, do *it* justice?"

"I don't want to talk about it. The important thing is I left. I had to leave. He was so possessive, like he owned me or something, and all I could think about was you. I missed you so much.

I can't deny that this made me feel great. It was what I wanted and what I thought about lying in my bed, alone in the dark.

Does she miss me?

Does she think about me?

The answer to both was yes, but there was more.

"I told Jacob that I loved you, and that I was going back to you. He refused to let me go. He said leaving him was not an option. I would always be his, he promised. He grabbed my arm and threw me down. So I ran. God, I hope he didn't follow me."

She stared at me, hoping for some sort of reassurance. But I was no fighter. And a conflict with someone I didn't know, well let's just say it wasn't my cup of tea. It kinda scared me. But I would never let anyone hurt her. Especially not the man who stole her from me. I felt a tinge of anger and jealousy. But I pushed it back. She was here with me now and that was all that mattered.

She stared at me, silent for a moment. She pushed back her tousled—casual but not sloppy—black locks from her face.

With eyes of hope and anticipation, and with tears resurfacing, Karen asked the question.

"Do you still love me?"

Could she not look at me and see it? Was it not written on my face the first day we met? I would always love her, not so much by choice, but by necessity. I would like to have stopped, many times and during many lonely nights, but my love for her was as much a part of me as my brown eyes and black hair, as much a part of me as my smile and the way I laughed. Forget the differences. Forget the fights. The one thing I had learned during our time apart was I didn't want to be without her. So I answered the question with the only answer there was and the only answer there would ever be.

Yes.

The word brought her even more tears and she ran to me. We held each other tight. This went on for several minutes as we relished each second of our reunion. I took her hand and led her to the room we once shared. She looked at the picture of us, still on my nightstand, as I ran my hands through her hair and kissed her lips. Our tongues danced inside her mouth. She moaned uncontrollably while I kissed her neck and ripped at her blouse. She forced herself on top of me, grinding her hips against my stiffness. We kissed again, harder this time; she bit down on my lip, drawing blood. The salty taste ran down my throat, but only for a second. Like an infant to its mother's nipple, Karen sucked my lip, savoring each precious drop. Jacob had certainly changed her. Never had our foreplay been so animalistic. But how could I complain?

"I want you," Karen begged. We ripped off each other's clothes.

Her hips lunged to meet my every thrust; our eyes intertwined in something so fiery that every inch of my skin burned with desire. I again kissed her neck, tasting her sweat as we picked up rhythm, her moans transforming into screams. She tossed me off of her with surprising strength and climbed on top of me with great force. I took hold of her breasts as she slammed down on me, harder each time. I tried to show restraint, but it had been a while. I could not stand it another second. Climatically I came inside her; my own screams of pleasure overtaking hers. She collapsed beside me and fell asleep in my arms. Once again she was mine.

Early that same morning, before the sun came up, there was a noise at the window in the bedroom. I rose up in the bed. I stared in disbelief as the window rose, apparently by some hidden force. The sounds of the street assaulted the room, followed closely by its stout odor. The wind howled. The temperature was much too frigid for fog, but from the open window it rolled in, thick and blinding. *Invite me in*, a voice inside my head demanded. Before I could even think about it, my lips slowly mouthed the words "Come in." For the second time in the course of the night, I questioned whether I was awake or not. It was all so dreamlike. I rubbed my eyes and opened them again. A naked man stood at the foot of the bed. His skin was a pale silhouette against the fluorescent glow of the moonlight flooding the room through the open window. The fog continued to roll, disguising his face while showcasing his tall, slim body, toned and firm. He stood erect in the silence of the dark.

"It is time," he said.

Karen sat up in the bed. "Jacob?"

"Yes. It is time."

Karen grabbed my arms and held me still with the power of ten men. My attempts to move were futile. She opened her mouth, displaying large sharpened fangs, and I stared into her eyes, once brown, now red. I opened my mouth to scream but it never quite made it out of my throat. Jacob waved a finger in the air and shook his head. His nails were long and sharpened like the blades of a knife. He hissed and I saw his teeth were longer, sharper than Karen's. He floated above the bed and eased down on top of me. I was unable to move, blink or even breathe. He ran his long nails across my neck seductively, never taking his eyes off mine. He pushed his lengthy, curly black hair away from his face. He smiled down at me. Though his fangs still showed, I felt no fear. His skin was soft and flawless. A tranquil stillness swept over me. After this moment of playfulness, he sank down on me, first licking and then burying his teeth into my neck, lacerating the flesh and bringing with it excruciating pain. Yet I lay still, unabashed.

The first gush of blood splashed Jacob's pale face. He lavishly sucked from the wound to avoid another such waste. Lustfully torn between pleasure and pain, I grabbed the back of his neck, pulling him close. This reaction startled him and he pulled back, staring at Karen, blood dripping from his ripe, rose lips. She looked down at me, aching to taste. *This can't be happening,* I told myself. Outside thunder rattled the sky and a cold November rain brewed. Karen wiped my forehead with her palm, ridding me of my perspiration.

"Jacob owns my soul, but you own my heart. This is the only way we could be together. Now close your eyes, love, it's gonna rain"

I wanted to speak, but couldn't. A single tear escaped the corner of my eye and rolled down my cheek. I felt blood drip from the incisions on my neck.

"You were right. Love conquers all," Karen whispered as she gently licked the tear from my cheek and sank down on me, enclosing the holes and beginning to feed. I shuddered from the chill of her icy lips, stared at the ceiling and prepared to be reborn.

BRIAN W. KEEN lives and writes in the mountains of West Virginia. His fiction has appeared in various outlets including *Dark Animus*, *Macabre*, *Scared Naked*, *Maelstrom Volume 1* (available from Lighthouse Media One), *Night Shopping*, *Shadowland*, *Blood Moon Rising*, and *Deep Magic*. His story "The Dance" is scheduled to appear in 2005 in *Chimera World 2*. You can contact him at keenbrian2002@yahoo.com.

BAD HAND MAN

Karen Koehler

For Ace and the boys at the saloon.

–Shuffle–

A murmur went up in the town of Gehenna the day the Bad Hand Man rode in. He came in out of the Skillet on a massive, barrel-chested Suffolk as black as a raven's breast, its nostrils exhaling smoke and sand like a machine on full power. Its riveted breastplate bore the signet of the Omega Powers, and again the horseshoe-like symbol sat between the creature's flat, triangular ears. The creature bared its teeth at passersby, and those who saw creature and rider at first glance swore one of the Four Horseman of the Apocalypse had stepped out of a netherworld portal to move schismatically between the mortal and the alive.

But then the deathland sun was refracted by the animal's joint rivets, and soon enough the scouring wind plucked at the edges of the rider's duster to reveal a dusky purple silk lining. Women took their laundry in early that day, and the First Church of the Divine Restitution welcomed fifteen new Believers into its folds. The bingo parlor was closed for the first time in almost ten years. What had been visited upon the township of Gehenna was not a Horseman, yet somehow its presence was no more reassuring.

Gehenna waited and watched.

–Shuffle–

"…and there was these here metal dactyls who carried folks around in their pouches, not like the 'borgs—bigger, kiddo, bigger," Indian John was saying between pitching forkfuls of freshly scythed brome into the winter loft of the Crayton's barn. "And a pair of golden arches that rose straight outta the ground, and as God is my witness, they—"

"Would lead you to a pot o' gold," fourteen-year-old Jake Stryker finished with a nod as he curried the Crayton's alpha broodmare in the hey-strewn aisle.

"Shows what you know," Indian John sniffed and stopped to lean on his fork, always a sure sign he expected his listener's full and undivided attention. Jake complied, leaning back against a tall divider and crossing his arms. He waited patiently, knowing the old Indian would finish the telling of his vision when he felt Jake had suffered enough.

"A happy meal," said Indian John after a full minute.

"A happy meal, John?"

"As God is my witness."

"How in world's end can a meal be happy?" Jake asked. Then after a few minutes he burst out laughing at the sight of the concentrated scowl on John's face. "Funny man," Jake said and went back to work.

Just in time, too, as Rilk Crayton's hulking shape filled the doorway of the barn astride his overfed devil of a mount. Lucifer's eyes rolled to show the silvers, and his master followed suite as his gaze pinballed between Jake and Indian John. "Whatta you two pigeon-dicked fag-faces getting off on?" Rilk grunted.

Jake lowered his eyes.

But Indian John wasn't so tolerant. "Go fuck the dog in the corner, Rilk," he muttered as he threw down his fork and began climbing the rope ladder to the loft's trap door.

Rilk dismounted, his expression resembling the soft stone idiocy of a macabre cherub. He hitched up his trousers with two thumbs and swaggered forward. "What did you say, Injun man?"

At the top of the ladder, John was struggling with the trap's rope, trying to loop it through the ring and tie the door shut. Stupid, John, Jake thought as he watched the highbrow Crayton firstborn stop to grip a rung of the ladder. "What did you say to me, old man?" Rilk repeated, his voice a notch higher.

John managed to knot the rope. "You heard me right 'n clear, boy. Or are you as deaf as I am blind?"

Jake's eye caught a glimmer of a steel boot knife. He tried to warn John, but it was already too late. The ladder was cut and John hung by one arm from the trap. Rilk stood watching and smiling just below the struggling man, the knife in one fist.

Indian John whimpered, his booted feet flailing in search of purchase as his one-handed grip began to slip. The fall was a good ten feet, just enough to pulverize old bones and turn old flesh into bruised purple sponge.

"Stop it, Rilk! World's sake, he's an old blind man!" Jake cried, emerging from behind the mare's flank.

Rilk's shadow drenched Jake like black paint. "Well lookee here," Rilk drawled. "The one-inch dick finally has a voice."

Rilk cut him.

Jake threw up an arm to protect his face and a narrow thread of red agony arrowed from between his second and third fingers to the knob of his wristbone. Jake moaned and cowered back.

Rilk smiled, his upper lip drawn back in a feral cupid's grin. "A gift from me to you, you little whore's son. Think of me whenever you look at it."

Blood poured down Jake's hand like water out of a leaky spigot. He looked away from it and saw Indian John lying very still on his side in the aisle. Ignoring the pain in his hand, he went immediately to John and knelt down, taking the old man's hoarfrosted head into his lap. "Leave us alone," he said. "Please…just leave us alone."

"Sure," Rilk sneered as he tramped past the two of them. "I know how you two get off on one another."

Jake put his cheek to the crown of John's head, and John's hair trapped the baptism of Jake's tears.

Rilk paused in the doorway and turned back. He laughed. "Hold up. You two were giving me so much entertainment I almost forgot—a Bad Hand Man's in town. Probably lookin' for a couple faggots like you two." He laughed once more, harshly, before he left.

–Reshuffle–

"You're playing the house, son," said Jake Stryker the Elder, once, in another life. He posed before the hotel's full-length vanity mirror with its frosted etchings of cities in the sky and brushed the lint off the sleeves of his black frock coat, set his gambler's hat fashionably askew on his head.

Jake the Younger saw his father's half-sweet, half-villainous smile peek out from under his handlebar mustache in the wonderful, milky-etched mirror. It was to be a good night in the casino for his father, Jake knew. He'd played eleven sets of poker against himself and won nine. A very good night. By dawn they ought to have enough greatcoins to get them out of the Skillet.

"You play the house all the time, and the banker's keepin' score," Jake the Elder continued as he smoothed the lines of his waxen mustache. "Nothin' wrong with a little evil, so long as it's being scaled out with your inside good. Remember that, son, else your heart's gonna sink that ol' feather of Maat."

–Shuffle–

Jake walked Indian John inside their cropper's hut and eased him down onto his pallet, removed his boots. John swallowed and blinked up at the ideogram of rafters over their heads.

"John."

"I'm okay, kiddo. Nothin' broken."

Jake brought the old man a canteen of water and settled at his side to help him drink. "You sure don't look okay, John."

"Nothing to it. Fall and the arms of Gaia will catch you."

Jake smiled at the old man's crazy philosophy, then grimaced as pain wrapped its fiery tentacles around his hand.

"Here, let's have a look, son," John said.

Jake let him "look".

"Bone wound," Indian John declared as his callused fingers played over the puckered edges of the wound on the back of Jake's hand. "Gonna need needlework on this one, kiddo."

"Great."

"Better'n through the heart," John said before sending him off to fetch the hook needle and wire sutures. When Jake returned with the supplies, he found the old Indian holding a clear bottle with a dark yellow label on it. Ether.

"No," Jake said.

John scowled. "You wanna be awake for this massacre?"

"I'm not a child."

"As you will."

Jake found an old bridle strap to bite down on, then let John go to work. Sweat ran down his face like tears. How he hated his indentured servitude to the Crayton ranch, the feel of stale and unwashable sweat on his skin and straw in his eyes, the pulled tendons and the cranky mares. He was his father's son. Five years of labor hadn't squelched his partiality for soft goosedown beds and ballroom floors, for etched mirrors and the minty-smelling fabrics and furnishings in the hotels he and Dad once lived in, or the smoky, fluorescent casino halls with their clicking dice and magnetic cards. This had been Jake Stryker's milieu for the first nine years of his life, the very weft of this universe. Even now, half a decade later, it didn't seem fair to him that that weft be broken. He hated the ranch, this life, this pain in his hand, and cursed whatever god had ordained such a cruel joke by played on him, the oil-soured leather in his mouth gagging off the words and sending them back down his throat like vomit. He nearly choked on the feast.

The gods were not fair and the Law was no better. It wasn't fair that a man kill another man and be awarded his son, the way Old Man Crayton killed the gambler Jake Stryker and was apportioned a new stablehand. They called it responsibility for the orphaned. Jake called it one hell of an indenturing system. He was still too young to hit the circuit with a deck of magnetic cards, but the day he turned twenty-one and was released by the system there would be a wind in the door named Jake Stryker whom none would hold back. It was a vow.

He wept ashamedly, wondering if it was possible to go mad from pain.

"Easy, kiddo, easy. Almost there."

"I'm sorry."

"Don't be."

Jake looked into Indian John's dead gaze, his leatherworn face, and wondered what it must be like for him. It was for some unspoken-of sin that John had spent almost four decades of his life in servitude to the Crayton clan. And though he owed John more in the way of care and protection than any other person alive, Jake found he could hate John too, his soft complacency, the stagnation of his life which he seemed to embrace with all the passion of a lover. What could do such a thing to a man?

"Done," John said as he finished swaddling Jake's hand. The elephant wrinkles in his face had smoothed themselves out at last. He looked almost at peace.

Jake spat out the leather. The pain was still bad, but the bandages made it endurable. Cradling his hand close, Jake rose silently from John's pallet and put corn porridge on the brazier to boil. He worked slow, reaching for the question which threatened him like a roiled rattler just a little too far to be taken by the tail. He didn't manage to wrangle it until he found himself sitting at John's side once more with their supper.

"What Rilk said...do you suppose he was lying?" he asked as he studied the clumps of meal on his spoon.

Indian John had not yet touched his supper. "I think even a bastard like Rilk wouldn't joke 'bout a Bad Hand Man." For a moment the mood in the cropper's hut darkened almost to the shade of a funeral, then he slapped Jake's thigh companionably. "Your gamblin' daddy ever teach you Bad Hand poker, kiddo?"

He was changing the subject, but suddenly Jake didn't mind in the least. "Two men and a deck of surgery cards. A barbarian's game. Even Dad never played it." He remembered, o yes. The kinds were distorted in Bad Hand poker—skulls for spades, bones for clubs and tongues for diamonds. Hearts were hearts. The two unfortunates trapped in a game threw out continuously until one or the other called a show, which meant hands were high, always. Highest hand took the prize, and that prize was denoted by the greatest card in the loser's hand. Jake still shivered a little whenever he thought of the mute, one-armed Bad Hand victims his father had played occasional games of straight-up poker with. Once, he even played a complete amputee.

Barbarian game. Yeah.

Jake tried a spoonful of porridge, but it was too bitter to swallow. He set his supper aside.

John was studying the clapboards of their hut that too much time and too little repair had worn down to no-color reed wood. The old legends and inscriptions cuniformed into the wood by younger Indian John hands had long since eroded away. All that Jake could clearly see now were the horseless coaches and stacked glass adobes that Indian John believed in. Squinting, he could almost make out an upside down U, or what might possibly be a horseshoe.

"D'you think it's true...about the Bad Hand Man?" Jake persisted, whispered.

John sighed, his face crinkling in on itself. "'Suppose Rilk wouldn't have made mention of him were he any runner-the-mill gambler, would he?"

"'Suppose not." Yes, it certainly might be a horseshoe. "Who d'you think he's after, John?"

Who, John?

John smiled, a pinched, horrible expression. "We'll know tomorrow when the poor bastard gets the signet. Now, go on, kiddo, and get me one of them readers," he said, shooing Jake toward his sagging shelf of books, "and find me a good tall tale to chuckle over. Go on."

–Reshuffle–

"The smaller the stuff, the bigger the bluff," declared Jake Stryker the Elder as he laid down his third straight flush of the evening.

The one-eyed mountain of a miner who had seemed so cocksure of himself only a moment ago let out a string of muttered curse and shambled up from a felt table laden with a dragon's trove of valuables.

Jake Stryker winked at his son.

–Shuffle–

The next morning found Jake sitting quietly at the table and watching Indian John wake slowly. Slowly, he rose from his pallet, hobbled outside, then returned. He joined Jake at the table.

"John…"

"Taking a piss," Indian John said.

"Liar." Jake took the black iron Omega from his coat pocket and dropped it clankingly to the tabletop. John sat perfectly still, his face a stone obelisk to serenity. But Jake knew it was a bluff, for John's scaly old fingers quaked lightly as if his hands carried a static electrical charge. "Don't lie to me, John," Jake said.

"You don't want to know."

"Yeah," he said. "I do."

"It's not your trouble!"

"I say it is! Why in world's end was there an Omega nailed to our door, John? What does a Bad Hand Man want with us?"

"Not you. Me."

"Why, John?"

"It's not y—"

Jake stood and smote the wall behind Indian John with the iron Omega. The curve of the signet stuck in the wall like a shuriken star from one of the old historical reels that sometimes played in town. The impact sent a visual tremor up the clapboards. A single custard cup toppled off a high shelf and shattered like a bomb.

"Tell me," Jake whispered resonantly, the voice of a whole other person. "Tell me. I want to know."

John shivered, swallowed. He would tell; Jake knew him too well and needed only to wait. He prepared a pot of coffee and set it on the brazier as Indian John began to speak with hesitant strength.

"The Great law given us by the Omega Powers states that whosoever touches one of its Lawgivers or draws his blood shall play a Bad Hand Man to the punishment of one of the parties."

Jake nodded as he stirred some cornmeal into a pot. He knew the Laws by rote. Everyone did.

"I was a boy like you once, Young Jake Stryker," John continued on at a sigh. "Strong and posolutely burstin' with ambitious energy. I bussed table at a saloon in a town called Harmony, deep in the burnt old heart of the Skillet. A real egad for non-excitement, I 'member. 'Cept this one dislucky day when an Omega Man swaggered in and ordered up ale. I bussed it over to -him in what turned out to be a damned-cracked schooner. Stupid bastard cut his mouth on it. And later that same night a young Indian took the reins and rode east. I weren't no fool. I weren't gonna play a Man or nothin'. You lose, you lose...you win, you lose too, coz you become one of them Omega-programmed monsters."

Hesitation. "For couple years I moved myself around a lot. 'Ventually I comes upon Gehenna and the Crayton clan in search of slave labor. But an Injun's luck is rottener n' dead dog left out in the sun, and turns out Old Man Jimberly Crayton's the Omega Man's cousin, twice removed..."

Here Indian John's voice faded, as if reluctant to epilogue his story.

The meal was burning. Jake moved it off the burner with little enthusiasm. "That's the reason you stay on? The Craytons shield you from the Law?"

"'Round these parts the Craytons *is* the Law, kiddo."

Jake absently played with the bandages on his hand. "But they're not shielding you anymore."

"Who needs a crazy, blind old Indian when you got young blood?"

Jake looked away.

"Not your fault," John stated. "Jimberly Crayton's fault, kiddo."

"But this—"

Indian John hissed for silence. He said low and even, "I will play the Man tonight down at the Dead Horse Saloon, Young Jake

Stryker, as I was always meant to do, and I will win or I will lose. 'Tis easy's that."

"You'll lose, John."

"I can play."

"Not blind. Bad Hand Men don't use brailled cards."

"I'll cope." John's chair screeked back. He stood, a sure indication that their discussion of his future was over. "Mare's need shoein', boy. You gonna stand there all day and look lost?" He left the cropper's hut for the barn.

Jake Stryker wiped at his burning eyes and followed soon after.

—Reshuffle—

Jake Stryker the Elder stopped at the end of the mud-slathered swine rut which passed for a coach road in this shithole of a town and dropped his sack of deeds and trinkets before the feet of a naked, long-haired child playing with the bones of some small animal. The child dug into the sack and immediately found the tiny silver horse pennant that Jake Stryker had adeptly liberated from the bodice of the local Countess and added it to her play trove. The macabre and the exquisite mixed romantically.

Jake the Elder offered up his empty hands to his son. He raised his arms and sighed with a great expressive breath as if to beseech the sky or some unseen deity. Closing his glittering blue eyes, he asked, "Do you feel it, son? Lighter than Maat's feather."

—Shuffle—

The question was: Could he do it? He wasn't tall like his father. And he didn't have four decades of workman's sinews the way Indian John did.

No. The answer was no.

He could not.

He would have to be clever.

He left the milo field they were chaffing early, before sunset, and returned to the cropper's hut. He hid inside the closet, standing on Indian John's old boots, the bottle of ether in one hand and a bandanna in the other. He waited for almost an hour. Finally, just as he was about to nod off, he heard John shuffle in. He listened to the old man rattle around the hut as he prepared to go into town tonight.

Now! It had to be now!

He stepped out and reached for John. He clamped the soaked cloth around John's nose and mouth. John grunted, flailed. He was uncommonly strong for an old man. An arm struck Jake across the face. A foot mule-kicked him.

Jake held on.

John forced him back until Jake's back struck the closet, the impact almost driving the living breath out of him. Something porcelain hit the floor and shattered.

Jake held on.

John was strong, but Jake was young, had more endurance.

Jake held on and John weakened.

It was over. John went as limp as a scaring straw man in Jake's arms. Jake dragged the old man to his pallet and laid him out as if for a wake, but the symbolism was all wrong, reversed, the irony vulgar. Jake removed his boots and kissed Indian John's crinkled brow, knowing the old man would dream of silver dactyls carrying passengers and glass adobes standing against the sky. "Forgive me," he said.

He took John's iron Omega and left him.

–Shuffle–

The Dead Horse Saloon teemed. The usual shell men and working girls were there, of course, as well as various castes of villains, from barons and troubleshooters to banditos and hired guns. They milled across the sawdust-strewn floor or wobbled uncertainly at the plankwood bar and tried to avoid crashing into spittoons or the minefields of broken glass left behind by brawlers. There was darts and roulette and billiards in various levels of play and cheating.

No one looked his way. The patrons of the Dread Horse were expecting Indian John, not the dead gambler Jake Stryker's brat.

So Jake passed unmolested through the gambling hall, letting a cold calm fill him, letting the voices first drone together, then disappear completely. He could hear nothing now but the greasy slide of cards, the chittering of weighed dice, the whirling of the wheel of fortune. He smelled nothing but the clear white burn of fermented grain whiskey and husky breaths full of sarsaparilla tobacco.

He saw nothing but a witch's figure in black at the end of the hall. The figure looked up at his approach, and for a moment Jake was almost struck blind with fear. This was death, the final, terrible residual of his every waking nightmare. The creature was a white skeleton wrapped in a black shroud of a duster lined in faded royal purple beneath. Its long white hair seemed to move like sentient albino serpents with its every little gesture. Its eyes looked yellow.

Great gods, *yellow*.

Jake dropped his eyes and found himself staring at the titanium hilt of the laser scalpel on the creature's belt…and that was almost too much to bear, then, almost enough to send him fleeing into the night, a child forever.

But he had nothing to lose. He had lost everything a long time ago. His life or limb or tongue would only be a compliment to those things. He lifted his gaze.

There were groupies there, of course. That wasn't unusual. They were the usual cretin lackeys addicted to violence like sucklers of the cheapest rum, human refuse who followed Bad Hand Men around like a retinue of hungry vultures. Rumor had it that on occasion a Bad Hand Man could be impressed with a particularly savage act of vigilante justice and take an apprentice under his wing. Such were their terrible hopes, these mulling barbarians. Yet with only a flick of the creature's hand they cleared out like flies, leaving the creature and Jake staring at each other with rapt reptile attention across the table.

Jake looked the Bad Hand Man in his subhuman yellow eyes, challenging him to speak, but the Man remained silent. His tongue had been extracted a long time ago.

Riding on a wave of fear, Jake plucked the iron Omega out of his pocket and flung it to the tabletop. The ringing of iron seemed to smother all over sounds in the gambling hall. For a full minute all that remained of the former hubbub was the silver roulette ball rolling once around the wheel and finding its nook. The games were at an end.

A new one was about to begin.

It didn't matter that he wasn't Indian John. He who carries the Omega must play the Bad Hand Man. The Man nodded; he, too, knew the Laws by rote.

All for a cracked schooner forty years ago, thought Jake with poetic irony as he took his seat. The gods were not fair. Then all thoughts were erased as he watched the creature, this Charon of Gamblers, produce a deck of surgery cards. He cut the deck, then shuffled it, once, twice. That was all. There was no mysticism here, no gambling gymnastics, no magic that Jake could see.

The Bad Hand Man dealt them both five cards.

A lull had settled like the whispering, self-conscious murmur inside a funeral parlor. The townsfolk of Gehenna were watching him closely, but Jake could not see them, their faces mysteriously unfocused and distant. There was only the hand he held.

The ace of Skulls. Jack of Tongues. A Skull and Bone trey. A five of Skulls.

He studied his hand impassively. He must be impassive. Any other emotion would show. He had the makings of a flush...but the ace of Skulls disturbed him. A sensible man would cast it away immediately, lest it denote his fate. He wanted to worry his bottom lip undecidedly but decided he could not afford to allow the gesture.

The Bad Hand Man's yellow overgrown fingernails tapped the tabletop impatiently, and the tremor was conducted by the warped wood plants into Jake's arms, making his hands tremble. The creature had thrown out a low Tongue and Bone card.

The Man was going for a high-risk or bluff hand: it was Jake's first gut-instinct.

Jake felt the sudden need to be sick, but swallowed that impulse as well.

The Bad Hand Man smiled emotionlessly.

Jake instinctively broke his pair and threw out the Bone trey and the jack in the hopes he could finish his flush.

The Man dealt him back a queen of Skulls and a Heart trey.

Jake felt his own heart die in his chest. He could have had three of a kind! He felt the need to vomit right over his surgery cards and scarcely managed to restrain himself. He knew Dad would call him pigeon.

Hell, he *was* pigeon.

But he was playing the house.

Can't let it show.

He watched the Bad Hand Man's baleful skeleton's face, wondering if the thing would call a show.

The Man didn't call a show.

Jake muttered an internal prayer. He threw out the useless trey. The creature threw out an ace of Tongues.

This was curious What in world's end did he have? Not a...royal flush?

The Man's soulless smile grew infinitesimally, as if he had just read Jake's mind somehow. Jake looked away. He knew the Bad Hand Man had won. He had a better hand and he wanted Jake to fold and finish this foolishness at once. It would be for the best to finish this and end the purgatory, this prologue to the agony which was somehow worse than the agony still to come.

He had been playing a Bad Hand Man for jeezusssakes...was he crazy?

But still...

The smaller the stuff, son, the bigger the bluff.

"No," Jake said, low. And then again, louder: "No." Again: *"No!"* He looked the creature in its ancient reptilian eyes and spat the proclamation out like venom. "Get the fuck outta my head and deal!"

The Man dealt.

A nine of Tongues.

That fifth Skull card wasn't coming.

"Call," Jake said, his voice hoarse.

He was amazed. The surface of the creature's face remained unaltered, yet the expression beneath his poker mask was hollow, almost surprised. This was perhaps the first time the creature had ever been called to show by his opponent.

He was a bluffer, and Jake realized his first instincts about the Man—such as he could be called a Man—were right.

The Man laid down his hand. A bad hand, indeed. All low mixed card with a single royal card, a jack of Skulls.

Unlucky bastard.

A tremor passed through Jake's limbs that seemed to carry with it every over-contained terror. He wondered briefly if he would weep or simply fall to pieces from relief. He did neither and simply set his own hand down.

A tide of surprised cries ripped the expectant audience wide open.

Too numb to speak or move, Jake watched as the defeated creature rose into a tower of gangling bones and black sand-washed fabric. He removed his laser scalpel and set it on the table before Jake. Jake expected fear, reluctance—the expression of a sane man. But Bad Hand Men were not sane. They were not *men.* What Jake saw impaled him on a peculiar kind of terror: it was the ambiguous, immaterial weariness of, not a creature of Golgotha, but only an old, old man not so terribly different than Indian John. He nodded once at Jake, as if to bless his efforts, removed his battered black gambling hat, then kneeled and placed his ear to the table as if it were a chopping block.

The patrons of the Dead Horse began chanting, cheering Jake on to take up the scalpel and perform the deed that he had so ardently earned, had inherited. To defeat a Bad Hand Man. To become a Bad Hand Man himself...

The power of the audience seemed to animate him, and Jake found himself taking up the scalpel and standing. It was so well balanced an instrument that he could imagine wielding it in his sleep. With the barest touch of the lighted controls the instrument sang alive, a shining rod of justice that turned the air electric.

Expectant faces followed his every move. He saw the shining eyes of sadistic cats everywhere he looked.

But he was his father's son. Not one of Omega's programmed monsters. Maat's feather would not sink his heart, he vowed. He bent low and kissed the crown of the Bad Hand Man's head. Then he rose and turned away from the proceedings.

And stopped.

Not ten paces from him stood Rilk Crayton in his overfed bulk and his arrogance. And the sight of him was bad. But what he had brought with him was worse. For he carried over one shoulder what looked at first to be a fool's scepter. But then Rilk swaggered forward through a cleft in the crowd and Jake saw, finally *saw*.

It wasn't a scepter. It was a pig-sticker. And from atop it, crowning it like an icon, Indian John's head seemed to survey the hall with sagging, sleepy-lidded eyes. For a moment, as Rilk moved, the eyes seemed to find Jake, to see Jake.

Someone was screaming.

Jake discovered it was he, a wordless barrage of noise in blind defiance of the evil supplication wrought by this barbarian. He could feel nothing superficially, but that didn't surprise him in the least. His emotions had at last been boiled down to the bone and nullified. He would never feel anything ever again.

He spun, wielding the perfectly weighed instrument he had won with arcane precision. It cleaved the Bad Hand Man's ancient head from his shoulders so cleanly the creature continued to scrabble at the tabletop with dirty, untrimmed fingernails for a full half-minute before toppling to the floor.

The audience shuffled back as if poisoned by Jake's presence. Only Rilk remained, staring at Jake with wide-eyed, cherubic surprise. Then he jerked, dropping his supplication to the Bad Hand Man to the sawdusty floor. He'd seen something he couldn't negate, something he couldn't look away from even a moment.

Like a rabbit mesmerized by the emotionless gaze of a snake, he was fully incapable of escape.

The old man lay crucified in the dust. Come morning he would be stripped down to the bone for souvenirs, and even his bones ground for gris-gris by the town magician. Only his purple-lined coat would remain untouched, for like the iron Omega, this was the signet of the Bad Hand Man. None would dare touch that.

The Laws forbade the touching of an Omega Man's coat, the drawing of his blood.

Rilk Crayton knew the Laws by rote. Everyone did. It was the reason he now stared in petrified horror at Jake Stryker's hand where the bandages were pink sopping straps coming undone. They revealed the knife wound which had become unstitched in the execution.

Rilk raised his hands. "Please," he said.

But Rilk Crayton's fears were grossly unfounded. Jake Stryker would never dream of rushing a man with this slender and exquisite instrument. He was no barbarian. He was a gambler. And besides, he no longer bore any ill will toward the vast Crayton clan. He bore no feeling of any kind toward anyone.

Jake shut down the scalpel and returned to the table. He doffed the Bad Hand Man's sun-faded gambling hat and shuffled and reshuffled his new set of surgery cards with absent grace as an evil, emotionless smile corrupted his lips.

"Let's have a hand, Rilk," he said.

KAREN KOEHLER is one of the youngest and most influential authors of her generation. Her versatility in many different genres has helped her to write a number of compelling science fiction, fantasy, and horror novels. Her past works include the critically acclaimed industrial gothic novel *Slayer*, *Slayer: Black Miracles*, *Slayer: Stigmata*, *Scarabus*, and *The Maiden #1: Out of the Ashes*, all from Black Death Books. *Slayer* is the cornerstone of the new Industrial Gothic movement. Her forthcoming novels include *Shredder: Iron Angel*, *The Blackburn & Scarletti Mysteries Volume I*, and *Slayer: Armageddon*. Her short work has appeared in the anthology *The Blackest Death Volume I*. When she is not writing, she works as an editor, publishing consultant and all-around coffee girl. Visit her home page at http://www.khpindustries.com/covenhouse.html.

KEEPER

Aurelio Rico Lopez III

A vector of evil—
Sleek and black,
She spreads her wings
Like a shadow come alive.
An empty soul
With blood-filled desires,
She tastes the air
With her forked tongue.
Driven by an insatiable hunger,
She takes flight,
And the children hide.
—Hell's Angel

For Nacianceno "Kiddy" Rico.

"That's bullshit," Pete said.
"Well, that's what I heard," Vincent countered.
"Bullshit," Pete dismissed.
Salvador smiled as he listened to them. He picked up a piece of bamboo from the ground and tossed it in the fire. Sparks leapt out of the flame like a swarm of fireflies.
Salvador glanced at his wristwatch. He had led this group up Mt. Matutum. Vincent, Misao, Pete, and Dianne—two young couples from the States. After hiking for most of the day, they had arrived at the base of Kasadyahan Falls where they set up camp. Pitching their tents beneath a large mahogany tree, both couples had changed into their swimsuits and dashed towards the basin of

the waterfall. Salvador had sat on a nearby boulder and stood watch.

Night had engulfed the mountain, so they built a campfire and cooked dinner. After feasting on hotdogs, grilled chicken, bananas, and a pot of rice, they began telling ghost stories.

Foreigners.

Vincent had just finished telling the tale of the vengeful man who murdered unsuspecting couples with a meat hook. Obviously, no one believed a word of it.

"Oh, come on," Misao said. "Back in Japan, we have stories like that too."

"Exactly!" said Pete, peeling another banana. "There can't be *that* many psychos with hooks."

"Well, there's Captain Hook," Dianne said, smiling.

"And that guy from *I Know What You Did Last Summer*," added Misao.

Vincent groaned. "That movie sucked."

"For once, I agree with you," Pete said. He took a bite out of the banana and smiled. "That Love-Hewitt chick's got great tits, though."

Dianne punched him on the shoulder.

"Ow! What gives, Di?"

She wrinkled her nose at him. "You figure it out, Einstein."

Pete put his arm around Dianne. "Awww…Jennifer's got nothing on you, babe. I swear." He looked over at Vincent and grinned, his right cheek puffy with banana. "Vince, doesn't Di have the greatest boobs you've ever seen? A helluva lot better than Jennifer Love-Hewitt's, don't you think?"

Vincent could feel himself blush. Misao tried not to laugh.

Dianne pushed Pete away. "Asshole," she said, but everyone could see she was smiling. The truth was, Di wasn't bad looking at all, and there must have been a lot of guys who would have thought she *did* have better breasts than Jennifer Love-Hewitt's. Vincent certainly thought so, though he'd never admit it. Not in front of Misao. Definitely not in front of Pete.

The fire crackled.

"What's the scariest monster you can think of?" Misao asked no one in particular.

"Vampires," Dianne answered, relieved at the change of topic.

"They scare you?" Misao asked.

"Are you kidding? Vampires have scared me ever since I saw *Salem's Lot* when I was in the third grade."

"I've got a question," Pete said, raising his hand like some schoolboy. "The Count character in Sesame Street is a vampire too, right? How come no one's afraid of him?"

"Okay, wiseguy," Dianne said. "What are *you* afraid of?"

Pete stuffed what was left of the banana in a garbage bag and grinned. "Werewolves."

"Werewolves?"

"With a vampire, all you get are little bite marks on your neck. A werewolf will rip your body into shreds."

Dianne smiled at Misao and Vincent. "Werewolves, he says."

"Hey, I'm not the one who's afraid of a Muppet," Pete said and poked her playfully on the side. Dianne jerked in surprise and said something the others couldn't hear.

"What about you, Vince?" Pete asked.

"Linda Blair."

"You mean the character she played in *The Exorcist?*"

"No, I mean Linda Blair."

Misao giggled.

"Your turn, Misao," Dianne said.

"Wait, wait! I know this one!" Pete said excitedly. He pressed his index finger against his temple for effect. "Godzilla!"

"Very funny, Pete," she said.

Salvador checked his watch again. It was a few minutes past eleven. He tossed another stick into the fire. Gray smoke rose steadily and disappeared among the branches of the tree's large crown overhead. In the distance, a bamboo tree creaked. Crickets chirped from their underground burrows.

"What about you, Sal?" Pete called. "Any monsters lurking on the mountain?"

Salvador grinned. "Maybe."

"Oh? What kind?"

"Lots of them. *Tikbalangs, tiyanaks, manananggals...*"

"Sounds like a menu."

Misao sat up straight. "What exactly is a mana... manana..."

"A *manananggal,*" Sal finished for her. He risked looking at his watch again. Eleven fifteen. It was getting late.

"According to Philippine folklore, a *manananggal* is a Filipina possessed by a demon. During the day, she appears normal. But when night comes, she transforms into a monster, growing enormous, bat-like wings. What's most unique about a *manananggal* is its body. You see, during the transformation, a *manananggal* detaches itself from the waist down. It leaves the lower portion of its body, feeds, and returns to it before dawn."

The burning firewood crackled.

"The *manananggal* usually feeds on animals like pigs and chickens, but it is said that over the years, it acquires a taste for human flesh. However, decades of progress and development have forced *manananggals* and others of its kind to inhabit forests and mountains."

A twig snapped behind them. They all turned to the direction of the sound. Dianne yelped in surprise, and Pete got up with a start.

Standing a few feet away was a young woman.

Salvador stood up. "Everyone, relax." He walked over to the woman, put a hand on her shoulder, and presented her to the group. "I'd like you to meet my sister Maria."

"Your sister?" Misao asked. "I didn't know you had a sister."

Maria smiled.

"Shee-it, Maria," Pete said. "You almost gave me a heart attack."

Maria turned to her brother. "Only four?"

"It's been a slow season," Salvador explained. "Tourists are worried about the Abu Sayyaf rebels, and reports of terrorist bombings in the city have only made things worse."

While Salvador and Maria talked, Vincent stared at Maria. She couldn't have been more than 25 years old. Vincent couldn't put his finger on it, but something about Maria's presence was wrong, out of place. What was Maria doing here?

The night was strangely silent. The night birds, the frogs, the crickets—all the animals had become still. The whole mountain suddenly seemed threatening. Like the silence before an explosion.

"You're late," Salvador told Maria. "Are you alone?"

"The others will be here soon."

"Others?" Pete asked. "What others?"

Ignoring Pete, Salvador kissed Maria's forehead, reached inside his jacket pocket, and pulled out a flashlight. He switched it on and started walking away from the camp.

"Hey, Sal! Where're you going?" Pete called. When Pete tried to run after him, Maria stood in his way and pushed him back. Pete stumbled backwards and fell on the ground.

"Shit!" he cried out. "What the hell did you do that for?"

Maria only smiled.

They called for him, but he wasn't going back. After a while, they stopped yelling. When Salvador eventually reached the foot of the mountain, he would tell the local police that they had encountered Abu Sayyaf rebels. He'd say that they had abducted his group but that he had managed to escape in the cover of night. The local government would conduct a search to try and locate the tourists, but they would find nothing.

He swung his flashlight left and right, but the beam did little to hold back the darkness. He came across a group of five dismembered bodies partially hidden behind a grove of bamboo. The upper portions of the bodies were missing.

He blocked out the screams and kept walking.

AURELIO RICO LOPEZ III is a self-diagnosed scribble junkie. His fiction has appeared in venues such as *Night to Dawn*, *Horrorfind*, *Dark Corners*, *Werewolf*, *Lunatic Chameleon*, and *The Blackest Death Vol. I*, to name a few. He is also the author of *JOLTS*, a collection of horror-ku (Sam's Dot Publishing). Aurelio hails from Iloilo City, Philippines, where he drinks way too much coffee during his spare time.

MINION

Andrew L. MacKinnon

Dedicated to my wife, Karen.
My reason to exist and evolve.

Preface

Sometimes—after you've been told a ghastly story and prostrate in the greying light of darkness—what you've been told starts to become reality.

Did something actually move in the corner of the room? What was it that slithered under the carpet in the shadow? Was it the mental ability to create visions that are undeniably true, or was it a real creature of the black evil void?

The realisation of the power that is, for the normal, dormant in the brain, comes to those who, unfortunately, have these visions persist their devilment in the sheen of light. If the aforementioned is true, it would be a nightmare with eyes wide open.

Fifth of July, in the year of our Lord, 1834

I'm excited. When Lord Lingbo invited me to research his complete family history, I was enthralled, to say the least. My hobby realised into practice. Except for my posterior being bruised and numb when I arrived, I feel in tip-top health. I do hate travelling in those wretched stagecoach contraptions; my travel sickness you know. I even had to administer sips of elixir to myself all the way here.

What were my main objectives? I would certainly like to grasp any information that was unbeknown to the Lord. Without a doubt, I will receive gossip from these scraggy peasants that are strewn around the village, and all for a coin or two. Certainly, I will have to orally excavate a few minds to obtain the desired legends.

I must extend my gratitude to my dear friend Robert for asking that Hob's chap to speak with Lord Lingbo concerning my aspiration. Without his intervention in the matter, I would still be in search of an opportunity.

I do wish Robert wasn't so modest. He is a dear friend, taking care of Elizabeth for me whilst on my quest. She seemed very disappointed at the prospect of me leaving. When I told her that Robert would be on hand to entertain her, she perked up a little. I feel Robert will take good care of her for me.

Let me tell you of the sight I beheld in the grounds of this estate; they are awe-inspiring, with the blood-red roses, bright creamy yellow tulips and daffodils. The variety of shrubbery is quite staggering. Wondrous.

Upon entering the main hall of the manor; manor, that's quite an underestimation of its magnitude. Never have I seen such ornate craftsmanship except for the intricacies in cathedrals.

So far as my eyes would permit, sculptures the heights of small children were perched in a crouching position. These were crammed into a niche high on the pillars to each side of the entrance, and seemed so crude and out of place.

The grotesque stone infants seemed to be trying to evade the savage winds that—so I've been told—swell up from nowhere and take everyone unawares. They do look so very real, I swear they moved. Probably just my imagination.

Please, don't think of me as pretentious if I have one criticism of the Lord, but the manor is very grimy and the smell of rotting fruit and spent Lucifer's hangs in the air. Does he not have a maidservant? They are inexpensive and keep you warm at night. They dare not refuse or they are sent back to the village, disgraced as a thief of some sort.

These questions among others I intend to have clarified at a later stage. I must say, though; Lord Lingbo certainly supplies ample sustenance and spirits for his guests.

The great hall was disgusting; an intricate mass of cobwebs encompassing the ceiling with the odd strands that would ensnare against my face, giving me an expressed sense of dread. Like chunks of ice sliding down one's spine. A sensation I would not like to encounter again at any cost.

Once the food was consumed and darkness crept down the windows, it was time to retire. The Lord took his leave to the back of the north wall. I felt my left shoulder absorbing a moist heat, making me feel physically sick. I turned to rise, but was confounded with a being so deformed it was almost unrecognisable as that of a human species. The thing was approximately four feet of tortured flesh and bone.

Please let me elaborate, so you may envisage the horrendous sight that hunched before me: its hair was a tangled mat, and by close inspection, if one dared, would undoubtedly contain an infestation of flea's and other mites leaping around in better health than their host. The creature's face, to me, seemed the most terrifying of all. It was amass with skin-straining boils of a seeming potent nature if they exploded near a person.

God, what a thought, all that congealed blood, jaundiced yellow and mouldy green pus, embedding on your skin and pulsating with revulsion. My heart felt as if it were pounding on my ribs to be released and free of this frantic situation. It was only when, at last, the creature made a gesture toward the swirling staircase that I knew what it was trying to relate in its slobbering, gibberish language.

Please forgive me; it's an awful-looking beast. One does not want to be seen with a peasant begging for a crumb of food, but to be gibbered at by an imbecile is too embarrassing to contemplate. Do you not agree?

While climbing the stairs, the being insisted on urging me forward to the top by constantly tapping on my arm. I found that quite irritating.

Once at the corridor to the rooms, he pointed to the second door to my left. I'm positive I heard it say, in a slurred way, "Bed."

I could have been mistaken as there was so much saliva dripping down its chin, and the source of which was squeezing and bubbling betwixt teeth that were twisted, rotten and putrescent.

The claw-like hand of the thing caught my forearm as it turned its head to one side and spat on the floor, then turned and gravelled to me, "You s'eep 'ight."

I haven't any idea what it was trying to relate as its little beady eyes stared into mine. It didn't seem as if there was any malice in those lethargic orbs.

Once the thing lit a candle in the room and departed my presence, I was alone with the macabre dancing of the candle's shadow on the wall panels, and the foul stench of tallow. At the left by the door is a writing desk where I sit at the moment, next to which is a plush four-poster bed with one of those large oak chests at the foot of it.

Well, I feel quite tired now after the long journey and large meal today. I hope tomorrow will bring some satisfaction to many questions.

May God be with me in all I do, and I send dear sweet Elizabeth my deepest love and yearn her constantly.

Sixth of July, in the year of our Lord, 1834

Well, its late evening and I've a lot to tell.

This morning I was awakened by rapid knocks at the bedroom door. Without a doubt by the being I presume is the Lords servant, as there doesn't seem to be anyone else in the manor assisting in the daily chores to be carried out.

Last night was quite astonishing. I dreamt of the dank room in which I slept. Obviously, trying to remember a dream is a great feat for the normal, but mine was so vivid. I will try to explain.

I remember awakening to a very loud ticking, accompanied by some grumbling voice, then a sudden slapping sound to break the monotony. I don't know how, but I was in another position on the bed, peering down at the floor. With the assistance of the moon's glow, I observed thick, black and shiny cockroaches scuttling across the floorboards. They tapped on the skirting in extreme panic, trying to escape from—SLAP—from near the window. Just cloaked by the shadow, I could make out a creature sitting on the floor with its knees up and holding a cockroach betwixt its fingers.

One thing I did notice was that the beast only had three fingers on each hand, with approximately three-and-a-half-inch nails. What transpired next amazed me. The creature brought the bug to its mouth and crunched the head off, leaving an insect with legs pumping and kicking to escape this devastation.

I do believe these creatures are known as goblins, you know, like trolls. The kind of mythical monster you read in children's fairy stories. As any mature adult knows, it was certainly not reality, but its face was too detailed to be a phantasm. It had a pointed chin, long globular snout, pointed ears and a scrawny body, but with a stomach that nearly warmed the floor. The body of this creature was covered in warts and sores. There was an intense smell of ammonia that crawled across the room from the apparition, pulling at my stomach.

After it devoured a few more insects it seemed to sense me watching in bewilderment. Its eyes widened and began to leer, baring long slender teeth. The being then used its elongated arms to lever itself from the ground, leaving the feet dangling in mid-air for an instant, then it waddled off in another direction, searching out more fleshy victims.

Once the pernicious thing let the cockroach's body fluid permeate its mouth, it inclined its head and sniffed the cold air with flared nostrils. He turned slowly to face me.

It began slobbering obliquities into the dark. The talons on its toes scraped into the floor's varnish. It moved slowly at first as if it were wary of me, then it fettered toward me with its arms waving in a frantic motion that made its nails click together. It was getting closer. The smell becoming stronger and I couldn't move a muscle, as if I were lashed down to the bed by invisible bonds and my face hanging over the bed's footboard. The goblin leapt upon the chest and grinned from ear to pointed ear. He raised his index finger and rested it against my temple, then drew the nail down my check and under my chin, exposing my warm flesh and blood to the night air.

The goblin withdrew its finger and protruded a long, thin grey tongue which it dragged the bloody nail across, to leave a residue of my blood for it to taste. I found sanctuary; the beast seemed to lurch into convulsions, my blood obviously didn't agree with the inferior slurry the beast used to stay alive.

I was wrong.

It lunged toward my face, tearing pieces off with its teeth. Chewing a part, then spitting it out as its claws ripped another section of flesh from my carcass, in preparation of the feast. Alas, I awoke to sweat-sodden night cloths. My heart pumping blood around so fast I shook with terror—or was it excitement?

Once I've played my charade of politeness at breakfast tomorrow, I will undoubtedly have the freedom of the manor, facilitating my investigations. My elementary plan is to splice the manor into manageable sections, one each day. I will then verify or amend the information I collect in the village. I think I shall work from top to bottom. The attic will be first.

Something I have always enjoyed, ever since I was a child, was to explore in the uncharted waste-lands of attics. I don't know what the attraction was to me then—or even now. Maybe it's the musty and decaying relics that give the grimy aura of mystery. Perhaps it's the deathly silence that calms some people. No sound, but you swear you can hear the spider weave its cadaver clock high up there in the rafters.

I look forward to tomorrow and all it might hold for me, so I must say goodnight and get some rest.

Seventh of July, in the year, 1834

The attic was exultant. Everything I ever dreamed of attics being. There was a wall to my right that was saturated in books of all shapes, sizes and textures. Behind me was a skylight that looked out into the grounds at the front of the manor. To my left, blackness. The light couldn't penetrate the dark side of the room. So, once I equipped myself with a length of tallow, I ventured into the uncompromising and desolate black void.

When the lamp became engulfed in the darkness, there was a sharp manic scream that seemed to emit from all directions. I plucked up my courage and began to sneak further into the inexorable blackness. I was hardly able to peer two feet in front of me. The darkness seemed like an ethereal eternity.

My shin cracked against something hard. My head followed the glow from the lantern as I slowly raised and moved it around, unearthing items of interest. I found what caused the throbbing in my leg. It was an antique table. I couldn't see the type of wood it was fashioned from for the layers of dust and the cocoon of webs that embraced it. I wondered if the dirt and webs were preserving the table in this stagnant form. A leather-covered tome was first to be uncovered by the soft light. As I gently opened the tome, I heard the spine crunch; severing the fragile pages of history contained in this cemetery of words.

A dusty scriber devoid of ink lay hidden behind the tome, and a candelabra standing close by resembled a volcano, spewing its flesh-dispersion of ire on an unsuspecting land of peasants. My vision was distracted by a white object the lantern toned to my right. When I turned from the lava of wax, there was a skeleton slumped in a large chair. I ventured forward for a morbid close inspection of the bones. As my hand rested on the arm of the chair, spiders came crawling out of every orifice: nostrils, extruding between the teeth and where the ears used to be. Most came scurrying from their nest in the eye sockets, which startled me into a few involuntary backward leaps.

I snatched the tome, damning this light for not showing more area than it does. I tripped and faltered on the way to the trap door in the floor of the attic.

This unease was increased by what seemed to be things slithering across my path, as if they were deliberately trying to make me keel over.

Now, as I try to remember a resemblance of the sound, I can only describe it as rubbing two pieces of kelp together. Actually, from the glimpse I caught of them, that is what they looked like, large sticky lumps of breathing seaweed, squeaking along the floor.

Eventually, after seemingly hours in turmoil, and slipping on the slimy trail left behind those things, I managed to reach my destination.

I didn't venture into the gardens or beyond the gates today. It looked as though someone had tried to dilute the amount of evil in hell by drowning it in water, creating a blanket of fog that engulfed the land and its inhabitants. I couldn't even observe the gardens from the bedroom window, just outlines of statues when the fog decided to creep down, leaving its wet residue on everything it devoured.

As a trip outside was out of the question, I decided to further my exploration of the manor.

After a fruitless afternoon of searching dead-end rooms and gaunt closets in the lower half of the building, I dressed for dinner. There were the usual variations of fruit and meats on the table to choose from. I had chosen some luscious meat from the banquet laid before me. It was pinkish-brown in colour on the outside, with an orange type of sauce in the middle of it. The meat looked juicy and raw. You know, just the way any red-blooded human prefers their meat.

"What type of animal do I eat, Sir?" I questioned the Lord.

"That, my dear Mr Bastion, is a special combination of meats that only my cook has the secret ingredients for. It has been passed down through many generations of his species, and never once been or needed to be altered in any way. It is perfect."

"Would he be the swine who escorted me to my room last night?" I asked.

"No, certainly not," the Lord replied in a grumbling sort of laugh. "That was Carrion that you met last night. He is just my personal servant."

"Then, my Lord, I do not understand what you imply by 'species'? What have you got preparing your food down there in the kitchens?"

"I am sorry," the Lord apologised. "Please excuse my evasive demeanour. What I meant to say was race, not species. You see, he is rather like an animal himself, as he is so hideous and deformed, and takes with the mannerisms of a beast. You do understand, don't you?"

I did partially understand the Lords burden, so I gave him my forgiveness. The Lord also apologised for the first night I arrived at the manor. He was quite rude and did not speak too much, but said he had urgent work to finish and certain things required his constant attention at all times. It was such that, if the preparation was not to the imperative perfection required, the whole experiment would spoil.

Darkness battled twilight for a prize of the stars and the night as we ate our meal. At the end of the meal and cigars, the Lord excused himself so he might return to his work.

"Yes, certainly, Sir. May I ask what it is that you work at?"

I was dumbfounded by the abrupt reply from the Lord. "Sir, I don't think that is any of your damned concern. I will take my leave of you now."

The Lord stormed out of the great hall, slamming the heavy door behind him. The positive reverberation seemed to quake fear into the foundations and walls of the whole manor.

What had I said to upset him? Were his experiments so precious to him that he resorted to fits of rage when simply asking about them? Might it possibly be the way I had asked the question that traumatised him? Was he screaming at me in order to evade probing questions I might have asked if I wasn't being hit with a barrage of insults? Could it be something that's so advanced and intelligent that even I could not comprehend it?

Enough of this macabre train of thought. I do not wish to bore you with my morbid fantasies.

I ponder my sweet Elizabeth's health.

Damn, I can't think of any real pleasantries to comment on. This bloody manor is consuming all my thoughts and time. I am ensnared betwixt the lust of two evils: The devil's pillows of Elizabeth's bosom and the spellbinding intrigue of the Lord's past.

The Lord has had a varied and unusual past, as I found from the tome in the attic. This book reveals no dates in it to ease my task, but the black ink states the following on the first page:

> He has not a heart, he need not a heart.
> Can not and will not, kneel to the God's hand.
> Char the soil and reap the land,
> burn the bodies and keep the souls.
> Six times six times six men fold.
> Six men dead, six men's souls
> six men wish to be cold.

I am not quite sure what this inscription means, if it's relevant to my quest or some meaningful warning to be learned. The next few pages tell of some spiritual war and of someone fleeing to earth. Banished. To fester on this planet, but gaining strength for the future onslaught. He vowed that, through time, man will pay for Gods actions. That man will suffer under Lucifer's reign of eradication, so your God will weep in shame and sorrow to see his creation destroyed, slowly.

That was as far as I read tonight. I will read more tomorrow. I tire now. So again, I bid you farewell until we meet again in these pages tomorrow night.

Eighth of July, 1834

Horrendous visions were seen in my dreams last night. The dream was pleasant in the beginning. I was having a picnic in a field with Elizabeth when she started teasing me about Robert's desires for her. Obviously wishing a game of hide and seek, she ran from me into the woods. As I stepped through the woods, my feet crunched on dry dead wood, discarded by an injured tree.

The more ancient barks I passed, the deeper the shade of light plunged until it resembled the colour of a monks' cowl. I shouted for an answer from Elizabeth, as this game had lost its humorous element now. Only the sound of secret messages being whispered by the leaves above indicated any life. Just a constant noise, like a cacophony of singers not sure of the words to sing and always out of tune with each other.

I searched out this curious noise until it became so deafening I had to cover my ears in protection.

To my disgust, the source of this was emitting from a swollen mass, propped against a tree's trunk. A swarm of various species of flies, bees and wasps flew around excitedly. Their only intention was to extract the last of Elizabeth's beauty and life from her now excessively bloated carcass.

I could only stare in awe. The drone grew in volume. Louder and louder. As I let out a multitude of ebbing screams of sorrow, I awoke.

The sight on opening my eyes tempted me back to my nightmare. Surrounding the edges of the bed slouched a gaggle of goblins that leered from drooling teeth. I noticed the bed covers seemed to move, but I was not moving my limbs, so I threw back the covers to free a black mass of flies that filled the room with buzzing. The goblins all yelped with joy as they started chasing and jumping after the airborne snacks. On closer inspection of the bed, I found woodlouse crawling without any positive direction on the white sheets upon which I lay.

My heart was ready to burst with pain, as they were feeling their way up through the hairs on my legs and I could feel them running, confused, in my pubic hairs. I could only stare with opened mouth as no scream would come to my lips. I could feel earwigs massing and wriggling under the length of my spine, trying desperately to find a warmer place to breed. Maggots in my hair were escaping via a path down my face to meet with the spiders looking for a new home, their hairy legs brushing against my goose-fleshed face.

All the excitement soured the liquid and food in my stomach, throwing a stream of hot sticky vomit over the bed. The chunky liquid started sliding down the wood and bedclothes, pulsating with the movement of the maggots and worms that began to gorge themselves on the free meal.

The goblins were closing around the bed. Each grabbed a part of my body and started pulling and ripping my flesh.

At the extreme point of limbo, I saw Carrion grinning and pushing me in a rocking motion. I lashed out with my hand, knocked him sliding across the floor.

"Why you hurt me?" asked Carrion.

"You should be grateful I don't kill you. Don't ever touch me again, you ugly little bastard, do I make myself understood?"

There was no answer from Carrion. He only stood with shamed eyes examining the floor.

"Do I make myself understood, idiot?" I shouted.

Still no answer from the beast in front of me.

"Answer me, damn you."

"Yesh, shir," Carrion replied.

I ordered the deformed imbecile to continue about his business and leave me alone.

I read more of the tome today and found that every hundred years, a new Lord takes over the running of the manor. Actually, it isn't a new Lord, but a new person. One Lord is not related to another and the paper for each one is of different quality to the previous guardian of this gaunt building.

All the protectors of this place tell of the multitude of servants hiding behind every evil stone used to create this embodiment of Lucifer's haven.

At dinner tonight, the Lord told me that I was brought here by telling me untruths, helped by my so-called friend Robert. As I am not to leave, Robert will eventually receive the love I once had from Elizabeth.

"Elizabeth has no love for you, only for Robert, as it has been for the past year and a half," The Lord told me.

"Why do you tell me this, Sir. Is this part of a test or plan of some kind?"

"No," said the Lord. "I thought I would tell you the bad news as I am fond of you and would like you to know the truth. They didn't know that I would enlighten you to their secret life. I hope you understand and I would prefer you to stay, as I enjoy your company."

I could not understand this news. There was too much to believe.

"I'm sorry, Lord, but I shall want to leave at first light, to attend this problem at home."

"You have no life outside, this is your home now," The Lord almost whispered.

"I will retire for the night, if you'll excuse me," I said disgustedly. I could hear the Lord's laughter echo all the way though the manor as I left.

I went to my room where I write this diary. Hopefully, I will feel better when this manor is far behind me and in the past. I feel with all the pressing matters today, sleep will not be an easy luxury to find.

Date: July, 1834

My sleep was plagued with flesh-crawling sights on the eve of my departure, as I predicted. I thought I was awake in my first dream of the night. I will try to extrapolate on my fantasies.

My eyes grew accustomed to the moonlight blending through the window. I sat up erect and saw the Lord flanked on both sides by goblins against the wall directly opposite my bed. They all stood there just laughing and laughing.

The light began to flicker in the room, like the fingers of a tree waving in front of the moon's glow. As I turned my head, I noticed that the window was open, sending in a breeze that chilled my skin. I rose out of my warm bed and ran bare-foot to close the window, when I realised my body was smeared in slugs, all shades of black. Sticky slime trailed down my body.

Before I could reach the window, the room was invaded by death-head moths which engulfed me with their powdery wings and hairy legs adhering to the slime. Some were bad navigators and crashed into my face in a puff of dust, while others caught in my hair. I tried hard to keep my mouth closed, but a scream escaped and was soon gagged by an orb of moths entering my mouth. The hairy little bodies tickled the back of my throat and the pumping action of their legs and beating of the wings made me retch from the pit of my soul.

The last sound I heard was someone saying, "You have passed and gained; one task remains."

While merging into another vision, I was awakened by shouting, screams and laughter. Dragging my body from the bed, I put my dressing gown on as I made my way to the location of the noise.

The festivities came from the great hall, which was overrun with those goblin creatures. They didn't notice me, so I edged closer and saw the Lord sitting at the head of the table. The goblins seemed to be rejoicing in the only way they knew how, demonically.

One of the creatures was on top of the table, its arms not fully extended, so that his rectum was touching the varnish. He began to drag his body across the table, leaving a trail of worm-ridden excreta smeared from where he started to where he rested. This made the wood steam in the chilled air.

Others were clawing at their warts to relieve the itching, some wildly fornicated over chairs, and one pair chased each other around the great hall. Why, I do not know. The Lord raised his voice above the mayhem.

"Please, will you join us, Mr Bastion. My children are quite harmless."

A goblin bit a finger off another beast as the Lord finished speaking. I walked to the table, but there was no space to sit. As I tried to sit betwixt two goblins, they bared their teeth and hissed violently at me.

"Remove them from your chosen place," The Lord advised.

After swiftly kicking one from a chair, I sat next to the Lord. He spoke with deep sincerity.

"You are not leaving the manor, ever. There's no existence outside these gates. There is nothing for you outside this arena except a cold dark void. Just now you are but a tyro in my domain, but you will learn all that is required. I have been conditioning you from the day you arrived at the manor. Do you recall any visions in the night?"

"Yes," I replied. "But, they were more like nightmares than visions. I thought..."

"No," the Lord interrupted. "No, my friend, they were to test your physical endurance, and I was interested in finding out if your mind could take the constant torture. I must say, the result was unexpected."

The Lord tipped his goblet of wine to his mouth and drained the contents.

"You see, Mr Bastion, there have been so many I have experimented with in the past; and they all failed miserably. They didn't even make it through the first night. "

The Lord hung his head low in disappointment.

"What happened to them—when they failed?"

Lord Lingbo raised his head slowly.

"Their minds were unbalanced. They could not speak, and eventually they regressed to idiots. They were all disposed of."

Curiosity ate at me, like a lion ripping at the inside of its prey.

"Where did you bury the bodies?"

"Oh, my dear Sir," the Lord spoke with an acerbic tinge to his voice. "They have not been laid to rest, and never will be. They have been stored in salt barrels by Brock and myself in the lower cells of the manor."

The Lord and I stared at each other in an elegy of pause that seemed to last an eternity. My head began to spin and sharp pains began to fluctuate through every nerve in my body. Suddenly, there was blackness in my eyes. The harder I strained to prise open my eyes, the more daylight flooded the room.

Date: 1834

I was still feeling perplexed this morning as I dressed and ate breakfast. After which, I questioned the Lord concerning my coach home.

"I am afraid, Mr Bastion, you will be unable to return today as …"

"Sir," I retorted. "I wish to leave today. In fact, immediately."

The Lord seemed quite anxious as he tapped his cane on the floor.

"The fog is too thick. No one will travel here in such conditions. You'll have to be my guest for a little while longer."

"Dammed inconvenient," I exclaimed as I pulled off my jacket and hat.

After giving Carrion my jacket and thumping my hat on to his chest, he emitted a sniggering sound that infuriated me further. I twisted around and slapped Carrion with the back of my hand.

"Don't you sneer at me, you little bastard."

Carrion lay on the floor, bleeding at the mouth. The Lord wore a wry smile on his face as I pounded the flight of stairs to my room. I screamed an echo through the hallway of the naked manor.

"I want the first available coach out of this dammed mad house."

The Lord had much to say at dinner that night.

"Mr Bastion, do you remember last night at all?"

"What do you mean, Sir? I had a nightmare about you and some beasts, here in the great hall. That's all, just a dream."

"No," exclaimed the Lord. "What you saw last night wasn't a dream, nor a vision. What you saw was real. In the flesh."

If that was true, what about the things the Lord had told me about? So I questioned the Lord.

"So, what you spoke of concerning Elizabeth and Robert—it's true?"

"Yes," The Lord almost shouted. "But that's not the whole story. Elizabeth is a courtesan—has been for most of her life."

I felt anger and pity and shame, but mostly embarrassment, all rolled into one, huge, explosive emotion. I didn't know whether to cry for sorrow or anger.

Knowing my own selfish nature, it was probably tears or ire and self-pity that soiled my face. Carrion came shuffling behind the chairs with bowls of broth for the Lord and I, giving me a wide expanse as he passed. The idiot probably thought I would challenge him again.

The Lord was telling me some spectral stories about how he became the guardian of the manor. The tales were informative. At last, the Lord is opening himself up to me.

"Mr Bastion," said the Lord. "As you may have found out, you have minimum powers in your possession now. If you stay, these powers will increase and whatever you desire will be at your feet, to do with as you see fit."

I searched my mind for something out of my ordinary, everyday life that I could relate to the powers that Lord Minion spoke of. I couldn't, and told him so.

"Sir, I do not understand what you imply by 'powers'? What are these powers? How do I use them?"

The Lord impatiently closed his eyes and pursed his lips. The Lord almost whispered the question. "You dislike Carrion, do you not?"

"That's true," I agreed.

"Well, imagine in your mind what you would really like to inflict on him. Focus all your thoughts and all the anger that has built up inside you. It will swell up inside your mind to become a combined force, then direct the power toward Carrion. Please, try it."

The Lord called Carrion from the corner of the great hall to come to the table where we sat. When Carrion approached the table, the Lord told him to sit facing me.

"I not want to, Lord." Carrion pleaded. " Mr Bast'n hurt Carr'n."

The Lord spoke softly to him.

"It's going to be fine, Carrion. Mr Bastion won't harm you. I'm here to protect you."

Carrion sat down cautiously; his hands were white-knuckled on the edge of the table. Ready for a quick dash to the nearest exit. The Lord turned to me and raised his eyebrows expectantly.

"Get on with it, Mr Bastion," he demanded.

I tried to remember all the irritations that Carrion inflicted upon me: his tap, tap, tapping at my arm. His smell. The way he sniggers at nothing in particular, the way he leers, with all his sores and blemishes of the skin. His inferior slouch and gait added to the irritations.

My body started to tingle and my breathing grew heavier. I feel quite intoxicated. Carrion is nothing but a subspecies of beast. Filth that is ready and willing to be eradicated. He should be grateful of the pain I will inflict. Good enough for dirt on noble feet.

I felt my head was getting lighter and I was becoming confused with all the various thoughts running around in all directions. As I used my hands to steady the raging disturbance in my mind, I felt my skin start to crawl underneath my fingertips.

My vision was clear as I saw Carrion directly in front of me. His eyes were weeping bloody streams of fear and panic. Instead of salty sweat, blood seeped out of every pore of Carrion's skin. His fingernails turned black. His eyes opened so wide the spherical shape of his eyes could be seen.

The veins on his face and hands expanded and protruded from the skin. His body decayed rapidly, like being crushed in a drowning mass of grain surrounding his being. A body press, depriving him of life or human form.

The Lord spoke as he gazed at the blood dripping on the floor. From the depleted corpse strewn from the chair to the chilled flagstones. "You are in need of better control of your gift, Mr Bastion," the Lord chastised. "He was a good servant to me, it's a great shame. You will also learn how to make death cleaner, as the smell of blood gets sweeter in your memory the longer you exist. You crave it more and more with each passing day."

I sat in awe at the sight. I couldn't believe that I, Joseph D. Bastion, could be responsible for the death of this being, or any form of being. Be it human or otherwise, just by direction and focus of my own morbid thoughts. This was a strong weapon I possessed. How could I control it? Would I use it wisely? Most importantly—do I wish to use it again?

I was quite tired, but the Lord and I talked late into the witching hours.

Date: Unsure. Can't think.

Time is an unsure element in the manor; the lapsing of days or hours are not required. It's difficult to grasp any concept of reality and fantasy. The timeless existence in this place gives you pervasive comfort; nothing to rush for, nowhere to be at a specified hour. You just accept life or death as it's destined to be.

I had slept quite late this morning, and then wandered around the manor in a daze, I think. I heard a slow scraping sound from below me. The vestibule was dim, but I could make out a grotesque figure glowing at the bottom of the stairs as the tallow was fed with fire.

I was wakened at the table in the great hall. The Lord sat at the table, staring at me, which made me feel drowsy again. I lapsed into unconsciousness and began some spectacular visions of the carnage and atrocities from past decades.

"Mr Bastion..." repeatedly filtered my ears as I strode back into reality. The Lord was still gazing at me. "Mr Bastion, are you awake? Mr Bastion?"

"Yes, I'm here," I bawled.

"We still have much to discuss," The Lord pressed.

"What is there left to say, my Lord?" I questioned.

The Lord shifted in his seat, preparing himself for the answer to my question.

"There's much to discuss yet, Mr Bastion. We have still to deal with the acceptance of your destiny as the next Minion."

I inclined my head to the side, showing interest in the words he spoke.

"You know what you must do to claim your prize, Mr Bastion?"

"No," I retorted. "But you may tell me, if you wish."

The Lord inhaled deeply and his face leaked submission to a visual extent.

"You have to replace me; I must be eliminated in order for you to take my place. You must aspire this command."

"I cannot harm you, Lord. You have more strength than I."

"Yes, that is true, Mr Bastion. Alas, my added gifts will leave me before the battle begins. I am not permitted to use them."

The Lord took a long drink of wine and continued.

"Although I like you, Mr Bastion, I have come to accept this existence of mine for a long time and would hate to loose it to you."

"What do you mean, 'them,' 'the gifts'? Sir?" I mused.

"My dear Joseph. I may call you Joseph, yes?" the Lord continued his verbal instruction before waiting for an affirmation. "I have the six souls of the master in my being, which give me sustenance so that I do not become infirm, until my saviour is sought. So, I will now release them, and the battle may commence."

Hanging his head low, the Lord began to shake. Black shapes slid and pulled from his ever-dwindling arid body before flying and swooping around the great hall. They eventually came floating down to rest around the table, emitting deathly groans of depression.

The sound made one feel so full of sorrow that death would be welcomed with opened arms to escape this sinking of emotions. Before I became entangled in a feud with the Lord, I had a fight in my own mind to contend with first. Would I be able to win over the Lord, or will I be the one to lose my life and soul?

Eternal limbo will be expectant.

What kind of existence will I endure if I become the masters' minion? Do I really want all this dread? Can I cope with the beasts? So many questions, and yet no answers prevaricate.

My eyes began bulging from their sockets. The Lord had begun.

"No, Lord!" I screamed. "Not now, please."

The pain in my eyes grew excruciating. My body exploded with tingles; like that new medical treatment found in the east, small needles being pushed under my skin, all over my body. These all came racing up to my head, then pushed forward to my eyes. My vision turned the colours of a rainbow as a stream of blurred lines shot toward the Lord. His muscles were sent into a continual jerky motion and his back arched into a severe, spine-crushing hollow.

If he didn't have his hands clamped on the edge of the table, he would have screeched across the floor in his chair. The Lord let an escalating squawk exit his throat as his neck was forced over the headrest on the chair. The veins on my face and hands began to swell and deform under the sensitive touch of the skin on the palms of my hands.

I bolted to a standing position, throwing the chair backward and exploded all my energy at the Lord, trying in vain to exorcise the distortions running through my body. The pitiful wreck of a man in front of me began to tremble. White foam squeezed from his lips. His muscles began to tighten rapidly, racking his body before the skin that covered his skeleton was stretched to its limits.

The Lord's bones started snapping and muscles tearing as the joints squeaked loose from the bones that hosted them. Limbs were ripping off as the skin decayed and entrails poured out onto the stone floor, filling the great hall with a goblin's stench.

It was over. The Lord was dead.

His face was wearing a leer. Why?

I looked around in triumph. The hall was filled with goblins, from wall to wall and across the damp flagged earth. They crept up and surrounded me. I sat down in the nearest chair to catch my breath when, suddenly, goblins grabbed my arms and pinned them behind the back of the chair. Others snatched and held my legs.

One large goblin appeared at my right and brandished his long, three pronged claws of devastation.

"Why," I wept. "Why am I being punished? I did what was expected of me."

The goblin shredded the shirt from my body, then it turned to face the black forms sitting around the table and nodded repeatedly.

"No, no…Oh Lord no…"

The black forms began a menacing float above the table, sounding melodious moans.

One at a time they came, their screeching laugh echoing in my head, hurtling toward me. They slammed into my chest, which made my ribs expand and my stomach shrink. Each form that pounded into my chest felt like a heart attack without any time for recovery. My physique became more muscular and younger. I felt warm exaltations as I faded in mind.

Upon opening my eyes, I was confronted by a smothering crowd of grinning goblins waiting patiently for me to steer them all in a direction of deprivation and destruction.

"I am now a minion of the master, just as you are now my minions. We have a tiresome task ahead. There are still many souls out there to be stolen. But, working together, we can have the feeble humans that are not pure in mind and soul."

The goblins crept closer, pushing against my legs. I reached my hands down and stroked the heads of two siblings. They purred with contentment.

"You are the best friends I have ever had or ever will need. There is a lot I need to learn yet. But with your aide, we can become all powerful and aid the master in taking this lifetime of souls as well as the previous and future centuries of man."

I spoke to my servants all through the cowled skies, making plans for Man's future and the new guardian reading this tome. It is now your time. You will never leave this Manor again, with your soul.

Before closing this chapter of my miserable existence and entering it into the tome, I have one last task to complete. I must extend an invitation to Elizabeth and Robert for a few well-deserved meals. I will relish that immensely.

Lord Bastion, Minion Manor.

.

ANDREW L. MACKINNON may be contacted at: ShortShocks@Yahoo.co.uk

IN SHADOWS

Paul Melniczek

In the corner.

A shroud of suggestion at the edge of his bleary vision, Roger grips the bottle with a sweat-moistened palm, spilling beer onto his shaking hand and the mahogany stained bar beneath, the wood tainted with bitter fluids and wasted lives. Snapping his head around like a shiftless watchdog kicked out of idleness, and there's nothing to be seen...

He chokes on the bile quivering at the back of his parched throat, the dry tickle, dry despite the three shots of gin and half dozen slammers, poison-kisses to welcome oblivion, harsh, biting drinks to fight back the loathing that follows him wherever he goes.

"I think you had enough." The drawling words of the beef-mitted bartender remind Roger that he still lives in a very real world, one which is gradually slipping away from his feverish grasp.

"No, I'm fine. Did you see something over there?"

The man swings his head patiently like a sloth looking for fresh greens. When he returns to stare at Roger, his eyes speak more clearly than any caustic-laced comment ever could—another lush, dime-a-dozen loser, stinking up my pub...

"Should I have seen something?"

Roger stands up, feeling the head-buzz from the liquor. With false confidence, overdoing the fabricated scene, he looks more a drunk by the second. "Keep the change."

Stiff legs, overemphasizing each carefully planned step, never looking back as he leaves the temporary comfort of the drowning hole, except his nightmares can't be drowned tonight, or any night.

One more block to his apartment, the bleak buildings loom beside his shuffling figure with grim watchfulness—reassuring concrete, familiar and friendly. He asks himself, I'm not insane, am I?

What's that?

Roger stumbles, clumsy feet stubbing into the cracked cement—the crack in his forsaken life. Beneath the lamppost, across the street, a shadow hunkers down—lurking, observing, waiting.

It's not real.

Rubbing his eyes until they moisten, Roger can rake his hands across the orbs until blindness strikes, but he can't excoriate the truth. He looks, the dim light illuminates an empty sidewalk, deserted street, no sinister shade lurks in hiding.

Nothing.

drifting thoughts, tired, of everything

houses pass by, the ghosts of fleeting dreams, homes of pathetic people who belong,

bitterness at the world and men, chances he failed to take, spiteful regrets at his own inadequacies,

"Don't care."

a figure appears from out of nowhere

Up the beaten steps leading to his room, Roger hears the whispers behind locked doors—about him? Do they know, see it in his slouched posture, the depressed curve of stooped shoulders? Scared. The whole world shouts accusations at him, screaming at him.

Ignoring him.

In his mind, all within his tortured thoughts, they exist only in chastising conscience, the self-purgatory of his heinous act, withering him to ashes. He turns around, looking down the staircase, there it is—brooding at the edge of Roger's awareness, stroking the chords of retribution, plucking the strings of condemnation. Eating away at the remnants of his will, a scourge on his weakening strength.

Roger blinks and the shadow is gone, banished into the dark recesses of a destitute imagination.

It never existed.

The kennel-small room is bright from the glare of dusty light bulbs, shadeless lamps to repel dark spots, and shadows. Television reminds Roger of an orderly current revolving around him, in which people walk, laugh, and cry.

And live.

The conscience can be a treacherous scorpion if prodded too many times.

He turns his head.

In the bathroom, skulking like a malevolent, leering voyeur, a shadow. Sentient, intelligent, full of black purpose, sightlessly observing him. Roger's chest heaves in ragged, dragging bursts for air, white lips gulping like a fish washed up on a beach of caked, gritty sand, eyes bulging in suffocation.

The phantom shifts, moving closer, the end approaches.

He waves a hand across his febrile brow…

…and nothing is there, only the wall tiles glinting dully from pink fluorescent bulbs. Static, flickering above a greasy porcelain sink. The image lingers in Roger's mind, the scorched grains of his sanity.

There is no shadow, never was.

the frantic figure, hands waving madly at the twin beams of death speeding towards him,

"No, no." frightened animal-whimper, nauseating thump,

body laying on the ground, in the icy frame of his rear view mirror, pain, blood, fear,

guilt,

mind shrieking, "don't stop, keep driving, wasn't your fault, no one will know…"

escape

run from the gaping maw of guilt, into a lifetime of guilt,

something moving, above the crumpled form, or just his imagination?

Sleep comes—unbidden, unknown, wrapping him within its cloak of distraction, teasing him with the promise of forgetfulness. So alluring, teasing, dreams become reality, pleasant sensations of a normal, carefree life, everything is fine.

Eyes bleeding wide open, the sweet wine of false bliss suddenly transformed—Roger's waking world is the foundation for nightmares. Vacant pupils staring up at the plastered ceiling, tiny pieces ready to break off and splatter onto him like corrupted stardust. Crawling slowly is a tiny spider, a wandering nomad in the desert of Roger's room—the desolation of his life.

A black figure, directly above him. The shadow, its vitriolic presence hovering over him like a demonic bat, preparing to descend upon his pathetic form. No time to move, think.

Endgame.

Eyelids closed, the voiceless scream will have no release. Roger awaits the inevitable.

Nothing happens.

He pries apart the bleak cavities of bloodshot eyes, shock registering on his pale, gaunt, face.

...and the ceiling is empty.

So very tired, can't sleep. Pangs of hunger ripping through his stomach, has lost any desire to eat. Wants to forget the world, himself, but his mind prevents such amnesia—that, and the haunting fear. Roger leaves the dreary apartment, wanders the streets, less a beggar, more so an outcast. Beggars at least have kindred, he doesn't. Defeated chin glances up seeing a newspaper stand, stark in the night, brimming with conviction, the reality of meaning, structure. He has lost both.

Young man pierces him with suspect eyes, wary feelings of distrust.

"Looking for something?"

Yes, but nothing you can offer, he thinks. On the wall, across from the stand, the foul shadow waits, imprinted on the granite surface, an affliction on Roger's being.

"There, what do you see?"

A frown of displeasure, a sneer at the rambling vagrant.

Roger lifts a callused finger at the ghastly vision, growing larger now, separating from the wall, coming towards his broken frame. The man shakes his head, staring at the blank stone. It's empty. Nothing.

Cramped legs churning wildly, directionless, the only thought in the scattered mind is retreat, but to where? Every refuge is unearthed, no haven remains. All are visible to the relentless dark stalker.

It doesn't even exist.

Roger staggers across the street, senses blind to the outside, closing away the inside. What is left for him?

Pale headlights bear down on his stricken, wasted figure, tires screech in protest, nearer—too late, Roger's body is flung to the side, a weightless marionette—but where are the tightly held strings? The man behind the wheel gasps, frightened beyond words, revulsion strangling his abdomen, the pressure enough to burst his heart. Motionless, the wreckage of a ruined man, laying in the trash-filled gutter, another piece of discarded material coughed up from the city's tasteless gorge. The driver snakes from the car, a new pair of lines etched into his forehead, never to be smoothed away. He watches, trembling in horror at the achievement of his grisly handiwork, and the revelation which ensues.

Further away along the wall, beneath the revealing lamp glow, a pair of shadows recede in the distance, one pursuing the other.

REVENGE OF THE ROACH KING

C. Dennis Moore

I pulled up outside my brother's building the night after he called. He'd said the noises were finally too much for him. Said he couldn't sleep with the constant scritching and scratching in the walls and over the floors. The heat was bad enough, but those sounds were likely to drive a man crazy. He said as long as I was coming over anyway—we did have a funeral to discuss—could I bring my equipment?

My brother's building was a dump. I'd only been there once before and I must have forgotten what a hole it was. I went in the front door, stepped over a puddle of…something, and climbed the stairs, passed a door covered in police tape, and knocked on Jerry's door. When he let me in, I was reluctant to take the offered seat—who knew what was living in that couch—and instead walked around inspecting the place.

Jerry's kitchen, really just a sink, stove, and refrigerator along a far wall of the one-room apartment, was a haven for the bastards, trash can full, dirty dishes on the counter, some with food dried onto them, open cans half-full of sticky, sugary bait for the little things. I wanted to tell him he probably wouldn't attract them like he did if he'd just clean the place up a little, but in the end, in a place like this, I knew that wasn't true. This building was infested and Jerry emptying his trash and wiping off the counter wasn't going to change that.

"I can take care of the problem in here," I told him, "but you really probably ought to get the landlord to call somebody."

"You're somebody."

"I'm not on the clock. This is a favor. I'm only here so we can decide what we want to do with our mother."

"Later," he said, "just get rid of them, will you? I can't take them anymore. If it's money, I got some money, I'll pay you."

"It's not that, it's just you should get the owner involved. It's his building, make him foot the bill."

"Landlord's a jackass. For me, okay?"

"Alright," I said. "I'll start in here, then check the basement, that's a common area, while you think about how you want to go on Mom's funeral." I took a shaker of boric acid powder from my pocket and explained to him that it's harmless to people, but it's about as effective as you can get when dealing with cockroaches.

I put some behind his trashcan, sending a small wave of roaches scurrying under the refrigerator, away from the light. I tried to stomp them all, but only managed to get two. A few things fell from the overflowing trashcan, bits of crumpled paper and a couple of empty beer cans. Roaches love beer, I don't know why. I put them back, shoved the trash down further.

I sprinkled more around the sink, then started moving away from the "kitchen", around the room. When I reached the closet and was about to open the door to put the powder in there, Jerry quickly said, "What are you doing?"

"Cool dark place," I said, indicating the closet. "One of the first places to check."

"You don't need to worry about the closet."

Now I was curious. Was he hiding something? I wanted to ask, but with my little brother, I figured that's where he kept his weed. Extermination isn't a glamorous job; some of us go into it because we hate them that much. What Jerry was dealing with was cockroaches, and anyone who's ever had a problem with them can tell you, they are one of the most persistent of insects, difficult to get rid of, more difficult still to keep out once they're gone.

The basement turned out to be a wash. I found nothing down there except a washer and dryer that probably didn't even work. I sprinkled boric acid powder into the corners and along the walls anyway.

The problem remained of finding the nest. I decided to return upstairs to Jerry's apartment, but first I made another circuit of the basement, just to double check. On the way to Jerry's door, I passed the taped-off apartment again. I'd have to ask about that one.

I found Jerry in his closet, shoving something aside, cursing, and tumbling over something, like he wanted to get whatever was in there out of sight before I saw it.

Unless it was a giant cockroach, I wasn't interested in any of Jerry's dirty laundry.

"Did you find them?" he asked, shutting the closet door and turning to face me again. Whatever was in that closet, his face was all the admission anyone would need; it was something good, and he didn't want anyone else to get it. Yeah, I thought, probably his weed.

"There's more to it than that," I said. "Besides, I didn't find anything in the basement. What's in that taped-off apartment?" I asked, figuring an undisturbed room, dark and empty, might just be the perfect place for a nest.

"Um, I don't know," he said.

"I wonder if I should talk to the landlord about checking it out for infestation."

"You can talk to him but he won't let you in. It's sealed off for a reason."

"I know that. But you let a bug problem get out of hand and it can become a health hazard. I'm not saying I wanna inspect a crime scene—" that was obviously the reason for the tape, whatever the crime was. Murder was my guess, but that's nothing new in this town "—I'm just saying I want to check for a nest. I mean, so far, I've only seen roaches in your apartment. Far as I can tell, you're the only one with an obvious problem, but that can't be because roaches, once they get in, breed and infest the building. If I'm gonna get rid of them, I need to find out where they're coming from."

"Can you just get rid of them, please? I can't help you with that apartment, just forget that one, and please find them and kill them."

I'd already spent more time in this building tonight than I wanted to.

"They're all over this place and I can't take 'em," Jerry said. "I can't even sleep at night."

"I'm not doubting they're here," I said. I wanted to tell him the big surprise would be if a dump like this *didn't* have bugs, but instead I said, "Before I go door to door asking to check for nests, I think we should discuss Mom. She said she wanted to be cremated, but I just don't know if I can."

"Don't worry about the funeral," he said. "I got it covered."

His eyes flashed to the closet—I don't even think he noticed it—and I wondered after all just what was in there.

"I'd really just as soon discuss it first, if you don't mind."

His reluctance shone through, but he agreed.

There was no way I was knocking on any doors anyway, not until we'd settled the matter. I came here tonight for our mother's funeral, and we were going to get it out of the way. What did he think, that I just wandered around town at night looking for infestations to exterminate? I was doing him a favor here; the least he could do was hear me out.

So we settled it. Our mother wanted to be cremated, but neither of us wanted to do that deed just yet. We thought maybe we'd have a viewing first, a nice affair like she deserved, with all her family and friends, a last chance to see her. We could have her cremated afterward, couldn't we? The only problem I could see was the cost. She hadn't left much in her will, barely enough to cover the costs of a bottom-dollar funeral, a ten-spot away from a pine-box affair, but we were giving her better than that. If we could afford it.

By my watch it was after nine when I started knocking on doors. Still fairly early, so I wasn't worried about waking anyone, but late enough I wasn't disturbing them during dinner. I'd have to interrupt a few sitcom reruns, probably, but other than that, I figured the tenants wouldn't mind too much in helping to get rid of the bug problem.

Shows what I know.

The first door I came to was answered by an old man in a dirty tank top who thought I was the police and slammed the door in my face, yelling, "I didn't hear anything, leave me alone."

The next door was different, but I still didn't get in. I'm not surprised, not many people, especially in a neighborhood like this one, are going to let a stranger in this late at night, no matter who he says he is, or what he wants. I could have come to the door bleeding and half-dead and I still wouldn't have made it inside. From the few apartments I'd caught glimpses of from the door, they didn't look half as bad as Jerry's, so chances were none of them were being used as nests.

I tried three more apartments, all unsuccessfully. I stood in the hall, looking at that taped apartment door, covered in strips of yellow. Then I went down to the entryway.

I went to the row of mailboxes and found the one I wanted. Whatever'd happened in the cordoned apartment, no one had changed the mailbox label. Apartment 3B was rented to Ronnie Gallagher. As I read the name, a sense of déjà vu came over me. I knew I'd seen that name before, and I stood there trying to force the memory, to remember where I'd seen it. Then it hit me, it had been written on something in Jerry's trash can. Ronnie G., it said. Had to be the same guy. But so what? What was I trying to prove?

Only that Jerry'd lied to me. He might not know what happened to Ronnie, and probably he didn't, not everything, but if he'd known the man, he had to know something, right?

Again, so what? I know, it was no big deal, none of my business. His life is his, I told myself. I don't tell him everything.

But dammit, if he'd known the man was dead, he could have just said it.

"Yeah, guy I know used to live there. He died, though."

Simple, right? But he hadn't said that. He'd lied and said he didn't know anything.

Why?

I didn't know, but now that it was on my mind, the question was burning into me and I wanted to find out, wanted it more than I wanted to find the nest and get out of here, even, because I could tell already that I was on to something.

So I did a little lying of my own. I was glad I'd worn a button-up shirt because they look more professional when you're pretending to be a cop.

The first floor apartments were out of the question, I'd already knocked on them, so I climbed the stairs, went to the door furthest down the hall, and asked if I could speak to them about Ronnie Gallagher.

"We already talked to you guys," the old woman said when she opened the door. "There's nothing else to tell. Go away."

"Ma'am," I said, putting my foot in the door before she closed it, "we're just here to make sure we've got it all straight. People remember things over time, you know. We just want to get all the facts we can."

"Well if you want all the facts," she said, "you ask that man down there." She motioned with her head. I turned around and saw she was looking at Jerry's door.

"Does Mr. Boyer know what happened?"

"He ought to," she said. "He was there. I heard 'em come in together that night. Out all night at the bars, I'd say. Both of 'em so drunk it's a wonder they got up the stairs."

"I see. So then, when it happened—"

"When he was killed."

"Yes," I said, "when Mr. Gallagher died, was Mr. Boyer actually in the apartment with him? Or did they part company before that?"

"'Part company'? Where you from? No, no, they went into that man's place together. Don't ask me what they was doing, I mind my own business around here. But it was probably something queer, you know, I always said there was something wrong with those two. I bet they was doing something nasty together."

"Fine, thank you, I think we've got enough for now."

I pulled my foot back, but I guess she wasn't finished.

"You tell him," she said, "nothing good comes from that kind of sin. He's going to hell, you just wait and see."

I nodded, said thank you again, and backed away.

Then I stopped and went back to her to ask, "Ma'am, have you had any problems lately with pests? Cockroaches? Anything?"

"Of course not," she almost cried. "I keep a clean house, you better believe that. I wouldn't let nothing like that into my place, who are you talking to?"

I turned around and let her keep going as I left. I glanced down, then, and saw it.

A cockroach scurried under the door to Ronnie's apartment.

I stood in front of it, wondering what was on the other side, put my ear to the door to see if I could hear anything, then realized it would have to be one huge nest for me to hear it, and with the former occupant dead, there wouldn't be any other sounds in there.

But there was.

As hard as it was to believe, I did hear something, a scraping, and a low hum. I couldn't say what the noises were, but whatever they were, they sure as anything shouldn't have been there, because this apartment was not only empty, but sealed off as well.

I looked around, looked at everything, waiting for an idea to come to me. Then I saw the stairs leading up. I glanced out a hallway window to the street, and there it was.

I took off up the stairs, climbed past the third and fourth floors, and got outside onto the roof. From here, I had to figure out which direction I was looking for—Ronnie and Jerry's apartments were on the left when you came in the front door—and when I was oriented I went to the fire escape.

Now, this might be a little risky because the fire escape that covered Ronnie's window would probably be the same one that ran in front of Jerry's, and when I left his apartment last he'd been standing in front of the window. If I was quiet and careful enough, he might not notice me. Unless he was still standing at the window.

The night was hot, no breeze blew, nor did any clouds threaten rain. It was one of those summer nights a person suffers through in bed, tossing and turning, searching for the cool spot on the sheet, the cool side of the pillow, the few seconds of air as the fan sweeps past.

The streets were about as empty as they ever got.

Strange for the city to be so quiet. Like everyone knew something was coming, and they were trying to stay out of it. Even the prostitutes had abandoned their posts tonight. The junkies had stayed home. The bums had found some other alley to live in for the night.

From here it was four stories to the second floor. As I made my way past the fifth and fourth floors, I was trying to make out from above where I was in relation to Jerry's and Ronnie's apartments, trying to figure out which one I would pass first. On the third floor, I had it pretty much figured out. On the second floor, I had to stop before I went in front of Jerry's window.

It figured I'd have to cross his to get to the one I wanted.

I tried to use the light from inside to tell if he was standing in front of the window, or if he was further inside. But even if he was back further in the room, he could still be watching out the window. How could I be sure?

Then I heard something I hoped was coming from his room and not from next door, or above, or from anywhere else in the building. A toilet flushed. I prayed it was Jerry's as I leaped across the fire escape, past his window, and stopped in front of Ronnie's. I didn't bother to look inside and see if Jerry was there or not, I just wanted to get across.

I cupped my hands over the glass and tried to see inside the supposedly empty apartment.

I would never be able to unsee what I'd seen.

Instead of an empty apartment with a few bugs crawling across the floor, I saw that black room, every inch of it moving, writhing and shifting as if the walls and floor were alive, but it wasn't the room that was moving. It was the bugs. They filled the room. I'd never seen so many damn bugs all at once, and I had to stand a second staring and force myself to breathe.

It was 10:30 by that time and the whole world was dark, but I saw their black and brown bodies reflecting in the streetlight. Seeing them like that, with something so innocuous as a streetlight mingling with their wretched little selves, somehow made the scene more grotesque.

My pathetic little shaker of boric acid powder wasn't gong to do any good in here.

I backed away from the glass.

Before I could turn from the window, though, I saw something even worse.

There was something under the bugs, something big and sprawled, and when a naked knee raised up, followed by a shoulder and then a head as the body sat up, I wanted to scream.

The body stood. Bugs fell from it, clattering onto their brothers in the dark before rejoining the scurrying mass on the floor. The streetlight shone on the body's eyes, and those eyes were directed at me. The body took a step and I could already feel its fingers grabbing my shirt collar, even through the window and across the room I knew what it would feel like.

I darted away, pounded on Jerry's window, screaming "Let me in! Open up! Jerry, open the window!"

I spotted him kneeling in the closet, and when he heard me, he leapt up, slammed the door, and ran to the window.

"What is it?" he called through the glass.

"Open the fucking window!" I yelled again.

I heard Ronnie's window go up.

Jerry got the lock on his own window undone and hauled up the pane.

Before ducking inside I glanced over. The foot was on the fire escape, one hand curled around the ledge to pull himself out.

I threw myself into Jerry's apartment, telling him, "Close it, close it!"

He did, then locked it again, and before Jerry could even step away, the naked man was at the window, smiling in. His eyes found Jerry and his grin went evil, as if he knew a secret about the man and was glad to tell it to anyone who'd listen.

"Shit," Jerry said.

The man outside turned his head toward Ronnie's apartment and we heard the bugs over there growing angry, loud, clattering over the floor as they hurried toward us. I expected to see them racing under the door, gathering to cover and eat us. Roaches will eat anything.

Jerry turned toward the sound, then back to the window, and I heard him say, in a very frightened and breaking voice, "Ronnie? Please."

I looked at the man outside, and echoed Jerry.

"Ronnie? Gallagher? I thought he was dead."

Jerry looked back at me, and Ronnie followed, staring at me with dead eyes and his wicked grin. Jerry's face was the opposite, slack with fear, twitching around the mouth and eyes, ready to cry with dread.

"What did you do?" I asked Jerry.

Before he could answer, the walls began to crack. Roaches spilled from them like water, out of the walls, and down them, crawling for the floor. I had a second to wonder where they'd go once they got there, for me or Jerry, before I regained my senses, got to my feet, and grabbed Jerry's shirt.

I hauled him toward the door, threw it open, ready to get downstairs and outside, out of this place, and away. I didn't know how soon I could get the police here, but I was gonna find out.

We got as far as the hallway.

When I opened the door and made for the stairs, I saw the hall was full of bugs, too. The sound they made clacking over the floor, and worse, over each other, made my stomach turn.

From down the hall, the old woman I'd talked to earlier opened her door and yelled, "What the hell is all this noise out here? What in the world is going on?" But when she got out there and saw what it was, she screamed, flew back into her apartment, and slammed the door.

"Call the police!" I yelled, knowing she wouldn't. You live in a neighborhood like this, you see all the bad stuff that goes down day to day, and you slowly lose faith in the ones who are supposed to take care of you.

I heard something slam, then rattle behind me, and I turned in time to see Ronnie throw a punch at the window. His fist cracked the glass. Another punch and he'd shatter it. Jerry and I didn't have much choice; no matter how horrible their crunching bodies were going to sound and feel under our heels, we had to get out of here.

I needed to think, and I desperately wanted to know what the hell was going on.

"Come on." I grabbed Jerry and pulled him out. He shook loose and ran back into the apartment, nearly slipping on the moving bodies under his feet. I wondered what the hell he'd gone back inside for, until I saw him head for the closet. He pulled it open, sweeping a pile of roaches out of the way. They gathered, fell over each other, and kept on crawling, oblivious. Jerry stepped into the closet and came back out with a suitcase in each hand.

He glanced over at Ronnie who was climbing in through the open pane. I half expected rain and thunder to start any second, adding to the ominous mood, but the outside was calm and dark. Ronnie set his foot on the floor and the roaches parted for him.

I looked at him, then at Jerry. The last ten seconds had seemed to take minutes. The bugs were still spilling from the cracks in the wall, as well as coming now from under Ronnie's apartment door. The hallway was flooded with them, a glistening wave of shiny bodies.

"Let's go!" I yelled at Jerry. He'd stopped in the middle of the room and was staring at Ronnie, but my voice brought him back and he got moving again.

Bodies crunched under us as we ran for the stairs.

I was only too happy to leave the mess and weirdness behind and get outside into the nighttime city and fresh air. I got into the van and unlocked the passenger door for Jerry. He climbed in beside me, locked his door, and put one suitcase between his feet, the other on his lap.

I started the van and took off.

I didn't know how long we'd been driving or how far we'd gone, but Ronnie and his cockroaches were behind us and right then that was all that mattered.

But after a while, the silence got to me and, because it was all connected somehow, I said, "You wanna tell me what's in those cases that warrants what just happened?"

"Not really," Jerry said.

I rephrased.

"Tell me what's going on or I'm driving you back and you can deal with it on your own."

He was silent for a while, breathing and looking out the window.

Eventually he said, "Money, of course. Isn't that what it's always about? Money or women, and I don't have a woman in here."

I looked over at him, then back to the road.

I'd ended up on the other side of town, somehow, and I wondered if I should go to the police. But did I really think they could take care of Ronnie?

"I'm listening," I said.

He kept his eyes on the suitcase in his lap as he laid it all out for me. Jerry, Ronnie and some guy named Brown had done a job a few weeks back. Brown had been the brains, Jerry and Ronnie the muscle, and the money had been meant for a big man who ran a few illegal operations around town. Brown and company had intercepted the transfer, made off with the money, and should have been long gone by now. Except Brown was fingered and disposed of. Jerry and Ronnie had been pretty confident they hadn't been ID'd, but they also wanted to hold off spending any of the money just yet in case someone put two and two together and came after them.

But, like all things of this nature that involve more than one person, Ronnie got impatient and wanted to split with his half of the cash. Things got bad and he and Jerry got into it pretty bad one night. Jerry knocked him on the head and Ronnie went down. Not knowing what to do next, Jerry left him there. He took Ronnie's half of the stash, but he'd left the body.

I was glad our mother hadn't lived to hear any of this.

He said he wasn't afraid of fingerprints in the apartment or anything, he and Ronnie'd been partners a long time, everyone knew they hung out. But no one knew about the money, so hopefully, he reasoned, no one would have reason to suspect him. As simple as that reasoning was, it worked, and Jerry was never arrested. He was questioned, of course, so was everyone in the building, but never was a finger pointed at him.

"But what's with all the bugs?" I asked. "How does he do that with them? And more important, why isn't he still dead?"

"I don't know how he's still alive," Jerry said. "He was dead and gone, I know it, everyone did. And I don't know about the bugs. He'd always had roaches real bad, but he didn't seem to mind and they had only just started working their way to the rest of the building."

"I didn't see them anywhere except his place and yours."

"Maybe he was sending them to watch me."

"He can talk to them?"

"I don't know," Jerry said. "That's kind of stupid, isn't it? Talking to bugs? But so is Ronnie coming back from the dead."

I didn't tell him how I'd seen Ronnie emerge from the mass of bugs back in the dark apartment, or how I saw them part to let him walk on the floor.

"Just give him his money," I said. It was the only thing I could think of that might make this all go away. What else were we supposed to do? Kill him again? Have him arrested? Sprinkle him with boric acid powder?

"And what's he gonna do with it? Spend it in hell? No."

"Then what do you suggest? You think he's just gonna let you go like that?" I asked. "He came back for something, and I bet he's only gonna be satisfied leaving with one of two things, his money or you."

"He's not getting the money," Jerry said. "He can try to take it, but he's not getting it."

"How much is it?"

"Half a million."

I stopped the van. I stared at him.

"You're life isn't worth two hundred and fifty thousand? You could keep your half and still live better than most of the folks in this town. Just give him the money and be done with it."

"No."

I started the van again, but made a U-turn in the middle of the street.

"Where you going?" Jerry asked.

"I'm taking you back," I said. "This is stupid, you'd have more left over than I'll ever see in my life and you won't even do it to save yourself. You know I hate it when you're being an ass. You're dealing with this on your own."

He looked at me, incredulous.

"You can't take me back," he said. "He'll kill me and take the whole stash."

I glanced at him a second, then turned back to the road.

"Isn't that what you did? Grow up, man," I said. "You got yourself into this mess."

"Are you crazy?" I saw him try to get the door open, probably wanting to jump out and save himself, but the street was packed and when I swerved further to the right, he knew he wasn't getting the door open. I ran a stop sign, sped up, and ignored his pleas to let him go.

Okay, so it might not have been the most brotherly move, but I grew up with him, and anyway, I wasn't going to let him face this alone. He's still my brother, right?

When I pulled up in front of his building, he was still trying to convince me.

I turned off the engine and got out. He was trying to open the door and take off before I got to him, but I ran around, cut him off, and grabbed his shirt, hauled him from the van and shoved him toward his front door.

I took out the suitcases, held one in my hands and tossed the other one at him.

"Take that to him," I ordered. "When you come back empty-handed, you can have the other one."

He looked up at me from the stoop, like a child begging for another chance before being sent to the corner. But his eyes met mine and he knew I was serious. He wasn't going anywhere except back inside that building.

"What if I take off with this? Up to the roof, then down the fire escape in back?"

"Then I'll take this one inside and give it to Ronnie. Either way," I told him, "he's getting what he came for."

"You can't do this. It's not your money."

"Because I didn't steal it fair and square? It's not yours, either, if you want to get technical."

He stood up, put out his chest and was about to say something, but the front door opened and we both turned toward it. The entryway was covered in roaches.

"Go on," I said.

He looked at me, no longer like the punished child, now like the one who knows his parent is going away and doesn't want to be left in the classroom alone.

I shook my head, telling him I wasn't helping him, that this was his to deal with.

He picked up the suitcase and turned toward the door, but didn't step inside.

The bugs parted for him, clicking along the backs of their brothers as they moved out of Jerry's way.

In the second before he stepped in, I wondered how they'd opened the door. How did they turn the knob?

And then Jerry was walking, very slowly, almost shuffling forward like his legs were heavy steel, but he was moving at least. He climbed the two steps to the doorway, then took a deep breath before crossing the threshold. Another two steps and he was well inside.

The door closed behind him.

When Jerry was up the stairs and out of sight, I got in the van and grabbed a canister of insecticide. What was I going to do with this, spray Ronnie with it? He wasn't a cockroach himself. He wasn't even alive. But at least his army would be stopped by it. I pumped the handle and carried it with me to the fire escape. I'd told him this was his problem to deal with, but if history had shown him anything, it should have been that I'd always be there to back him up.

The fire escape was a challenge, but I finally managed to wheel a dumpster beneath it, balance the canister on the edge while I climbed on, then hit the ladder with the sprayer in one hand. Climbing a fire escape with what amounts to three or four gallons of liquid isn't something I'd recommend to anyone, and when my fingers almost slipped off the rung, I thought for sure I was going to end up with my back broken over the side of the dumpster. But I managed to hold on and finally make my way up to the first fire escape landing. From there it was a lot easier.

I had to stop once and wonder where I would find them, in Jerry's apartment or Ronnie's. It made sense they'd be in Ronnie's, though, that being where the deed had taken place.

I found Ronnie's window, crouched outside it, and tried to look in.

All I could see was dark, with specks of what I can only call "less dark" breaking through. I didn't understand it at first, then I realized I was seeing the darkness in the room through the cockroaches that covered the pane. They were crawling around each other, making what little light there was dance as it broke through the spaces between their bodies.

I imagined for a second how horrible it would be to have them crawling over my skin and I shuddered, trying to shake off invisible roaches.

I couldn't hear anything inside, but I didn't want to put my ear to the glass. If I heard anything at all then, it would only be the clack of their tiny feet against the glass. Instead, I moved as close as I could without touching the glass and tried to hear anything I could through their horrible sound.

I put the canister between my feet, held the nozzle close to me with my hand around the trigger, just in case.

I waited, for what I wasn't sure, but I knew something had to happen.

And then it did.

I heard the yelling from inside, even over the clack of the roaches on the window, and the whine of the city sounds all around me. Jerry's voice came through first.

"You're not getting it," I heard him say. "You can't take it with you, isn't that what they always say?"

Didn't I just tell him to give the man his cut of the money? Was he insane or just stupid? I wanted to kick his ass right there for not doing what I said.

"You're not just taking off with my share," Ronnie said. It was the first time I'd heard him talk. "You do what you did to me, and then expect me to let you just take it from me?"

"Life ain't cut and dried. Things happen, man. I can't help the way things went down."

"You're the one who caused it!"

I heard a noise and looked down. A roach was crawling over the bars that made up the floor of the landing, swerving toward my feet. Without thinking, I aimed the nozzle at it and fired a blast of bug spray in its face. It tumbled off the rail, tried to cling to the side, but couldn't, and vanished into the dark as it fell. The roaches on the window didn't seem to care for what I'd done, or maybe they were reacting to what was gong on inside, I couldn't tell, but they were certainly a lot angrier than they'd been. They swarmed over and around the windowpane, clacking like mad, and I thought if they'd had voices they'd have been roaring.

I moved to the window again and tried to listen, but the voices were drowned out by the roaches. All I could hear was something being smashed and a voice crying, "No, don't!"

I grabbed the canister by the handle and swung it up, shattering the window, and causing the bugs to fall out, covering my hands and arms until I shook them off in a near-panic, their tiny legs a disgusting reminder of why I usually wore the coveralls. I wished I'd left them on.

When the rush of bugs had fallen aside, I looked into the room, but could make out nothing in the dark. Whatever or whoever was in there, I stood there like an idiot, frozen, and giving anyone a clear shot at me. After a second I forced myself into the room, knocking out the jagged glass with the canister and stepping onto the pane, then into the room.

More roaches crunched under my feet.

Without seeing anything in the dark—it seemed none of the meager light from outside had found its way in—I began spraying everything in front of me, dousing anything in my path.

The bugs scurried away from the poison, but I still crushed hundreds of them as I walked through the room.

I looked around, trying to find Jerry. I was beginning to rethink sending him in here.

The room appeared empty, but it had also appeared empty when I looked in earlier and saw Ronnie rise through the bugs like a vampire leaving his coffin at night.

"Jerry!" I called out, but no one answered.

Ronnie's apartment was a one-room, like Jerry's, so when I didn't find anyone in the bathroom, I figured they'd left. Hoped, anyway. If Ronnie'd pulled the Rising From the Bugs routine in reverse, and if he'd taken Jerry with him somehow, I didn't know what I was going to do or how I could follow them.

Getting out of the apartment was a chore, having to keep the spray trained on the knob to keep the bugs off it, and still grab and turn it to open the door. In the hall, I wiped my poison-coated hand on my shirt, and went to Jerry's door. I didn't bother knocking. More bugs were shoved out of the way as I opened it.

And more bugs died under my feet when I stepped in.

The light was out, and when I used the spray nozzle to hit the switch, nothing happened. I left the door open for the hall light.

Jerry was across the room, lying on the floor, covered in swirling brown and black bodies. I couldn't tell if he was alive or not, but I prayed for merely unconscious. I hated to think I'd sent him inside only to kill him. My mother would have killed me.

Ronnie was nowhere.

I went to Jerry and kicked bugs off him, sprayed them, crushed them, anything I could.

The door slammed shut and I whirled. Something was moving toward me, I felt it, but couldn't see. The spray nozzle went out and I hit the trigger, splashing whatever was out there in poison. Roaches skittered and clacked. The thing in front of me advanced, oblivious of the spray, and knocked me in the chest. I flew backward and fell to the floor.

Bugs covered me in seconds.

I managed to stand and wiped frantically at my body to wash the bugs off it, but the second I moved one, another took its place.

I heard a groan, and Jerry was moving. Thank God he was alive.

"Get up," I told him. "Get out of here, hurry!"

I heard him moving, but saw nothing. The bugs had made it to my face.

I felt them trying to crawl into my mouth, and I rubbed my shoulder against them, crushing and smearing their tiny pus-filled bodies against my cheek and chin.

He groaned again. I heard something move on the other side of the room and I stumbled toward it in the dark, blind for the cockroaches.

The canister was still in one hand. I'd been holding it like grim death.

I reached the mass, grabbed it. It was a man, Ronnie, and I held his shoulder, took him to the ground and, through the haze of bugs on my face, I straddled him, opened his dead mouth and shoved the nozzle of the spray can down his throat. I wasn't careful like a doctor, searching for the right tube, I just slide it into his throat like a sword, not caring where it went. I heard him under me, struggling and gasping, gurgling in his throat, trying to scream. But I wasn't letting him get away. Even returned from the dead, this had to work. I found the trigger, squeezed it. With the nozzle filling Ronnie with insect poison, I stood up and held the trigger with one hand while I used the other to pump the handle, making sure the pressure never slackened, that the poison never stopped spraying.

His struggles grew more frenzied for a second, then, after his fight, he stopped moving.

The bugs clacked no longer. They seemed to fall away from my body, my skin, my eyes. I heard them hit the ground, then scurry away.

I'd done it. Whatever hold he'd had on them, it was over now that he was dead. Again.

I wiped away bug smears from my face and took a deep breath, stifled a little by the stench of insecticide filling the room, but it was still a sweet breath nonetheless.

I let go of the handle, looked around. The room was still dark and I couldn't see Jerry anywhere. I wondered if he'd gotten out while I was at work on Ronnie. Then I spotted him. He was standing near the door with the suitcase in his hand.

"I guess the whole thing is yours, after all," I said.

"You keep the other half," he said. But it wasn't Jerry. Ronnie opened the door and I saw him full length in the hall light. Naked and dead, but moving and carrying the suitcase with a quarter million dollars in it, hijacked from a big man in town. He closed the door behind him, and a second later I heard him enter and close the door of his own apartment. I didn't want to know where he was going from there.

I went to the wall, flipped the light, then remembered it didn't work.

I opened the door again and saw him there from the hall light. Jerry lay dead and straining, his eyes bulging and spit and poison spilling from his mouth.

I left the apartment, knowing I had a few hours still to get away. There was two hundred and fifty thousand dollars in my van and that would help in getting out of the country. I didn't see being able to explain any of this and expect to be believed, so I really didn't see any other option.

I got in my van and drove off. I had to get home, clean up, hide the money, then come back and do something with Jerry's body to make sure he wasn't found for at least a few days. I couldn't skip town just yet; I had a very big funeral to plan first.

C. DENNIS MOORE is 32, married with 3 children, and he lives in St. Joseph, MO, where he works as an inventory control clerk. He's published over 40 short stories, 2 novellas, a poetry collection, and edited the *Book of Monsters* anthology. His website is at www.cdennismoore.com

VEILS

Marc Paoletti

B efore the darkness took Eva Tanguay that night, she was a theater manager's dream.

In 1905, at the tender age of twenty-three, she was dubbed the "Youngest Burlesque Star of the American Stage" by the San Francisco theater press, an accolade that drew people in droves. Moreover, she was as sweet as devil's food cake to second bill performers. As a headliner, she made sure they got the money and moral support they were due, which made it easy to book other acts.

But desirability and demeanor aside, Eva's career was still very much in doubt. As a critic from *Variety* wrote, "It remains to be seen whether Ms. Tanguay's talent for titillation is as fleeting as the public urge it slakes."

A valid question for the fickle world of vaudeville, people knew. Especially Eva.

She was consumed by the question, most notably during the blackouts before her signature act. Waiting offstage in the dark, the stress of it would cause something deep inside her middle to go tight and threaten to unearth memories she could not recall but knew lurked there nonetheless. She would keep these memories at bay with thoughts of lavishly colored costumes, breathtaking set pieces, and the downpour-patter of applause until the footlights flashed and she could burst onstage to leave them behind forever.

Until the next time.

That night at the Orpheum Theater, crown jewel of San Francisco's Barbary Coast, Eva burst onstage in much the same way to perform her signature act for a crowd of boomers and the caviar set. With a blare of trumpets from the orchestra, she emerged wearing a lavender princess that adorned her ample breasts with two spangled peacocks whose bodies wrapped her narrow waist in a knee-length plume of emerald feathers.

She strutted across the proscenium, hips and feathers pumping in time with beating drums and whining strings, as she twirled a pearl necklace around her first finger. When she reached center stage she stopped, feet shoulder-length apart, and trembled like her body was coursing with current, which caused every voluptuous curve to jiggle and shake. Next she swirled her hips down in tight, languid circles until her knees splayed like the devil's horns and— boom!—shot her rump in the air to flip up the feathers and reveal the skin-colored satin underneath. Then she grabbed her breasts and spun them like propellers, so fast they almost popped free from the bodice, and as men craned forward, eyes wide, trying with mere thought to fray the thin fabric that kept those glorious mounds in check, Eva smiled.

This was *her* moment, her self-defined Tanguay Moment, when their heat, their attention, their bubbling want for her—and her aching need for them—was greatest. Her vision blurred with the joy of it, transforming their rapt, upturned faces into gauzy blooms of color like she was looking at them through a veil. She struggled to maintain the ecstasy of the moment, spinning, spinning, until her flesh began to pull and ache.

When finally she stopped, it was as though a spell had been lifted. Men smiled sheepishly at their wives, pretending to be just as intent on her closing number: a maddeningly chaste and breathless rendition of "The Whole Dam Family". And after her act was finished, while the audience gave its thunderous ovation, Eva cried to them with antic sincerity, "Thank you, my darlings! I am Eva Tanguay! I am Eva Tanguay!"

Later that night, while the theater manager was distracted with an Ethiopian act, Eva slipped out the Orpheum's backstage door. She'd heard that a house in a poorly visited area of the Coast never failed to pack them in, night after night. No other house, big-time or small, had that kind of consistency, and Eva needed to know why, as only the "Youngest Burlesque Star of the American Stage" would.

She'd changed into a silver gown slit to the hip and a zebra print waist-jacket, which she drew tightly against the San Francisco cold. She walked for several blocks along Pacific Street in the direction of the Bay, heels clicking loudly against cobblestone, until she came upon a modest vertical sign above a green pagoda that read THE EPITOME THEATRE, and below it, on a red marquee, "Continuous Late Performances starring the Dainty Dark Dancer. Seats 10¢."

Eva approached the box office attendant who was young and dressed like a Ming warrior. She slid him a dime, collected her ticket, and then sauntered between two Fu Dog statues into a lobby that was empty of people. She'd expected the same Oriental motif within, but the furnishings were discordant like someone's blind aunt had done the decorating.

In the far corner was a life-sized diorama of a tenement room with a kitchen table and black iron stove. Given its own arched niche nearby was a stuffed dog with a pile of sawdust on the floor beneath its unstitched belly. The ceiling was painted with a thick field of stars and two giant moons. And on the far wall, in large gilded letters, was the word "Become".

Eva swallowed around a knot in her throat, trying to focus past a sudden feeling of nausea. She had a sense that there was something at work here, something she did not quite understand. She admired the seeming irreverence of the place, but the lack of theme confused her. Wiping her mouth gently with her palm, she headed upstairs to where she knew the backstage area must be, intent on getting a performer's view of the show.

She kept to the shadows to hide her identity from the passing blur of stagehands, unionists and talent. But even in the shadows she walked with purpose like she belonged there—because she did and always would belong among the clutter and bustle of vaudeville. She was Eva Tanguay, after all! Youngest Burlesque Star of the American Stage!

She wove through a tight cluster of majestic elms, stepped over a bright red fire hydrant, edged around a monstrous brown camel—all props, of course, but rendered with meticulous care. She sidestepped to let a gaggle of harried-looking stagehands rush by, then walked alongside an olio of sand dunes before finding an out-of-the-way corner, stage left, behind a thick fold of curtain.

In front of her was the stage; its darkness was absolute.

No stray ribbon of light from underneath or between the closed curtains broke it, and her eyes wouldn't adjust to it no matter how hard she stared, not that she tried for very long. Looking at the darkness, she felt her middle go tight and nausea creep up from her stomach in a thick, sour snake. She swallowed, determined not to let a touch of fever—or irrational fear—prevent her from discovering what this strange little house had to offer.

She turned her attention instead to muffled sounds coming from behind the curtain: the familiar cacophony of rowdies clapping and yelling and whistling as they swarmed like ants to find their seats. She edged the curtain aside for a peek, relishing the way the coarse material tickled her fingertips—but saw no one. Just a stark, empty house.

She blinked in confusion. Where was the crowd? Where had the noise come from?

Before she could give the matter more thought, the house went dark, the curtain swished open, and footlights flooded a stage the size of a railroad car as enthusiastic horns and strings issued from an unseen orchestra.

In the center, a thin blonde woman wrangled a pack of black Chihuahuas up a tall ladder, and then ordered them TO leap though a brass hoop that she held with both hands. The dogs yipped as they launched themselves from the top step without fear, tiny legs paddling the air before landing on the polished wooden stage, nails clacking. For several moments the act remained disciplined until the dogs suddenly and simultaneously broke rank. They scampered toward Eva and then looped back toward the blonde woman in a frantic but discernable infinity pattern; they ran faster and faster until they became a black streaking blur—and then the footlights snapped off.

The stage plunged into darkness so suddenly that Eva didn't have time to shore her mental defenses. A memory welled up despite her best efforts to think only of spangled costumes, of nimble performers...*of Mother holding the small dog on the iron stove by a fistful of scruff. The dog whines softly as it stares at me with watery eyes.*

It's almost dark in the room, and so cold that my breath dissolves before my lips in weak clouds. I am eight years old. My dress is threadbare cotton and I can't stop shivering. The only thing that hurts worse than the cold is the hungry emptiness inside me. It won't go away, no matter how hard I try to think of the way father used to make me laugh. The emptiness makes my body go tight every time I move, like there's a wire lashed between my throat and belly.

I touch the dog tentatively with one hand, and then more confidently with the other. My tiny fingers sink deep into its soft black fur, and the warmth of its body spreads to mine like a secret, traveling up my fingertips to my palms, then all the way to my elbows. My sister, who is twelve, is too weak with emptiness to appreciate the surprise. She sits at the kitchen table with her cheek on the top of her hands, looking this way. The flickering candle on the table has turned her face into a dancing rictus of shadow.

I look up at Mother; her face is pale like the moon.

I feel the dog's body jerk, and then it yelps and leaps off the stove. Mother is too weak with emptiness to follow and props herself against the stove with her bloody knife-hand.

I run toward the dog, trying to ignore the wire tearing down my middle. I open the front door and pale moonlight from a window down the hall spills into the room. As the dog slip-scurries out the door, I notice that its wire—the one that connects its belly to its throat like mine—drags behind like a second tail…

Eva jerked from the memory. Streams of sweat tickled her forehead and stung her eyes. Her throat was dry and thick. She shrugged free from her jacket, let it fall to the floor, and with a sharp kick, sent it sliding away. She looked around timidly in the dark for anyone who might have a glass of water, but the backstage area was cavernous, black and empty.

The dog. She remembered the dog now. The dog and the terrible hunger. Mother had brought home the dog as a gift, and then had so cruelly taken it away.

Afterimages of the bloody trail shining silver in the moonlight lingered until she forced them away with thoughts of a bright and happy vaudeville.

Of *her* vaudeville.

Of a vaudeville that no one could take away.

Eva plucked a book of Diamond matches from her bodice, matches that she kept in case the power went out like it had in St. Louis last year when she needed to perform by candlelight. She tore free a match, struck it, smelled sulfur. She tried again and the match sputtered, barely alive.

She held up the flame; it lit only a tight circle around her hand. She extended her arm, hoping to see someone on the other side of the stage, when the match went out as though pinched by ghostly fingers.

"Vaudeville," Eva whispered to comfort herself. "My bright and sparkling vaudeville."

Before she could tear free another match, the footlights came up again to reveal an easel across the stage which read, "The Elegant Two." A man and woman, both with short hair and dressed in black evening clothes, twirled from the opposite wing, arm-in-arm, dancing a waltz. They spun like elegant dervishes, the woman's long dress brushing the stage floor with a hiss. They spun to every corner, first front, then back, before settling mid-stage, where they abruptly disrobed. The formals were attached to their bodies with ties at the waist, wrists and ankles, and fell away easily from their bodies to reveal black burlesque tights.

The performers bulged with such muscle that Eva could not differentiate between small breasts and swelling pectorals. The duo locked elbows and swung around so quickly that Eva lost track of who was who, and then one scurried up a towering metal frame to a trapeze that had appeared unnoticed during the disrobing. Eva assumed it was the male performer since it was traditionally the male's role to support a female in acrobatics.

But when she saw the performer's wide hips straddling the swing, she realized it was the woman up there with one end of a thick rope looped around her shoulders. When the woman dropped the other end of the rope to the floor, her partner scaled it halfway, and then, using his arms only, bounced and flipped with abandon.

It was like nothing that Eva had ever experienced. The revolutionary display of androgyny disoriented her, causing her vision to haze and the nausea to rise nearly into her mouth. Whenever the man's acrobatics sent him outside her circle of focus, he became a darting, whirling smudge.

Eva looked behind her with more determination this time, trying to spot by the light of the stage a unionist, a performer, anyone, but saw only props and the long shadows they created against the walls.

Back onstage, the man was hanging from the rope by his teeth now and spinning so quickly that his body seemed longer and thinner, shedding whatever masculine mass it once had.

Eva rubbed her eyes with her palms, and then was struck with a profound and growing sense of dread.

She'd always supported her fellow performers, but now realized what an empty course of action that was. For the past two years, no opening act could compare to her talent. But here, the openers were superior to any other acts she'd seen, big-time or small. And if the openers were this good, what would the Dainty Dark Dancer be like? Remain complacent, Eva thought, and she would soon be at the mercy of acts like these.

When the stage lights snapped off again she was suffused with envy and anger and thoughts of a vaudeville rightfully hers. The blackout hummed like a living thing, its influence rushing over her as though she were buried neck-deep in sand before a rising tide. It became thick and organic and *I can hear Father's breath rasping in his throat. The sheets are twisted like rope around his waist and stained dark in many places. His bare arms are nothing. His chest is nothing. Everything masculine that makes Father* Father *is nothing. His body is a pile of thin sharp angles and muted colors, not strong like Mother, who has grown thick from supporting the family at the mill.*

I am six years old.

Father's face is pale like the moon.

Mother warned me not to go into the bedroom because I might catch what Father has, but tonight I could not resist. I wonder if Father is sick from hunger, the same hunger that makes my middle hurt in a way I can't stop.

And now, in the cold and murky room, I see that his ribbed chest is no longer moving. The rasping sounds have stopped.

"Father?" I whisper, leaning over him.

He lashes out, clutching my elbow in a grip that hurts. His chest fills with air one last time, then deflates abruptly like a balloon, sending a thread of mucus across his cheek. His eyes close and his dark mouth gapes and his hand clutches my arm even tighter like he wants to pull me with him into death...

When Eva blinked from the memory her cheeks were wet with tears. Father had been so strong, and then he was nothing. She'd thought she could rely on him forever, but he'd left the family alone.

Left *her* alone.

Eva swallowed thickly, keeping the memory away with swirling thoughts of her dances—her *triumphs*—on stage. But the feeling of dread, the nausea, the blurred vision, and the assault of unearthed memories threatened to overwhelm her.

She had to leave the theater, she decided. Now.

She stepped back from the stage, and the wire between her stomach and throat pulled taut, making her gag. Steeling herself, she tried again but doubled over this time, coughing a warm, lumpy mouthful onto the floor. It was as though she was tethered to the darkness.

Eva groped around the coarse fabric of the curtain and swept her hands in large circles against the wall until she found the knotted bundle of curtain ropes. She wormed her fingers between the thick loops and pulled until her flesh rubbed raw, trying to send the curtain down, trying to do anything to sever the power the stage had over her, but the coil was too tight for her frail fingers to pry loose.

"Help!" she yelled as her eyes filled with tears. "Anyone! Please!"

She tried to run again but the tether tore at her throat and stomach so intensely that her vision went red. She gasped in hiccupping breaths and stumbled back to her place by the curtain—when a spotlight fingered the stage opposite her.

Eva could not see the Dainty Dark Dancer in whole, only a slender leg that was wrapped in black veil as it arced slowly into the light. Then the rest of her eased into view.

Eva had expected the usual shimmering colors of a seven-veiled dancer, but Dainty was a pale beauty covered in black veils that overlapped her voluptuous body in soft layers. There were no solid bits of costuming either, no cropped vest, no stiff skirt or belt with dangling tassels, only the black veils and jeweled strands that crisscrossed her pale décolletage, her ample bust, her narrow midriff. Dainty's nose and mouth were veiled too, but her eyes definitely were not; they flared like gas lamps between black-painted lids. Dainty moved with a graceful scissored step, passing one leg behind the other to land toe-heel against the polished wood until that foot supported her weight, then raising the other to scissor again. She moved across the stage smoothly with the spotlight, like her bones were made of water.

Eva watched entranced, realizing that the movements in her own act were amateurish and crude by comparison.

When Dainty reached center-stage, she raised her arms and pressed her palms together above her head. Left leg crossed behind the right, she began a liquid rotation of her torso that tightened and loosened the veils covering her. Then Dainty slowly outlined the supple contours of her body with both hands until the flip of a finger sent away the veil covering the smooth white flesh of her left thigh. Now Dainty lowered herself gently to one knee and shifted her weight onto her arm, which she slid across the floor until she lay on her side. She pushed her right leg straight up to form an L with the left, then with a flick revealed her right thigh as the free veil slithered to the floor.

Dainty shed the black veil from her stomach next and dropped it among the others like a charred snakeskin. Veil gone, the jeweled strands lay across her stomach like a sparkling caravan crossing a virgin desert. She pulled the veil from her nose and mouth, which revealed her chest too, and Eva could not decide where to look; both areas captivated her. Heavy breasts with dark areoles the size of plums or Dainty's sharp cheeks, unapologetic nose and black painted lips.

Dainty moved with an almost supernatural fluidity that Eva could only hope to match. No hip-flinger, no torso-tosser, no hooche-kooche or chorus girl would ever—could ever—compare. Even Eva's own Tanguay Moment paled before Dainty's darkly ethereal grace.

Eva wanted Dainty's talent. Craved it. Felt her middle go tight with the thought of owning it. Knew it would prevent other acts from taking away the vaudeville that was rightfully hers.

One veil remained on Dainty's body now, the seventh veil, and it cradled her hips. Eva crouched low on her haunches and watched, hypnotized. She found herself saying in a literal stage whisper, "Pull off the last veil, Dainty. Please, pull it off…"

Dainty heard the plea and stopped dancing. She stood slowly, looking at Eva, pale skin gleaming in the spotlight. Without breaking eye contact, Dainty reached behind her back and produced a prop head. It was the Baptist's head—pale, longhaired and bearded, eyes rolled up with the shock of decapitation, crimson felt decorating the stump.

Dainty held the head in the flat of her left hand, and then stepped out of the spotlight toward Eva. The darkness swallowed her. Eva could hear only her own ragged breathing and the slow slapping of bare feet coming closer when the white flesh of Dainty's face and the prop head faded up from the gloom before her like twin pale moons, *like the faces of Father and Mother when I was a toddler.*

Strong hands from one of them cradle my back. I see their moon-like faces fade as they lower me…where? I twist and see a box below. It's dark in the room, but the mouth of the box is darker still.

As the hands lower me into the dark mouth of the box, the cardboard edges tower around me. My vision tunnels. My face grows numb with cold. The hands slide from my back and my head bumps the ground, sharply hurting. My tiny fists flail and hiss against the stiff cardboard. And then I feel a grinding underneath my back as the pale round faces of Mother and Father blur away.

They are pushing the box, I realize. My whole body shakes as the box vibrates across the floor. I can see only a square of gray above me until the box slides underneath the iron stove, and then the gray goes black.

I hiccup in fear, inhale thick clumps of dust. I feel cobwebs and a crawling tickle across my face.

Have they pushed me underneath the stove to keep me warm?

Or to cast me away?

There is a sudden loud banging in the stove above me. The black iron turns a dull red. Heat washes down, singeing my face and sucking the breath from my lungs so that I can't cry for the strong hands to pluck me free...

Eva watched as Dainty used her free hand to pinch open the mouth of the prop head. The stage was dark but the open mouth of the head was darker still.

"Little Egypt?" Eva asked, though she knew it wasn't.

"I am the true daughter of Babylon," Dainty told her, and held out the head. Eva took the head in both hands and felt warm rivulets run from her palms to her forearms to drip from her elbows.

Eva knew what Dainty wanted her to do. Dainty wanted her to do what every seven-veiled dancer did with the severed head of the Baptist.

Do it, Dainty's eyes promised, *and I will always be with you.*

Eva looked into that darker than dark mouth and saw the pale face of her mother. Of her father. Both faces were sunken and stricken with fear. She saw herself there too, at the mercy of the cold, the stifling heat, the hunger, the dark.

I will never go back to that place, she vowed. *I will never be stolen from or abandoned or cast away again.*

She brought the prop head level with her own, and for years after that night, critics, the public and performers would wonder what had happened to Eva Tanguay.

Variety would ask, "What change has possessed this once gentle young performer?"

The New York Dramatic Mirror would describe her as the "Woman-o-War of Vaudeville" and note on more than one occasion that her eyes "flared with a fierce and disturbing darkness."

American Vaudeville would label her demeanor as "assault and battery."

She would be called The Cyclonic One.

The Tempestuous One.

Lady Dynamite.

Dragon in a Sequined Dress.

She would brutalize other performers, pushing one down a

flight of stairs, choking another almost to death and slamming the head of another into a brick wall.

But her talent would become irreproachable and timeless, particularly her "Dance of the Seven Veils" that featured serpentine, almost inhuman flexibility, and a seemingly live head of John the Baptist that leered at her from a silver platter.

The Courier-Journal would write, "The originality of her method, songs and costumes has put Eva Tanguay in a class separated from any other vaudevillian. She will be with us for a long time to come."

That night, the Epitome Theatre house lights came up and the seats were full of people with pale, blurred faces. Eva could feel their heat, their attention, their bubbling want for her. Dainty stood watching her too, face blurred, teeth shining white from between black lips. Eva brought the head of the Baptist closer. She looked deep into its darker than dark mouth and thought, *I am Eva Tanguay. I am Eva Tanguay.* Then she pushed her tongue into the darkness and through it.

MARC PAOLETTI is a graduate student at Columbia College earning his MFA in fiction. Before moving to Chicago, he wrote advertising copy in Los Angeles. In addition, he worked in the film industry as a licensed special effects pyrotechnician (he blew things up and got paid for it). His recent fiction can be found in the anthologies *Hair Trigger 27*, *The Book of Voices*, *My Angels and Demons at War*, *Cold Flesh*, and *The Best Underground Fiction Volume 1*.

PERHAPS I'M NOT DARK ENOUGH

Stephanie Simpson-Woods

Nightfall was approaching as Joanie stared at the blank document on her computer screen. She was trying to write a scary story for a contest she stumbled upon over the Internet. Not only would she gain recognition, but she would also win $100. It didn't seem like much, but it would definitely pay for a few months of Internet service. Her eyes fixed on the screen in front of her, she tried to dig deep into the darkest part of her mind. The more she tried to prod, the more distracted she became.

Her mind dwindled to her cozy afternoon watching the birds from a paint-chipped rocking chair on her front porch. She remembered a striking Blue Jay toying with a small Finch at a feeder she had put in her yard last spring. She also recalled watering the flourishing patch of flowers she had planted after the last winter frost.

"Hmm," she said with a sigh. "Perhaps I'm not dark enough to write such stories."

Joanie looked through her office window, out into the darkness that blanketed the sky. She tried to visualize something grotesque and evil peeping in: a flesh-hungry zombie or a moaning, white ghost. Instead, she noticed her neighbor, Mr. Williams, turning on the sprinkler system he had installed so his lush, untarnished lawn would get a refreshing drink of water.

An hour had passed by and all Joanie had typed were two words: 'Nightfall was'. As much as she brainstormed, nothing more came to mind. Her inner darkness was about as evil as a beef stew simmering in its own juices for seven hours on low in a crock-pot. "That would make a great meal for dinner tomorrow night," she said aloud as if it were the most brilliant idea she had come up with all evening. Sad to say, it was.

Slightly aggravated with her thoughts, Joanie went into the kitchen, fixed herself a cold glass of hand-squeezed lemonade and grabbed a few of the chocolate chip cookies from a batch she had carefully whipped together the evening before. She took a bite of one and smiled. The cookie was still moist and chewy, just like she liked them.

Returning to her chair, Joanie continued to munch on the cookies while she poked her brain for a horrific story idea. She turned her eyes from the screen once again and looked at a picture of her boyfriend, Alex.

Alex and Joanie had met six months ago at a bluegrass festival which was held a few miles from her town each year. She pictured the two of them dancing to a local band they had gone to see a week ago in a small pub the two of them frequented.

"I haven't called him tonight," Joanie mumbled to herself, running her fingers through her short, blonde hair.

Joanie shook her head out of frustration and looked down at her keyboard. She wanted to feel the light touch of the keys on her fingertips, but not one good, scary idea would push its way from her brain and into her thoughts.

Joanie left her station for the second time that evening and snatched her white, lacy apron from a hook in the kitchen. She figured she was wasting her time thinking and should go on with her nightly routine.

Apron tied snug around her tiny waist, Joanie walked down into the cold, dreary basement she visited nightly. Stumbling through the darkness, she finally found the chain to the lone light bulb that brightened the quarters.

"How are you tonight?" Joanie asked the strange gentleman she had gagged and shackled to the concrete wall that surrounded the basement. "I guess you can't talk, can you? Silly me. I knew better. Now if I could only find that…"

She removed the floral, cotton fabric she had spread over a card table in the corner of the basement and picked up a small handsaw.

"Here it is! I bought this baby at a yard sale for $1 and it saws like a pro," she snickered, moving toward the bound gentleman.

She pressed the sharp, tooth-like blades of the handsaw against his arm and smiled at the gentleman.

Squirming in the shackles, the gentleman howled through the cloth handkerchief Joanie had stuffed into his mouth earlier that night after she graciously invited him into her home when he stopped by to talk her into buying insurance.

"Oh. Don't worry. I will make this quick. I promise. I still have to go upstairs and find my dark side so I can write a story."

Once again, she smiled at the gentleman, quickly sawing the blades back and forth against his arm until she got to the bone, the man's flesh splitting in all directions. "See! That wasn't so bad was it?"

The man screamed as his sweat dripped into the bloody wound on his arm. He looked down at the cut, his breath quickening behind the gag.

"Now, now, don't be such a big baby. I hope you have life insurance," she said with a giggle, walking away from the man and taking hold of another instrument from the table: an axe.

Lifting it over her small head, she brought it down above him, chopping straight through the bone on his arm, it falling to the floor, his blood splashing onto her apron. "I should start investing in red aprons. These white ones never last through the night."

She put the axe down, picked up her handsaw, and then grinned at the whimpering gentleman. "Please don't cry. It's distracting. Besides, I only have one arm, two legs and your head left to dismantle. The less you distract me the quicker I can get back to my story."

Joanie spent the rest of the early evening removing the man's ligaments piece by piece. When she finished, she cleaned herself up and returned to her computer.

"Now then, where was I? Nightfall was…approaching," she said as she stared at the blank document on her computer screen. "Yeah, that sounds perfect."

STEPHANIE SIMPSON-WOODS is the author of the novel *I.M. Internet Message* and a variety of shorts on the web and in print. For more information, please visit her website at www.stephaniesimpsonwoods.com.

DEMON DREAMS

Lavie Tidhar

Slasher and the Uplink Twins

Slasher is standing outside the Dope Emporium talking to the Uplink Twins. It's raining, thick heavy drops that coat the street in an oily film and burrow into Slasher's clothes. The Twins, replenished in their black waterproof longcoats, merely look uncomfortable.

'Two for a buck,' says Upload, grinning and showing crooked teeth.

'Three for a buck,' says Download, scowling.

'It's a one-on-one situation,' Slasher says, flexing his razorblade fingers. 'One buck, one Demon Dream, and I'm doing you a favour.'

The Uplink Twins look at each other and nod simultaneously. 'Sort it out,' they say in unison.

'Done.' Slasher accepts the money, palms it and drops it into a hidden pocket in his trousers.

He leaves the Twins standing in the shadow of the Dope Emporium and gets on his bike, revving up the engine and shooting away in a cloud of dust.

'I want to kill him,' Upload says.

'Kill him later.' Download twitches, ready to go in and get some chemical shit into his system. 'After he delivers.'

Uplink shrugs, and they walk into the Emporium.

Slasher

He drives through Rape, through Jungle, through Blitzkrieg and Memory Lane, arriving at last in a dilapidated part of town where the eternal night seems deeper. There are almost no shadows, only a darkness as thick as sin and just as unpalatable.

Slasher stops at the end of Mortal Road, at the last house, which he cannot see.

It is a construction of inky darkness, as intangible as dreams.

This is where the last Demon lives.

Slasher walks through what he has came to think of as the door, an invisible portal into Pandemonium. He feels the temperature drop on his skin, which feels cold and clammy, as if scales are rubbing against it. The Demon keeps unpleasant concubines, some male and some female, but none entirely human. He brushes them off and walks further, until the faded outline of a grand staircase can be, not seen, perhaps, but imagined in the distance.

He stops before the stairs and stands, waiting. Time passes.

Later, the staircase shakes, as if something large, something unwholesome, walks down it. There is a smell of vanilla and cloves, cloying Slasher's senses.

I am tired, Slasher, the Demon announces. His voice echoes directly in Slasher's earbones, jarring. *What is it this time?*

Slasher doesn't move a muscle. Around him, the excitement of the concubines is palatable, but they keep their distance from him now that their master is awake. 'Twins,' he says. Words come out slowly and with an effort in the presence of the Demon. 'Want. Dream.' He takes a deep breath. Cinnamon. 'For Hokusai.'

Paid? The Demon's voice is uninterested.

'Yes.'

Hokusai, the Demon muses, *big fellow, isn't he? Hokusai...*

The stairs shake once more as he begins his invisible ascent. *So tired, Slasher. So...tired.*

'Sweet dreams,' Slasher breathes out as the smell of spices slowly evaporates around him. He turns his back on the staircase and walks quickly away, slashing through the air with his razors. The concubines slither, scales rubbing against his skin, fading into nothing when he slashes. They seem amused.

He steps into the true night outside, where rain continues to fall.

'I've got to stop doing this shit,' he says into the night. He gets on his bike and drives off, away from the Dark Slums.

The Uplink Twins

Upload is fucked.

He and his twin are sitting in an ill-lit private room inside the arcade. Download is smoking through a sheesha pipe, a noxious green smoke that turns his eyes, literally, into mirrors, silver balls in which the room, the smoke and the two naked Sex Workers are reflected eerily.

There are two Sex Workers, one for Upload, one for Download. The Twins have different tastes.

One is a man, his arms and torso black, his legs and penis white and somewhat shrivelled. There is a tattoo of a crocodile on his chest, looking somewhat like a pineapple, and a nametag identifying him, no doubt appropriately, as Janus.

The other Sex Worker is partially a woman, with a giant backside that glints wetly in the dim light, as if reflective oils were carefully massaged into it. Download likes butts, collects them like pinned butterflies, lets out his teenage angst on them and moves on to the next one. So far, only his fingers and his tongue have made the acquaintance of the woman's ass, and he is too wasted to expand the effort for further exploration involving his dick. Whatever nametag the woman carries is hidden, since she is sitting folded over, her ample buttocks facing the twins, her face resting on a cushion.

Download worries about his twin. Upload is so wasted he is close to dead: his body is melting and changing as more green smoke gets sucked into his unresponsive mouth, the pipe having come with pump for just the sort of occasion a patron was unable to continue by himself.

He is metamorphosing, skin turning into dull metal section by section, as if a burning metal is slowly pulled over his body. His Sex Worker, Janus, sits there looking bored, talking to the woman Sex Worker in a low voice. She nods on her cushion, from time to time, and farts, a low whistle that makes Download pause each time.

'Come on,' he says to Upload rather uselessly, 'I think you've had enough.' The air pump delivers more green smoke into Upload's lungs.

'Fuck this.' He attempts to kick the sheesha pipe and finds himself held up by the two Sex Workers.

'No damage to Emporium property, please,' the woman says in a pleasant voice. Her hands grip Download's like clamps.

'Sure, sure,' Download mumbles, and they release him and return to their previous positions: Janus looking bored on a stool, the woman's ass back in Download's face.

There is nothing he can do. Sergei The Undertaker doesn't like a mess, and you don't argue with Sergei if you value either your drugs or your life. Download shrugs and buries his nose in the woman's moist asshole, running his tongue against her sphincter and jerking off in slow, unhurried motions.

Upload is nearly all metal now. Janus snorts and gets up to leave. His services will not be required for the moment.

Slasher and the Professor

'Come in, come in,' the Professor says. His eyes stare vacantly into the air above Slasher's head, and he makes no move to leave the doorway.

Slasher sighs and pushes the Professor inside. 'Your salts, professor?' he says in a suffering voice.

'Huh? Oh yes, quite.' The Professor roots around in a cupboard, squinting, until he locates a small bottle of pills. 'Salts, yes, ha ha,' he says and measures out carefully two pills into his palm.

Slasher hands him a glass of water and the Professor swallows them quickly.

They wait.

'Oh, hello, Slasher,' the Professor says after a few minutes. 'Didn't see you come in. Would you like a tea or a coffee?'

Slasher smiles. 'No, thanks, we haven't got time for that now, Professor. I just came back from the Demon.'

The Professor's face lights up. 'Wonderful, wonderful! You know,' he says suddenly, his voice changing, 'you really don't have to call me Professor all the time. My real name is Morris Isaacovich.'

Slasher has heard this before. He likes the Professor, better than most of the denizens of University Mile, where the drifters and thinkers and the mad congregate. He likes the Professor, but there are rules.

'There are rules,' he says, in explanation. He shrugs.

The Professor shrugs. 'Pulp,' he says. There is venom in his voice. 'Bloody pulp, the lot of it.'

'I understand.' Slasher nods, waiting patiently for the outburst to finish.

'Anti-Semites, the lot of them. That Lovecraft son of-a-bitch, and his bloody Ewers.'

Slasher has no idea what the Professor is talking about, and time is running. The Demon is likely to start Dreaming soon, and they must follow Hokusai to find out how it goes.

The Professor calms down when Slasher says that, and nods, and puts on a coat. 'Bloody stereotype,' he mutters as he looks in the mirror. White hair sticking out of an aged face, a frailness underlain by purpose and spiritual strength. 'Bloody stereotype.' Slasher nods.

They leave, closing the door behind them.

Hokusai

He is the wrong man at the wrong place. The time, also, is wrong. Hokusai is a man pursued by demons, belittled by an intrinsic honesty, a barbaric sort of moral code that does him no good in this spatial and temporal anomaly of an urban landscape.

He sips his whiskey and wishes he could stop traversing narrative search spaces, and get laid.

There is a knock on the door, and a Blonde enters. Hokusai shudders. 'What do you want?' he says. 'There is nobody here?'

The Blonde smiles, a grotesque expression which makes her face appear even worse, as if an additional scar has been opened on her mutilated face.

'Nobody, or No Body?' she teases in a husky voice. Hokusai crosses himself. 'What do you want?' he asks again, tiredly.

'A Knight,' she says, promptly. 'A Knight in shining armour. A man who isn't tarnished or afraid. A man who isn't mean.' Her left eye cries blood.

Up to this point business is as usual. It's a charade that happens every day as he sits at his one-room office and waits for clients who never come. Only the Blondes, one every day, like bloody clockwork. They have picked him, the Blondes, as soon as he moved on their turf, and have since turned the morning's humiliation into a show, a sketch which never failed to amuse them.

They could have killed him as soon as look at him, but they laughed at him instead.

Then the usual script changes. Usually, the Blonde (whoever's turn it is) drags it out for a few more minutes, then kicks him around the room for a while, punching him about, that sort of thing, then leaves. To make it bad, they sometimes fuck him, which is worse.

Now, the Blonde's face melts and oozes onto the carpet, and in its stead is a smaller head, a baby's head, misshapen and pale and with two mischievous eyes that look at him in amusement.

'Find me,' it says. 'Find me, Hokusai.'

Then the head disappears, and the Blonde's body topples to the floor. Hokusai stares at the floor in horror. They are going to kill him. Really kill him, this time. The Blondes are not merciful. He almost shits himself, but appearances must be preserved, narrative compatibility must be compliant with the Dreaming. He coughs, his throat dry, but manages to collect enough phlegm to spit on the corpse.

'L-Looks like I g-got myself a c-case,' he says.

Slasher and the Professor

It is raining again, an acid rain that burns and turns the streets green with slime. Slasher and the Professor ride through the rain to the end of University Mile, passing through Blood and Gore and Sunshine until they reach the border of their destination.

Here, the walls are decorated in faeces and blood, random graffiti scribblings of the passers-by and the Child Gangs.

'I can feel it,' the Professor says, excited. 'The Dream. It's thickening.'

Slasher nods. Reality is shifting in subtle ways, marking the Dreaming of the last Demon, his failing grasp on the matrices of the city's continuum. Slasher lights up a cigarette and they wait by the wall as the Dream coalesces around them.

'Tell me about the Dreaming,' Slasher says. He likes hearing the Professor talking about it, which he does nearly every time they meet.

The Professor needs no further encouragement. 'Once,' he says in the tone of a storyteller, 'once there were angels.' His voice shakes with emotion. 'A plethora of angels, asleep in the heavens, Dreaming together a beautiful world. A hive-mind, if you will, of such power that their Dreaming took hold of the flimsy material of space and time and moulded it to fit the Dream.'

Slasher drags on his cigarette thoughtfully, blowing smoke rings against the wall of blood and shit. The Professor goes on, heedless.

'But slowly, in the passage of time, more and more angels stopped Dreaming. Perhaps they woke up—so they Wakers say—perhaps they simply slept on but were no longer able to Dream. Either way, the remaining angels became bitter by the dwindling in their numbers, became angry, became lost.'

Slasher nods and smokes, nods and smokes.

'The angels began to Dream themselves into the world they had created, walking its passageways even as they changed it by their anger and hate. They began to interact with it, and become lost in it, and more and more of them stopped Dreaming altogether.'

'The world changed,' Slasher states, grounding his cigarette into the wall.

'Yes,' the Professor agrees, 'the world changed. It's become smaller, and worse, and unimaginative. A universe had shrunk into the size of a city, peopled by absurdities and stereotypes, divided into parts and shuffled like a child's toy.

'And now, the last angel, the last Demon, is Dreaming his last Dreams before he, too, will stop. No longer Dreaming the world, only small strands of the whole, single narratives. You see,' he says earnestly to Slasher, 'the future of the world is in our hands, Slasher. Only we can save it.'

Slasher nods and lights up another cigarette and they wait as the Dream takes shape around them. They wait outside Dead Babies for Hokusai.

The Uplink Twins

The Sex Worker is looking bored, and Download is panting as he rams his cock in and out of her ass. Upload's skin colour is slowly returning to dirty green, the silver fading.

'Hungry,' Upload says. Download pants.

'Want to kill someone,' Upload says in a petulant voice. 'Let's go.'

Download moves faster and faster, trying to reach a climax despite his brother's return to annoying consciousness at just the wrong moment. 'Shut up,' he says through gritted teeth. 'Shut up, shut up.'

'Fuck you,' Upload moves to sit by the Sex Worker's face. They begin a conversation in low voices, ignoring Download's increasingly frantic sounds.

'Is he always like this?' The Sex Worker asks. Upload waves his hands in the air. 'Yeah, ' he says. 'Give him a bit more time and he'll be done.'

'Who are you going to kill?' she asks curiously. Upload winks at her and taps his nose. 'Why, you want to make some money at the bookies?'

She nods. 'Of course,' she says, 'if the tip is good.'

'Slasher,' Upload says. He imitates shooting a gun. Bang. 'Slasher and, if the Dream doesn't do it for me, Hokusai.'

'Why?' she asks, making a mental note to bet against the twins if they think of taking on Slasher. 'Why Hokusai?' She knows Hokusai, the mangy so-called Investigator who frequents the Emporium once a day like clockwork after his beating by the Blondes. 'What's he done to you?'

Upload taps his nose again, while behind the Sex Worker Download is screaming as he slams against her ass. 'No reason,' he says at last. 'Just don't like him, really. Besides,' he adds as Download stops screaming at last and lies spent on the couch, his flaccid dick covered in shit, 'it will piss the Blondes off if I kill their little toy, wouldn't it?'

The Sex Worker stands up and stretches. Her nametag, finally revealed, says Hi I'm Lynn. 'Thanks for the tip,' she says, 'I'll put a bet on as soon as you're off.'

'You do that,' Upload says. 'You do that.'

Lynn smiles and resolves to bet a sizeable portion of her morning's income that these two will be dead by the end of the day. As for Hokusai, she'll have to check the odds first.

'Yes,' says Download. He is stroking his dick absentmindedly. 'You do that.'

Hokusai

Hokusai can tell something is wrong. He is very perceptive, attuned for the subtle interplay of disjointed narrative and spatial disintegration.

Now he moves like a man possessed, abandoning the prone body of the Blonde in his office, descending the stairs, and driving away in his car, a gray and rusting box spray-painted on the sides by the Child Gangs.

'Little bastards,' he murmurs and speeds away. He passes through Squalor, through Love, along the shores of the Dead Lake, in which the bodies of U-boats float belly up in the icy, dark water, surrounded by the gaseous remains of what have once been people.

He drives through Alphaville and Necroville and Abundance, and all along the suburbs until he reaches the wall of Dead Babies.

A luminous green arrow is painted on the wall, with the word THIS WAY alongside it. Hokusai follows it, cursing as he steps in shit and pools of dark, luminous piss. There is a thickness in the air around him, like an infusion of disturbed sleep.

Hokusai reaches at last a door in the wall. There is a doll nailed to, a baby doll, with a knife holding it against the door through its chest where spray paint the colour of dry blood covers it like a blanket.

Dead Babies.

He pushes the door and enters.

Dark blue skies, as if just past sunset (though sunsets have been gone from the city for a long, long time), a breeze of cool air, and green shrubs and trees and gravel.

Hokusai breathes in the fresh air and worries at the implications. He has never been to Dead Babies before, and expected something different. Something didn't feel right.

He takes a few steps further, and his foot sinks into something soft and unpleasant.

'Ah', Hokusai says, looking down. Despite the revulsion rising in him, the bile threatening to come up his throat, at least this is more within the confines of the narrative.

Hokusai's foot sinks into the belly of a body, causing the eyes to pop in the face, and gas to escape from the rotting stomach. He lifts his foot up carefully, trying to wipe his shoe on something more solid, dislodge some of the corpse's rot and stench of it.

He doesn't find one.

As he looks around him, he sees the reason for the green, healthy shrubs. Their roots are sunk into the ground, which is itself composed of thousands of still bodies, and as he watches they suck noisily at the ground. A nearby tree waves its roots in the air, red and moist, with suckers the size of eyes on them. They nearly hit Hokusai.

He wants to leave. Right now.

But the door through which he came is gone, and the Dream now takes possession of his actions.

Step by step he moves through the dead bodies, breaking a finger there, smashing a head there (there, where the brain oozes out of the broken skull like cream through a tube), sinking deeper and deeper into the masses of dead bodies.

He throws up, once, all over his clothes, the retch of alcohol and canned food mixing strangely with the smell of dead bodies.

Then he plods on.

Slasher and the Professor

As if on cue, a door appears on the wall besides Slasher.

He taps the Professor, who startles, and points silently to the door.

'Quite, quite,' the Professor says, looking shifty. 'It's just that...' he hesitates, then says, 'the dead bodies, you know?'

Slasher is busy checking his gear. He finishes sharpening two large knives which he tucks back into his trousers, and gives the Professor a reassuring pat on the back. 'You know how it is,' he says.

The Professor takes a deep breath. 'Of course.'

'The Dreams today,' says Slasher, 'are like contract killings, you know? They're bad for a *reason*.'

'Come on,' the Professor says. He walks to the door and gives it a violent kick. 'Let's do it.' The door falls to the ground inside Dead Babies, and the Professor steps over it, kicking the baby doll away from him.

'I've got a bad feeling about this,' Slasher mutters to himself, and follows the Professor inside.

The Uplink Twins

'I've got a bad feeling about this,' Download says. He's pissed off at his brother. 'I don't particularly want to kill anyone right now, you know? First you get wasted on that green shit, then you disturb me as I engage in sexual intercourse, and now you're dragging me along to kill some people you have a grudge against. I mean, really.'

'Fuck you,' Upload says. His body twitches, and the two cannons in his hand respond, shooting a blaze of bullets in random directions.

'Besides,' Download says, 'it's as dangerous as anything to get anywhere near a Dream, you know that.'

'I want to see Hokusai suffer,' Upload says. 'Suffer, suffer, suffer.' Another twitch, and more bullets fly from his guns. 'And that little shit Slasher. I know he's going to be around there somewhere. Watching like the little perv he is.'

'Oh, fuck it,' Download says. 'What the hell.' They get into their vehicle, an old-fashioned rocket ship graced with fins, jet outlets and other sexually suggestive and technologically redundant components.

The strap themselves in and lift off the ground with a quiet hum. 'How does it do that?' Upload asks.

'Grav-jets? Anti-gravity?' Download suggests.

'Nah. No such thing, anti-gravity,' Upload says. 'That would require discarding the idea of an Einsteinian space-time continuum in favour of some fanciful, lurid and essentially non-workable hypothesis.'

'Oh.'

They fly over Rape and Jungle, past Memory Lane and into the Wilderness Gardens, where Zombie corps work day and night, battling the constant growth of the Eternal Tree. They weave through its branches and continue over Soldier Town and the Missile Silo.

Soon, they can see the clouds of Dreamstuff as they near Dead Babies, a bending and a twisting of reality, a broken darkness which is the sky.

They fly over the wall and settle down, compressing several tons of dead bodies into a pulp.

Hokusai

As he walks through the mire of dead bodies Hokusai changes.

At first he doesn't notice, but soon the changes become obvious: the extension of the arms into slime-dripping tentacles, the bulging of the forehead, the sharp, metallic extensions on his back. Hokusai accepts the changes as just one more facet of the nightmare he is in. His detective-mind analyses the problem and suggests to him, somewhat nervously, that he is under the influence of a Demon Dream.

Hokusai accepts this with the true logic of a Dreamer, and plods on through the stench, which is now somewhat flavoured with scents of cloves and cinnamon. If anything, this new shape his body is busy assuming is quite comfortable for this particular environment: like the trees and the shrubs, his arms now plunge into the mass grave and suck nutrition away happily. His legs, now growing strong, hard flippers, move more rapidly through the bog, and the fins on his back slice through the soft tissue of flaccid bodies like thin, sharp razors.

Hokusai glories in the new sensations as the scent of cloves intensifies. Somewhere close, he thinks, lies the solution to his immediate problem.

He smiles happily and dives into the ground of rotting bodies.

Slasher

Somewhere in Dead Babies Slasher loses the Professor. It happens gradually, as they wander deeper into the Dream.

'There's a method to it,' Slasher says, holding on to a tenacious tree root and swinging on it to the next clump of trees. 'You don't want to step on the ground if you can help it.'

But the Professor is gone.

'Professor?' he says. 'Morris?'

There is no answer. Slasher worries at this, looking up into a sky now burning like an image of hell. The scent of cinnamon is overpowering.

'Demon? Is this part of the Dream? Demon?'

There is no answer. Slasher grabs another tentacle as it comes out of the soggy ground with a sucking sound, and jumps with it to the next tree. His hands are covered in the slime of body fats and stomach juice and blood.

'Shit.'

Somewhere inside Dead Babies, Slasher knows, the core of the Dream is taking shape. Centring on Hokusai, yes, but now it seems that the Professor has been sucked in as well, and he himself is not far behind. He wonders who else may be attracted to the Dream, like flies to a rotting fruit, before it is all over.

A tentacle swishes past him and he slashes it with his blades, absentmindedly. Time to move on, then. Slasher jumps on another tree, slips, and nearly falls into the open bellies of two twins.

'Shit!'

He grabs at the nearest branch and hauls himself up. Twins. Interesting. He checks his equipment again, making sure the knives and guns are all still strapped securely, and heads deeper into Dead Babies.

The Uplink Twins

'This is fucking disgusting,' Download says, looking at the splattered brains on the windshield. 'I ain't going down there. No way.'

'Don't be a such a fucking pussy,' Upload straps more guns onto his person, so that he looks like a walking arsenal. 'Grab an Incinerator and let's go.'

They descend the stairs of their craft onto the ground, initiating the seals on their outfits, which transform into self-sustained scuba suits. The two brothers sink slowly into the ground and begin swimming through it, red flashes marking their progress as they blast a path through the rotting bodies.

'Are we there yet?' Download broadcasts on the suits' private link.

'Shut up.'

They swim through blood and shit and rot and intestinal gas, towards the centre of the Dream.

Hokusai and the Professor

Hokusai is surprisingly happy.

His new body swims through the bodies like a shark, and soon he reaches dry land. It is an island, dark and silent in the middle of the bog, like a cancerous growth on the flesh of the earth.

Hokusai's body is changing again, slowly, his skull elongating, his suckers turning into large, hairy arms, his fins to the legs of a reptile. He looks about him, sniffs the air with his new, enlarged snout, and nearly gags on the stench of vanilla pods.

'Come on!' he screams suddenly, scaring himself. 'Show yourself, *Demon*! Come on!'

'Shut up.'

Hokusai jumps as a small figure materialises out of the trees to his left. 'Who the fuck are you?'

'Morris Isaacovich.' The Professor's voice has lost its hesitation, its confusion, the characteristics Slasher is familiar with. Now, it is cool, calculated. In his hand he is holding a small handgun, pointing at Hokusai. 'You can call me Professor.'

Hokusai chews on this. 'What are you doing in my Dream?' he asks at last.

The Professor smiles. 'I'm glad to see you're not as stupid as you look,' he says. 'How did you know this is a Dream?'

Hokusai shrugs. 'The smell. Cloves, vanilla, cinnamon. The shape-shifting. The whole setup stinks. So, let me ask you again: what the fuck are you doing in my dream?'

'My,' the Professor says, 'I believe you're enjoying yourself.' He smiles nastily and throws Hokusai his gun. 'Take this. You're going to need it.'

Hokusai lets this one past. The gun feels like a toy in his now-massive hands. 'Why?' he says at last.

But the Professor is no longer there.

Slasher and The Uplink Twins

When the twins reach the island, Hokusai is gone. They inflate their suits and float over the bodies, stepping on heads and arms as they climb up to dry land.

'Something not right,' Uplink says. He points one of his guns at the mass of dead bodies and begins shooting, picking up heads which have remained whole, zapping them so they explode like moist, eaten-through fruits.

'Yeah,' Downlink says. 'You.' He joins his brother in shooting dead bodies, but you can tell his heart isn't in it. 'Can we go now?'

'Not quite,' Slasher says, stepping from within the hidden confines of the trees. He shoots both twins, stunning them, and methodically strips them from their weapons as they lie unconscious on the ground. Then, 'Wake up,' he says, slapping the two until they come around. Slasher's razors are very close to the twins' throats, a fact which is very clear to them. They speak without moving their heads even a fraction.

'Slasher.'

'Boys.' Slasher examines the Twins critically. 'What are you two fuckheads doing here?'

'None of your fucking business,' Download manages, then squeals as Slasher's hand cuts hard across his neck. 'Urgh...'

'You don't know what you're messing with,' Slasher says quietly. 'I should do you a favour and slit your throats now. What do you say?'

Download gurgles. Upload stares up at Slasher with hatred in his eyes. 'What do *you* want, dick-fingers, is what I want to know.'

Slasher smiles. 'What do I want? World peace, a house in the suburbs, sex with Japanese twins.' His razor blades press harder on the Twins' throats. 'Every other fucking cliché in the fucking book. What I want right *now*, however, is for the two of you to get the *fuck* out of this Dream before you regret it. Believe me, you'd much prefer simple, natural death to the shit that's going to happen to you if you stay. Understood?'

The Twins are outgunned. Slasher lifts his blades slightly and they nod. 'Good. Now get the fuck out of here.'

The Twins get off the ground meekly and wander off back into the swamp of the dead.

'Kill him?' Upload broadcasts on the suit's private channel.

'Fuck that,' Download's voice has a murderous quality to it. 'We're going to Mortal Road. We're gonna waste the fucker Demon.'

They wade through the mush of bodies to their craft.

Slasher

Slasher is following Hokusai at a safe distance. The monstrous figure has left Dead Babies, crashing through the wall as if it were made of brittle paper, and has been moving steadily in the same direction. Hokusai's body kept changing all the while, as Dreamstuff surrounded him like a cloud of flies. Fins, tentacles, spider legs, wings of various kinds, sprouting and dying on his changing body.

They pass unnoticed through Rape, where bodies, like an image of the condemned, hang naked and broken from rusting pipes and wooden stakes. They are surrounded by shadowy figures, gangs of men, women, and things which are neither, both beast and human. The naked bodies writhe in pain as they are penetrated, over and over, with organs, with metals, with medieval implements.

They scream, continuously.

Hokusai wanders through it all with only one thing in mind. He ignores the crowds, heading through the centre and border of Rape.

Slasher follows.

They cut across Blitzkrieg, where Slasher jumps each time an explosion is heard and felt, and Hokusai whistles; they roam through Memory Lane, where Slasher weeps, or laughs, or grows grim, while Hokusai is expressionless.

At last, they reach Mortal Road.

Hokusai ambles along the rows of dying houses, his footsteps sending the earth quaking. Slasher follows in his wake.

Here, the Dreamstuff is thick like a paranoid's sweat. Hokusai walks through the door of darkness that marks—or rather, in the absence of light, masks—the Demon's abode. Slasher follows, feeling the familiar sensation of reptilian touch diminished. There is a musky smell in the room. One of fear. The Concubines touch him from time to time, fleetingly, their touch faint. They're scared.

Hokusai makes his way in the darkness to the stairwell, and Slasher follows.

Then the silence explodes, as a putter of bullets like miniature thunder sounds from darkness.

And Hokusai falls.

One Big Happy Family

'Like one big happy family,' the Professor says.

He lights up a small oil lamp which spatters, casting grotesque shadows with the small illumination it provides. In the pool of light, Hokusai writhes on the floor, his body changing rapidly. Bumps rise and fall, fins appear and disappear, organs materialise only to be replaced, seconds later, by yet more bizarre appendices.

Upload and Download step toward the light from their respective corners, guns at the ready. Slasher and the Professor lock eyes for what seems like eternity.

Finally, it is the Professor who breaks eye contact, and Slasher finds his voice. 'What's going on?' he asks, succinctly.

'Shut it,' Upload says, and kicks him viciously in the groin. Slasher topples over, but as he does so his hand strikes out, low, cutting a wide gash in Upload's leg.

'Son of a bitch.' Download kicks Slasher in the ribs, then stomps on his hand, nodding his head in satisfaction at the sound of breaking bones.

'Gentleman,' the Professor says, 'please.' He walks over to Slasher and kneels down beside him. 'Don't do anything,' he says in an urgent, low whisper. 'This is up to me now, Slasher. Remember? I said it's up to us to save the world. And you can do that by remaining on the floor and not interfering. OK?'

He waits, and Slasher, out of loyalty or pain, finally nods.

'Good.' The Professor turns to the Twins and motions to the contorting Hokusai. 'I was hoping to make use of this man,' he says reproachfully. 'Never mind. I believe you and I have the same agenda in mind?'

The Twins look at each other, then back at the Professor. 'Sex, drugs and rock'n'roll?' Upload suggests. 'or killing that motherfucking gob of phlegmic puss Demon shit?'

'The latter,' the Professor acknowledges. Around them in the darkness the Concubines begin to moan, and Slasher feels their leathery touch increasing over his prone body.

'First things first,' Upload says. He walks over to Hokuai's metamorphosing body and points his gun carefully. As the thing at his feet twists and contorts Upload pulls the trigger.

Out of the large weapon slugs come out and fall on Hokusai. They are large, hairy creatures, their body emitting a green slime that soon covers Hokusai from head to foot. The crawl over his body slowly, their eyes blind, and probe him with their pointed heads. Soon, one or two find a particularly soft spot and begin to burrow inside, their teeth making clacking noises as they eat their way into their new host's flesh.

Several slugs reach Hokusai's pelvis and begin clacking loudly. Hokusai screams, once, then falls silent.

'A fitting end, don't you think, Professor?' Upload says at last. He has been standing still, watching Hokusai being colonised, and is absent-mindedly stroking his growing erection. 'When Private Dicks go Public, what?' He sniggers to himself, breathing heavily.

'Fuck this,' Slasher mutters. He pulls out a small gun from a trouser pocket and shoots the Twins in rapid succession. The bullets pass right through their head, scrambling brain in their passage, exit the skull with an explosion of bone and brain matter, and fly on, disappearing into the distance.

Upload and Download collapse, heads banging against the floor. Pools of blood gather around each like two puddles.

'Well,' The Professor says. 'Looks like it's you and me again, Slasher.'

'What do you want?' Slasher asks. His voice is bitter 'I thought you wanted to study the Dreams, not end them!'

'The Dreams are poison,' the Professor says. Some of his absent-mindedness seems to return to him, and his eyes momentarily glaze over. 'Poison to keep us in this dark, shrinking, twisted world. Only killing the last angel, the last Demon if you prefer, will release us.' His eyes ask mutely for help, but Slasher can't help but notice the Professor's hand sliding to his belt, and he reacts.

The Professor's brain explodes in a red shower, and he, too, falls. The oil lamp smashes on the ground and the burning oil splashes everywhere.

Soon, there are four small fires burning merrily in the hall, casting away darkness. Four Viking funerals, Slasher thinks, but he is tired, so tired, and soon his mind descends into a maelstrom and he passes out.

A Demon Dreams

When the fires burn out the Concubines approach. Children of darkness and invisibility, they touch Slasher with reverence and lift him up.

They carry him up the grand staircase in slow, ceremonial steps. At the top there is a small room, and inside it a large bed, empty and waiting.

They lay Slasher down on the bed, arrange his sheets, fuss over his covers.

Dreamstuff chokes the room like the smoke from a burning monastery.

The Concubines withdraw, closing the door softly behind them, and go back down the stairs, to wait for their master to awake.

And in the small room at the top of the staircase the Demon Dreams.

Assassin golems? Jewish vampires with a natural resistance to crosses and holy water? Immortal Tzaddiks with drug problems?

When he isn't re-imagining Jewish mythology in noir terms LAVIE TIDHARD exploits other cultures just to get paid per word (or per page. Or perhaps). He is currently poor enough to consider becoming a socialist. He is also the winner of the Clarke-Bradbury Prize (awarded by the European Space Agency), a reviewer for *Interzone*, a regular contributor to the *Internet Review of Science Fiction*, and a film producer in his spare time. Honest.

THE SPACE BETWEEN

Erik Tomblin

B rian first saw the door two weeks after he and his parents had moved into the two-story Victorian. It called to him on the tail of a light breeze that teased the hair on his neck. He was moving toward the bed, book in hand, when a chill and whisper from across the room made him look up in surprise. For a slice of a second he saw the door, but it disappeared before the visual even registered in his thoughts. He paused a few steps later, instant beads of sweat peppering his brow.

"Hello?" he said and blushed at the sound of his voice, the way it wavered in fear of nothing.

So he dismissed the incident.

He saw the door again just two days later. Once more he was walking toward his bed and his neck broke out in gooseflesh, an indiscernible whisper from no visible source finding his ear.

"Who's there?" he asked, this time not so stricken with fear but somewhat annoyed. He paused as before, but could still feel a breeze wafting across his neck. Brian took a step back and it became a bit stronger, but he saw nothing unusual. He took another step back and looked around the room.

There. Something.

Gone in less than a second, again in the far corner of the room. The breeze had gotten weaker. Brian moved toward his bed, much slower this time. He began to feel the phantom breath across his forehead, then against his cheek. It swirled around his ear and he stopped when the door faded into view.

Brian turned to face it. It remained there, against the southeast wall next to the window that opened into his backyard. He leaned his body toward his bed and watched the door quickly fade into the wall. He shifted back and so did the apparition.

There was nothing very special about the door. It actually looked as if it belonged in the old house, except for the fact there was nothing beyond the wall but a garden and trees. It was white like the walls and actually appeared to have the same old iron knobs as the rest of the doors in the house. The only difference Brian could make out was that this door looked newer, not as many scuffs and scars from years of use.

His mother startled him as she popped her head around the open door frame, calling his name. "Brian? Hi, sweetie. Do you want burgers or pizza for dinner? Your father's going to pick up something for us on his way home."

Brian's eyes twitched away from the door, which promptly disappeared. He moved his head to one side as if trying to shake a stray thread of spider silk loose. His eyes focused on his mother and he regained some composure.

"Pizza sounds good." He blinked his dry, stinging eyes.

"Are you okay?" his mother asked, stepping into the room.

"Yeah, I'm fine," he answered, quickly moving toward her to demonstrate his point. "I'm just thinking whether I like my room arranged this way."

Satisfied with his response, Brian's mother looked around the room. A small frown of concentration was quickly replaced by her big, loving smile.

"I think it looks great. Maybe we can get that aquarium you've been wanting. There's plenty of room."

Brian smiled, trying not to look back at the blank wall where the door had been. "Okay." The enthusiasm was forced, but his mother did not seem to notice.

"I think that's a good idea. Well, your father will be home in about an hour so we'll eat then."

"Thanks, Mom."

She smiled again, then left the room.

Dinner in an hour. Brian checked his bedside clock. It was only 4:53 PM. He could hear his mother leave through the kitchen door and watched her walk past his bedroom window. She would most likely be in the barn, going through the multitude of junk her wifeless, childless uncle had accumulated over his eighty-plus years on this earth. Brian would likely have the whole hour to himself.

Back near the bed, he adjusted his stance and let the breeze guide him back to just the right spot. It did not take Brian long to see the door again. He listened to make sure his mother was not returning for something she might have forgotten. He could hear nothing, not even his own breathing. The door remained in place, shifting only the slightest with every miniscule movement of Brian's head.

He began to walk toward the door, keeping the course of his movement as straight as possible. His head remained motionless except for its gliding advance toward the mystery. Even the possibility of sound seemed to fade and his ears popped from some unexpected drop in air pressure. At least he felt them pop, but did not hear them pop.

Within five feet of the door he noticed the dimming of his peripheral vision. Darkness crept in from behind and began devouring everything but the door as he moved closer. At three feet the door seemed to almost glow. When Brian's hand touched the knob he could only see the door and nothing else.

The knob was cold, far too cold for this room. It was smooth and worn in his grip, and felt so strange he couldn't quite explain it to himself. He could only think that it felt dead, unreal. He let go for a moment and the room blinked back into view around him, though dim and hardly visible. Brian grabbed the knob again and watched the room fade out. He looked around and saw nothing. And he couldn't really acknowledge it as darkness.

It was *nothing*.

Brian turned the knob and opened the door.

In the few seconds Brian stayed just inside the door he saw enough to make his stomach turn inside out. His breath caught in his throat. Beyond the blood, he couldn't make out much of the new room. He thought he saw a bed, maybe a dresser and a vanity with a chair knocked over in front of it. Only the larger details came through the wash of red that covered most of the room. The smell of it forced itself up inside his head, toppling him back through the door.

His own reality snapped back into place with a flash of light and air that hurt his eyes and ears. He could feel the floor under him vibrate, then settle into place. The stench of rancid blood still lingered in his nostrils, but a few panicked breaths dissolved the memory.

Before Brian could even begin to piece together an idea as to what had just happened to him, he heard a knock at his door and jumped to his feet.

"Brian? Hi, sweetie. Do you want burgers or pizza for dinner? Your father's going to pick something up for us on his way home."

It was his mother. He immediately realized she had already asked him this question, but under the circumstances, he found this odd occurrence to be less important. He shook his head and blinked, not sure she was actually there.

"Pizza sounds good." Had he just spoken?

"Are you okay?" his mother asked, taking a step into the room.

"Yeah, I'm fine" Brian replied, moving forward. "I'm just thinking whether I like my room arranged this way." The words came out of his mouth with almost no effort of his own. Again, a repeat of what he knew had already occurred.

Brian's mother looked around the room and smiled.

"I think it looks great. Maybe we can get that aquarium you've been wanting. There's plenty of room."

Brian forced a grin, trying not to look back at the blank wall where the door had been.

"Okay," he answered.

"Yeah, I think that's a good idea. Well, he'll be home in about an hour, so we'll eat then."

"Thanks, Mom."

She smiled that smile again and left the room.

Brian swung around to look at his clock, seeing exactly what he expected.

It was 4:53 PM.

Again.

Brian avoided the door for a month before he felt the familiar breeze tickle the hair on the back of his neck one evening. He looked up from his desk where he was reading about the fish he had chosen for his new aquarium. The door was there, but he could not see it yet. He felt it in the room, a presence that pulled at him.

He rose from his chair and walked to the same place as before, turned his head to the same angle. There it was, though clearer this time. He looked over at this clock. It was 11:58 PM. His parents were asleep and he had been allowed to monitor his own bedtime when he turned fifteen, two years ago.

Not knowing exactly why, Brian reached forward, opened the door, and entered into the darkness.

Brian's sense of relief was immediate. The blood was gone and he found himself in a room with a female. She sat on a bed with her back to him, her cotton gown half-covered by her golden hair, which she brushed with long, slow strokes. He felt the breeze come from behind him. The girl's hair shifted slightly and she sat up straighter, her grooming halted. She turned to face him with a visage so lovely Brian almost forgot how he had gotten here.

"Brian?" she asked, then dropped her brush and rushed to him.

Any natural instinct to flee such a strange situation was quashed by the girl's beauty. Her arms wrapped around his neck and she pressed her warm body against his, planting kisses along his face and neck. He held her to him instinctively and looked around the room.

It was not your typical teenage girl's bedroom, not that Brian had much to compare it to. There were no posters, no abundance of stuffed pandas or giraffes. There was one doll, perched atop her pillow. It looked as if it had been made from an old potato sack, with buttons for eyes and a patch of red yarn for hair.

There was no television, no radio. There wasn't even an alarm clock next to her bed. Noticing this, Brian realized the light in the room was not from a cute ceramic pony lamp but an oil-burning lantern, the kind his great uncle had collected out in the barn.

His face was suddenly squeezed between the girl's hands, her beautiful blue eyes gazing into his. "I've been waiting all week for you!" she told him in an excited whisper.

"How did you—" Brian began, but her kiss cut him off. Her lips were sweet and soft against his and she smelled of soap and skin. He let himself fall into the moment and kissed her back with a passion he didn't believe himself capable.

Suddenly she stopped and cocked her head to one side as if listening for something. Apparently satisfied she had heard nothing, the girl turned back to Brian.

"My father is livid!" She pulled him over to her bed and they sat down. "He is sure you are a devil. He says such horrible things to me. He won't even take me to church now. We sit here and he reads from the Good Book from sunrise until sunset."

Brian could only stare at her. She knew his name, and obviously felt comfortable with him, while he had no idea who she was. He knew he needed to say *something.*

"How did you know my name?"

She gave him a funny look, then smacked him on the leg. "Stop your silliness," she chided. "You must take me with you, especially now." She gave him such a serious look he felt he should know to what she was alluding.

"*Now?*" he asked.

She took his hand and placed it on her firm belly. Her look melted into one of such warmth and happiness he could not mistaken her meaning.

"We must go, Brian. Father will know soon enough. I cannot imagine what he would do to me." She reinforced this thought with a shaky sigh and pulled him close. "Please tell me I'm going with you, Brian."

He couldn't speak. He could hardly breathe, and when he tried he found his attempts short and shallow. He pulled her away to look at her from arm's length. Yes, she was beautiful, but he was sure he'd never seen her before. He glanced around her room again, searching for something to trigger his memory.

The girl frowned, beginning to look as confused as he felt. Terror conquered her face when she heard a noise from outside her room.

"Quickly! Go!" she hissed, pushing him back to where he had entered. He tripped over his own feet and tumbled through the door. As he did, he saw the door next to her vanity open. A man in his fifties stepped through the entrance, calling his daughter's name:

Laura.

Brian saw the mixture of fear and outrage on the man's face as their eyes met.

His world went black, the feeling of falling took him over, and the floor of his own bedroom appeared beneath him to stop his descent.

Brian jumped to his feet and looked at his clock. It was 9:45 PM. He was not surprised that it was earlier than when he had left. What surprised him was that it was almost *two hours* earlier. He was sure he had only been in that girl's room for five minutes, maybe ten. Brian moved over to his desk to check his calendar. The first ten days of August were crossed through with red ink, so it was still the 11th.

Just to be sure, Brian crept down the stairs to the living room where his parents sat together on the sofa watching the end of *American Gigolo*, the same movie he knew had ended at 10:00 PM earlier that evening. He realized they would be up to his room in ten minutes to wish him a good night and warn him not to stay up too late. Brian knew he would not sleep very well unless he would be able to push the night's events out of his thoughts for later perusal.

This would not happen.

For another two weeks Brian forced himself to avoid the door. He would occasionally feel the light wind beckon to him, but he would move out of its path to avoid the temptation. No more was it his curiosity he fought but the promise of another visit with Laura.

Granted, he hardly knew her. But her touch, taste and smell remained at the front of his thoughts. Even the way that prudish nightgown graced her figure made him want to be with her in a way he had never felt. And she obviously felt the same way, though he worried about her allusion to being pregnant. This, Brian knew, was not possible. She surely meant something else, perhaps an illness or nervousness that could not be helped until she was out of that house, wherever that house really was.

By the time Brian had decided to return to Laura he was ready to reciprocate her amorous actions, but just as ready to discover who she was and why she thought she knew him. Hopefully, when the truth became clear it would not jeopardize any possibility he had of getting to know her.

When he stepped through the door again, Laura was on her bed, this time lying on her stomach, facing him. He stepped from the shadows and her face lit with such joy his heart melted. He moved cautiously toward her bed, listening for her father or anyone else that could pose a problem.

"Brian, my angel! You're back!" She rose to her knees on the bed and held her arms out to him.

"I couldn't leave you," he said, grasping her hands in his. "I can't stop thinking about you."

"Nor I, you," she answered.

"Are you okay? Did your father hurt you?" She looked well, but he thought it best to ask.

"Of course I'm fine. Though Father did want to know to whom I had been talking in my room alone. I told him I was praying to my angel, which is not far from the truth."

"Laura, I'm no angel. But I do want to help you. And…well…" He was new to this and the words would not come through.

"What is it? Tell me, Brian."

"I think I'm falling in love with you."

Brian didn't know whether the look of surprise on her face was a good thing or not. Laura confirmed his hope by wrapping her arms around his neck and giving him another of her sweet kisses.

"I feel the same. I knew I was meant for this."

Brian thought that was a strange thing to say, but soon did not care as Laura rolled onto her back and pulled him on top of her.

"You may take me, Brian," she offered.

And he did.

He laid there in bed after the act, spent and confused but deeply in love. He went over the details of her supple breasts and strong legs in his mind. Other things, like her whispered prayer of thanks to God, tried to vie for his attention, but he pushed those thoughts away and reveled in the moment.

Laura lay sleeping next to him in full, splendid beauty. The lamp was almost burnt out. Her tiny puffs of cinnamon breath tickled his ear. She was more beautiful in this moment than he ever imagined, more vulnerable as well. He would have to talk to her about coming back with him, though he had no idea what consequences that could entail. Surely his parents wouldn't let a stranger move into their house. Even if they did, they would need to know who she was and where she was from.

Lost in these thoughts, Brian did not hear the footsteps until Laura's father was stepping into the room. Brian rolled out of bed, onto the floor, and scooped up his clothes.

"Hey!" the father yelled, shifting his step to dart around the bed after Brian. Laura had awakened and had begun to scream.

"No, Daddy! Don't hurt him!"

Brian ran to the corner where his door appeared, floating just a few inches above the floor and shining with that eerie luminescence. Laura's father had stopped at the end of the bed, his mouth agape. He held his hands to his chest and stammered out a prayer.

Brian leapt into the darkness and was gone again.

It was just after midnight. There were a few boxes sitting around Brian's room that shouldn't have been there since the first week he and his family moved into the house. A quick look at his calendar confirmed Brian's fear. It was almost a full two months before the evening he last visited Laura. It had only felt like an hour, maybe two, but his time had looped back on itself again, though at a faster rate than before. The risk was becoming greater on both sides now, with Laura in definite danger from her father or someone else and Brian's own time being turned back on him with uncertain consequences.

He laid down in his bed to go over what he had learned thus far, if not to make sense of it then at least to calm the buzzing confusion in his mind. This would not be easy. He knew he would not be able to explain what was happening in this room and beyond that door, at least not on a deeper level. But he might be able to make sense of his experience and the beautiful girl that needed his help.

Brian closed his eyes and saw his hand placed on her belly as he had on the first visit. The significance of this was not missed. Laura was pregnant, or believed she was. And she believed it was his child. Granted, he knew this was impossible at the time she had hinted at it, but how possible was it that he'd been traveling to another place or another world through a magic door in his bedroom? And now that they had lain together, just how impossible was her pregnancy?

Laura knew his name. She trusted him. He saw no signs or omens to prevent him from doing the same. Especially if she was in as much trouble as she wanted him to believe. Her father had seen him twice now, and this second time was surely enough to send him over the edge.

The blood. It was her room that was rotten with blood on his first trip through the door. Was it her blood? Was her father going to cross the line that Laura was afraid to imagine? And if her father was the imminent source of this danger, then it could already be too late. He might have to bring her back with him. He would definitely have to warn her.

And he would have to do it *now*.

By the time Brian was convinced he had to return to Laura and had formulated his simple plan—get in, get out—it was after one in the morning. He hadn't even noticed the breeze starting up an hour before. He stood in the spot and found the door easily this time. He noticed he had more play in his position before the door would disappear from view. He opened it and stepped through.

Laura was on her bed, this time lying down and reading what looked like a Bible. The lone lamp stood guard against the shadows. A golden glow surrounded her, accentuating the curve of her breasts under the cotton gown. The pages of her Bible fluttered in the wind he brought with him.

She looked up and saw Brian appear in the corner. He could tell she was instantly afraid and confused by his arrival. He rushed over to her and knelt at the side of her bed. She pulled her legs up and began to jump from the bed, obviously not recognizing when he called to her.

"Wait, Laura! It's me." He instinctively talked in the same hushed tone she had used with him earlier. It worked. Laura halted her escape and turned to face him, grabbing a quilt from her bed to cover her body. He would need to calm her quickly to convince her of his plan.

"It's me," he repeated, "Brian." He stood and moved across the bed toward her.

Her fear was subsiding. She sat across from him on the bed. Recognition, with a strange afterglow of melancholy, lit up her face.

"I wondered if I'd ever see you again," she said.

Brian knew time was of the essence. "I'm here to help. I want to take you with me."

"Help? Why would I need help?"

"Your father. I think he's going to hurt you. Something terrible." Brian could tell his sense of urgency was lost on her.

"My father," she laughed. "The only harm he would cause is a good flogging with a hickory branch if I don't study The Word when I'm supposed to." She smiled at Brian, and he couldn't help but believe her, regardless of his previous concerns. Her eyes reflected the unmistakable belief in her own words.

He put his hands up to Laura's face and pulled her closer. Her beautiful eyes spoke of such innocence and kindness he could only think of what a paradise it would be to live in them. Brian stroked her hair and tried to find the words he had rehearsed so diligently before stepping through that door.

"Are you an angel?" she asked.

He was surprised by this question. Was she oblivious to their previous conversation? Now it seemed the tables were turning.

"An angel?" He let his hand drop to her thigh. She gasped lightly, then placed her own hand on his, guiding it to her waist.

"I think you are," she said, not letting him answer. She pulled him closer for a kiss as sweet as the first, if not sweeter.

A door closed in the distance.

"That must be my father. Should you stay?"

Brain jumped up from the bed and moved toward his exit. "Look, you can come with me if you want, but we can't let him find me here."

"Why? He is a godly man. Could he not see you?"

"Listen, Laura, I'm not an angel. I'm Brian and I came back to help you."

Footsteps were approaching her door. He knew he would not have time to convince her to come with him. A knock at the door was his queue to escape. The door began to open.

"Laura? Who's in there?" It was a man's voice.

"I'll be back. Be ready!" he whispered, though not sure she heard, and disappeared into the darkness from which he had come.

In the morning, Brian's parents came into his room. He had not slept all night and declined their offer for a trip to town to pick up some cleaning supplies for the new house.

"Are you sure, son?" his father asked. "Stay up too late reading again, huh?"

"Yeah. I'll be okay. You two go ahead."

Assuring them he would be fine after some breakfast, Brian was able to get his parents out the door and on the road. He was anxious to get the house to himself. If he could get into Laura's room and get her to come with him quickly enough then the time factor might not matter as much. If she were not sure, he would just take her and convince her later. He still felt her life was in the balance and would do what was necessary to preserve it.

Brian watched from his window as his parents left a trail of gravel dust in their wake. He turned and found the door. It seemed so strong, so real this time he hardly had to try. With a deep breath he stepped through for what he hoped would be the last time.

Laura's room was lit with natural sunlight this time. It was the first time he had seen it in this way. The furniture was a lighter colored wood. There was no closet. Just a matching armoire that stood a few feet away, near the corner where his door always brought him. Brian walked to it and opened its doors. The strong smell of its cedar lining reminded him of the scent of Laura's skin. Her clothes, though dated by his standards, conjured up new images of her slender form undressing before him.

Brian laid down on the bed and imagined Laura giving herself to him once again. Her warm skin, her trusting eyes, her comforting smile all made him want her so fiercely. With these thoughts, he fell asleep waiting for Laura's return.

Brian awoke to the sounds of someone approaching the house outside. Along with voices and cheerful laughter, he could hear creaking wood and animal noises.

Was this a farm?

There, the unmistakable whinny of a horse. Someone was calming the animal while others entered the house. Brian jumped from the bed and slid under it, cursing himself for being so stupid as to fall asleep.

There was more laughter just outside the door. It was Laura's, and it rang in Brian's ears like the sweetest angel's song. She opened her bedroom door and entered, closing it behind her. Brian waited, wanting to make sure no one would follow her into the room. He watched her feet move over to the vanity, where she sat down. Removing one shiny black dress shoe, then the other, Laura stood again to remove her heavy dress.

Brian thought it best not to let her get so far. If his parents were in his room when he returned, he would definitely not want a half-dressed girl appearing with him out of thin air. He stuck his head out from under the bed and whispered.

"Laura."

Her head whipped around in his direction, not seeing him until he began sliding out from under her bed. Before Brian could even show his face she was screaming with a fear so intense he realized she did not recognize him. Laura's arms were crossed in front of her chest, though she was still fully clothed. She gasped for breath as he stood up before her, then continued screaming, this time for her father.

"Father! Father!" she yelled, backing away from Brian as he advanced. "Someone is in here!"

"Laura! Please! It's me!" Brian pleaded, trying to keep his voice low. It did no good and she jumped back from his reach.

The bedroom door burst open behind him. Laura's father came through, his eyes locking in on Brian. There was no recognition in those eyes. Brian could tell her father was trying to get as much grasp on the situation as he could before acting. Her father's hand dropped to his hip where a large knife was sheathed in leather.

Brian looked back to Laura, who had stopped screaming and now cowered in the far corner, waiting for her father to subdue the intruder. The door, unseen by Laura, hovered just behind her. There was only one thing for Brian to do if he were to save the girl he had fallen in love with. The rest would fall into place later, he was sure of it. But for now, he would have to act against her will and do what he believed was right.

The father advanced, pulling the knife from the sheath and lunging toward Brian. Brian leapt for Laura, who yelped with a fear that struck at his heart. She held up her arms to protect herself. It did no good. Brian's force carried them both through the door and into the darkness.

The time spent in the space between his world and hers seemed to last much longer this instance. Previously, once released Brian would quickly lose the sense of timelessness from that interlude. But for now he felt suspended in that strange place for an eternity, and it was the sweetest eternity he could imagine.

In that everlasting moment, he and Laura were in synch. Their minds and bodies meshed into an inexplicable entity, climaxing with a complete pure knowledge of each other. The most powerful sense of love could not compare with what he was feeling. Brian felt his thoughts and body give in to her presence. He felt his mind mingling and merging with hers, sharing feelings and facts of which both had been unaware until this slice of forever.

When the darkness broke and they fell to the floor on the other side, the sense of loss was enough to bring even the happiest person to his knees in a fit of despair.

Brian looks up at the face of Laura's father, who blinks twice—dazed by some strange aberration in the shadows of the room—then focuses again on Brian. Laura is sobbing on the floor, the wound of her separation with Brian still fresh in her mind. Brian looks into the corner of the room.

The door is gone. Not even a trace of its previous existence.

The first attack is a jab to Brian's torso. Laura's father lifts Brian up by the hair, removes the blade from between his ribs, then slides it deep and fast across his neck. Brian falls to his knees, grasping at his throat and feeling the blood run between his fingers. He watches Laura's father go to her, occasionally glancing back at Brian to ensure his incapacitation.

"Everything's fine now, Laura. Look. It's me, your father. He can't hurt you now."

Brian gets back to his feet and heads towards the door. He doesn't know where he can go and stumbles around the room in his confusion, spraying blood in wide swaths as his arms wheel around madly. Grabbing the chair for balance, Brian knocks it over and falls on top of it, breaking two of his ribs.

Laura is coming around, reaching up to stop her father from stroking her hair. She lifts her face to his, fresh tears streaking down in shiny rivulets. Recognition sets in, then realization. Her eyes dart around the room, looking for Brian. When she finds him lying on the floor he has but a few breaths left in him to grace her with a smile.

She can only give him the same, but that is enough.

ERIK TOMBLIN holds a B.A. in Psychology and a Masters in Information Technology. He is married and has three daughters. His first novel is in its final stages and he is working on a second. His novella, *Riverside Blues*, has been picked up for print release. A detailed list of Erik's publications, both print and online, can be found at his web site: www.eriktomblin.com.

KEEPSAKE (A TALE OF THE NAMELESS)

Ray Wallace

"Feeding time," said Jeremy as he pulled back the curtains and looked out over the innumerable lights of the night-shrouded City below. It was a breathtaking view, one that never ceased to cause a tiny thrill to surge through his body. Jeremy had to hand it to Nicolae; he had chosen well when he had decided to house his Coven here. The place was old, built more than a century earlier, still in immaculate condition thanks to Nicolae's oversight of its constant upkeep. The place was also big, a sprawling manor that covered most of the hilltop upon which it perched. And the location was wonderful, isolated out here on the edge of the City, away from any curious neighbors who might become suspicious at the odd, occasionally frightful sounds that often emanated from the house's interior.

For a few minutes Jeremy looked out the window, thought about all the people down there going about their tiny lives, acting on their whims and jealousies, suffering through their tragedies, finding in their hopes and dreams the strength to endure. All of those people, millions of them, oblivious to the fact that he was here, standing at his window, looking down at them, imagining just how good they would taste…

Jeremy let the curtains fall back into place, turned away from the window, skirted the king-sized bed from which he had recently arisen, and approached the desk located next to the room's lone entranceway. He reached out and flicked the switch on the wall there, blinked against the sudden luminescence that bathed the room. Then with an eager light in his eyes he opened the desk's top right drawer, removed what appeared to be a black jewelry box.

Setting the box on the desk he tilted back its hinged lid, simply stared for a moment at what was contained within.

Teeth.

Gleaming, silver teeth.

Very sharp, gleaming, silver teeth.

Razor sharp, as a matter-of-fact.

Each tooth pointed like a tiny chrome dagger.

One had to be careful when handling these teeth, even more cautious when wearing them. It would actually be quite foolhardy for anyone without Jeremy's resiliency, without his supernatural ability to heal himself and superhuman tolerance for pain, to make use of them at all. For causing damage to oneself with them was unavoidable. As most everyone has managed, at one time or another, to bite his or her tongue or the inside of the cheek while eating; with these teeth in place, such minor wounds were not so minor anymore.

Jeremy slowly, almost reverently, lifted the teeth from the box's padded interior, took a few steps to his left to stand before the full-length mirror bolted to the wall there. For a moment his vanity took over, as it always did, and he had to just stand there and soak in his naked reflection. He was tall, just over six-foot-three, his body composed of lean, wiry muscle, his skin the pale perfection that all the members of the Coven had in common. The type of body Michelangelo would have loved to capture in marble. His light brown hair hung to his shoulders and surrounded a face that was almost absurdly handsome. In high school and college a number of girls had called his eyes "dreamy". And many more had willingly climbed into his bed.

After college he had decided that whatever job his business degree could have gotten him would have to wait, and he had moved to the City, found an apartment and a roommate, had pursued a career as a male model. He had quickly risen through the ranks, within a year-and-a-half had become one of the most sought after faces in the industry. How weird it was to see himself on billboards and magazine covers, to have so many people adore him, to suddenly have more money than he knew what to do with. And the parties, the women, VIP lists at every club in town.

It was at one of these clubs that he had met the man with the Russian accent, the man who had introduced himself as "Nicolae", the man who then introduced him to three of the most beautiful women he had ever seen: Sara, Mary, and Judith.

And the rest, as they say, was history.

Nicolae had asked Jeremy if he wished to experience a night he would never forget. Nicolae's three companions had smiled at Jeremy, one of them licking her lips. What red-blooded American male could possibly turn down an offer like that? So the five of them had left the club, had stepped out into the City's warm darkness, had all piled into the stretch limo waiting for them out front. A couple of drinks and a short while later Jeremy realized they were leaving the City, were taking one of the bridges to a nearby suburb, were climbing through the rolling hills that led to some very exclusive and reclusive estates.

Then they were there, at the old and sprawling mansion, the limo sent on its way, Jeremy ushered up the front steps and through the front double doors. One of the girls took his hands and gently pulled him into the house, led him beneath the giant chandelier in the entrance hall, up the wide and sweeping staircase at the room's far side. Jeremy followed without question, his thoughts a little hazy, as though he had been hypnotized. A part of his mind wondered if he had been drugged during the ride over here, something slipped into his drink. The rest of him didn't care, was concerned about one thing and one thing only: getting to fuck these girls.

They reached the top of the stairs, the girl before him—*Judith, her name is Judith*—still holding him, pulling him along. Something odd about how cold her hands were, but he just couldn't summon the will to be concerned about it. The other two women followed behind him, lightly pushing him along, giggling and laughing like this was some sort of wonderful game. He found himself laughing in response, trying to remember the last time he had felt this good, this happy.

Then they were in a room, a spacious bedroom with a massive four-poster bed near one wall, a love seat and vanity near another, huge cushions thrown about the floor, silk drapes covering the windows and hanging from the ceiling. He found another drink in his hand, a tiny mirror with lines of a white powder cut onto it held before him, a short straw held to his nose. And a pill, he was given a little red pill, took it without a moment's hesitation.

After that it all became a blur, a phantasmagoric series of memories:

Delicate hands pulling his clothes from his body, pushing him to the cushioned floor... The three women naked above him...

beside him... beneath him... He felt hot, so hot, like a fever burned within him, the cold skin of the women a soothing balm to the fire that threatened to consume him... Then he was on the bed, looking up at the mirror he discovered on the ceiling there, gazing with a detached awe upon the sight of himself and the three beautiful women, their skin so pale next to his, writhing about with something approaching total abandon. *Like some strange creature*, he remembered thinking, taking in the vision of all those entangled limbs moving to their own silent rhythm, occasionally spasming as a jolt of pleasure shot through them. *A sea creature pulled from the waters and left to die in the choking air...*

And there was Nicolae, seated on the love seat, drink in hand and a grin plastered on his face as he took in the action, raising his glass at times in a salute. Then there was the release, the mind-numbing explosion of his climax, the fire pouring out of him, leaving his body suddenly weak as that of a newborn child...

He remembered lying there, eyes closed, moaning, so thirsty, unable to move, one thought spinning through his overloaded mind: *What the fuck? What the fuck?* It was impossible to organize his thoughts. He briefly wondered about the pill he had taken, but he couldn't concentrate. He was so damn thirsty... Then a male voice with a Russian accent said, "Here, drink," and something cold and wet was pressed to his lips. He drank deeply, greedily, the liquid soothing the parched dryness that had threatened to consume his being. It was the most wonderful thing he had ever tasted, a thick, salty liquid that almost immediately restored the strength that had been all but entirely sapped from his body. Then that voice again: "Come, my dears, let us leave him now." He heard the door close, forced himself to open his eyes.

The mirror showed him lying there, alone, body slick with sweat, a red smear across his mouth. He licked his lips, tasted again the drink that Nicolae had given him: Salty. Coppery. Blood. *Oh, shit.* He thought about what had been pressed to his mouth. Not a glass, no. Something else entirely. Something softer. With a tear in it. A piece of rubber? Not quite. Something organic. Something alive. Or something that *had been* alive. Skin. Cold skin. Cold as the women he had bedded. But different. A man's. Nicolae's, of course. More than likely his wrist.

The sick bastard had cut his wrist and let Jeremy drink his blood!

"Oh, shit," he said aloud this time.

He sat bolt upright, momentarily amazed at his strength's sudden return, stood from the bed and ran across the room to the door, ready to storm out of there and kick him some weirdo Ruskie ass. The door was locked. "Motherfucker!" he shouted and beat at the door, pulled on the handle as hard as he could. It was a thick door, heavy, solid oak probably, the handle made of some black metal. No way he was going to be able to open it. In a rage he turned and stalked to the room's other side, tore at the curtains there, exposed the hidden window. Iron bars covered it at six-inch intervals. "Son of a bitch!"

A trickle of fear found its way in past his anger and he was just starting to wonder about what sort of trouble he was in here when the pain hit him. In the stomach. Like he had been punched. Hard. No, stabbed was more like it. He grunted and doubled over. Now what the hell was this? For a moment the pain lessened. He stayed bent over, taking deep breaths, afraid to stand up immediately. And then it came again. Twice as bad this time. He stumbled over to where the cushions littered the floor and collapsed on top of them, moaning, curled himself into a fetal position.

"Oh, God… Oh, God…" he whispered.

He hoped that the terrible feeling would let up, but it didn't; instead, it intensified and spread outward, moved up into his chest, down into his legs, invaded his hands, his feet, his head. He screamed, a primal sound without words, a simple expression of his agony. Like a great wave the pain rolled over him, through him, threatened to drown him in its brutal intensity. He forgot where he was, who he was, what he was, knew that he was simply this thing that hurt, wished only that the pain would go away. And when it seemed that this agony could not possibly get any worse, it did. The great wave became a tsunami. Mercifully, he passed out.

At some point he felt hands on him, lifting him, carrying him to the bed. He whimpered and tried to speak but a soothing female voice shushed him, told him that everything was going to be alright, that he had to fight it, had to fight the pain just a little while longer, that if he did, everything would be so much better than he could have ever imagined. Again he slept. And awoke to the sickness.

In some ways, this was worse than the pain, left him hot and weak and delirious, filled his mind with the most horrible thoughts. *I'm dying*, a voice said over and over in his mind. *Dying… Oh, please, God, don't let me die…*

Someone pressed a cold rag to his head. Ran it over his naked body. It felt good, so good, helped quell some of the heat that threatened to boil him alive but did little to rid him of the awful thoughts, the certainty that he was about to die.

Then the voice again: "All right, Jeremy. Here it comes. This is the part that matters most. Your heart is slowing, your breath growing weaker. Do you see it? The light? The little pinpoint of light? See it growing? Do not fear it. Go to it. Embrace it. It is the end. It is the beginning." The voice was fading... fading...

"We'll be waiting for you on the other side..."

He reached out to the light. It took him in, washed away the sickness, the pain, the fear. It held him, comforted him, bathed him in its brilliance. He felt like an unborn child in the womb, warm, safe, protected.

Then the light spit him out.

He opened his eyes and gasped, forced himself into a sitting position, a feeling of terrible dread washing over him. He was still in bed, still naked, and the women were there. Nicolae was there. And there were others, eight more of them, standing about the bedroom, all of them looking at him. He felt that he knew them, all of them, even though he had never seen most of them before in his life.

"I told you," said Nicolae to those gathered. "I told you he'd make it."

"What the fuck happened to me?" asked Jeremy in a voice barely more than a whisper.

"Why, you passed through, my boy."

"Passed through?"

"Yes, you are one of us now. Feel your chest."

Jeremy did, looked a question at Nicolae.

"What do you feel?"

"Nothing."

"That's right," said the Russian with a smile.

Then it dawned on him. Nothing. No heartbeat.

"Welcome to the Coven," said Nicolae.

"*Welcome,*" echoed the others present in a single voice.

"Holy fucking shit..."

Jeremy shook the memories from his head. That had all happened only a few months ago. Oh, the things he had seen and done since that night... He brought his mind back to what he held in his hands, to what the evening ahead held in store for him. He smiled, watched his reflection smile back at him, then he opened his mouth wide and inserted the teeth.

They were a perfect fit, made from a mold of his own teeth and gums by a master sculptor he had hired specifically for the job. Hired, then thanked by brutally murdering with his bare hands, by tearing into the man with his newly-made chrome dentures. After all, his new purchase needed to be broken in, didn't it? And he needed to know just how well the teeth worked. Just fine, it turned out, as he bit into flesh and muscle and internal organs, as he shredded through them with no more effort than one would normally exert while masticating a perfectly boiled piece of shellfish. Chewing and swallowing with wild abandon, he gorged himself on the body parts and fluids necessary to sustain him and his kind. No simple vampires were the members of his Coven. No. Their hungers ran deeper, their tastes more varied. Sure, blood was fine but served only as a sauce for the meat through which it coursed. And how could the many other treats of the human body be ignored? The eyes, the tongue, the liver, the kidneys, the spleen, the testicles... Jeremy ravenously partook of them all. But not the brain. He was warned about that, but had experimented once, anyway, out of curiosity. Never again. He had immediately felt as though he were on the worst acid trip of all time, had been sick for days afterward. Only Nicolae ate the brain, and rarely at that. He said it gave him visions, allowed him to see the future. Yeah, well Nicolae could have his visions.

When Jeremy's hunger was satiated, he sat on the floor next to the ruined corpse, leaned back against the wall there and thought about what it was that he had become. What Nicolae and his Coven had turned him into. Nameless. That's what Nicolae said they were—"the Nameless"—the creatures of the night who had never been named, who masked their true natures so diligently, who disposed of the remains of their victims so carefully, that their human prey was all but unaware that they even existed. And those few who *were* aware would never do anything so foolhardy as call attention to the fact.

"I am one of the Nameless," Jeremy had said aloud to the deathly silent room.

And he had found that he was content. No, more than that. Happy. Delirious. What power Nicolae and his children—as he liked to call the members of his Coven—had given him! More power than he could have ever comprehended as a mere mortal.

Unimaginable strength and agility. Resistance to all known diseases. The ability to live for centuries. Who wouldn't be ecstatic with these newfound gifts? He was an unstoppable force, a god who strode through the mortal realm, selecting victims on a whim, dragging them kicking and screaming into dark alleys where he fed and left the remains. He didn't have time to care about the scraps he left behind. There was so much to do in this nocturnal world he ruled, so many others upon whom he wished to feed. So what if a few mauled corpses were discovered? Who would guess—or be taken seriously if they did—that it was the work of a supernatural creature? And what did it matter if the humans *did* know? What could they possibly do about it, anyway? The care with which the Coven masked its presence seemed silly. If the humans ever became aware of the Nameless, they would simply tremble in fear at the knowledge. Of course, Nicolae felt differently on the subject. In one of his visions he had seen a panic-stricken mass of humans hunt down and destroy the Coven.

Let them try, Jeremy had thought with a red and silver smile while relaxing there in the sculptor's shop. *Let them try…*

With an effort, Jeremy pulled himself away from the memories, from his reflection in the mirror, skirted the bed, opened a closet door and pulled forth a pair of black slacks and a long-sleeved black shirt. His "killing clothes", as he liked to call them. Blood was much harder to detect on dark fabrics. It was no coincidence that his wardrobe was almost entirely black. Once dressed, he thrust his feet into a pair of black boots and then he was out the door, one thought drifting through his mind: *feeding time…*

A short while later found him downtown, driving around, then pulling over to the curbside when he saw what he was looking for.

Hookers were easy targets as Jack the Ripper had discovered all those years ago. Even easier, these days. All one had to do was pull up, flash a little green, open the passenger side door, take them somewhere nice and secluded.

"Get in," he told the girl standing on the sidewalk who couldn't have been much older than eighteen. Pretty, probably hadn't been on the streets all that long. Dark hair and big brown eyes, tight skirt and top that demonstrated her wares as effectively as possible.

With a resigned shrug that seemed to sum up her life, she got in.

"Nice car," she said around a piece of chewing gum, taking in her new surroundings appreciatively. And it was. A 2004 Lexus.

The Coven kept a few cars in a garage behind the mansion, all expensive models, of course. Nicolae wouldn't have had it any other way. And he could afford it, that was for sure. Staying young for more than a hundred years gave one plenty of time to amass a fortune. "So watcha got in mind, Mister Rich?"

"Oh, we're gonna go all the way," Jeremy said with a tight-lipped smile. After some practice he had learned to speak almost normally with his special teeth in. No sense letting his next meal see them too early, though; might scare her, make her do something stupid, like try to get away.

"Yeah? Well that'll cost ya. Fifty bucks."

Jeremy gave a low whistle. "Fifty? Wow. You must be one hot piece of ass."

"Plus twenty for the room," said the girl with a confirming nod of the head. "There's a little motel up here around the corner. Cheap place and they don't ask no questions."

"Is that so? Sounds good to me." And it did. Somewhere new and different from the piers and alleys and other dark spots where he normally fed. After all, variety *is* the spice of life, isn't it? Or un-life, as the case may be.

Jeremy gunned the car out into traffic, followed the hooker's directions for a couple of minutes until she said, "Over there on the left, just before the traffic light." He pulled up in front of the place, two of the letters of its garish, yellow neon sign burned out so it simply read MOE. He gave the girl the twenty dollars, let her out to go pay for the room. Then he went and parked the car in an empty space near the end of the building, waited for her to come out. A short while later she came walking over to where he stood leaning against the car, jangled the key at him, said, "Room seven, honey." He pressed a button on his key chain, heard the car's alarm chirp, then followed the girl over to the room. She opened the door, and then they were inside. Jeremy closed the door behind him.

"Nice, huh?" said the girl as she crossed to the queen-sized bed that dominated the room's interior. She sat on the corner, facing him.

He took a moment to look around. There was the bed with its orange spread. Next to it, a small faux mahogany nightstand with a black phone perched atop it. Located on the far side of the bed was a second door that presumably led to the bathroom. A white plastic table and two chairs sat near a window covered by an ugly green curtain. Stained beige carpeting covered the floor and smoke-stained white paint covered the walls. All in all, a less than appealing place.

"Yeah, nice," said Jeremy.

"You got the money?" she asked.

"Sure do," he said and pulled out his wallet. He was in a good mood. Might as well play along for a few moments. As he took a fifty from his wallet, held it out, he showed the girl his shiny silver teeth.

She didn't even flinch, simply reached up and took the money, said, "What the hell are you, some sort of white gang-banger wannabe?"

Jeremy had to laugh. He liked this one. Eating her was going to be a special treat.

"No. What I am... well, you wouldn't believe me if I told you."

"Is that so?" She lay back on the bed, hiked her skirt up, let him see that she had nothing on underneath. "Why don't you show me instead, Mister Rich?"

Jeremy could feel the hunger within him like the mouth of a great beast yawning open. He stopped smiling, let his voice go deep with lust, although it was not of a kind the girl on the bed could ever imagine. "I think that's a wonderful idea."

Then he was on her.

She screamed. Oh, how she screamed as he tore into her with his teeth and his impossibly strong hands. He was often amazed at just how long they struggled, how long it took for them to die even after they were ripped open and some of their vital organs were no longer in the places or shapes they were supposed to be. This was something that he only thought about afterward, however, once he had taken his fill and the hunger had been satiated for the time being.

She was still screaming when the room's front door burst inward. Even then he did not want to stop, did not wish to pull his head free from the cavity he had excavated in the poor, dying girl's abdomen, down where all the choice meats lay. But some part of his survival instinct managed to override the hunger and he lifted his head up and turned, stared out from the red, gore-streaked mask that covered his face toward the line of intruders entering the room.

Looks like I've been followed.

It was the Coven, of course. Half of them, at any rate. Nicolae was there, approaching the foot of the bed. Taking up positions to his right were Marcus and Justin, two of the older, stronger males. To the left were the three women who had been present at Jeremy's conversion. Judith stood at the center of the trio, shaking her head, a look of profound sadness etched across her features. She had tried to warn him, had told him that his reckless behavior was unacceptable, that Nicolae was worried that he was arousing suspicion, starting to draw unwanted attention. But he hadn't listened. Drunk with power, fueled by the omnipresent hunger, he hadn't listened at all.

The Coven leader motioned toward Marcus and Justin. "Take him," was all that he said. The two immortals pounced on Jeremy.

The struggle was vicious but brief, the room in shambles by the time it was over. Then Jeremy was dragged half unconscious out to one of the pair of cars the Coven members had driven down to the motel. The trunk was opened and he was bound tightly with the chains hidden within. He was then unceremoniously dumped into the trunk, and then the trunk was closed, sealing him in a tiny space of absolute blackness. The car was started and driven off just as the sound of police sirens drew near, then faded as the motel was left behind.

Jeremy was afraid. He didn't want to die. Not now. Not when there was so much ahead of him. Thousands of years. Millions. Who knew? The thought of a second, final death weighed more heavily on him than the first one ever had.

All too soon the car came to a stop, was turned off, the trunk was opened and he was pulled out, carried through the yard that led around to the back of the manor. There he was dropped to the ground on an open expanse of lawn. All the while he begged and pleaded, said how he was sorry, that it wouldn't happen again, that he'd learn to restrain his appetite, that he'd be more careful.

But Nicolae wasn't having any of it.

All twelve members of the Coven were there, standing in a circle around his prone form. The night sky was so clear above, the stars so many, so bright.

"I'm sorry, Jeremy," Nicolae said. "You don't know how sorry I am. But I've seen this before. The hunger... It's beyond your control, will always be beyond your control. It is a danger to us all. A danger that must be dealt with."

With that the Coven melted into the darkness, made its way back toward the house.

"No!" Jeremy shouted. "Noooo!" The fear was on him, a thick and terrible thing. He yelled until his voice was hoarse, until the stars began to fade from the sky, until he accepted the fact that his cries for mercy fell on deaf ears. By then it was nearly dawn.

He told himself there would be no more screaming, that he would face what was to come like a man. But when the sun broke over the horizon, it burned all such empty promises from his head. Its light was a searing, scalding thing that caused him to writhe like an insect trapped beneath a magnifying glass. Smoke rose from his body as his pale flesh began to melt then burst into flames. The noises he made found their way into the house, echoed through its corridors, were the sounds most members of the Coven would hear for years to come in their darker dreams. Thankfully, the sunlight was quick and efficient in its brutal work. Within a few minutes the worst of it was over and the screaming had stopped. The once beautiful Jeremy had been reduced to an unrecognizable, twitching thing within a shroud of burnt clothing and fire-blackened chains. Eventually, even the feeble twitching ceased as the Coven's youngest member was claimed by final death.

The following evening, when the sun was once more absent from the sky, Nicolae ventured out again into the backyard, over to the spot where Jeremy had met his demise. Nothing remained but the chains and a roughly man-shaped burn spot on the grass and a scattering of ashes. Oh, and something else, gleaming in the moonlight.

He knelt down and picked up the teeth, set them atop his palm, stared into their wicked, razor grin. Immaculately, they still gleamed, seemingly untouched by the fire that had consumed their master. A truly magnificent piece of craftsmanship, to be sure. After a time, Nicolae sighed and stood, put the teeth in the breast pocket of the silk shirt he wore. "A keepsake," he murmured to the darkness and the ghost of a dead immortal he was sure he sensed somewhere nearby. With that he turned and wandered back to the house and the Coven that awaited him within.

RAY WALLACE hails from Brandon, FL, a suburb of Tampa where he runs a record label with his brother, composes electronic music, and writes his fiction. He has published more than twenty stories in such magazines and anthologies as *The Blackest Death Vol. 1, Small Bites, Erotic Fantasy: Tales of the Paranormal, Monster's Ink, Whispers from the Shattered Forum,* and at *Bloodfetish, Dark Muse,* and *Delirium Online.* A few of his other stories have appeared at The Chiaroscuro website where he took first place in a fiction contest. He also wrote a long running book review column for The Twilight Showcase webzine and now writes reviews for Chizine and SFReader.com. He is currently working on his first novel and is a member of the THWN and Underside writers groups.

Printed in the United Kingdom
by Lightning Source UK Ltd.
107548UKS00001B/439